Two Sides of Destiny

RUTHIE MAJOR

PublishAmerica
Baltimore

Softcover 1-60836-524-7
PUBLISHED BY PUBLISHAMERICA, LLLP
www.publishamerica.com
Baltimore

Printed in the United States of America

I would like to dedicate this book to all the young people I have taught, mentored, fostered and parented throughout my life, as a Sunday School teacher, Youth Counselor, Mentor, Foster Parent and Aunt. They were the sole motivators in writing this book and I pray that their lives are changed as a result of our relationship, because they have truly changed mine and special thanks to my niece, April Grant

I would like to acknowledge Jesus Christ, who is Lord of my life. I want to thank my pastors, Charlie and Marian Redish of Life Changers Covenant Ministries in Charleston, SC, whose dynamic and electrifying teachings encourages and imparts wisdom in me weekly from the word of God and pushed me to finish this book and get it published. I want to thank my former pastor, A.R. Bernard, of Christian Cultural Center in Brooklyn, NY, who through his extraordinary teaching laid the foundation for my faith in God and has caused me to be rooted and grounded in the word of God. I want to thank my mother, Maple, and sister, Rena, for their love and support throughout my life. I thank my brothers, esp. Jerico, aka Rod, who has encouraged me in their own ways. I thank my god-mother, Frances, for her prayers and spiritual guidance and all my friends that have been a constant in my life, especially Lillian and Denise. I would also like to give a special acknowledgement to someone, who in his own way, caused me to pursue my own dreams of writing and in his own way, supported my efforts. I pray the will of God be done in your life. I would like to give special acknowledgement to Maria Cordrey for the cover design. You can contact Maria at *originalideasdesign.com*.

"Now there was a day when the sons of God came to present themselves before the Lord, and Satan also came among them." Job 1:6 (NKJV)

"Then I heard a loud voice saying in heaven, Now salvation, and strength, and the Kingdom of our God, and the power of His Christ have come, for the accuser of our brethrens, who accused them before God day and night, has been cast down." Rev. 12:10 (NKJV)

"Who is he who condemns? It is Christ who died, and furthermore is also risen, who is even at the right hand of God, who also makes intercession for us." Romans 8:34 (NKJV)

Prologue

The creature slithered its way from room to room, gliding its long red form, while using its tongue to smell its way. Every now and then he rose its slimy, sticky, scaly body up on its belly and hissed at the angelic beings that watched it slither its way around them and through them; staring at them with his small beady eyes. The creature arrived at a gate where two giant-angelic beings stood guard. The angels had wings as wide as the sea to engulf the gates that they were standing guard. Their hands were firmly fixed across their chest as they stood in military attention. The creature stood on its belly as he raised his head and spoke to the angels at the gate.

"I am here to see the Master," hissed the serpent.

"Not in that form you will not!" roared the angel, whose name was Michael, the chief prince of the angelic beings. "Change your form or you will not be allowed to enter."

Satan, also known as the devil, was once the most beautiful angel in heaven, but his pride and his beauty got him thrown out of heaven because he wanted to be like the Most High God. Because of his sin, he was now deformed and horrible to look upon, but he had the power to change his form for periods of time, which he used often to deceive many. He tried to slither his way through the gates of heaven on numerous occasions to remind the Holy One of what He had done to him. Michael chuckled at the thought, knowing that on the few occasions he did manage to slither his way through in another form; the Holy One only threw him out of His sight as fast as lightning. Some things never change, Michael mused. Satan then took on the form of an upright angel, without the wings, but his face would always be distorted.

"Do you have cause to be here today?" the angel Gabriel inquired, he was the messenger archangel.

"I always have cause!" roared Satan. "Now step aside and let me through!"

The two angels scowled at Satan, but reluctantly began to close up their wings. As their wings closed through the thickness of the clouds, a door began to open. As Satan walked through the gate, he saw the door opening up and he let out an involuntary shutter. He had gone through this door plenty of times, but the glow and the air that was fresher than anything any one could imagine always made him shutter. He took a quick look back at Michael and Gabriel and Gabriel commented, as Satan knew he would, "that Satan is the air of righteousness, lest you forget."

The two angels shook with laughter, as Satan turned a deeper color of red as he slowly began to walk through the doors. The huge doors were made of pure gold. They were carefully designed with artifacts from the Ark of the Covenant. Satan's beady eyes darted from side to side as he fumed with jealously, at what he thought should have belonged to him. As Satan began to walk slowly toward his object of hatred, his head was bowed down, for he was not allowed to look directly into the eyes of the Holy One.

Satan suddenly stopped cold. There was still a considerable distance between himself and He who sat on the Throne. The first voiced he heard was like a trumpet.

"Come closer Satan!"

As Satan looked up to be able to guide himself closer, he saw a glimpse of the One that sat on the throne.

"His appearance was like jasper and sardius stone; and there was a rainbow around His throne, in appearance like an emerald. Around the throne were twenty-four thrones, and on the thrones were twenty-four elders sitting, clothed in white robes and they had crowns of gold on their heads. And from the throne preceded lightnings, thundering, and voices. Seven lamps of fire were burning before the throne, which were the seven Spirits of God. Before the throne there was a sea of glass like crystal, and in the midst of the throne, and around the throne, were four living creatures full of eyes in front and in back. The first living creature was like a lion, the second living creature like a calf, the third living creature had a face like a man, and the fourth living creature was like a flying eagle. The four living creatures, each had six wings, were full of eyes around, and day and night they say, "holy, holy, holy, Lord God Almighty, Who was and is and is to come!" Whenever the four living creatures give glory and honor and thanks to Him who sits on the throne, who lives forever and ever, the twenty four elders fell down before Him who sits on the throne and worship Him who lives forever and ever, and cast their crowns before the throne saying, "You are worthy, O Lord to receive glory and honor and power, for You created all things, and by Your will they exist and were created."

As he came close to the throne, he diverted his eyes, so that he would not look on the Holy One, which meant he had to focus on the second object of his hatred. On the right hand of the throne sat Jesus, the Son of God, who would be interceding on behalf of the believer.

"What is your business here today Satan!" came the thunderous voice of God. Satan cowardly recoiled.

"Stand before my father you coward!" came a voice that was a little mellower, but spoken with strength and authority.

Satan knew that voice and it irked him that this Jesus, whom he once killed was there giving him orders, but Satan knew he had better do as he was told or he would be out much quicker than he came in and through another entrance. Once again Satan stood before the Holy One with his eyes averted from His face.

"I've come to request permission to send..." Satan started but the thunderous voice cut into his statement.

"You've come to what!?"

Satan knew this was an attempt to make him run like a coward, but he stood his ground and spoke a little louder, very little.

"I've come to request permission to send out a death angel."

"You do not need my permission for that; you have authority over the death angels!" the voice shook the throne. It was clear that Satan had interrupted an important meeting between The Holy One and His counselors and was feeling the heat for it, even up here.

"Your Majesty," Satan continued, undaunted by the comment, "I need permission because it is one of your own, a believer." Satan recoiled slightly again, because he knew what would come next.

"Who is it?" spoke Jesus as he stood up out of his seat and his voice seemed to be even louder than that of The Holy One Himself. He spoke so loud Satan thought he felt the floor trembled beneath him, but the floors of stone beneath him were sturdy and strong; it was only the weakening of his knees that shattered together. Satan gave the name and Jesus adamantly replied, "You have no right to be here to make such a request. Leave at once, or I will throw you out!"

Satan looked at Jesus recoiling even more; he knew Jesus did not make idle threats, but he had never been threaten to be thrown out by him before, so he decided to tread his ground carefully by turning to the Holy One, who was just and said, "Your Majesty, please, consider my case." The Son was now thinking that he wanted to crush Satan as the little bug that he was, but he knew his Father was just and would allow Satan to make his case. "You see Your Excellency…" Satan began to lay out his reasoning before The Holy One.

After he laid out the facts, as he saw them, The Holy One said, "Step aside Satan! Son, sit down," he spoke to Jesus. "We will take a look at the events that has led up to this day."

Satan was really annoyed now; he wanted to be in and out. This was clearly going to take some time and he had a host of demonic imps waiting for his instructions. They could do nothing without specific instructions, such stupid little creatures they were, but they were all the Holy One gave him to work with.

"If you are wrong about this Satan, you will be commanded to take ten of your highest ranking demons from out of the earth."

Satan trembled where he stood, while The Most High and His Son looked on. The clouds began to open up revealing a little town in Brickenbrat, Tennessee, where Jewel Stone and Lois Johnson were raised.

Chapter One
Jewel and Lois

The Johnsons' van pulled into the church parking lot approximately ten minutes after the Stones pulled in. Lois waved at Jewel, as she was getting out of the car and Jewel waited for Lois as her dad parked the van and they got out.

Jewel, the eldest of Paul and Theresa Stone's three children, was four feet and eleven with a small petite frame. Her complexion was a rich creamy bronze like her father, with round light brown eyes and silky blue, black hair like her mother.

She was an honor roll student and president of her school's student body and debate team. She was well liked amongst her peers and her teachers. She was the student every teacher wanted in their class and they told her parents every opportunity they got. She had a good relationship with her parents and could get her father to agree to almost anything on her behalf. She had high self-esteem instilled in her by both her parents, who made her believe she was their very own princess of the Nile and could be whatever she wanted to be.

Lois was five feet and four, light complexion with pretty white teeth that showed pink gums, when she smiled. She was the eldest of Richard and Stephanie Johnson's seven children. Her hair was endowed with lots of red highlights that heightened her slanted eyes to give her a mischievous look. She was well figured, with curves all in the right place. She put on a tough exterior, but underneath she was a scared young lady constantly crying out for attention. She had the ability to be an honor role student, but that would please her parents, which was the last thing she wanted.

Her attitude got her kicked out of regular high school in her sophomore year. She was sent to a school that was more interested in keeping trouble teen-agers off the street during school hours, than on education. Lois was miserable there and did what she needed to do to get herself back into the regular public school. She was always unsure of what tomorrow would be like for her and went to bed many nights dreading the next day. She looked forward to being on her own, believing that then she would be able to control her life and what happens the next day.

Jewel went to one of the best private school in their county and Lois went to the worst high school in her district. The only thing the two had in common was that they went to the same church and both had personalities that drew people to them. Jewel made her peers feel good about being around her and Lois made them feel like they were missing out on a lot of fun, if they weren't hanging out with her. When Lois did not sign the agreement her youth counsels put together to get them to agree to remain virgins until they were married, it became rumored that it was because she was already sexually active. This was not the case, however, but Lois never said anything to correct the rumors and when she was asked by her parents concerning the reason, she simply said, "believe whatever you want. You are going to anyway, regardless of what I say." When the rumors reached the Stones, Jewel's parents grew concerned about their daughter's relationship with Lois and what kind of influence she would be on Jewel. In the end, they decided to let Jewel choose her own friends and trusted her to make the right choices.

When Lois and Jewel first met, Lois was cold towards Jewel and did not want to be part of their click, but Lois intrigued Jewel and she was determined to pull Lois into their group.

Jewel began to invite Lois along when they went out and insisted on her coming when she seemed reluctant. Soon Jewel and Lois clicked and became good, if not, best of friend. Jewel never judged Lois and accepted her for who she was, which set well with Lois.

Stephanie waved and smiled at Jewel warmingly.

"Hi, Jewel," Richard greeted Jewel as he got out of the van and headed inside the church with Stephanie.

"Are you ready for New York?" Jewel asked Lois, as they headed for their routine makeup, check-up in the ladies' room.

"As ready as you are for college. Are you still going a month early?"

"Yeah."

"You must like school."

"I'd rather be in school, than to be on my own."

"You're going to be on your own someday Jewel, might as well start now."

"Actually, I think I'll start later, besides I think college will prepare me more to be on my own."

"If that's what you believe, then that's what you believe."

"Well, I do have a plan you know."

"Oh yeaah I forgot, you wanna be the next Johnny Cochran or somebody."

"Not funny."

"Wasn't trying to be. You still want to be a lawyer don't you?"

"Yes I do, and what's wrong with that?"

"Nothing girl, go for it. I'll need a good lawyer friend, because I intend to get in all sorts of trouble in New York."

"Lois, you are so full of it."

"Shhhhh," one of the greeters said, as they left the ladies' room to enter the main sanctuary.

They passed notes through most of the praise & worship and announcements. After they ran out of things to say, they were left to listen to the remainder of the Pastor's message. This Sunday was youth day and Pastor Fisher prepared a special message for the graduating seniors. As they finally settled down and began to listen in, they heard him say, "One day you're going to realize that your life is the sum of all of the decisions you made throughout your life time. Decisions that were like roads, some were straight, some threw you for a curve, some will be steep and dangerous, some narrow, some may have many lanes and some may have intersections. Today you're at an intersection. At the intersection, you must decide which road you will take. Some will be unsure and some have already decided and are ready to go. One thing you can know is that your road has already been predestined by God to get you at your ultimate destiny. There are two sides of destiny, but the decisions you make will get you to only one of them. So in order to make sure that you begin on the road to the destiny that God has ordained for you, I want all graduating seniors to please come forward. Let us stand and join in prayer with them."

"Oh come on," said Lois annoyed, she hated when they were made to come up for prayer.

As Jewel got up, she had to nudge Lois, who was still sitting, "Get up," she said. Lois reluctantly got up and walked to the front of the church.

The Pastor stood in front, while the ministers of the church stood behind the group of graduating youth and told the youth to repeat after him and he began, "Lord Jesus, I stand before you today, as one not sure of what is going to be at the end of the road that I am about to chose, but I can make sure of my destiny today. I want to repent of my sins and confess Jesus Christ as my Lord and Savior and ask him to come into my heart. According to your word in Romans ten and nine, you said that if I confess with my mouth the Lord Jesus and believe with my heart that God raised him from the dead that I shall be saved. I thank you Father for saving me." He continued to pray for the youth and lay hands on them for God's guidance throughout their lives. At the end of his prayer, his wife stood by him and they hugged the children and presented them with gifts from the church.

After the presentations, Pastor Fischer blessed the food that was prepared for the graduation class in the fellowship hall and then dismissed the congregation.

Chapter Two
Satan's Den

As Satan sat on his makeshift throne, he changed his appearance into the beautiful creature that he once used to be, except his face was still distorted. Some of the little demons, called imps, were late and would be severely punished because Satan had no tolerance for tardiness. After all the demons made their reports on their assignments, there was one that caught Satan's attention.

"Bedeekle!" he roared, and a slimy bulging eyed imp approached. Looking over the report, he inquired, "What's the significance of your report?"

"Well, your highness," the imp began in a screeching whining voice, as he bowed before Satan, "Jewel and Lois will be leaving home soon, and I have my doubts that either one of them have any true alliances with, well, you know." The imp did not want to even mention the Holy One, because he knew how intolerant Satan was of His name being mentioned. "I think I can persuade them to our side, or at the most destroy them before they choose a side."

"Yes, yes" Satan said rubbing his long wiry hands together, "this could prove most advantageous to us. If we can accomplish this, it may make many at the Ekklesia church depressed and discouraged and ripe for our attack. I like it. If you can pull this off, you could earn your demon wing."

This was exactly what the little imp was hoping for, as he stood there pleased with himself, Satan roared, "Well, Why are you still standing there! You got work to do! Get to it! All of you get to it," he roared even louder.

The Intercessor

The morning has arisen, and yet I pray; yet I pray...

Chapter Three
Lois

As Lois boarded the plane to New York, her seat was next to the window. She was not sure if she was going to like that or not; maybe she should try to change with someone. She looked around for a likely victim, but everyone seemed occupied with boarding and finding their own seat, so she settled into hers and hope for the best.

She sat watching the ground people put the luggage in the plane and the other activities on the ground. The plane began to move and she heard the pilot clearing for takeoff. The flight attendant began their pre-flight safety lecture saying, "In case of an emergency…" and Lois thought they might as well say, "in case the plane begins to go down," what other kind of emergency would there be on a plane thousands of feet from the ground. She smiled at herself as she imagined her mother, as a stewardess, saying, "in case the plane crash, I will lead you into a prayer of salvation." Well, Lois thought, it would certainly be appropriate. Lois shook herself, now was not the time to be thinking such thoughts.

As the plane began to lift off the ground, Lois ears went deaf again and she began to shake it.

"Gum?" the passenger next to her offer.

"No thanks," Lois said.

"Is this your first time flying?"

"Yes," Lois replied, "how did you know?"

He smiled and said, "gum will help your ears to stay open on takeoffs."

"Oh," said Lois, "then thank you very much," she said as she took the gum from her neighbor's hand. He went back to reading his magazine and Lois began to look out the window again. "Wow!" she thought this was quite amazing. The airport beneath her began to get smaller and Atlanta began to look like a miniature dollhouse, then the clouds came in view and Lois regretted not having a window seat on her flight from Tennessee to Atlanta. She would have loved to see Tennessee beneath her getting smaller and smaller. Lois was already feeling homesick. This was a new feeling for her. She could not wait to get away from her family, so she thought, and now she missed them. How could that be?

The scene with her mom and dad on Monday night played back in her head. They were giving it their last try to convince her to stay and go to a community college. Lois thought, even if she had chosen college it would not have been a community college. She needed to get away. She missed her siblings, but they were so annoying most of the time and she always felt like the odd one. She was their half sister, not that anyone made her feel like half of anything, even Richard never made her feel like she was a stepdaughter, but then again for years, Richard did not make her feel like anything. He was so caught up in drugs and alcohol, he could only think about himself. When he became saved he wanted to make amends, but Lois felt it was too late for that. He hugged her at the airport terminal and said he loved her and that he was going to miss her so much, matter of fact, he said, "I miss you already." Lois felt like crying, which she did on the plane, but she was not about to allow herself to cry in front of him. Her mother didn't say much, except "be good, help your aunt out when you can, take care of yourself and we'll be praying for you."

"We'll be praying for you," that was her mother's cure all phrase.

At some point Lois fell asleep, when she awoke the flight attendant was taking up trays and cups. When she got to Lois, she asked, "Would you care for something at this time? You were asleep when we came around."

"No thank you," Lois said, suddenly glad she ate something at the Atlanta terminal. Lois decided to spend the rest of the flight awake.

Feeling homesick again, she tried to refocus her thoughts to something lighter, her friends, who were more Jewels' friend than hers. Brian and Ashley only tolerated her because of Jewel, but Jarod was different. He didn't go to the same church as they, but he always met them at the mall and the movies to hang out. She really liked him and maybe it could've been more to their relationship, if his mother didn't dislike her so much. Thinking about Jarod and Jewel made her sad. She would probably keep in touch with Jewel, but she knew she wouldn't with Jarod.

The Captain came on over the intercom, cutting into her thoughts saying, "ladies and gentlemen we are now over New York. The weather is overcast at seventy degrees."

He began to give out the gate and flight numbers for connecting flights, for those who were continuing their trip to another destination. He instructed the flight attendants to prepare for landing in ten minutes. They were then instructed to sit upright in their seats and fasten their seat belts. Lois sat up straight, placed her seat in the upright position and prepared herself for the landing. She suddenly felt butterflies in her stomach. Soon she would be in New York starting a whole new life outside of the Johnson family.

"Visiting?" the passenger next to her inquired.

"No," Lois said, "I'm here to stay."

"Well let me be the first to welcome you to New York. My name is John."

"Lois," replied Lois.

"Nice to have met you Lois, enjoy your new life."

"Thank you." John went back to his paper and Lois went back to looking out of the window. It was dark and Lois never saw so many lights, except at Christmas. It was about ten o'clock. She saw the wings of the plane opened as she felt the plane descending. Soon they were on the ground and the Captain was welcoming everyone to the beautiful and exciting city of New York.

"Exciting," Lois thought.

As they were deboarding, there were flight attendants saying goodbye to them and telling everyone that they hope they enjoy their stay in

New York. Once inside the terminal, flight attendants were giving out helpful directions, pointing people in the right directions and confirming connecting flights. Lois smiled at one as she walked by. A flight attendant may be a good job, but she soon thought against it, thinking of all the flying they do. She did not want to make a career of flying. It took all the courage she had to get on this plane.

"Lois! Lois! Over here!" As Lois looked in the direction of the voice, she recognized her Aunt Deb. There was someone else with her, but Lois did not know her. Deborah caught up to Lois and gave her a big hug. "How was the flight?"

"It was okay," Lois said.

"Your first time flying and it was just okay. Were you scared? Did you meet anyone on the flight? That helps, to past the time. Was the food good?"

"Okay," Lois said. "The Flight was great. I was a little scared at first and I did meet someone named John, who was the first to welcome me to New York and I didn't eat, because I fell asleep."

Deb looked at Lois and smile, saying, "well, I guess that sums that up. Oh, I apologize Lois; this is Karen, my friend. She volunteered to bring me to the airport, so that we won't have to take public transportation, otherwise, it would take us over an hour to get home this time of the night."

"Hi," Karen said, "nice to meet you and welcome to New York. I hope you like it here."

"Thanks," said Lois.

"Why don't I go get the car, while you two pick up Lois' luggage," suggested Karen.

"Great idea," said Deb, "see you out front," she turned to Lois and said, "You look tired."

"I am a little," replied Lois feeling the tiredness coming down upon her. It had been a long day for her.

After Lois and Deborah retrieved her luggage, they met Karen out front. They got in the car and off Karen went, like a horse in a race, Lois thought. No wonder they say it's safer to fly than to drive. Well, I guess, Lois laughed to herself, if everyone in New York drives like

Karen; they were probably proving that statistic true. Karen was driving like the airport was on fire and they were making a great get-a-way.

As tired as Lois felt, she wanted to stay awake to see everything she could, even if it was too dark to make out most of the things they passed. No one said anything to each other in the car, except Deb mentioned that her parents called to make sure that she remembered to pick her up and to give Deb the flight number and time of the flight, for the fifth time.

"That's your mom," Deb stated. "We're here," Deb said, as Lois stared at the tall building surrounding them.

"Do y'all need help carrying the bags?" Karen asked.

"No, I think we got it, right Lois?"

"Yes maam," Lois replied. Lois looked around her at all of the tall apartment buildings, "is this like the projects, Aunt Deb."

"Like nothing," replied Deb, "this here is the project, welcome to it," she said sarcastically.

"How many floors are there and what floor are you on?"

"There are seventeen floors and we're on the tenth."

"Tenth, wow!" Lois said.

"Wow indeed," responded Deb, the door to the building was unlocked and they walked right in. Deb made mentioned that it was broken again. They walked up to the elevator and Deb punched the button for the elevator to come down. It seemed like they waited at least ten minutes before the elevator came.

Inside, the elevator smelled like urine and Lois frowned. Deb caught the frown and said, "don't worry about it. You'll get use to it."

Lois thought, "hope not."

Finally they were inside of Deb's three-bedroom apartment. Lois stood by the door as she took a quick assessment of the place. It was nice with a warm look to it. It didn't look like it belonged in the building. It was apparent that Deb took care in decorating her home.

Deb was motioning her to a room, "You can stay in Bridgett's room for the time being. She can sleep with me. She pretty much sleeps with me anyway. She doesn't know the joy of having her own room yet. Kevin and Mike are in here," she pointed to the room across from

Bridgett's, "and I'm in the last bedroom down the hall. Here is the bathroom, only one." She flicked a light in another room and said, "and this is the kitchen."

As the lights went on, bugs began to scatter about and Lois flinched.

"Unfortunately, you will get use to them. It's a battle between them and us and no matter how clean you keep your apartment, if your neighbors don't you will always have them in the projects."

Lois smiled embarrassed at her reaction. It wasn't like she had never seen roaches. They had them in the projects back home, as well. She was just surprised to see them in New York. Deb showed Lois the dining area and the living room. It was sort of an, all in one, room.

"That's it," Deb said. "The grand tour has ended," she said as she gestured openly with her hands. "You're tired. I'm tired; let's get to bed. Oh, by the way, call your mother before you go to bed, or she'll be waking us in the middle of the night."

After the call home, Lois went to her room and flopped on the bed. Richard was already sleeping, but her mother was anxiously waiting for her call.

"I was just about to call," she'd said. They didn't talk long. She was just glad that Lois had arrived safely. As Lois stared up into the ceiling, she realized that for once in her lifetime, since she was five years old, she had a room to herself. She thought Deb shouldn't be so generous she may never leave, but she knew she would. She loved her aunt Deb, but living in the projects was not why she came to New York. She was going to get a good paying job and a nice apartment in a nice neighborhood, not that she was not grateful to her aunt, but she already knew she wanted more.

Lois changed into her gown and realized how sticky she had become, but she was not about to take a shower; she was too tired for that. She looked around for the air conditioner and didn't see one. She called out to Deb and asked would it be okay, if she turned the air conditioner up a little.

She heard Deb mumbling something, as she came down the hall and she was almost sorry she asked. Deb came into her room, went to the window, pulled it up and said, "Air conditioners are an expense I can't afford. We live on the tenth floor, at night this is all the air we need. During the day, we have fans. Is there anything else?"

"No maam." Lois, embarrassedly replied, "thank you."

"You're welcome," Deb replied, but Lois doubt that she was. Lois finished getting dress for bed, got under the covers, decided against that and decided to sleep on top of the covers. She was soon sound asleep.

Deb took the children to her neighbor, so she could give Lois a brief tour of the Bronx the next day.

It was a hot and muggy day in the Bronx and Lois said, "I thought New York was always cold."

"No, we have two warm months," laughed Deb, as her emphasis was on the two. "Today is one of those rare hot and humid days in the Bronx."

Lois asked many questions that left Deb exhausted from answering them. She finally suggested that they go into a nearby McDonald's for some fries and a soda, so she could sit down and rest.

By the end of their outing, Lois knew what train to take out of the Bronx. She knew where Deb went to buy grocery and what areas of the projects to stay away from. She was also told, as much as possible, never be outside in the projects at night by herself.

Lois bought a roll of tokens and they walked back to Deb's apartment. Lois was exhausted; she never walked so much in her life.

"This is how it is, when you can walk, walk," said Deb, "because cabs are expensive and if you let them find out that you are new here, they will take you around the state and back. I can't stress that enough. Stay away from the cabs, unless someone else is paying."

As they approached the section of the project where Deb lived, people were out and music was everywhere. "That's how it is around here," explained Deb. "If you see a guy with a girl, no matter how good he looks, look the other way. These girls will cut you up for someone else's man. The man they're with aint theirs, but they act like he is."

Lois and Deb suddenly looked in the direction of a screaming woman. She was yielding a knife and screaming, "Heffa! That's my man and I done told you once to stay away from him, and I aint gonna tell you know more. It's on now, you %##*#!" She was yelling profanity at a woman walking with a man.

The woman with the man turned and put her hand on her hip and was waiting for the woman to approach, when someone yelled, "she got a knife!"

At that, the woman who was with the man said, "you aint worth all that," and she took off running.

The woman with the knife walked up to the man and they got into a heated argument. The woman began to cry and the man walked away and the woman began yelling after him, "but I love you! I love you!" The man didn't look back he just kept on walking.

"Wow," said Lois. "Is that his wife?"

"Nope," replied Deb. "He aint married, but he stays with another woman who have two kids for him. She supports the kids and him."

"I guess he's what they call a player," said Lois.

"I got ya player," said Deb, "that's what you call a poor excuse for a man and an even poorer excuse for a human being. These women degrade themselves like this all the time around here."

"Has anybody ever been hurt?" asked Lois.

"If you call dead, hurt, then yeah."

Lois only response was, "wow."

"Stay away from married men niecy and as much as possible stay away from men that are already involved with someone else."

When they were inside the apartment, Lois headed straight for the bathroom. She needed a nice long warm bath. While she did that, Deb went to get the children.

After Lois was finished in the bathroom, Deb got the children all ready for bed and they all headed to the living room to watch TV before bed. When they got around to the living room, Lois was out, holding the remote control in her hand. Deb took the remote and told her to go to bed, "you had a long day," she said. Lois didn't argue; she got up and went straight to bed and was soon asleep, but this time she remembered to put up the window to let in the night air.

"Lois, Lois."

Lois turned to face the door with her eyes half shut wondering who was calling her. She still hadn't adjusted to the reality of being in New York and not in Tennessee. Lois eyes were barely opened and filled with cobwebs, as she realized that it was Deb calling her.

"hmmm?" Lois sleepily asked.

"We leave for church in one hour," said Deb.

"I'll skip church today." Lois replied.

"No skipping church in this house. Get up. You got one hour."

Lois thought, "God, some thing never changes." She lay in bed for another ten minutes and realized that she had better get up. Her aunt was doing her a favor by letting her stay with her and she did not want to break any house rules; she had to find her own apartment soon. She didn't come all the way to New York to go to church at someone else' command matter of fact, she didn't come to New York to go to church. She wanted to enjoy life.

Deb was true to her Word; she was standing by the door calling for Lois within the hour. Lois grabbed her purse and ran out the room and said, "Present."

"Funny," Deb replied.

"What time does your church starts?" asked Lois looking at her watch.

"It starts at nine," answered Deb.

"Then why are we leaving at eight?"

"Because on the weekends, the trains run on a different schedule and it takes twice as long to get around on the weekend as oppose to the week days," explained Deb.

The service was different than what Lois was used to. The people in Deb's church jumped up and down and danced through most of the service. The Pastor's sermon was short. Lois wondered if it was due to all the time they took jumping up and down, dancing and running up and down the aisle. One person would start and set off at least three or more others. It was a small church, so ten people jumping up and down, dancing or whatever seemed like a lot.

After the service, Deb introduced Lois to her pastor and some of her church members. She let them know that Lois was looking for a job and if they hear of anything to let them know.

Karen, Deb's friend also went to the same church. After service, she offered them a ride home, but Deb declined, knowing it would be too cramped, with all five of them in the back of her small car. Karen lived alone, but she picked up her mother every Sunday and Wednesday for services. Deb usually accepted on Wednesdays. She didn't like riding the trains late at night.

Deb decided to take everyone to BBQs. The children jumped up and down and scream.

Lois asked, "Is that there favorite place?"

"Not really," said Deb, "their favorite place is Mickey Ds, but we don't eat out often."

"I see," said Lois.

She could understand that. They never ate out as a family. It was too many of them. When they did, the most they could afford would be a family pack from KFC.

The restaurant was nice. Deb ordered for everyone except Lois, who chose the same thing Deb ordered, so they brought them the family special, with a big jug of lemonade. While they were waiting on their food and the kids were coloring on their mats, Deb asked Lois, "Have you ever caught the holy ghost?"

"No, I don't think so. I've never even heard of 'catching the holy ghost' before," responded Lois, knowing Deb was referring to the way the people were acting in her church.

"I know better," said Deb, "you teens are just in your own world. You probably just didn't pay attention."

Lois was about to explain to Deb what she did learn about the Holy Spirit, but she didn't want to offend Deb. The waiter brought their food and Lois was glad for the diversion. They ate practically in silence, while making small talk with the children and after the meal Deb paid and they left.

They heard the phone ringing as Deb was putting the key into the door.

"Watch it stops as soon as I get this darn door open," Deb said annoyed. When Deb finally got the door open, she dropped everything in her hand and ran to the phone. "Hello. Hello," Deb yelled and all she heard was the click of the phone. "Never fails," Deb said as she flopped herself on the couch and began to take off her shoes.

"I'm going to change, unless there is something you want me to do first?" Lois asked.

"No, but thanks for asking," Deb said. "All we do after church and dinner on Sundays is watch whatever is on TV, or the TV watches us, because we fall asleep as soon as we get comfortable."

Lois went into her room to change clothes and decided that today's event deserves a page in her diary, so she took out her diary and began to write. She also wrote that she wanted to share with Deb over dinner about what she learned concerning the Holy Spirit. It wasn't much, but she did remember that they were taught that the Holy Spirit is gentle. As Davida, her youth leader, would put it, "He's a gentleman and will not make you act unseemingly and out of order and He will definitely not make you do anything that you don't want to do."

There wasn't a TV in Bridgett's room, nor the boys. Deb had a small 13-inch in her room, but the kids were not allowed in her room. Lois decided to go out and watch TV with them.

When she walked into the living room, she heard the noise of the television and snoring. She decided she didn't want to watch the television alone, so she returned to her room with the paper she bought to look in the want ads. She did not have a clue on how to look for a job in the paper. The want ads had so many jobs it was overwhelming. She finally turned to the comics and read it, until she fell asleep.

Everyone was awakened to the sound of the telephone ringing. Lois heard Deb picked up. "Hello," she said groggily and then she livened up. "Hi Sis." Unless it was a sister from her church, Lois knew that it was probably her mother calling to check on her. "Did you call earlier?"

"Yeah, we heard the phone ringing while we were walking through the door." Lois heard Deb pause after each comment. "No, service was over its regular time, but we went out to eat because I didn't get to cook last night."... "Its okay, Sis, you know I would let you know if it wasn't.".... "Yesterday I spent the day showing her around, so that she will know what trains to take.".... "Well, yeah, I have to work, so she is on her own.".... "She is going to be fine.".... "Yes, anything can happen, that's the risk you take everyday living in New York, but I'm sure that anything can happen in Brickenbrat, as well.".... "here, talk to her.".... "Yeah,".... "wait a minute."

Lois was standing in the living room when Deb turned to call her, so she gladly passed the phone to Lois, sighing a relief that her interrogation was over.

"Hi Mom.".... "huh, huh.".... "um hmm.".... "Yes maam." Those were the first decipherable words Lois spoke. "I will.".... "okay.".... "I love you too mom.".... "okay."

The next voice Lois heard was Richard. "Yeah, I am doing fine.".... "So far it's great.".... "I'll let you know." Richard said I love you, but Lois didn't respond to it. "Can I talk to Maggie or Ritchie?".... "Oh, okay. Tell everyone I said hi then. Bye." Lois slowly hanged up the phone.

Everyone had resumed watching TV. An hour had almost past since they all took a nap.

"You can watch TV in my room Lois, if you don't want to watch what we're watching," Deb offered.

"Thanks, but I'll just watch whatever you guys are watching."

Lois suddenly felt homesick again and did not want to be alone. Deb's floor was carpeted, as was her custom at home, she got on the floor next to Bridgett who was lying on her stomach with her two hands holding up her face. Lois squatted in Indian position next to her and watched TV, until it was time for the children to go to bed.

"That's it you guys. Let's get ready for bed. There's a good movie coming on later Lois." Deb said. "I'm going to watch it in my room, so that when I fall asleep, and I will, I will already be in bed. You are welcome to watch it with me."

Lois did and true to her word again, Deb fell asleep half way through the movie. It wasn't really that good anyway, so Lois got up to get ready for bed. She was excited and anxious about tomorrow and wanted to get a good night rest.

Chapter Four
Jewel

Jewel lay in her bed wide-awake looking at the time ticking away on the clock. She knew she had to get some sleep. The drive to Atlanta was about three and a half hour, but sleep deluded her. Tomorrow she would be starting a new phase in her life and she felt much anticipation. Her stomach felt like butterflies were swarming around in it. She was excited, nervous and scared.

She was pleased with her choice of car and even more pleased at getting her parents to agree on her choice. She was now the proud owner of a brand new red mustang coupe. She also convinced them that taking her car to school with her for the first year would be to their advantage. They had originally decided that it would be best if she did not have a car for the first year of college, but that plan changed when her grandma Lynnie presented her with a check to buy a car, as a graduation present from her and her late husband. This was her grandmother's way of making up for the years of resenting her.

On his dying bed, Jewel's grandfather, who adored her, made her grandmother promise to make things right with Jewel. For years, she shunned Jewel, because Jewel was dark complexion.

Her own daughter, Mae and her granddaughter was dark like Jewel and she treated Mae like one of the servants, yet she refused to believe that she had anything to do with Mae's suicide and murder of her daughter. Jewel, like Mae, was dark like her father.

In her latter years, Lynnie was beginning to think that maybe she wasn't right about light and dark skinned blacks, after-all, look what happened to her Junior, he could pass for white and yet he wasted his life with alcohol and drugs and ended up overdosing. She decided that she was going to embrace her Nubian princess granddaughter, as Paul so often called her. She wanted to be a part of Jewel's life and hope it wasn't too late.

Jewel began to wonder what college life would be like. It's a wonder, she thought, that she was leaving for college at all. Her father was so protective of her and was against letting her go away to college, but after days and months of discussions and research, they all were able to agree that Georgia State University was the best choice, especially since Jewel agreed to attend Georgia State University College of Law after her undergraduate studies. She would be close enough to home that, if necessary, her parents could just get in their car and drive down. She wanted to go to a New York school, but her father was dead set against that. One of the reasons, Jewel knew was because Lois was going to New York and she was sure that her dad saw college as an opportunity to separate them.

Jewel agreed on Atlanta because it was said that Atlanta was like a little New York, maybe she would even stay after law school and find a job.

Atlanta had 730 fortune 1,000 companies and many of them had their headquarters in Atlanta. Georgia State was downtown, right in the middle of Atlanta. Atlanta also had a reputation of being the "city too busy to hate."

The van and the mustang were already loaded with everything Jewel would need while away at college. Jewel and Theresa were in and out of stores all week getting last minute items. They were all going to take the drive up to Atlanta the next day to help Jewel get settled in. She was already registered for summer classes and was hoping to find a job on campus before the fall semester began.

As the alarm went off at 6:am, Jewel was already wide-awake looking at the minutes on the digital clock change minute by minute until it arrived at 6:am. The music went off to her favorite station and she hurriedly got out of bed and headed for the shower. All her things were already packed. Theresa suggested buying everything new, hair brush, comb, curling iron, even her robe, so she wouldn't have to carry her personal items back and forth when she came home on breaks.

Jewel was excited about the day and began to sing a tune so she could quiet her mind. Everything was going through her mind this morning. Would she like being away from home? Would she find a job? Was she ready for college? What if she made no friends? She knew that was a silly thought, because it was not hard for her to make friends.

"Jewel, are you up?" Theresa called while tapping on the door.

"Yes, I'm getting into the shower."

Theresa left and went to the kitchen to prepare some breakfast for them. She began to wonder where the years had gone. Did they teach Jewel everything she needed to know to make it without them? Did they instill enough good values in her? It was a lot to think about. They originally planned to spend the night at a hotel and leave the next day, after making sure Jewel had everything she needed. It wasn't necessary for them to do that now with Jewel having her own car; she wondered if they should stay with the original plan or drive up and come right back.

"How can you expect people to sleep around here with them bacon and eggs doing all that talking," Paul said, as he came into the kitchen and opened the refrigerator to get a glass of orange juice.

Theresa smiled at the comment and was glad for the interruption into her thoughts. It was Paul's favorite line from one of the little rascal's episode.

"Everyone up?" Theresa asked.

"Yep," replied Paul, "even David."

Soon everyone was dressed and sitting around the breakfast table and Paul led them in prayer, "Thank you Father for this day. We call the food that is set before us, bless. I thank you for another opportunity to have a meal together with my entire family. Give us a safe trip to Atlanta as Jewel leaves our home to embark on college. We call her bless, amen."

Paul felt like he should have prayed more, but he did not want their breakfast to get cold and he wasn't one for a lot of words. There was not much conversation at the table, except for Theresa checking now and then to make sure that Jewel packed everything she needed. Everyone left the table as soon as they were finished with their breakfast to get last minute items they wanted to take with them on the trip.

Paul drove the van and David, the middle child, and Tessa, the youngest, rode with him. Theresa rode in the mustang with Jewel.

"Sweetheart, the first thing you do once you get settled is to find you a good church." Theresa said. "Matter of fact, after we get you all settled in today we could probably drive around Atlanta and see what churches are in the area."

"I'll find my own church mom, thank you very much." Jewel replied a little annoyed.

"What's the matter sweetie?" Theresa asked picking up on the annoyance in Jewel's tone

"I'm sorry mom, I'm just a little anxious. The idea of having to make new friends and getting use to staying in a room with other people, I don't know. All these thoughts just keep going through my mind."

"Sweetie you'll be fine. You're easy to get along with and you are very impressionable. You'll make friends easy. You are going to shine. You are going to dazzle people with your charm, your winning smile and your abilities."

"I hope so." Jewel said.

"Sweetie, I know so," Theresa replied with such enthusiasm that Jewel's fears almost dissipated.

They drove in silence for a while and then Jewel heard a noise. She looked over at her mother. She was asleep snoring quietly, so much for company, Jewel thought. She decided to let her mom sleep; besides her thoughts were keeping her up and alert.

She couldn't believe that she was still awake. She hung out late with her friends the night before, with the exception of Lois, who was already pursuing her dreams in New York. She was going to miss them. Brian was going to a community college and Ashley still didn't have any plans. Jarod was going to college, but he had several choices and hadn't decided yet. He said he needed a break from school. He also seemed sad, but it was probably because Lois left without saying goodbye to him. She never knew what happened to those two. At first it seemed as if they were going to hit it off, but then Lois just started to back away. Jewel realized she didn't get a number or an address from Lois. She would just call Lois' mom later and get it from her. She wanted to keep in touch.

She didn't dare tell her father that she practically stayed awake all night, because he wouldn't let her drive. This was her first time driving on a major interstate this long. Paul was keeping a little above the speed limit, so that Jewel could stay right at the speed limits and he was thoughtful to put on his signal every time he changed lanes or passed another vehicle.

As they saw the exit sign for Georgia State University, Jewel checked her watch. They had made good time, even with a stop for them to stretch and use one of the rest area facilities.

As they pulled into the Atlanta traffic, Jewel became a little fearful. Her mother noticed it and said, "You want to pull over, so I can drive sweetie?"

"No mom," Jewel replied, "I have to get use to driving in Atlanta's traffic, so I might as well begin now."

As she saw signs directing them to where to park, Jewel felt relieved to be out of the traffic. This wasn't the first time that she was at the college. She and her parents came one day for a tour, before deciding on the college, but somehow the college seemed larger and taller now. Jewel pulled out her information that the college mailed to her with instructions for when she arrived on campus.

"I need to check in and then we will be able to get a cart or something to carry my stuff to the room." Jewel announced.

It took two hours for Jewel to check in and get all her things into the dorm room. It was afternoon and everyone was hungry, so they decided to go get something to eat before they checked into their hotel for the evening. Jewel parked her car and they all went in the Van.

It was Saturday afternoon before the Stones decided to pull out of Atlanta to head back home. Jewel was already feeling homesick. She had insisted on staying in the dorm that night by herself, even though Tessa pleaded with her to let her stay. She wished she had. She realized that it was going to be awhile before she saw them again. Thanksgiving seemed so far away. She tried hard not to cry, but when Theresa hugged her so tight and began to weep, saying, "How can I leave my baby here in Atlanta. You don't know anything about Atlanta. You don't have to stay if you don't want to. You still have time to register to a local college at home," tears began to stream down Jewel's face and Paul realized he had better put a stop to Theresa emotions, before Jewel did decide to pack up and come back with them tonight.

"Theresa, stop it." Paul said gently as he pulled Theresa away from Jewel and hugged her. "She is going to be alright."

"You promise?" Theresa asked. Paul knew that if he said she was going to be all right, then she had better be all right, or she would hold him responsible.

"I promise," Paul responded knowing it was ridiculous to promise something for which he had no control. Having no control over his daughter's life suddenly hit him and he almost wanted to turn to Jewel and utter the same words that Theresa had just spoken.

Jewel reading her parents well, as she usually do, spoke up, "You guys I'm going to be just fine. I promise."

Jewel promising seemed to make more sense to Theresa, as she began to wipe her tears and look for tissues in her purse to blow her nose.

"See ya sis," Tessa said as she hugged Jewel.

"Yeah, see ya," David echoed, as he headed for his seat in the Van.

As they pulled off, Jewel waved until she couldn't see them anymore, tears suddenly came streaming down her face like a rainfall.

Chapter Five
Lois

After months of answering blind ads, Lois decided to go to a job agency. This was her first trip to Manhattan and she was proud of herself for taking the right trains and getting off at the right stops, but she did a lot of walking before she realized she was headed in the wrong direction.

She entered a tall pretty building and suddenly felt very nervous and out of her elements. She found the agency she was looking for. As she entered the room, almost every head turned her way and then back to whatever it was they were doing. She walked up to the desk where a girl was sitting and typing on a computer.

The girl looked up and smiled at her and said, "Yes, may I help you?"

"I'm...I'm here about a job," Lois said, not sure herself of whether she could help her.

"Which job is that?" the girl asked.

"Excuse me?" Lois looked confused.

"You said that you are here for a job," the girl said, "which one? We advertise many in the paper."

"Your ad said that you would help me find the job that's just right for me." Lois said, showing the girl the folded piece of paper she tore out of the Sunday's paper.

"I see," the girl stated, and Lois wondered what she saw. She handed Lois a clipboard with a paper and pen attached and said, "please fill out this application. Don't leave anything blank. If there is a question that does not apply to you indicate it, not applicable."

"Not, what?" Lois asked. The girl wrote 'na.' "Oh," Lois said, still not sure if she understood.

Lois began to fill out the application while standing in front of the receptionist, so she further explained herself, "you may take a seat over there and bring it back when you're finished."

"Oh, okay," Lois said as she looked around and found a seat next to a well-dressed woman. The woman was wearing a well-tailored gray suit, with sheer black stockings, black pumps and she smelled good.

Lois was suddenly aware of the black slacks and orange blouse she chose to wear. She did not have that many nice things. Her wardrobe consisted of mostly Jeans, big shirts, tee shirts and sweatshirts. Lois had a few nice dress and skirts that her mother bought her for church. Ever since she was old enough to work, she bought what she liked and if her mother wanted her to wear something else, she would buy it for her.

As Lois began to fill out the application, there were a lot of questions that she could not answer. Her work history consisted of working at the age of 13 as a junior youth counselor at the city camp, because she was too old to attend. She was a youth counselor in training, which meant she didn't get paid. At 14, they paid her less than minimum wage and called it training wage. She was really annoyed, because she worked the year before free, as a trainee.

As soon as she turned 15, she got a job at Mr. Riley's "Homemade Ice-cream Shoppe." She worked there every summer since. Mr. Riley even wanted her to work this summer. She felt bad about letting him down, but she wanted to get a head start on looking for a job in New York, even though Deb said it would be better to look for a job after the summer, when all the high school and college kids gave up their summer jobs to go back to school. That didn't make any sense to Lois, especially since she worked at Mr. Riley's after school, as well as the summer.

Lois filled out the application to the best of her knowledge and got up to give the girl at the desk the completed paperwork.

The girl took the clipboard and looked it over. "Thank you," she finally said to Lois "you may have a seat until you are called."

As Lois headed back to her seat, another woman who was filling out an application took it. Lois looked around for another seat and found one at the door. She was glad not to be sitting by the well-dressed woman, because she could feel her occasional stare.

Lois began to look around and check out the office. There were men and women sitting behind desk talking to other people in offices with doors and large see through windows. She heard typewriters going in one room, but you could not see in that room. The waiting area was cold. The furniture was burgundy, the wallpaper was flowery with slashes of burgundy on a beige background. The burgundy carpet on the floor was a little darker than the chairs. There were nice paintings on the wall. There was a picture of the Statue of Liberty, one of a bridge, Lois wasn't sure what bridge and she couldn't read it from that far. There was a pretty painting of clouds, water and people on a boat. Across the painting the word "T E A M W O R K" was written in bold white letters.

A woman picked up a manila folder at the front desk and called out her name. "Yes, that's me," Lois said as she stood and walked towards the woman.

The woman extended her hand to Lois and Lois did the same. "Hi I'm Valerie," the woman said as she shook Lois' hand. "I'm going to be working with you today to see if we can find the job that's right for you."

"Okay," said Lois.

"Let's see," the woman said as she looked into the manila folder in her hand. "Let's start by giving you a typing test. Follow me please."

Lois followed the woman into a room where people were clicking away on typewriters. She gave Lois instructions for the typing test.

"You can take about ten minutes to practice. When you are ready, just pressed this timer down and the clock will begin. When you are finished, Beverly," she pointed at a woman who was walking around observing the typers, "will take your paper and show you back to my office. Okay?"

"Okay," Lois replied.

When Valerie left the room, Lois placed a paper in the typewriter and wished she took typing in high school more serious.

"Too late now," she mumbled to herself.

Lois practiced for a little and then Beverly tapped her on her shoulder and reminded her that her practice time was up and that she needed to begin.

As Lois began to type, she felt like she had two left hand and she could not remember what keys should be lined up with what fingers, but she typed anyway. The bell ranged and she stopped. Beverly came over took her paper and pointed her in the direction of Valerie's office.

"Have a seat," Valerie said to Lois. She looked over the typing test and said, "You'll probably need to practice your typing for accuracy. People want accuracy more than speed, although it's to your advantage to have both."

Valerie finally looked up at Lois and said, "Lois, I don't know that we can help you at this time. How long have you been out of high school?"

"I graduated this summer," Lois answered.

"Have you considered going to a technical, or business School? The clientele we service are looking for a little more than a high school education. It does not have to be college, but some kind of structured training in a particular field. There are schools for receptionist-typist, bookkeepers and office managers."

She looked down and pulled open a drawer and pulled out some pamphlets, "here are some that will actually help you get a loan to go to their school and will help you find a job when you're finished. If you're interested, I could call some of them for you now."

"I may be interested, but I need money now," Lois answered. "I'm living with my aunt and she has three children. She can't afford to support me while I go to school."

"Some of the schools offer night programs Lois. You could get a day job, or a night job and go when it's convenient for you," Valerie stated.

"That's why I'm here," Lois said, "to get a job."

"I see," acknowledge Valerie, "where does your aunt lives?"

"In an apartment," Lois answered.

"No, I mean what borough."

Lois wasn't sure what Valerie meant. Valerie looked at Lois' confused look and asked, "How long have you been in New York?"

"About a month."

"I see," Valerie said. Lois thought if she could see so much then why wasn't she trying to help her find a job, instead of sitting there asking her all these questions.

"What I meant," Valerie clarified, "is do you live in Queens, the Bronx, Brooklyn…," before she could finish naming the five boroughs Lois said,

"Oh, my aunt lives in the Bronx." Valerie smiled and reached down to open another drawer and began to look through some files.

She began to write something on a piece of paper. "Here is the address for the job service in your borough. They specialize more in finding jobs for people without skills. Why don't you check them out?" Lois looked at the piece of paper, not registering what Valerie was trying to tell her.

"You mean you can't help me find a job?" Lois asked, sadly. Valerie didn't respond, so Lois showed her the ad she cut out of the paper.

"Your ad said that you would help me find me a job that would be just right for me."

"Yes, our ad did say that," Valerie agreed, "it also says," and she took the folded paper from Lois and looked at it more carefully and then showed it to Lois, while she pointed at something written in very small letters at the bottom of the ad, "some skills required, sweetie. You don't have any skills that we can work with," Valerie said apologetic, "but like I said, job service specializes in helping people without skills find jobs in other sectors of the workforce."

Lois had no idea what she meant by that last statement and since she wasn't going to help Lois find a job, Lois didn't bother to ask her to clarify what she meant about sector.

"Can you tell me how to get to job service?"

"Even if I could," Valerie said looking at the time, "it's probably too late to go down there today. They close at five and since they are a state operated agency, they don't care if you have been standing in line forever, when it's time to close, they close. I could tell you how to get there from here, but I couldn't tell you how to get there from where you live."

Valerie got up out of her chair and said, "I'm really sorry we can't help you Lois, but if you decide to go to one of those schools come back and see us and ask for me." She gave Lois her card.

"Thanks." Lois said, as she left Valerie's office feeling rejected and disappointed.

The next day, with new enthusiasm, Lois got directions from Deb and headed down to job service.

The building was old and grayish looking. She needed to go on the second floor of the six-story building. She walked into the huge room and looked around for what to do next. There were long lines of people waiting. No one stopped what he or she was doing, not even for a moment to acknowledge her present.

"You need some help?" a man dressed in a uniform came up to her and inquire.

"I, I'm here for a job."

"You want to apply for a job here, or you want them to help you find a job?" the man asked and Lois saw his name written on a badge with 'security' underneath.

"I want them to help me find a job." Lois said.

"Pick one of those blue numbers there and find yourself a place to stand or sit until they call your number," the security guard instructed Lois.

"More like stand" Lois thought as she looked around for a seat and decided to stand against the wall.

Deb told her that she thought the place open at 8am, but wasn't sure. Lois looked around for a sign with the hours of operation on it and she saw one that read "Open Monday thru Friday 8am to 5pm." Lois arrived at 10am.

Lois also saw signs instructing people what line to stand in and whether or not they needed to get a ticket. There were different colored tickets for different things. She heard calls for, green 10, or yellow 15. They repeated the call, waited a few seconds and began to call another number.

One man came back from the bathroom and went to the desk and asked if his number was called.

The woman said, "Yes, and where were you?"

The man became angry and raised his voice at the woman. "What do you mean, where was I? I have been waiting in this line for almost two hours! I'm a diabetic and I had to take a leak! I'm not taking another ticket!"

The woman changed the tone of her voice when she saw how upset the man was at missing the call for his number.

"Sir," she said, "there is no need to get upset. You will be next."

"You danggone right, I'll be next," the man said as he walked back to his seat mumbling, "they make you wait here for hours and soon as you go to the restroom, they call your number. What kind of junk is that?"

As he looked at people sitting, they shook their heads in agreement with him. It was right before noon before Lois' number was called.

The woman name on her desk read, Laura.

"Have you ever been here before?" she asked Lois.

There was no formal greeting, the woman just got right to the point.

"No," Lois said.

"Then you will have to fill out this application."

Not another application Lois thought, she wished she had the one she filled out yesterday from that other agency so she could copy from it. Lois took the application.

"Find a seat over there and fill it out please. When you finish, place it in that box and someone will get back to you."

"Today?" Lois asked in all sincerity, but Laura obviously thought she was being sarcastic.

"Look," the woman began, stopping what she was doing to make sure that Lois understood her, "we do the best we can and we have to go to Lunch too. Look around you at the people in the lines, the people sitting and the people standing against the wall. Half of those people will not be seen today and will have to come back tomorrow. I suggest if you want to get interviewed today, you fill out your application as quickly as possible, put it in that box over there and wait," the woman finished emphasizing "wait."

Lois was about to apologize, but decided that may waste more of her time. She didn't intend to insult the woman, but when the woman said to put her application in a box, she assumed that she would not get seen today and would have to come back tomorrow.

To Lois' surprise she found a seat. She sat down and began to fill out the application. She did it quicker than yesterday, because they were mostly the same questions.

When Lois went to place her application in the box, she looked towards Laura's desk, but Laura was gone. Her name plate was turned around and it read, "Out to Lunch." Lois laughed to herself, "at least she gets to go to lunch, I have to wait here for my number, or my name to be call while my stomach cries out, "eat."

"Lois Stone?"

Lois got up and went to the window where her name was being called. Lois thought, "I guess I graduated from a number to a name, which must be a good thing."

"Hi Lois, I'm Eileen. Please sit down."

At least she introduced herself, Lois thought.

Before Lois finished sitting down, Eileen began, "now Lois, the only jobs we have right now for people with little skills like you, are jobs in factory. I may be able to get you into a fast food place. Let me see if I can set up some waitress' interviews for you."

Eileen began to look through books. "Here is how it works. We will send you on job interviews and you will report back to us on how it went. You don't have to come everyday. Let me see. Why don't you come back every Tuesdays and Thursdays to check in. I'll try to schedule all your interviews for Mondays, Wednesdays and Fridays. If you start working before your day to check in, drop us this postcard."

She took a postcard out of her desk and gave it to Lois, "all you have to do is put your name on it and write, 'I am working'. If you get a job through us, the company will call us and let us know that they hire you. Okay."

"Okay," was the first word Lois spoke, since she sat down.

"Let me make some phone calls. What time do you prefer to go on interviews?"

"It doesn't matter. Anytime is good."

"Good," said Eileen, "because quite honestly, if you are coming to us for a job you should make yourself as available as possible. People will be more willing to work with you, if they see that you are flexible to their schedule."

Without saying another word, Eileen picked up the phone and began to make phone calls to companies. She called restaurants concerning waitress jobs, hotels concerning housekeeping jobs, factories, etc.

When she got off the phone, she began to give Lois one card after another. The cards had the name and address of the company, a name of the person Lois was to see, the time and day of the appointment. She had at least three interviews for Lois that week.

"I think that's enough for one week. If you have any questions about the interview before you go, just give me a call." She gave Lois her card. "When you come back, you will take a purple card, that's me. If for some reason I am out, someone will be here to help you. Do you have any questions?" Eileen asked Lois.

"No," Lois replied.

"Okay then," Eileen said, "good luck. I hope one of these works out for you, if not; I'll see you back next week."

"Thanks," Lois said, even though she felt somewhat enthuse about her prospect, she was realizing for the first time that she probably was going to need more than luck to land a job, maybe she'll call her mother later to pray for her, she thought.

She looked at the cards in her hand, at least she had some interviews.

Lois was backed the next week and the next.

"Lois, I know you don't want to hear this," began Eileen, "but I've received calls from some of the places that I sent you and they are questioning my judgment on sending them someone with no experience."

"Some of the people said that the jobs were just filled, or call back tomorrow and when I call back they say, well we had you and someone else in mind and we chose the other person, sorry, we'll keep your application on file." Lois said in her defense.

"I know," said Eileen, "but what I am saying is that maybe you need to go back to school and get some training. Most of the jobs that I am sending you to are dead end jobs anyway. You seem much too intelligent for that. What are your plans, anyway?"

"Plans?" Lois never thought of any plan. Her plan was to make a lot of money and buy all the things that other people had that she didn't.

"Listen Lois, you are too young for this, you need a plan. I can help you with that."

"How?" Lois asked.

"I can help you get state funding to get into a technical college."

"That would take me two years," Lois stated and Eileen shook her head in agreement.

"What about a business school?" Lois asked remembering what Valerie told her yesterday.

"That's a choice. There are certainly plenty of them out there, but there are no state funding for those types of school, but they will help you get a loan. Most of them are legit. We can look up the ones with the best statistics at finding their graduating students a job."

"Let me think about it." Lois said feeling rejection all over again from her first interview with Valerie, except Eileen was much more helpful and sympathetic.

"In the meantime, here are some more interviews," said Eileen as she gave Lois about three more cards with interview schedules on them. That seemed to be her limit with Lois, three a week.

Lois got up and left, as Eileen called out her next client. She wished there was more she could do for Lois, but Lois didn't have any skills or experience that she could work with, but she stilled wished she could do more.

Another month past and Lois did not have a job. She was going through the paper when the phone rang.

"Hello."… "Hi Mom."

Stephanie got right to the point. She was concerned that Lois had not find a job yet, and did not want her to be a burden to Deb.

"I know Mom."… "I really did not promise to come home after a month."… "You and Richard decided that would be best."… "Mom, there are lots of jobs out here. I just have to find the one that's right for me."… "I am helping Deb out."… "No, I don't baby-sit for her during the day. The boys are in a summer day program and Deb said it was better to keep Bridgett in daycare, because they charge her the same price, regardless."… "Well, because I don't stay home everyday. I could get a call from the job agency anytime to go for an interview and I need to be able to pick up and go."… "I'm not going to promise you that. I will find a job. It's not like I'm not looking."… "There are jobs."… "There are jobs for everybody."… "Okay, Mom." Lois was getting agitated with her mother's call. She called once a week to monitor Lois' progress. "Okay Mom, I'll talk to you later."… "I love you too."… "I will think about it." Lois hanged up the phone.

The last thing her mother asked her to do was to consider her other options, if she did not find a job soon. She said she would, but she had no intentions of going back to Tennessee to go to a technical college. Eileen had given her some paperwork on some business schools in the area, maybe she would consider getting a loan to go to school for six months. With a loan, Eileen said she could probably borrow enough to pay for her transportation to school and back. They would help her find a job at the end of the six-month and then she would pay back the loan. Maybe that was her best option, if Deb didn't mind her staying longer. She would talk to Deb about it tonight, Lois thought to herself. She could go to school at night and baby-sit for Deb during the day. That way Deb could save some money on Daycare.

As the children sat with their bowl of ice cream in front of the TV, Lois and Deb was cleaning up in the kitchen, when Lois made her proposal.

Deb thought for a minute then replied, "I think you should go back to school Lois, but it isn't necessary for you to baby-sit for me during the day, besides I think it's best for Bridgett to be around kids her age."

Lois felt her heart sank. She couldn't ask Deb to let her live in her apartment free of charge, while she went to school at night, besides her parents wouldn't allow her to impose on Deb like that.

Deb saw Lois face sank, and said. "I think the factory where I work have some openings posted. Matter of fact, my supervisor asked me the other day if I knew of someone who worked as hard as me who needed a job."

This was hard for Deb to do. She did not like the place where she worked. She didn't want any one to have to work there, especially her niece, but she knew Richard and Theresa would not allow Lois to stay with her if she was not helping out.

"I'll see if I can put in a word for you tomorrow, but you have to promise that you will go to school at night, so that you won't have to work their for long." Deb stipulated.

"I will Deb, but you sound like you don't want me to work there."

"Baby, I don't want anyone I know working there."

"Then why do you?" ask Lois.

"Right now, it's a job and it pays the bill and put food on the table. I can't afford to work during the day and go to school at night with three kids. It's just not reasonable."

"Maybe when I finish school and get a good job during the day, I can stay home with the kids at night and you could go to school at night."

Deb smiled at Lois and said, "That's a nice thought Lois, but you have your own life to live. You had nothing to do with me being so stupid to have three kids out of wedlock with fathers who don't even know how to spell responsibility. My time will come."

Lois had always wondered how Deb ended up the way she did, but she never wanted to ask, maybe one day Deb would feel comfortable enough to talk to her about it, but she felt uncomfortable pursuing the issue.

Deb saw the look on Lois' face and mistook it for pity.

"Don't feel sorry for me. I love my kids. They are the best things in my life and I loved their fathers. I was just too stupid to realize that they didn't know anything about love." Lois nodded, as if she knew what Deb was talking about, but she didn't.

Deb wanted to change the subject, so she said, "With that settled let's get our deserts and sit before the TV."

"Lets," said Lois as they laughingly began to dish out ice cream in bowls.

It didn't take much for Deb to convince her supervisor to hire Lois. The paper factory was known for hiring teens right out of high school. Deb met her children's fathers at the factory. Now that Deb was saved she saw the factory as a cesspool for sin, adultery, fornication, lying, stealing, hatred, lust, backbiting, gossip, and every other sinful acts and deeds.

Lois was nervous her first day on the job. She did not want to let Deb down, or embarrass her in anyway. Mary, Deb's supervisor, said she would get Lois in her department, but Laura, who was a supervisor of the Pasting department, insisted she needed Lois more. They said that it would be better for Lois to work on slower machines at first. When she mastered the slower machines, she could move to the faster ones. They paid fifty cents more, when you worked the faster machines.

Everyone was nice to Lois, but Lois who was never considered shy found a lost for words, mainly because most of the workers in her department were Puerto Ricans and Haitians and she couldn't hardly understand a word they say, especially when they began to talk in their own language.

Lois found herself just smiling, nodding her head and agreeing to everything they said.

When she messed up, they started speaking in their own language. Lois knew that meant they were cursing her out, talking about her, or both. Lois thought, thank God for Laura. She was African American and seemed very nice. She came over to check on Lois every now and then to make sure everything was okay. She had a good relationship with everyone in her department and she made Lois feel comfortable.

Every time Lois messed up something, she would say, "It's your first day; don't let those women get to you with their gibberish. They're just intimidated by someone new, especially because you're an American.

"Why?" Lois asked.

"Because half of them are probably illegal," Laura responded

"What do you mean?" Lois asked.

"When you are not an American citizen, you need a work visa to work in the States and most of them probably don't have one and are probably not American citizens," Laura explained.

Lois wasn't sure what all of that meant and she didn't want to ask anymore questions, because a small Puerto Rican lady was yelling, "you no talk, you work, you first day, work, work, work!"

Laura looked at her and told her to turn around and mind her own business. She pouted, but obeyed. They obviously respected Laura as well.

The machines kept breaking down and none of the ladies on her machine would call the mechanic assigned to their machine to fix it. They just used the opportunity to talk, so since Lois did not have anyone to talk to, she called Joe over, who was introduced to her by Laura. That didn't sit right with the women. They gave Lois a hard stare, as Joe began to work on the machine. Soon Joe had the machine up and running.

"What was wrong with it?" Lois asked.

"You want my job too?" Joe asked.

"Too?" Lois asked confused. "I haven't taken anyone job, yet," said Lois, with an emphasis on "yet."

Joe laughed and said, "I think I'm going to like you little girl. Pastes get clogged up in the machine and the machines choke," Joe began to explain, "all I do is take this little scraper and scrape the glue off and VOILLA!" Joe exclaimed, "and the machine starts to work again."

Except for the occasional visit from Laura and Joe, Lois day seemed long and boring. She was glad when it was time to go home. Maybe one day she may make a friend or two, Lois hoped.

They rode the Factory bus to and from work for a small fee, which meant they did not have to wait on public transportation. Lois fell asleep on the bus and had to be awakened by Deb at their stop. As they walked home, Deb asked her about her day and how she liked the work and did she make any friends.

When she got to the apartment, she went straight to the bathroom to run water for her bath. She knew Deb and the kid's routine and it would be at least an hour before Deb started giving them their bath and then she would take hers afterwards. Lois was not big on baths, but she felt like she needed one tonight. It wasn't that she worked so hard, but it was her first day on an eight-hour day job and her body was feeling it.

Lois found out that she couldn't register for the business school that she wanted to attend at night, until December. She planned to go in the spring, because the fall session was full, until then, she spent the afternoons helping Deb with the preparation of dinner, the boy's homework and getting the kids ready for bed. Deb and Lois had an agreement. Lois would contribute to the grocery bill while she lived there, pay for her phone calls and give something towards the electric bill. Deb didn't want to put too much responsibility on Lois, because she knew she would be saving to get her own place.

Chapter Six
Jewel

Jewel went from calling home every day for the first week to every other night, then once on the weekend.

She made an "A" in her course, and was pleased that she was starting college off on a good note. When she went to apply for a job, there weren't many more openings on campus, but she did have the advantage of being there early enough to choose from a select few designated for freshmen. It was a toss-up between being the hall monitor for her dorm, or an aide in the Library. Both offered an opportunity to study at work, but Jewel felt the Library would be quieter and handy when she needed to do research.

She left the Registrar's office annoyed because she didn't get all the subjects she wanted. She couldn't pre-register for the fall, because upper classmen had first picked, so by the time she could register one of her classes was filled, so she headed back to the dorm to review the fall manual again to choose another subject to fulfill her semester hours.

She had it all planned out on how many courses she would have to take during each semester to finish her undergraduate studies and move on to graduate school within three to three and half years.

When she returned to the dorm, there was a tall girl at her door searching for something in her bag and cursing through her teeth.

"Excuse me," Jewel said standing behind the girl.

The girl turned around and asked, "Are you in this room too?"

"Yes, I'm Jewel Stone. Who are you?"

With everything in her hand the girl held out her hand to Jewel and introduced herself.

"Hi, I'm Kimberly, but everyone calls me Kim."

It suddenly dawn on Jewel that today was the day freshmen would be checking into the dorms for fall semester.

"I'm sorry," Jewel said. "I forgot what day it was. Do you have your keys?"

"Yeah, somewhere in the bottom of this bag that holds the secret to my beauty," explained Kim.

"Let me get the door," Jewel offered pulling out her keys and unlocking the door.

"Thanks," Kimberly said, glad to have the search for her keys come to an end, at least for now.

Kimberly looked around the room. There were three beds in the room, a bunk bed and a twin bed, both on opposite sides of the room. The room was big enough for three people, which was fine with Kim, because she had four sisters and had to share a room with one of them, but Kim wasn't sure which bed was Jewel because there were clothes and things on all three of the beds.

Jewel didn't pick up on Kim's confusion, so she asked, "Which one of the beds have you chosen?"

"Oh, this one," said Jewel pointing at the twin bed closes to the window.

"I'll take the top bunk bed then; I would rather not have someone step over me."

"Good choice," Jewel agreed, but didn't make any attempt to move her things.

Finally Kim asked, not wanting to assume, maybe the other girl had already arrived. "That is, if it's not already taken. Has the other girl arrived yet?" she asked after Jewel still did not make an attempt to claim the things on the top bunk bed.

"No," Jewel replied, "she hasn't."

"Then I guess those are your things," Kim said pulling the things off the bed.

"Oh, I'm sorry," Jewel apologize, finally understanding, "those are my things. Let me move them out of your way," she said reaching past Kim to pull down clothes that she had thrown over the bed.

She took the clothes and threw them on the bottom bunk bed.

"Maybe you should put them somewhere else," suggested Kim, "I'm sure the other girl will be here today."

"Yeah, she probably will be," Jewel agreed, as Kim looked at her out of the corners of her eyes.

"Do you know the other girl?" Jewel asked Kim.

"No, I don't, but I sort of hope she's a sister."

Jewel didn't know how to comment on that. She never thought about things like that, although her parents were constantly concerning themselves with making sure that she had as many black friends as white.

"I'm going to get the rest of my things. I'll be back in a little bit."

"Do you need any help?" Jewel offered.

"No, but thanks for asking. My dad and brother are waiting downstairs for me, so they can help bring up the rest of my stuff."

After Kim left the room, Jewel remembered why she had come back to the room. She found the college fall semester guide and was looking through it for another course to take.

She began to wonder what it was going to be like to live with two girls that she didn't know. She had her own room at home. She used to share a room with Tessa, but when she turned 13 she convinced her parents that she needed her own space. They agreed and she moved into the guest bedroom, but because her father had relatives out of town, it seemed every summer and holiday she was replaced and had to move in with Tessa. Finally, her father built a guest suite over their garage. It had a bedroom, a bathroom, a small kitchenette and a small sitting area. She tried to convince her parents to let her stay up there, but to no avail. They felt she would be too separated from the family. In the end, she was glad she didn't, because once her dad's relatives found out about the suite over the garage, someone was always visiting. Her dad loved having his family and friends over, but she knew her mother felt put out, but she would never say anything about it.

It seemed like hours before Kimberly came back. When she did, there was an elderly man, a young boy and a white girl with her.

"I'm back," she announced as she open the door.

"I see you found your keys," Jewel commented.

"Yes I did, and I found our third roommate." She turned to the girl, "Jewel, this is Jennifer."

Jennifer held out her hand to Jewel, "Hi Jewel, call me Jenny please."

"Great, I guess I'm the only one that doesn't have a shorter name." Jewel observed.

"Jewel doesn't need to be shortened," said Jenny, "It's a nice name. How do you spell it?"

"J.E.W.E.L," Jewel spelled out her name for Jenny.

"That's different. I don't think I've heard it spell that way before."

"Check out her last name," Kimberly said.

Jennifer looked at Jewel puzzled and Jewel replied, "Stone."

Jennifer smiled, "were you teased a lot about that in grade school?"

"No," Jewel answered, "and I don't expect to be teased about it in college."

"And I'm sure you want," Jennifer said, "it's just interesting, that's all."

There was an awkward silence as Kimberly broke in to introduce the other people she had brought back up with her.

"This is my daddy and my brother."

Both girls acknowledge Kimberly's relatives, as Jennifer looked around the room and Jewel explained the sleeping arrangements to her.

"That's my bed over there. Kim is on the top bunk bed and we left you the bottom."

"Great," said Jenny. "Hope you don't mind the bottom?" Kim said only to be polite. She had no intentions of giving up the top bunk bed.

"No, the bottom's fine," Jenny replied.

Jewel noticed that Kim was being nice to Jenny, despite her earlier comment about hoping their roommate was a sister.

With everyone settled in, Kim took the initiative to call a room meeting.

"I think there are some things that we need to talk about. Our ways are going to be new to each other. Some things are going to be good and some things are going to bad, so why don't we set some rules."

"That sounds great!" said Jenny, "I'll get a paper and pen and write them down, and then we can type it up later and put it on the wall as a reminder."

"Is that okay with you Jewel?" Kimberly asked noticing Jewel was being non-committal.

"That sounds great." Jewel said.

"Okay, each one of us will take turn to come up with a rule. It's three of us, so let's make it fair and list nine rules with each one of us choosing three. I'll go first," Kim volunteered. "Rule number one. Clean up after yourself. Jewel you go."

Jewel was a little reluctant. She didn't have many rules at home, so she didn't know what to say. "I don't have one," she said.

"Just say something that really matters to you, or something that could really get on your nerves, you know," Jenny said trying to help Jewel out.

"Okay, we'll come back to you," said Kimberly, "go ahead Jenny."

"Rule number two, absolutely no boys in the room."

Jewel didn't understand that rule, so she interrupted by questioning Jenny's rule. "I thought dorm policy didn't allow for boys in the room."

"Policies are made to be broken," Kim said, "we're just reinforcing it. Your go Jewel"

"Okay," Jewel said, rule number three, no borrowing without asking." That was a rule she had to enforce on her little sister.

"Very good Jewel," Kim encouraged, "that's a good one." They went around two more times until they had their nine rules.

"Now," said Kim, "Is there any rule that anyone think is too ridiculous, or you want to debate it?"

The other two girls nodded negative, so Kim continued, "I decree that these are the rules that will govern the way we live with each other. These rules will remain in place until one of us leaves and then we will decide on new rules, if we get a new roommate, agree?"

Both Jewel and Jenny said, "agree" at the same time.

"Now, we have to set consequences for breaking the rules." It was obvious that Kimberly was taking charge as dorm room leader and Jewel wondered who gave her the authority to do so, but Jennifer didn't mind, so she went along with it.

"Each one of us will choose one. You go first this time Jenny."

"Okay, if a rule is broken, then the person should do our laundry that week."

"Good one!" exclaimed Kim.

Jewel was getting a little annoyed. Kimberly acted like she would never break a rule. Maybe she lived by rules like these and would be a pro at not breaking them.

"Jewel," Kim said as she was still writing down Jenny's rule.

"The person who breaks a rule would make the bed of the other two people."

"I like that one too," Kimberly said. Jewel felt good about coming up with a consequence, but she knew she was not going to like making up someone else' bed, but it was the only one she could think of, and she wanted to get this over with; she was getting tired.

"Okay, last one. The person who breaks a rule have to take the other two girls out to breakfast the following weekend, Saturday or Sunday, which ever day is convenient for the other two girls and they do not have to agree to the same day."

"How will this work, do we have to do all three if we break one of the rules?" Jewel asked, not sure if she wanted to be governed by rules and consequences.

"Well, let's see," said Kimberly. "What do you guys think?"

"Why don't we do it this way," Jenny suggested, "If someone breaks one of my rule then they have to suffer my consequence."

"That'll work," said Kimberly "and if they break one of Jewel or my rule then they will have to suffer our consequences. You agree with that Jewel?"

"That's fine." Jewel stated, wanting this to end, but Kimberly wasn't finished.

"Let's meet once a week at first to discuss issues that we have with each other and if once a week becomes unnecessary, we can move it to every other week or something. Is that okay with you two?"

At this point, Jewel would've agreed to anything to put an end to the meeting. When both Jewel and Jenny agreed, Kimberly moved to bring an end to their first meeting.

It was late and Jewel went straight to bed. The other two girls stayed up for awhile putting their things away, but Jewel knew that would end soon because one of the rules were that the lights would be out by eleven, but they could use their personal lamp as long as needed, but there would be no talking after twelve midnight, unless all three girls were up.

It was Saturday morning. A week had past since Jewel new roommates arrived. The week had seemingly gone well, or so Jewel thought.

At home Jewel was accustomed to sleeping late on Saturday mornings and having brunch with her family, when there wasn't some activity that one of them had to attend, but if it was not her, she would sleep late and get up and prepare herself a bowl of cereal. Dorm life meant being up and getting to breakfast before ten in the morning. She knew she would miss breakfast many Saturday and Sunday mornings, but obviously this was not going to be that morning.

Kim was shaking her to wake up. She had vaguely heard murmuring before the shaking began, but she was too out of it to hear what they were saying. She didn't know that they were discussing which one of them would tell her about a rule she had broken.

"Jewel, wake up!"

Jewel opened her eyes to see Kim towering over her. She looked up, rubbed her eyes and answered, "What is it? Is the Dorm on fire?"

"Very funny," said Kim, but she was not laughing. "Jewel, you have broken rule number one."

"What?" Jewel asked not knowing what Kimberly was referring to.

"Rule number one, Jewel. Rule number one says that you must clean up after yourself."

"I have," Jewel said defensively.

"Look around you Jewel, your space looks like a war zone."

"My space? I didn't know that it matter how I kept my space."

Kimberly rolled her eyes not believing Jewel could be so naVve, "well it does. We have to live in this room with you and that means we can't help but to be aware of how you keep your space."

"I can't stand a lot of mess Jewel," said Jenny, "I have a phobia and you're breaking your rule as well, because you don't respect us when you don't care about your space."

"I apologize," Jewel said, "give me a break."

"The break is that if you get up and clean this mess up right now, then we'll buy into your ignorance and accept the fact that you really didn't know that rule number one meant your space as well."

"Okay!" Jewel said as she got up out of bed, picked up her toiletry bag and headed for the bathroom.

When she came back Kim and Jenny had left. She thought better of skipping the cleaning until after breakfast. It took her until noon to put her things away and sort out what was clean and not. Jewel decided to go to lunch.

As she was walking out of the door, Kimberly and Jennifer returned. "Wow!" said Kim, "she does have a bed."

Jenny laughed and said, "I told you she was not sleeping on the floor."

"Okay," Jewel said. "It's clean. Are you two happy now?"

"Yes we are," said Kim. "Where are you going?" Kim asked Jewel.

"I've worked up an appetite. I'm going to lunch."

"Want some company? We just came back to get our lunch tickets. We're going down as well."

Jewel was having mixed feeling about these two, but she did not want to alienate herself, so she said, "let's go."

It was not long before Kim and Jenny were not happy with Jewel again. Unfortunately for Jewel, they did not know that this was how she kept her own room at home and her parents stopped bothering her about it and decided that as long as she did not bring her mess in the other parts of the house, it was not something they were going to fight about all the time. As long as she cleaned it periodically, that was fine with them.

Jewel did get her moments when she felt like cleaning her room, but it wasn't that often. Jewel realized this was going to be a problem with her roommates.

Chapter Seven
Lois

Lois had been working at the Paper Company a little over six months, when Kelly arrived.

Lois was promoted to Christine's department, feeding, catching and packing bags on a faster machine. She was working with Edith, a tall light-complexion young woman. She wanted to make friends with Edith, but Edith didn't talk much, nor smile much for that matter, so her communication with Edith was limited to work relations. The women that worked in Christine's department felt superior to the women in Laura's department. Lois never made it to Deb's department. In Deb's department, the women felt superior to the women in Christine and Laura's department. The irony of it all was that the pay was comparable. The other women made about fifty cents or seventy-five cents more than the women in Laura's department.

Kelly was placed in Laura's department. She was very pretty with a deep tan complexion, long black hair, huge round eyes and full lips. She was about Lois' height with a body that made men look twice and women frown and she wore very revealing clothes. She flirted with the mechanics and they fell over themselves to get to her, or make her notice them.

At Lois' machine they had to sit on a high stool that enabled them to feed paper into the machine. Lois already liked feeding into the machine, but now she got to watch "The Kelly show," as she began to call it. The machine Lois worked on was constantly breaking down, for one thing or another and while Lois waited for the mechanics to fix it, she would take the opportunity to watch Kelly. Kelly would occasionally look up and see her and smile a warm smile. She began to wave at Lois in the morning and Lois acknowledge by waving back.

One day Kelly walked over to Lois' machine.

"Hi," Kelly said.

Lois responded, "Hi."

"These machines are fast. I watch you from over there. You are really good at keeping up with this thing. You like working over here?"

"Yes, I do."

"By the way, my name is Kelly." Kelly introduced herself even though she knew Lois knew her name.

"I know," said Lois. "I'm…"

"Lois." Kelly finished Lois' introduction, "well I'd better get back to my station, or…"

Before she could finish her sentence, Flora, one of the women that worked on the machine with Kelly yelled, "Kelly, back to work now! You hold up work! Come!"

Kelly rolled her eyes and it made her look animated, "as I was saying, someone will be calling me soon." Kelly and Lois laughed and Kelly went back to work.

After that day, Kelly and Lois began to take their breaks together. They met in the women's locker room and find a bench to sit and talk. Their supervisors became aware of their routine and issued them a verbal warning about spending too much time on their break, so they began to meet outside for lunch. There was a food truck that came around every morning, lunchtime and two fifteen-minute break time. At lunchtime, they would find a place to go for lunch. The company had a little park area where the workers could go and spend their lunchtime.

During the winter months, there was a break area inside where they went to eat their lunch. Lois was bringing her lunch to work, but that ended when she began to spend more time with Kelly, who usually went out to lunch with her boyfriend, Steve. Kelly began to invite Lois along. Lois didn't care for Steve that much, but she wanted to be with Kelly so she ignored Steve's constant brooding moods. His moods didn't seem to bother Kelly none, so Lois didn't let it bother her.

Deb didn't care much for Lois' friendship with Kelly, matter of fact, she didn't care much for Kelly.

When Lois started to hang out with Kelly, Deb was too much like her sister not to say anything. When she finally found the right opportunity, or so she thought, to say something, Lois didn't receive it in the manner that she hoped.

Lois and Deb's relationship suddenly changed, as Lois' began to see Deb as another authoritative figure in her life instead of a friend. Deb liked the idea of Lois seeing her as a friend, but she knew the time would come when she would have to be to Lois what Stephanie expected her to be when she agreed to let Lois come to stay with her, a guardian.

It was one Sunday morning, when Deb realized how much of an influence that Kelly was making on Lois.

Deb entered Lois' room and Lois still had on her clothes from the night before.

"Lois," Deb called tapping Lois lightly on the shoulder.

Lois turned over and rubbed her eyes and looked at the clock. It was 7:30am. "Yes?" Lois replied inquiring of Deb the reason for her intrusion in her sleep.

"It's time to get up," Deb answered her inquiry.

It seemed to have just registered to Lois that it was Sunday and that Deb was waking her up to get ready for church. They usually left the house at 8:15, so they could be to church by nine for Sunday school. Thirty minutes was all the time Lois needed to get ready, but she usually got up a little earlier to have breakfast with Deb and the Kids, but since she started hanging out with Kelly, breakfast was sacrificed for sleep.

"Oh," Lois replied, "I'm not going today. I'm too tired. I didn't get in 'til 5 am this morning."

"Lois you know my rules," Deb said trying not to show her

annoyance; she knew what time Lois came in that morning, but Lois' was over the age of 18 and they never talked about any curfew. Deb was at a lost on how to handle this new situation with her niece, so she decided to let it ride and pray about it.

"Okay," Deb reluctantly acknowledged Lois' statement, "but we'll have to talk about this when I get back from Church."

Deb didn't wait for any more replies from Lois. She left the room agitated and went to her room and prayed asking God to give her understanding and wisdom in this new situation with Lois. She stayed on her knees until she felt the peace of God. She got up and began to get herself and the children ready for church.

Deb could barely concentrate on the service that day. She was constantly going over in her mind what she would say to Lois when she returned home. When she opened the door to the apartment, there was silence. She couldn't believe that Lois was still sleeping.

She was about to go to the room when the phone rang, so she turned to pick up the phone, "Hello." Deb answered. "Hi Stephanie."… "How are you doing?"… "How are the kids?"… "How's Richard?"… "Good. Tell him I said hi."… "Lois?"… "Yes, she is here. Hold on. I'll get her for you." Deb started to yell, but she decided to put the phone down and go to Lois' room.

"Lois?" Deb called as she knocked lightly on the room door. She called Lois two more times, while still knocking. She decided to open the door to the room. Lois was not there and her bed was made up. Deb's peace left her immediately. She did not know what she was going to tell Stephanie, because she had no idea as to Lois' whereabouts.

She picked up the phone and said, "I'm sorry Stephanie, Lois just stepped out to go to the store."… "Yes, we did just get in from church, but when I said just, I didn't mean that we had just walk through the door. Lois said that she wanted to get something from the store, so when I went into my room to change, the boys said that she left."… "Yeah, we do past a store on our way from church, but she just thought about something else she wanted for dinner and decided to go right back out to get it."… "Yes, I will do that."… "Yes, as soon as she gets in."

Deb was really upset with Lois. She did not like lying to her sister. She went to her room to change, so she could reheat dinner and feed the children.

As she was walking out of the bedroom, she heard Lois' keys turning in the door. She stood by the door and waited until Lois came in.

"Where have you been Lois? Your mother called and silly me, not knowing that you were not in your room told her that you were home, so then I had to lie to her about where you had gone."

Lois looked at Deb as if she was seeing another side to Deb. She knew Deb would be annoyed if she found out that she went out with Kelly, but was too tired to go to church, so she tried to get back early enough to beat them home.

Lois looked up at the clock in the living room and Deb noticed and responded, "I see, so you thought you could sneak out of here while we were at church and be back before we came back. Well, little did you know that your staying home from church today bothered me so much that I accepted a ride from Karen today, so I could get home as soon as possible to resolve this issue."

Lois did not like Deb's attitude, or the position she was taking. She felt the need to stand up for herself, or Deb would think she could order her around.

Lois was trying to find the words to say, when Deb asked, "what do you have to say for yourself?"

"First of all," Lois began her face flushed red with anger to match Deb's rising temper, "I do not have to answer to you. You are not my mother and I'm not a child. I'm nineteen years old. Secondly, I did not make you lie to my mother, maybe the devil made you do it."

With that remark, Deb was furious. "You're in my home young lady and I'm your aunt and you will not talk to me like that!" Deb screamed at Lois.

"Then you need to mind your own business," Lois yelled back.

Deb felt a tug on her pant leg and looked down to see Bridgett tugging at her pants saying, "mommy don't fight Loie."

Deb was so furious with Lois; tears were welling up in her eyes. She managed to calm herself down and say to Bridgett. "Mommy is not fighting Lois sweetie, go over there and sit down. I'm about to get you guys something to eat. Go on," she slightly pushed Bridget, who reluctantly walked away looking back as she walked back into the living room. "This is not the time to finish this conversation," Deb said to Lois, "but I assure you, we will finish it."

"Whatever," Lois responded, as she did a quick turn on her heels and went to her room.

Deb went back into her room and got back on her knees. She repented, because she knew she didn't handle the situation the way she should have, but she was fuming at Lois' ungrateful attitude. Finally she got up, realizing no peace was going to come to her right now concerning this. She needed to feed the children and come back to pray later.

Deb was in the kitchen when the phone rang and Kevy answered the phone. It was for Lois.

Lois came out of her room, picked up the phone and pulled the long cord into her bedroom. It was Kelly. "No, I didn't make it back home before them, and my aunt went off."... "It's not your fault." Lois was saying to Kelly's apology. "No I better not go back out tonight. I have to call my mother, if I don't, she will call back and only God knows what my aunt may tell her, then she'll get all bent out of shape and try to make me come home, or something. Worst than that, I guess, is that my aunt could kick me out of her apartment."... "I know. Let me get off this phone Kelly. I need to call my mom, before my aunt does."... "Okay, I'll talk to you tomorrow." Lois pressed the button for a dial tone and dialed her parent's number.

"Hi Mom. How's everybody?"... "I'm great."... "Everything is okay."... "I can't read aunt Deb's mind, Mom."... "She didn't say that anything was wrong."... "Mom, no, she isn't acting strange to me." Lois allowed her mother to go on and on trying to get her to confess to something. She knew her mom and she had a knack for knowing when something was bothering someone. She called it discerning of spirit. Lois didn't care what her mother said. She was not saying anything. If Deb decided to tell her about their argument, then she would just have to tell her side of it, but until then she'll just let her mother speculate, because she knew nothing for sure. "Okay mom. I'll talk to you soon. Bye." Lois wandered when these calls from her mother would end.

The next day Steve picked Kelly and Lois up for lunch and they went to McDonalds.

"Did you and your aunt resolve anything last night?" Kelly asked.

"No," Lois replied "the tension was so thick you could cut it with a knife."

"What are you going to do?" Kelly wanted to know.

"I guess I'll just wait until she says something to me about it, until then I'm just going to let it ride. And my mother," Lois went on, "she calls me all the time, as if I was still a little child. It's so annoying. It's driving me nuts. I don't know what to do?"

"I guess as you get older and a little more independent, maybe she'll let up," Kelly said sensing Lois' frustration and trying to ease her mind.

"I hope so," Lois said.

The tension between Lois and Deb lasted a week.

Lois was glad when Friday came. Steve was in a band and had a gig that night and Kelly asked Lois to tag along with them.

"It'll be fun. You can be a groupie."

"What's a groupie?" Lois asked, "sounds like a fish."

Kelly laughed, "no that's a grouper, I said groupie silly. It's just someone who hangs around a band."

"I don't know if I want to hang around Steve's band. I don't think they like me," Lois said.

"Are you kidding? Steve's friends think you're hot."

"Really?" Lois asked, surprised.

"As if you didn't notice," Kelly said.

Lois did notice how some of the guys looked at her and a couple of them even asked her to dance last week when she went with Kelly to a party at a friend of Steve's.

"I don't know…after last week I don't want to make my aunt more upset with me. How late will we be out?" Lois asked.

"Late," Kelly came right out and said. "Lois you are an adult. You can't let your aunt run your life and stop you from having fun."

"I know," Lois said. "Okay, I'll go," Lois decided.

"Great!" said Kelly, "then it's set, we'll pick you up about nine."

Lois knew she would have to tell Deb about her plans, but she wasn't looking forward to it.

Lois got home before Deb, because Deb had to pick up Bridgett from daycare and the boys from their after school babysitter. She was sitting on the couch when Deb walked through the door.

Deb and her children had routines for everyday of the week. On Fridays, the boys had playtime in their room and occasionally they let Bridgett play with them. Lois was glad that this was one of those days.

Deb went straight for the laundry. They took turns with the laundry, while the other one stayed in the Apartment with the children.

As Deb was headed for the door, Lois got up and said, "I'm going out with Kelly and Steve tonight."

Deb stopped and was about to say something, but she thought better of it and continued out the door to do the Laundry.

After the Laundry was done, Deb bathe the children and put them in their nightgown.

Lois took a shower after they were finished in the bathroom and put on her robe until it would be time to get ready for her night out.

Deb ordered pizza and walked down to the nearest video store and rented the children a movie. When the children were all settled down, eating their pizza and watching their movie, Deb asked Lois to come to her room.

Deb pulled the door partially close, so she could hear the children, as she started the conversation by asking Lois, "What time do you expect to be in tonight?"

"It's going to be late," Lois replied, "We are going with Steve and his band has to stay until the dance is over."

"I see," said Deb, "Lois," Deb went on "I know we didn't talk about you going out and what time I expect you back in. Honestly, I didn't feel it was necessary. You were practically raised in church and I know your mother has instilled good values in you, so I didn't see the need to have that conversation, but I was obviously wrong."

Deb was calm. She had regained her composure and was focus on the issue.

"Aunt Deb," Lois began, using aunt so that Deb knew their relationship had taken on a new tone. "I don't know what you might have thought, and yes, my mother did drill in me a lot of things, but those were her beliefs, not mine."

That statement caught Deb by surprise and she understood a little more than she wanted to.

"I'm an adult now," Lois went on to say, "I'm nineteen." Lois said emphasizing the "nineteen."

"I want to live my life the way I see fit, not the way my mother or you or anybody else wants me to. I know you think that Kelly is a bad influence on me, but how do you know what kind of influence I am on her."

Deb didn't know how to take that statement.

"Kelly is a good person, no matter what people think or say about her. One thing I do remember from our youth group back home is that you shouldn't judge someone before you get to know them."

Lois remembered Jewel and how she made friends with her, in spite of Jewel father's opinion of her. She and Jewel had become best friends and she missed that and wanted that with Kelly.

"I don't want to go to church every Sunday. I'll go some Sundays, when I want to, not because someone is making me go. I'm sorry if I have disappointed you."

Deb was lost for words. She had planned to lay down the rules to Lois about how late she should come back into the apartment at night. She also wanted to reinforce the rule about going to church on Sunday, but suddenly, Lois sounded a lot like her when she left home, off to make it own her own.

Deb saw the look in Lois' eyes and realized her mind was set. She came to New York to do her own thing and no one was going to stop her. Deb knew the look. She just hoped that Lois wasn't headed down the same road that she was on, or worst, but she also knew that there was nothing she could say at this point to change Lois' mind.

Feeling like she should say something Deb replied, "Lois I know something of that road you want to take. I've been there. I finally got turned off that road, three children later and no real man to say to my children, this is your daddy. Yeah, they have some man whom they see every now and then, but he is just someone for them to call daddy, but he isn't even a real man, let alone a real daddy, so I'm left to be both mother and father to my children. I don't want to see that happen to you."

With all sincerity, Lois looked at Deb and said, "It won't happen to me Aunt Deb, I promise," and Deb knew she meant it, but she also knew there were some promises you couldn't keep, because you can't see the end of the road until you get there.

"You can continue to stay here Lois, until you can afford a place of your own. I owe that to my sister, but because I know where you're headed, I want you to start looking for a place of your own as soon as possible. You're my niece and I'll always be here for you, but I have left that life you are longing for and I don't want any parts of it, not even seeing you live it." Deb got off the bed where she was sitting and hugged Lois and said, "I love you and I want nothing but the best for you. I will be praying that one day you will find what you are looking for."

This time it was Lois' who had tears in her eyes. She expected Deb to put up more of an argument.

That night Lois didn't have much fun at the dance. She caught a cab and came home early. On Sunday, she went with Deb and the children to church.

On Monday, she and Kelly caught a ride to lunch with one of the guys from the job.

"What's the matter?" Kelly asked Lois. "You have been in a sour mood all weekend. That's why I didn't stop you when you said that you were going to get a cab home Friday night. You having your period or something?"

"No." Lois replied. "I'm sorry I've been in a sour mood, but my aunt and I finally had our talk."

"How did it go?" Kelly asked. "Did you stand your grounds?"

"I guess," Lois half-heartedly replied.

"Talk to me Lois," Kelly insisted, "tell me all about it," and Lois did.

After Lois was finished, Kelly had an idea, "Lois, why don't we get an apartment together?"

Lois was not expecting that response, but her face lit up at the thought of having Kelly as a roommate.

"Really?" Lois wanted to make sure Kelly was for real.

"Yeah." Kelly said.

"Can we afford it?"

"I think we can. Let's start looking in the paper and asking around. I'm sure we will be able to find a place that we can afford."

"Okay," Lois said, suddenly feeling much better.

Everyday after that, Kelly or Lois bought the paper and began to search.

One morning Kelly came running up to Lois' machine and whispered into Lois ears, "I think I have find us a place."

"Where?" Lois asked. "I'll tell you all about it on our break. Meet me in the back."

When Kelly had something that she wanted to tell Lois and did not want to risk anyone hearing it, she would always request that Lois meet her in the back. They would walk to the back and go outside of the Factory.

The back led to a view of a river and in the winter it was too cold to be out there, but during the summer a lot of the workers would take their break out there to catch the breeze flowing in from the river.

When Lois came out, Kelly was already there rubbing her hands together, holding herself and walking back and forth to keep warm.

"What took you so long?"

Lois didn't want to waste time being interrogated by Kelly, so she didn't bother to answer; instead she got right to the point, "tell me about the apartment."

"My sister's boyfriend has a sister who's getting married. Her roommate has decided to live with her boyfriend, because she does not want to live with another female. My sister told her that I was looking for an apartment. They have a rent control apartment. The roommate doesn't really want to give up the apartment, because she isn't sure how living with her boyfriend will workout, so she wants to sublet the apartment."

Lois was confused. "Sublet? What does that mean?"

"It means, we rent the apartment from her. Their lease is up for renewal this year. I will sign the lease as her new roommate, but actually you and I will live in the apartment."

Lois heard enough to ask, "what if it doesn't work out with her and her boyfriend. It seems that I will be the one without an apartment."

"The deal is for one year," Kelly went on to explain. "If she decides before a year that it isn't going to work out between her and her boyfriend, she gets to move back into the apartment, but we get to stay there until we find a new apartment."

"Will there be room enough for three people?" Lois asked.

"There are two bedrooms and since this is my idea, she'll stay in my room until we find something else, if it comes to that."

"Or, until y'all kick me out. My name is not going to be on the lease, remember," Lois stated. "How will I know you two won't kick me out?"

"Hey," Kelly sounded offended. "You my girl. I got your back, even if that was to happen, I wouldn't just kick you out and I wouldn't let her either."

"Kelly, you don't even know this girl and you're acting like you can trust her."

"Hey, I got people." Kelly said, doing a bad imitation of a gangster.

Lois laughed and said, "Okay, Ms. Capone, but we better head back in before we get fired or freeze, or both."

This time Kelly laughed, at her even worst imitation of a gangster, but she was in agreement that they should go back in.

At lunch, they agreed to go over to the apartment after work to check it out. The apartment building was not in the projects and for Lois that was a big plus. It was next to a fairly decent subdivision in Queens. It meant they would have to take a train every morning to catch the company bus to work. The apartment building was clean. The intercom and the elevators worked. The apartment had two large bedrooms, a small living room and a walk-in kitchen. The girls loved the apartment. It was on the second floor, so if the elevator broke they could walk up and down the stairs.

The girl, who was getting married, was not there, but Teri, the roommate was. She explained the arrangement. It wasn't any different from what Kelly explained to Lois. Lois left feeling good about it. The lease was up in a month and Teri's roommate was getting married the week after that. Lois and Kelly could move in within five to six week. The girls were excited. Lois made Kelly promise not to tell anyone until she had time to tell Deb.

Lois stared up in the ceiling for almost an hour. Her mind was spinning. She finally got up and began to write in her diary. Tomorrow morning she was moving into her own apartment. It was an exciting time for Lois, another phase in her life was beginning, but her joy and excitement were overshadowed by her families' doubt and skepticism.

Deb surprised her with a lecture on how she felt that it was too soon for her to move out on her own, how it wasn't a smart idea to move in with someone she only knew for a short period of time. Lois didn't understand where Deb was coming from, since she was the one that told her that she would have to move, but Lois didn't bother to bring that to her attention. She obviously said it to scare Lois into doing the right thing, which only backfired.

When they got on the subject of school, Lois said she was putting it on hold until she got settled. Deb was not happy. Her parents were even more upset. They accused her of being irresponsible, not thinking things through, but none of what they were saying registered with her. She had her mind made up and there was nothing any of them could say to change it. Her eyes finally became heavy. She closed her diary and soon was fast asleep.

When she woke up Deb was up and cooking breakfast. Lois got up to take a shower, so she could be ready when Kelly and Steve arrived to pick her up. The idea of spending her first night in her new apartment with Kelly, where she would be paying her own rent and bills made her feel a sense of accomplishment.

As Lois was doing a final look through of the room to make sure she didn't leave anything, she heard the doorbell. She grabbed two of her bags and went to open the door, but Deb had gotten to the door first and invited Kelly to come in.

"Hi Kelly," Lois said behind Deb to let Deb know that she was standing behind her.

"Good morning," Kelly responded.

"Why don't you come in and have some breakfast with us," Deb offered Kelly.

"I don't eat breakfast, Ms. Hall," Kelly responded.

"Please call me Deborah, or Deb, and no wonder you're so skinny."

Kelly just smiled. No one had ever called her skinny before. She definitely didn't think she was.

Deb looked at Lois and said, "Lois, don't tell me you can't stay for breakfast. I got up early to make breakfast, so that we could sit down and maybe talk a little before you go. I thought maybe it would be less painful for the children."

Lois knew Deb was intentionally trying to make her feel guilty about leaving the children, because they had grown attached to her and her to them, but she wanted to leave without a production.

"I'm sorry Aunt Deb, but I don't want to keep Steve and Kelly waiting," Lois explained.

Kelly was feeling awkward just standing there, so she grabbed the bags that Lois had sat by the door and ask, "Do you have more bags?"

"I have two more," Lois answered and went back to the room to get them.

"I'll be back to help you with the rest," Kelly said.

But Deb spoke up and said, "I'll help her bring down the rest of her things."

When Kelly left, Deb called to the children, "come and say bye to Lois you guys."

The boys came running up to Lois and hugged her saying, "bye."

Bridgett who had grown especially close to Lois began to cry, "don't go Loie."

Lois picked her up and said, "I'm not going far Bridgett. I'll call you and I'll come by to visit a lot. You'll see me at church and some Sunday afternoons I'll come over to eat some of your mom's good home cooking."

She gave Bridgett a big blow kiss and put her down and said to the boys, "Remember to let her play with you guys, Okay."

"Okay," they both said in unison.

"I'm going to help Lois take her bags down stairs. I'll be right back, okay." Deb yelled at the kids, as they were going back to the living room to watch their cartoons.

When Steve saw Lois and Deb coming towards the car, he got out to open the trunk of the car and Kelly ran around the car and grabbed Lois bag out of Deb's hand and placed it in the back of the car as Lois did the same with the one in her hand.

Steve and Kelly got back in the car, while Lois stood facing Deb with her hands in her back pocket. Deb finally broke the ice and grabbed Lois and hugged her.

"You be good Lois. I'm sorry if your mother and I came down on you so hard about moving. It's just that we love you and want the best for you. Remember, you always have a home here. Don't be a stranger."

All Lois could manage to do was shake her head in agreement. She didn't trust herself to speak. When Deb let go, Lois got in the car and as Steve pulled off, Deb began to wave and Lois saw her wiping tears from her eyes. Lois waved back trying hard not to cry.

Kelly noticed Deb crying and said, "she acts like you are going far away. She's going to see you every day at work."

Lois knew Kelly's statement was for her benefit. No one said anything after that. They drove in silence the rest of the way listening to a tape that Steve had placed in the tape deck.

Chapter Eight
Jewel

It was the beginning of the spring semester and Jewel had just about enough of her roommates with their rules. She was spending all her Saturday mornings taking them to breakfast, because she forgot to pick up something, or made up her bed before rushing off to her morning class.

During the winter break, she complained to her parents about the situation. Theresa tried to be understanding, but she also wanted Jewel to consider the other girls point of view as well. Paul made it clear that he was on Jewel side in the matter. He told Theresa that he didn't send his daughter to college to do house chores, but to get an education and an occasional sloppiness is always to be expected. Theresa told Jewel to discuss her feelings with the other girls and to work out some compromise. Jewel knew that wouldn't work. She could hear Kim saying something like, "tough, you agreed to the rules, and the rules stand so stop being such a B.A.P." B.A.P. was Kim's new slang for calling Jewel a Black American Princess, which she knew Jewel hated being called.

Jewel decided to see if she could change rooms, but she didn't want to be placed in another room with girls she didn't know, which meant she had to make some friends, for Jewel that meant doing more with her free time than just studying and sleeping. Although her hard work landed her on the Dean's list, she decided she was going to lighten up a little and make some friends.

One afternoon after she got off from work, she went out to the track field to study on the bleaches. There were students out running, jogging and practicing for track meets. A blonde hair girl stopped in front of her and began to stretch, as she cool down from her run.

"You got the time?" She asked Jewel.

"Yes, it's 4:30," Jewel said looking at her watch.

"Are you on the track team?" Jewel asked.

"No, I just come out here to run sometime. How about you?" The girl asked.

"No, not me," Jewel responded as if it was unheard of. Then she thought about her comment and added. "I ran a little in high school."

"Yeah?" The girl seemed interested.

"Yeah, we even won second place in my junior year."

"That sounds a little more than a 'little' to me."

Jewel laughed, "I guess it was."

"Why don't you try out for the track team here?" The girl asked.

"No, I need to keep my focus on my studies." Jewel explained.

"So what do you do for activities? Statistic shows that a lot of girls gain weight in college for lack of exercise and extracurricular activities."

"Really?" Jewel asked, finding the girl's statement interesting,

"I do feel like I've gained a few pounds," Jewel said looking down at herself, "probably from having to endure breakfast with my roommates practically every Saturday or Sunday morning."

"What?" The girl asked, confused.

"Oh, nothing," said Jewel, "it's just that we came up with room rules and consequences and buying each other breakfast is one of the consequences for breaking a particular rule."

"I see," said the girl, "whatever works, I guess."

"It isn't working," Jewel said.

The girl looked at Jewel and they both began to laugh.

The girl stood up straight extended her hand to Jewel and said, "I'm Dawn, Dawn Hartman."

Jewel took her hand and said, "I'm Jewel Stone."

"How do you spell that?"

"J.E.W.E.L."

"That's interesting."

"In what way?" Jewel asked.

"A jewel is a stone. I like that."

Jewel and Dawn spent the next forty-five minutes talking.

"It's getting dark," Dawn commented looking up at the sky, "we'd better head back to the dorm."

"Yeah, we'd better." Jewel agreed, "maybe we could get together and jog sometime," Jewel suggested.

"I would like that," said Dawn, "let's exchange numbers."

They exchanged information and agreed to call each other.

Jewel and Dawn spent at least one afternoon a week running. Dawn had only one girl in her dorm room and she liked her, but she was getting to like Jewel better and they discussed how great it would be if they became roommates, but neither one was sure how they should go about accomplishing it.

Jewel called her mother one night and told her about Dawn and asked her to pray that something would work out, so that she and Dawn could room together the upcoming fall semester. Theresa agreed, but not before pointing out to Jewel that she should be praying for herself and attending church services. Jewel made the same old excuses about having too much homework to do and only having Sundays to rest. Theresa tried to get Paul to talk to her, but of course he only saw her side of it and told her to lighten up, because Jewel had a lot on her plate right now and she would get around to going to church. Theresa wanted to know when that would be.

One day after jogging, Jewel and Dawn were sitting on the bleaches talking.

"My roommate is transferring to another college in the fall." Dawn announced.

Jewel heart leaped, but she didn't know if Dawn still wanted her as a roommate. They mentioned it once, but never really discussed the possibility of it happening.

"I'm sorry to hear that Dawn. I know you guys get along very well. Why is she leaving?"

"Homesick."

"Where is she from?" Jewel wanted to sound interested.

"Ohio."

"Wow, she is far from home. I'm from Tennessee and when I get homesick, I can just get on the interstate and head home and be there in a few hours.

"How about you?"

"Right here. My parents couldn't afford to send me out of state to college and I didn't get any scholarships, so here I am."

"But you still got a good deal. This is one of the best colleges," Jewel added.

"Yes it is," agreed Dawn.

"Jewel, did you really meant it when you said that you wouldn't mind being my roommate?"

Jewel laughed and jokingly said, "I considered it, but I don't know what I would do without Kim and Jen." They laughed and got up and head back to their dorms.

Jewel had no problem telling Kim and Jen that she was changing dorm rooms in the fall. When the two girls came in for the night, Jewel was wide-awake.

"Kim, Jen," Jewel addressed the girls, "I'd like to talk to y'all about something."

"We are not doing away with the rules Jewel. Learn to live with it."

Jewel knew that if she wanted to; she could easily make friends with Kim. Kim just wanted to seem tough and hard. She acted like she had a chip on her shoulder for white people, but she seemed to have made friends with Jen, or maybe she was just joining forces with Jen against her, but her sarcastic remarks was just an annoyance to Jewel. After she started calling Jewel a BAP, Jewel decided that she had better things to concern herself with than Kim's criticism of her.

When Jewel told Kim and Jen that she had made the Dean's list with straight A's, Kim's reply was that, "it's not an accomplishment when you don't have to work hard for it."

Kim would stay up late at night telling her and Jen about what she did to get where she was, which to Jewel was not that big of a deal.

Jewel knew of people who had it harder than Kim and she really was tired of hearing Kim go on and on about how hard she had it.

"No, keep your rules, but I won't be here to suffer anymore of the consequences."

"Ha, ha, ha," Kim laughed, "so the little princess can't take a little discipline."

Jewel figured she might as well clear the air while she was at it.

"No Kim, what I can't take is you. I've had enough of your criticism. You know nothing about me, or who I am and what I want out of life. All you care about is your stupid little rules. Granted, I may be a little messy, but is it really that important? We are here to get an education, not to play house." Jewel breathed out, feeling some relief for saying what was on her mind.

"Jewel, I hate to be the one to tell you this, then again I'm not." Kim began. "You've had it your way all of your life and your mommy and daddy has catered to your every need. You probably have a maid, so you have never had to make up a bed or sweep up a floor, but the reality of it all is that you're not home anymore. There are no maids here. Jen and I are certainly not your maids and you couldn't pay me to be. You are not living at home in your own little world. You are living with two other people, who care not to see your underwear left where you step out of them. So go on and move out, I'll give it one semester before your new roommate kick your behind out."

"Come on you guys, there is no need to get into an argument about this," Jen jumped in, "Jewel, you act like we don't like you. That's not the way it is. Everybody has their own little pet peeve. Cleanliness is Kim's thing. It was how she was brought up."

Jewel jumped in before Jen could finish, "I understand Jen, but I wasn't brought up that way. It's not that I lived in a pigpen. I cleaned my room, when I got around to it. My mother didn't make a big issue of my room being clean every minute of the day as long as it got cleaned. I have always been taught to focus on my education and that's all I'm doing, but Kim makes it seem like it's a federal offense to have a piece of clothing hanging out of a drawer, or a cup left over night by the bed."

Jewel turned to Kim who was standing there feeling good about having said her peace, "I apologize for not being more considerate. I understand where you're coming from. You have every right to want a roommate that will abide by the rules. I did agree to the rules. I guess I didn't realize what it really meant. I don't dislike you. That's not why I'm moving out. I just think it's better to move in with someone who I am more compatible with."

After Jewel finished talking, Jen looked at Kim and gesture that she should say something.

"I guess you're okay, Jewel, but you are right we are not compatible and I can't overlook clothe hanging out of drawers, but I do wish you the best with your new roommate."

"Now hug and make up," Jen said.

Kim cut her eyes at Jen and said, "let's not get carried away. I think Jewel and I understand each other. When are you leaving?"

"I'll be here all summer and then when we get back from summer vacation, I'll move into the new dorm. Until then, I will do my best to keep my side of the room clean."

"And I'll do my best not to be on your case so much about it," Kim agreed.

Both girls did their best to keep their words. They even became a little closer with things out in the open.

Jen suggested that since they were getting along better that maybe Jewel didn't have to leave come fall, which both Kim and Jewel replied, "Naaah."

Chapter Nine
Lois

Lois woke to the sound of Kelly yelling and crying. She looked at her alarm clock and the red light glared two in the morning. Lois knew this meant she wouldn't get back to sleep, if Kelly and Steve didn't quiet down. She tried to pull the pillow over her ears, but she couldn't muffle the sounds of the two of them swearing at each other. Lois knew not to interfere.

She did that once, but Steve threaten to do to her what he was doing to Kelly and the next morning Kelly asked her not to butt in anymore. She chalked it up to a lesson learned. When she asked Kelly why they were fighting, she said that it was nothing. Lois knew Steve did drugs, which made her shy away from him even more. Kelly always made up excuses for his behavior. She said he only smoked a little marijuana to calm his nerves before a gig. After every gig, Kelly and Steve ended up in fights.

Kelly did everything she could not to provoke him, but she could not control the stares she received from other guys, or being asked to Dance, while standing around waiting for Steve to take a break. Kelly wore loose clothing to hide her shape, but it didn't stop the guys from hitting on her.

At Kelly's pleading, Lois went along on many of the gigs, but she soon got tired of being a groupie of Steve's band. She ended up going only on some weekends, because it was hard for her to get up and go to work the next day when she hanged out with them during the week, especially when Kelly and Steve spent the rest of the night fighting, after Steve worked himself into a jealous rage.

The night she tried to break up one of their fight, Steve knocked Kelly across a chair in the living area and smacked her in her eye. Kelly spent the rest of the weekend in the apartment because she didn't want her family to see it.

Kelly was the fourth child of five, which included two older brothers who were big. They suspected that Steve and Kelly had fights and told Kelly, if they ever found out Steve was hitting on her they were going to take care of him and show him what it felt like to be a punching bag, so Kelly did everything to keep her fights with Steve her secret and now Lois felt that it was her secret as well, if she wanted to continue to be Kelly's friend.

Kelly was very close to her family and she usually spent part of her weekend visiting her sisters, brothers, or her parents. She had two nieces and a nephew and she was always buying them things. Kelly had a good heart and it was hard for Lois to understand why she would put up with Steve. She could probably date anyone she wanted. When Lois asked her why she put up with Steve, she just shrugged her shoulder nonchalant and said, "you'll find out when you fall in love."

Lois hoped that falling in love wouldn't make her forget to love herself.

"What was the fight about last night?" Lois asked Kelly as she walked in the kitchen to make herself some breakfast.

Kelly was an early riser, especially on Saturday morning, because she wanted to get up so she could visit her family and be back by the time Steve came by.

"For your information it wasn't a fight, we just argued." Kelly said, already annoyed that Lois was bringing it up.

"Kelly..."

"Look, not this morning okay," Kelly jumped in before Lois could finish her sentence.

She knew what was coming and was not up to it this morning.

Lois threw her hands up and said, "fine Kelly it's your life."

"Exactly Lois, it is my life. Speaking of life, you should get one yourself."

"I have a life." Lois responded.

"If you call staying in the house all weekend and going to church on Sunday and having dinner with your aunt a life, then you need a head check."

"You are a fine one to talk and where are you headed this morning?"

"To my sister's," Kelly answered.

"Then don't criticize me for spending time with my family."

"Understandable, but visiting my family is not all I do on the weekends," Kelly said. "Why don't you go out with Troy? He's cute."

"Monkeys are cute," Lois responded.

"Well, then he's handsome."

"Don't let Steve here you say that. He will accuse you of liking him."

"Don't get off the subject Lois, you are not going to take me there with you this morning, okay."

"Okay," Lois said, "as for Troy, I agree. He is cute, but he talks to every girl in the factory."

"That's true," Kelly agreed, "but maybe if you give him the time of day, he wouldn't be talking to every girl."

"Maybe," said Lois.

"Hey why don't you call him up and ask him out," Kelly suggested.

"Are you kidding me?"

"Oh, I forgot, that is sacrilege for you country girls." Kelly remarked sarcastically. "Hey," Kelly said as if she just thought of a great idea.

"Oh, Oh," Lois said, "I'm in trouble now."

"Oh come on Lois, here me out."

"Okay, speak your peace."

"Why don't I ask Steve to invite him to this party we're going to tonight."

"First of all," Lois began, "I don't want to go out on a first date with you and Steve. You guys always end up fighting. secondly, Steve is going to be suspicious of why you are wanting him to invite Troy."

"For your information," Kelly said, "Steve knows that Troy has a thing for you. Steve and Troy are friends, besides we are invited to a friend's birthday party and Steve's band is not playing, which means I can devote all my attention to him.

"I see," said Lois, "that way he'll have no reason to become jealous."

"Come on Lois. You might have some fun," Kelly said ignoring Lois' comment. She was determined not to let Lois turned their conversation into one about her and Steve's fights.

"I'll make sure Steve let Troy knows that it's a general invite and not a date for you."

"Promise?" Lois asked.

"I cross my heart," Kelly said.

"Okay then, I'll go."

"Great!" Kelly said as she jumped out of her chair. "Let me get out of here. I'm taking my niece and nephew to the park."

"Why don't you let me know when you do things like that?" Lois said with a little whine. "I would love to take my little cousins and tag along."

She was also disappointed with herself for not thinking of doing anything like that for Deb's kids.

"You can still join us," Kelly offered.

"No, that's okay. I think I'll go shopping for something to wear tonight."

"That sounds great. Pick me up something nice."

"You don't need anything. You have a closet full of nice things."

"I know," agreed Kelly, "but more isn't going to hurt."

Lois laughed, as she left the kitchen, "I'll see what I can do."

She knew she wasn't going to look for anything for Kelly. When Kelly wasn't at work, she dressed like a model and Lois knew she couldn't choose anything she would like.

Lois and Troy hit it off at the party and soon they became a couple. They ate lunch together and Troy came over in the afternoon to spend time with her after work. She was the envy of every girl that Troy used to talk to. He still talked to them, but they knew that she and Troy had become a couple.

When she asked Troy why he was still talking to other girls, he said it was just work and a way of passing the time. Kelly knew Lois was a little jealous about him talking to the other girls, so she tried to keep him occupied in mindless conversation.

Troy was a player and there were rumors that he had another girlfriend outside the factory. When Kelly asked Steve about it all he said was, mind your business and let Troy take care of his. Kelly liked Troy, but she liked Lois more and she didn't want to see Lois hurt, so she let Troy know that if she found out that he was seeing someone else that she would tell Lois, which Troy replied, "if you do, I'll tell Steve and it won't be so good for you."

Lois got caught up in her relationship with Troy, soon he began to pressure her to take their relationship to the next level, but Lois wasn't ready for that kind of commitment. It bothered her that he still flirted with other girls.

One Sunday afternoon, Deb tried to talk to her about her relationship with Troy. Deb didn't trust Troy and was hearing rumors about him being involved with someone else. She didn't want to get into details with Lois about it, because she knew Lois would think she was just showing her disapproval of another one of her friends, so she tried to make her comments and inquiries as casual as possible, but Lois was bothered by them more than she wanted to let on. She wanted to open up to Deb, but fear Deb would share their conversation with her mother. Even though she didn't signed the contract at her church to be a virgin until she got married, she still wanted to wait until she was married.

Her purpose for coming to New York was to make a lot of money and be successful. She never thought about falling in love and getting married.

She began to make sure that Kelly was always home when Troy came over, and when he came over and Kelly wasn't there, Lois pretended not to be there and she wouldn't answer the door. Troy asked for a key, because he knew Kelly had given Steve a key. Against her best judgment Lois thought, but they never talked about it. Kelly just assumed that it would be all right with her. The truth was that Lois felt uncomfortable with Steve having a Key to come and go as he pleases, especially when Kelly was not home. Steve seemed to come by a lot when Kelly wasn't home. Kelly reasoning was that it didn't make sense for him to leave and go all the way back home just to come back later. Lois argued that he could call first, but Kelly said she was just being paranoid. Lois felt that it was Steve who was being paranoid. She knew that on plenty occasions before Steve came over, Kelly had already told him she was not going to be home, but he came over anyway, just to make sure that Kelly wasn't brushing him off, because she was out with someone else. He would question Lois about Kelly's whereabouts, which Lois commented to Kelly that it felt like he was interrogating her.

Lois wasn't sure what Troy's reasoning for wanting a key, but she wasn't about to oblige him. Lois talked to Kelly about it and her response was that since she didn't know Troy that well, maybe she should wait a few more months before making that decision.

One night while Steve and Kelly were in their room making out, Troy said with an awkward smile, "I don't know about you, but this is a little embarrassing for me. Why don't we just go into your room to watch TV?"

Lois suddenly hated herself for having a TV in her room.

"I don't feel comfortable inviting you into my room Troy, besides it's a mess."

Troy arched his eyebrow and said, "Lois we have been going out for a couple of month now. I don't care about your room being a mess, besides it can't be any messier than mine." He reached over and kissed Lois and said, "I don't think I'm going to be paying any attention to your room." He looked at her and gave Lois a smiled that sent her heart pounding, "besides I think you know what you can do to keep my mind off of your messy room."

Lois pulled away, wondering if he could hear her heart pounding, "I don't think that's a good idea."

Troy became agitated as he said, "I have needs you know. Guys are not like girls, it's hard for us to hold out, and I've been holding out just for you."

Lois couldn't believe that Troy was going to be this predictable. It had been drilled into her the lines that boys use and Troy was using the same lines on her.

"Look Troy, I'm flattered that you are holding out for me. I would like to think of it as more than holding out. Maybe you could think of it as respecting me," Lois said.

"I do respect you Lois," Troy said, "but other girls are pressuring me and if I can't find some relief from my girl, then what am I suppose to do?"

Lois got up and said, "Maybe you're supposed to leave now Troy. I like you, but I will not be pressured into doing something I don't want to do, or am prepared to do."

Troy picked up on Lois words and said, "I have protection."

Lois was getting annoyed that she was not getting through to Troy.

"Look Troy, like I said, I think it's best that you just leave now."

Troy got up and said, "Okay Lois, but remember this was your call. I'm not going to wait forever you know. I can leave here right now and walk over to another female apartment and have my needs met."

Lois faced burned as she went to open the door and said, "Then why don't you just go ahead and do that Troy. Don't let little ole me stop you from getting some relief."

Troy didn't look at Lois as he walked out the door. Lois slammed the door behind him and the echo made it sounded like the big garbage dump truck they heard in the mornings.

Kelly stuck her head out of her room and asked, "is everything alright?"

"Yeah." Lois said as she walked in her room and closed her door behind her.

"Okay," said Kelly as she stuck her head back in and close her door.

The next day Troy was talking to every girl in the factory, who gave him the time of day, but Lois tried her best not to look in his direction, or let it get to her.

Kelly was itching to know what happened the night before, but neither Lois nor Troy would tell her anything. Lois went to lunch with

Kelly, while Troy had lunch with some of the girls outside in the picnic area. Troy underestimated Lois' stubbornness not to give in and finally he came over to Lois' station after lunch to talk to her.

"Can I come over this afternoon?" He asked.

Lois looked at him unbelieving.

"No pressures," said Troy, "I just want to talk to you. I'm sorry I acted like a jerk last night."

Lois didn't know what to say, she never thought that Troy would actually apologize to her. He didn't seem the type to admit that he was wrong.

"Okay," Lois said, "but only if you promise that it will not be a repeat of last night."

"I promise," said Troy. "I just want to talk. See you at seven?"

"Seven is fine," said Lois.

Lois felt better the rest of the day. She felt that since Troy apologized to her, then it meant that he probably cared more about her than she thought he did. After all, he didn't have to apologize at all. He could have left things the way they ended it last night and the two of them could just go their separate ways.

Kelly made a date with Steve, so that Lois and Troy could have the apartment to themselves. She hoped they would make up. She thought they made a cute couple, but she also knew that Troy would have made a cute couple with any pretty girl on his arm. Lois wanted the privacy, but also wasn't sure that she could trust Troy to be alone with him.

Her youth teachers constantly drilled in them the importance of not putting themselves in compromising situations with boys. She knew this was a compromising situation and felt uneasy at Kelly's suggestion to leave them alone for a few hours, but she didn't want Kelly to hear their conversation either.

Troy was prompt. They talked for almost an hour. They talked about their families, their dreams for the future, Kelly and Steve, their likes and dislikes, topics in general.

Troy looked up at the clock in the kitchen and exclaimed, "Wow! I didn't realize we were talking so long. It's almost eight thirty. I'd better go. We both have to get up early in the morning."

"Yeah, I guess we have been talking for awhile," Lois acknowledged.

Troy got up and held out his hand to pull Lois up off the chair. They walked to the door and Troy asked, "Is it okay if I kiss you goodnight on the cheek?"

"It's okay," Lois said, "but you could also kiss me on the lips, if you like."

"I would like that," Troy said, and he did. Nothing else was said as Troy opened the door and walked out.

Lois closed the door behind him and went to her room. She didn't want to do anything except lie there and reminisce on what had just happen. She didn't know what she enjoyed the most, Troy's kiss or the time they spent just talking to each other.

She was still lying on her bed, when Kelly came into her room.

"I want to know all the details. I've been patient long enough," Kelly exclaimed.

"Whatever happened to knocking?" Lois asked, one of their unspoken rules.

"Oh, I'm sorry," Kelly apologize, as she went back out, close the door and knocked.

"Come in silly," Lois said.

"Was that better?" Kelly asked sarcastically.

"Funny," said Lois.

"Well, do I have to repeat the question, or what?" Kelly asked.

"The details are…" Lois began, "Troy and I had an argument, he apologized, came over and we talked."

"Talked?" Kelly asked with a puzzled look on her face.

"Yes, talked," said Lois.

"You didn't make out?" Kelly asked.

"No, we didn't, and if we did, I wouldn't be telling you, besides, I'm not ready for that yet," Lois replied.

"Not ready for that as in, with Troy, or as in, you are still a virgin."

Lois knew this subject would come up between her and Kelly at some point.

"Both," said Lois.

"You have got to be kidding me."

It was more of a statement than a question, so Lois didn't reply.

"I assume you had done it."

"You assume wrong."

"Girl, what are you waiting on? Prince charming? Marriage? What?" Kelly inquired.

"Maybe both," Lois said. "Look Kelly," Lois began wanting to end the conversation, now that Kelly knew the facts they might as well discuss it, "it's not a crime to be a virgin. It's my decision and I will be one as long as I want. I won't let Troy pressure me into it and I won't let you make me feel like I have some disease because I haven't done it."

"So that's what the fight was all about," Kelly said as the realization hit her, "Troy wanted to make out and you didn't."

"Now that you have figured it all out, I guess you can leave my room now, so that I can get some sleep, okay."

"Okay sweetheart. I know when I'm no longer wanted, but I will say one thing before I leave."

"Surprise, surprise," said Lois knowing Kelly would not go away without having the last word.

"As I was saying," Kelly said ignoring Lois sarcastic remark. "You have a right to do whatever you want and to hold out as long as you want, but if you hold out too long on a guy like Troy, you may just be holding out by yourself." Kelly left the room before Lois could comment.

Lois went to bed a little annoyed with Kelly. It's one thing for Troy to pressure her, but she did not want to be pressured by Kelly.

Kelly reminded Lois of some of the girls she hung out with in high school; always trying to make her feel guilty because she was still a virgin, so she decided to make up a lie. She told them she and Jarod had made out one day at his house. It wasn't that big of a lie. Jarod did kiss her once when they were at his house. He was helping her with her math homework. They took a break and were lying across his bed talking and looking up at the ceiling. Jarod leaned up on one elbow and looked into her eyes. He asked her what she was thinking. She told him that she was wondering what it would be like to live in a house like his and suddenly out of no where Jarod bent his head and kissed her on the lips and that was it. He laid back down and continued to look up into the ceiling. Lois remembered her head spinning and her heart beating fast and when she looked over at him, she saw his room door closing slightly. She knew there was no one else in the house, except Jarrod's mother.

She later found out that it was his mother, who had been at his room door listening to their conversation. She said she came up to see if they wanted to take a break for a snack, but couldn't help from overhearing their conversation. When Jarod kissed her, she didn't want to embarrass them by coming in, so she left. However, she made it clear that she would never live in their home, or in any home with her son and that she was unwelcome in Jarrod's life. After that conversation, Lois began to brush Jarod off, even though she really liked him. Lois shook her head as if to clear it from the memories of her life back home.

The relationship with Troy escalated. They did everything together it seemed, except go to church on Sundays. Troy would pick her up after church and they would go out to dinner. Deb invited Troy over to dinner once, but he made up an excuse for why he couldn't come.

"What are you doing for Christmas?" Troy asked Lois, while they were sitting on the couch watching TV.

"I don't know yet, but I will have to make up some story to tell my parents about why I am not coming home again this year. Last year I told them I just got started working, so I had no time off. I don't know what I'll tell them this year"

"Why do you have to lie? Why don't you just tell them that you don't want to come home for Christmas. What can they do to you?" Troy asked.

"They can't do anything to me," said Lois, "but they'll be hurt."

"They'll get over it," Troy said matter of fact.

"I know," Lois replied, "I love my parents. I just don't want to go back to Brickenbrat," Lois admitted.

"You said that you and your old man didn't get along." Lois felt embarrassed now having told Troy so much about her life and her feelings. Hearing his words brought a sting to her heart. She must've sound cold and heartless when talking about her family. She knew she said some good things, or did she?

"Families fight Troy, but it doesn't mean that they don't love each other."

Troy didn't agree, "me and my family fight and believe me, I stay away from them as much as possible and believe me when I say, there is no love lost among us."

"I don't believe that," Lois said not believing Troy at all, "you just think there's no love."

"Believe your fantasy Lois, but I like to live in reality myself."

The two of them didn't say anything for a while. They just sat and watched the television.

"Hey…" Troy said, "why don't we spend Christmas together, just you and me. You could cook."

Lois stared at Troy as if he had just said something terribly wrong and Troy changed his statement.

"We could cook," he said, "then maybe we could go out to a movie or something afterwards. What do you think? You can tell your parents that you are spending Christmas with your boyfriend this year and it wouldn't be a lie."

Lois liked the idea.

"That sounds great Troy! Let's plan to do that."

When Kelly found out Lois wasn't going to go home for Christmas, she invited her to spend Christmas with her and her family.

"We always have a big dinner and one or two more really doesn't matter," Kelly said, knowing that Lois might want to bring Troy.

When Lois refused the invitation, of course Kelly wanted to know why, "are you spending it with your aunt?"

"No," Lois said and finally decided to tell Kelly her plans knowing she wouldn't stop with the questions until she found out what Lois' plans were for the holidays.

"Troy and I are going to spend a quiet day here at the apartment. We're both going to cook and then go out to a movie later."

"That sounds great," Kelly said, not really sure why she didn't think it was a good idea, except she always thought of holidays as being a time to spend with families.

Stephanie had some exciting news to tell her daughter when she called home to tell them she was not going to be there for Christmas.

"Hi Maggie. How are you?"... "I miss you too."... "No, I'm not going to be able to come home for Christmas this year."... "I know I didn't come home last year. Could you put mom on please and don't tell her that I am not coming home for Chris..."

Maggie had already put down the phone and went yelling out to Stephanie that it was Lois and that she was not coming home for Christmas.

"I'm having dinner with a special friend."... "Yeah, I guess you could call him that."... "No, we're not having dinner with his family Mother. We just thought that it would be nice to spend it together."... "Both of us will be doing the cooking."... "No maam, Kelly will not be here. She is spending Christmas with her family."

Stephanie gave Lois a lecture on the meaning of family at Christmas and voiced her concerns about Lois spending Christmas alone in her apartment with a boy she hardly knew.

"I do know him Mama. We have been seeing each other for months now."... "A big surprise? What is it?" Stephanie was hoping to tell Lois about their surprise at Christmas, but since Lois wasn't coming home, she decided to tell her now about the house that they were getting ready to buy.

It was a house in a new subdivision. She and Richard had been working on repairing their credit for over a year and paying off old bills. It was the best Christmas present they could receive, when the broker called a couple of days ago and told them they were approved for a home in a new subdivision near their church. It was a white aluminum siding home. It had an upstairs, a fireplace, four bedrooms, a dining area, a den, a big kitchen, and two full size bathrooms with a small one downstairs, which Lois knew was what her Mother always wanted.

She laid out the plan to her. The boys would share a bathroom with them. The girls would take the smaller bathroom and the extra bedroom was Lois' for when she came home to visit, or back home to stay. Lois didn't want to ruin her mother's surprise by telling her she never had any plans of coming back home to stay, but she would certainly have to come home for a visit soon to see the new house.

"Mom, I am so happy for you," Lois said and she was, "you finally got the home you want and deserve."

Stephanie explained to Lois that she didn't deserve anything, but that she was grateful to God for opening up this door of opportunity for them.

"I will Mom."... "As soon as you guys are all settled in, I'm going to come for a visit and stay in my room."... "I'll talk to you again before Christmas Mom. I want to send everyone a gift, but I don't know if I have enough money."... "I know I don't have to worry about that. One day I will be able to do it. Tell Richard I said hi and that I'm so happy for you guys."... "Okay Mom."... "I love you too. Talk to you soon."

It began to snow on Christmas Eve and Lois prayed that it would not snow everyone in and ruin her plans with Troy. She was looking forward to spending time with him.

The snow had stopped Christmas morning. Troy came over early, even before Kelly left for her parent's. He brought doughnuts and the rest of the grocery to make their dinner. As Kelly left, she made a comment about how good they looked together in the kitchen making dinner.

Dinner was not the greatest. Neither Lois nor Troy was really good at cooking.

Dinner consisted of ham from a can, stuffing from a box, string beans from the freezer, aunt smith's sweet potato pie and some brownies Lois made from a box mix. They both agreed that it wasn't too bad, but they were both missing some good ole home cooking.

After dinner and desert, they were watching an old movie on TV when Lois asked Troy if he was ready to go to the movies.

She was about to get up and get the phone book, so she could find out what time the movie started and which theater they were going to, when Troy grabbed her arm and said, "why don't we skip the movie." He pulled Lois into his lap and they began to kiss.

When Troy hands began to move faster than Lois' mind or heart, she struggled to free herself from his grip, once freed she stood there in disbelief.

Troy also looked at her in disbelief and asked, "what's the problem?"

Lois stood staring down at him on the couch, breathing heavily from her struggle and answered, "I hope there isn't a problem Troy."

"Then come and sit back down," said Troy.

"I think we should be going to the movies now. We both have to work tomorrow, so we don't want to be out too late."

"Skip the movie!" Troy said annoyed as he stood up and grab Lois around the waist. "I was only kidding about the movie. I thought we'd just spend a quiet time here all day. Come on, let's go to your room," Troy suggested.

Lois pried his hands from around her waist and took a step back and said, "Troy, I don't know what you had in mind, but I planned on going to the movie, now you can go or not go, that's up to you, but nothing else is going to happen here today. There's no reason that we need to go into my room."

Troy forehead creased as he began to shake his head.

"You little tease. What do you think a guy means when he suggests a romantic dinner alone?"

Lois was upset with Troy for calling her a tease.

"First of all," Lois stated pointing her index finger in Troy's face with one hand on her hip, "no one said anything about a romantic dinner. We decided that we would spend Christmas together and then go to a movie afterwards. That's it." Lois said bringing her other hand down to her hip.

Troy tried to calm down, "so are you saying that we are not going to make out?"

Troy was too annoyed to play with his words, so he came straight to the point.

"No Troy, we are not going to make out!" Lois replied.

Troy stared at her for a long time and then said, "I could take what I want from you and there would be nothing you could do about it."

Lois heart suddenly began to pound louder and faster than her mind was thinking. Was he talking about forcing her to have sex with him? Troy was a little taller than Lois and very muscular, with no visible fat on his body. He looked liked he spent all of his time in the gym working out. He said that it came from lifting boxes at the factory all day.

Lois just stared at Troy not knowing what he was going to do next, or what she would do. It would be hard crying rape, when everyone knew of her plans to invite Troy over to dinner. She felt she was in a no win situation and wished she could run away and hide, but she couldn't.

Finally Troy said, "but I won't. I don't have to. There are too many girls out there willing to be with me. Why should I waste my time, or ruin my life on you?"

Without another word, Troy got his coat out of the closet, picked up his keys off the table and walked out the door.

Lois was hurt and spent the rest of the afternoon crying. She finally fell asleep and wasn't even aware that Kelly had knocked at the door, then peeked her head in to ask how it went, but she didn't bother to wake her. She would ask her tomorrow.

Lois usually woke Kelly up, but this morning Kelly awoke, squinting her eyes from the light that was shining in through her window. She looked at the clock and jumped out of the bed.

"Oh boy!" she exclaimed, "we are so late!" She ran down the hall and knocked on Lois' door.

Lois was awake with the covers over her head. She suddenly felt bad for not waking Kelly. She also was annoyed that Kelly relied on her to be her alarm. She needed to learn to wake herself.

Kelly shook Lois and said, "Lois, get up! We're late! We're going to have to call a taxi, because we'll never make the bus!" When Lois didn't move, she shook her again, "Lois, get up!" Kelly was getting annoyed that Lois didn't move or respond.

Finally Lois said, "I'm not going this morning Kelly."

"Not going?" Kelly asked, "if you don't work the day after the holiday, you won't get paid, now come on, get up girl!"

Lois had forgotten that and realized she couldn't really afford to miss two days without pay. She got out of the bed and did everything backwards. She put on her clothes, washed her face, put her hair in a ponytail, instead of giving herself those candy curls that Troy liked to see.

When Kelly came out of the room, Lois was sitting in the chair in the living room waiting for her.

"The cab will be here in ten minutes," Kelly said looking down at Lois, "are you going to work looking like that?"

Lois looked up and asked, "what's the matter with the way I look. We work in a factory, not a fashion runway. We don't have to dress like models everyday you know." Lois was referring to the fact that she and Kelly liked to dress their best going to work, even though their clothes picked up so much dust from the factory and was practically ruin by the time they got home.

Kelly wanted to be a model or a movie star and she was determined that one day she would be discovered and since she didn't know when that day would be, she had to look her best at all times.

Lois didn't have any dreams of being either, but she didn't want to look like a bum next to Kelly.

Kelly didn't miss Lois' sarcasm and shot one back at her, "you're right, besides your clothes match your eyes."

She was referring to the puffiness and redness. Lois had been crying all night. Every time she woke up, she cried herself back to sleep. She wasn't even sure why. It wasn't like she was in love with Troy, or was she. The first time they had came to this point, they had hardly knew each other, but now after months of dating she had grown close to him. He treated her with respect. Lois wondered if it all was all an act. Now wasn't the time to dwell on it.

She got up out of the chair, grabbed her purse and said to Kelly, "are you going to stare at me all morning, or are we going to work, now that you have practically dragged me out of bed."

They headed downstairs as they kept bickering at each other.

"You know Lois, you could have stayed your butt in bed for all I care. I thought you'd overslept, or something because of your big date yesterday. At least you could have left a note, or something for me last night letting me know that you weren't going to work."

"What difference would it make Kelly? You still wouldn't have set your alarm clock."

"I don't have one remember," Kelly replied.

"I gave you one for Christmas, Kelly."

"Yes, but I didn't have time to set it up yet. I have to read the instructions."

"Yes, I forgot and that will take you a couple of days." Lois was being especially nasty to Kelly who was getting tired of it.

"Whatever," Kelly replied as she got into the cab. They didn't speak to each other all the way to work.

All eyes were on them as they came in late. Lois never turned around in Kelly's direction all day. She didn't want to risk seeing Troy staring at her, or Kelly for that matter. She wished she could wear sunglasses, but she couldn't while operating the machines.

Lois was disheartened as the day ended and Troy didn't say anything to her, good or bad. She was hoping that he would say something.

Deb came over to her machine on one of her breaks and asked her how her Christmas was and she lied and said it was fine. Deb asked her about her eyes, but she just said that her eyes were red from very little sleep, because they caught the midnight movie and got home late.

Deb would have bought that, if it wasn't for the puffiness of her eyes and the fact that Troy avoided looking her way all day. He usually said, "Hi." Kelly just smiled a sheepish grin when she looked her way, so Deb knew something was going on, but she wasn't going to pry.

As usual, Kelly tried to get Lois to say what was wrong, but she wouldn't, although Kelly believed she knew. She thought Lois was being silly with her Victorian way of thinking, but she wasn't going to say, because they had that conversation before. She decided not to pry, at least for now.

One afternoon Troy came to the apartment unannounced. Kelly was home, so Lois let him in.

"Can we talk?" He asked.

"I don't think we have anything to talk about," Lois said.

Troy began to talk anyway.

"Lois, I'm sorry for acting like a jerk on Christmas, but I just don't know what you want. I love you and I want to be with you. You act like you want to be with me, but when I try to step up our relationship you draw back. I just want us to be closer. I don't know what else to say."

Troy stopped talking and waited for Lois to comment, when she didn't he said, "If you think this relationship is worth saving then you will have to call me, I've already made the first step."

He turned to leave and Lois grabbed his arm and said, "don't go. Sit, please."

Troy sat down and Lois sat next to him.

"Troy, I really like you, but I'm just not ready to have sex with you. I can't explain to you why, just that when I'm ready, I'll know. I may not be ready until marriage."

"Marriage?" Troy said, "wait a minute," he continued throwing up both hands, "who said anything about marriage?"

"I do plan to marry one day Troy. It may not be with you, but that's what I want."

Troy allowed Lois' words to sink in before he commented.

"Okay, I hear you. I can't promise that I won't ever try again, but I'll respect your wishes every time." Lois shook her head in agreement.

They both felt like they had reached some type of agreement.

Troy was true to his words; he didn't stop trying, but he always backed off when Lois resisted. Their relationship was taking a different turn, instead of getting closer; they began drifting apart.

One day Lois received a phone call from a girl she didn't know. The girl claimed she was pregnant with Troy's baby and that if she let Troy go, then he would marry her. Lois was shocked.

She was sitting in the chair by the door when Kelly came in wiping tears from her eyes. She didn't want Kelly to see her crying, but for once she wanted to talk to someone and Kelly was the only one she felt she could confide in.

For the next couple of days, Lois continued to see Troy without bringing the subject up. She wanted him to tell her, but he didn't.

One day at lunch next to her machine, she said to him, "I know, you know." Troy looked puzzled, as she clarified, "I know about the girl you got pregnant."

"I can explain," Troy began. "After I left your apartment Christmas day, I was hurt. I went to this club and I met this girl. One thing led to another and we ended up at her apartment. She means nothing to me, Lois. I mean it, nothing."

Somehow that was not what Lois wanted to hear, but she wasn't sure what she wanted to hear.

"What are you going to do about it?" Lois asked.

"Do about it?" Troy asked, "I told her to get an abortion. I even offered to pay for it. She's talking marriage and I don't even know the girl. She's crazy."

Lois listened to Troy going on like he was the hurt party and she suddenly knew what she had to do.

"Troy, I think we should just be friend. I couldn't go on being with you knowing that there is someone out there having your baby."

"I'm not going to marry her," Troy said.

"That's your decision," Lois said.

They saw very little of each other after that, but they kept up a friendly comrade at work. Troy tried every now and then to convince her to let him come over to the apartment for a visit, but she was determined that that part of her relationship with Troy was over.

Kelly respected her decision and didn't give her a third degree about it, even though Troy constantly asked her to put in a word for him with Lois, but she didn't. Kelly still liked Troy, but she wondered what kind of game he was playing. He not only had a girl pregnant, but she knew from Steve that Troy had moved on to someone new and he was still seeing an older woman every now and then. The woman was married and Steve said it was someone in the factory. Kelly wondered if he was just using Lois as a cover up. She was convinced that Lois was better off without Troy.

Chapter Ten
Jewel

Jewel was on the phone with her mother when Dawn came in and she looked up and wave to her. Dawn was motioning something to her, but Jewel just shook her head indicating that she didn't understand.

"Yes Mom, I'm happy with her. She may be the best roommate I'll ever have. I hope I don't have to have another. Mom, I've got to go."… "Okay, I'll tell her. I'll see."… "Love you too," Jewel finally said hanging up the phone.

"Tell me what?" Dawn asked.

"My mom wants you to come home with me one weekend for a visit. She and Dad want to meet you."

"That's fine with me," Dawn said, "if we can get you out of the books one weekend long enough to do something sociable."

"What's up?" Jewel asked, ignoring Dawn's last statement in curiosity of why she wanted her off the phone.

"Talking about your social life," Dawn said.

"Actually we weren't," said Jewel.

"Well, let's," Dawn said flopping down on the bed where Jewel was lying. "There is this guy. He's very nice and good-looking. He wants to meet you."

"Do I know him?" Jewel seemed interested, after all she was getting straight A's and making the Dean's list every semester, maybe it was time to enjoy college a little. She wanted to do something that would get her out of her room, besides her usual track run with Dawn and work.

"His name is Ken. You've seen him running around the track with Robert. Robert finally asked me out."

Jewel was puzzled, "where does Ken comes in?"

"Well, I told Robert I'd go out with him, if he agreed to a double date, so we could include you and he agreed. Then, I told him there was one small problem."

"What was that?" Jewel asked.

"I told him that you didn't have a date and could he ask one of his friends to join us."

"I see," said Jewel, "so Ken doesn't really know that it's me that he will be tagging along with on this date?"

"I told Robert this was not a blind date and he could actually tell Ken who you were, and I would do the same, and if one of you decided not to go, then we would just have to call the date off, until we find someone that you would want to go out with."

"Okay, stop," Jewel said. "I think I'm getting the picture. Why don't you just find another couple to go out with you and Robert? You both have other friends. At least, I know you do."

"Because, Jewel, I want you to go. Get out of this room. It's not healthy you know."

"I thought so." Jewel said.

"Come on Jewel, say yes, please."

"Okay, I'll go if he wants to."

"Great!" Dawn said, pleased at her accomplishment.

"I repeat," said Jewel, "only if he wants to."

"Oh, he wants to." Dawn said, as she jumped up off of the bed.

"Figures," Jewel said looking at Dawn feeling set up, regardless of how diplomatic she made it out to be.

Ken was a track star and he was good looking, Jewel admitted, but she decided to keep it to herself. Ken seemed to already have many accolades, not to mention Dawn telling him that he looked a lot like a young Sidney Poitier. She could have said any actor, because he would not have looked like any of them as far as Jewel was concerned. She guessed it was the only black actor Dawn could have thought of that had an accent, which Ken did.

He was from the Island of St. Vincent. Ken's mother worked several jobs to keep food on the table and clothe on the back of her eight children. His father died when Ken was nine year old. He was the youngest son. His dream was to come to the United States on a track and field scholarship. He already won two awards in track and field and his ultimate goal was to go to the Olympics and win a gold medal.

"My mother wants me to focus on a good education and make running secondary," he was saying to Jewel.

"And you should," Jewel commented, "a career in sports is so unpredictable."

"You're right," Ken agreed, "but we mustn't let go of our dreams, correct?"

"I agree," Jewel said.

He won't get any argument from me on that, she thought.

Dawn and Robert hit it off. Robert was a criminal justice major, but unlike Jewel, he did not want to be a lawyer. He wanted to do something in law enforcement other than become a police officer, like his Dad.

"Not that I don't respect what my dad does. I do. My dad is the greatest, but cops don't get any respect."

"Cops?" Jewel was questioning the use of the slang, "I'm sorry. I don't mean to criticize, but isn't the use of slang terms like that the reason why police officers are not respected."

"You're absolutely right," Robert agreed, "police officers are the 'politically correct' term, but I'm the affect of TV and street slangs." Jewel guess that was his justification.

Dawn was quick to jump in and change the subject knowing that this could be the beginning of a debate as far as Jewel was concerned.

"Jewel is our future lawyer."

"I see," said Robert, "isn't it funny. You'd think that lawyers and police officers should work hand in hand but they are so often each others adversaries."

"It depends on what you mean," Jewel stated "I'm not so sure that they are."

"Would you like to dance?" Ken cut into the conversation clueing in with Dawn where the conversation was headed.

Jewel looked up at Ken, who was already standing with his hand extended. She took it and they went on the floor to dance.

Jewel found out quickly that Ken had not been subjected to any American dance. She began to laugh at him on the floor. He was making wild movements with his arms that made him look like a monkey swinging from branch to branch.

"I'm sorry," Jewel said trying not to laugh, "it's just that…"

"I said I came to the US to run tracks and win an Olympic gold medal, not to learn the latest dance," Ken said before Jewel could finish her sentence.

"Okay, granted," Jewel said, "here, I'll show you."

Jewel came close to him and took his hand "first, listen to the music, then move with the beat, not before or after. For now, why don't you just keep your hands to your sides and not swing them around, besides you may hit someone and start something that we can't finish."

"Just watch me, okay."

Jewel began to move her head with the beat, then her feet and slightly moving her hand. Ken followed.

"See, it's not so hard." Jewel said as she saw Ken picking up her steps quite well.

"No, it isn't," Ken said, pleased with his dancing lesson.

The evening turned out to be nice.

"I'm glad Ken asked you to dance. It seemed to have tame the wild beast in you," Dawn said.

Jewel laughed. She knew what Dawn was referring to, "I'm sorry. I did seem to be getting off on the wrong foot with Ken."

"And Robert," Dawn added, thinking lets' she forget.

"And Robert," Jewel admitted, "but it did turn out okay, didn't it?"

"Yes it did." Dawn agreed with a big grin on her face.

"Robert asked me on another date. I think we'll just do a couple's thing this time. How about you and Ken?" Dawn asked.

"I like Ken. He's a nice guy, but we'll see. If he ask me out, I may say yes."

"Or you could ask him out," Dawn said.

"That's not going to happen," Jewel said, definitely. "Why?" Dawn asked.

"Just wasn't brought up that way."

"I'll leave it at that, goodnight.

"Goodnight Dawn."

Both girls turned their night-lights off and were soon asleep.

Ken did ask Jewel out again and she accepted. They went to a place that played Reggae music and Ken teased that this was more his speed and he was the one giving the dance lesson this time around and like him, Jewel was a quick learner.

Jewel and Ken became a couple to everyone who knew them, except Jewel and Ken. To them, they were just friends. They enjoyed being with each other and decided that they were not ready for any thing more. They both were committed to their goals.

"A relationship would take too much time, effort and energy, which neither of us can commit to," said Jewel.

They began to run together on the days Ken did not have a practice or a meet and Jewel went to see Ken in his meets, when their were home games.

Dawn was engrossed in Robert. Although Robert and Jewel did not hit it off at first, they began to warm up to each other, mainly for Dawn's sake.

One night Jewel inquired of Dawn concerning her and Robert's relationship.

"Well Jewel," Dawn began, "we really like each other and have a lot in common."

"But you want to be a teacher, and he, a police officer."

"No Jewel, he doesn't want to be a police officer, he wants to be in law enforcement, maybe a DEA or something."

"A drug enforcement agent?" Jewel questioned.

"Yes, a DEA, and what is wrong with that?" Dawn asked on the defensive.

"Nothing, but have you consider the life of a DEA? They go undercover for weeks, months and even years." Dawn laughed at Jewel's comment.

"Don't be ridiculous. This isn't the movies, you know. I hardly think the life of most DEA are as glamorous as all that."

"I don't see anything glamorous about a man leaving his wife and children to go undercover, even if it is for one day."

"Wife! Children! Goodness gracious Jewel, who said anything about marriage?"

"Well you never know." Jewel said as she headed to the bathroom throwing Dawn a sly look.

Besides Dawn, Ken became Jewel's best friend. She began to confide in him concerning everything and so did he.

Jewel told her parents about Ken, but her father was not buying the, 'we are just friend' line.

"Just remember why you are at college baby, to get an education, not to fool around, besides I thought you have a friend. What's wrong with Dawn?"

"Nothing is wrong with Dawn, dad. She's just interested in this guy and well…"

"Well what?" Paul inquired.

"Well, it's nothing really. It's just that we don't really hit it off and I'd rather not be around him that much and Dawn spends a lot of time with him. I guess you could say they are going steady, or something."

"Or something is probably correct." Paul said. "Like I said baby, you just remember your reason for being in school."

"I know daddy, that's why Ken and I have decided not to go steady, because we both have things in life that we want to accomplish."

"I'm glad to hear that," Paul said, "and in that case, I would like to meet this young man someday."

"Maybe you will, if I can convince him to come down with me for Thanksgiving."

"That would be great," Paul replied. "Your mother and I will look forward to meeting him."

"I didn't say he was going to accept my invitation, besides I haven't asked him yet."

"Then ask him," Paul insisted."

Paul had an alternative motive. He wasn't buying any of this friend stuff and he wanted to see for himself whether they were, 'just friends' he told Theresa.

Dawn announced that Robert had agreed to have Thanksgiving with her and her family, and Jewel raised and eyebrow.

"What?" asked Dawn.

"Nothing," Jewel replied.

"What is the difference between me asking Robert to dinner as oppose to you asking Ken to dinner."

"First of all," Jewel began to explain, "Ken doesn't have family here, so it is out of the kindness of my heart that I am inviting him to dinner. You, on the other hand have an alternative motive for inviting Robert to Thanksgiving dinner other than feeding him a home cooked meal."

"You think you have the whole picture on me and Robert's relationship, and you don't."

"Okay," said Jewel, "by the way, Ken did accept my invitation to go with me to Tennessee."

Dawn was glad Jewel changed the subject. She knew Jewel was right. She was falling very much in love with Robert. She was waiting for Robert to say so, but he didn't and she didn't want to be the first to say it. When they get to that point, she would make sure she told Jewel exactly how she felt about Robert. She was just holding out to see how he felt about her.

Jewel was glad Ken accepted her invitation. The ride was much more pleasant with someone, as oppose to driving home by herself and Ken was such a character. He made her laugh most of the way, even though he couldn't help with the driving.

"Just one of those things that I have not gotten around to doing yet in your country," he explained.

It didn't bother Jewel. She was just glad for his company. He stayed awake and talked to her all the way. As they past through the countryside,

Ken was amazed at the beauty of it all, as they past farms, dairies, plants, tobacco and cotton fields.

"Wow, you have a lot of what we have in my country," Ken said.

"I imagine so," Jewel replied.

Ken was even more amazed when Jewel pulled up in front of her home.

"Where are we?" Ken asked.

"We're at my house," Jewel said.

"Your house?" Ken said. "You didn't tell me you were rich."

"I'm not," Jewel said, "besides this is my parent's home. I just lived here while I was growing up and now they let me come back for visits." Ken laughed.

"But wait," Jewel said, "one day I'll be rich and so will you. We will both have homes bigger and better."

"You're right," Ken agreed as Tessa came running out of the house. "That's Tessa?" Ken asked.

"Yes, that's Tessa."

"Mom and dad home yet?" Jewel asked Tessa.

"Mom is, and she's waiting on you to make the sweet potato pie."

"Oh great!" exclaimed a disgusted Jewel. "I don't know why she insists that I make pies every year. It's not like I really make them. She stands over me and instructs me through the entire process."

"So you cook?" Ken asked Jewel. "No, I don't cook," Jewel responded to Ken while opening the trunk of the car to get their bags out, "which reminds me, when I'm rich I'll make sure I hire a cook." Ken and Jewel laughed.

And Tessa not interested in knowing what the joke was, turned to ken and said, "by the way, I'm Tessa."

Ken took her hand and said,   "It is nice to meet you Tessa. I've heard a lot about you."

"I like your accent." Tessa said ignoring Ken's last statement. "Are you from Africa or something?"

"No, I am from St. Vincent."

"Darn!" Tessa exclaimed, "it sure would've been cool if you were a real African."

"Sorry to disappoint you," Ken said.

"I'm not disappointed. It just would've been cool if you were, that's all." Tessa said matter of fact.

They entered the house through the garage, which put them into the kitchen.

Stephanie was in the kitchen cooking, "Hi Mom." Theresa stopped mixing some dough and wiped her hand into her apron to give Jewel a warm hug.

"Hi sweetheart. Did you have a good trip?" She didn't wait until Jewel answered the question before she was addressing Ken, "you must be Ken. We have heard so much about you."

Ken grabbed Theresa's hand and shook it.

"Oh excuse my hand" Theresa said apologetic.

"Oh, that's alright Mrs. Stone," Ken said, "your wet hands in the kitchen means that you were cooking and there must be something to eat." Theresa laughed at Ken's frankness.

"There sure is. Why don't you two get settled in and I'll fix us all a little something for dinner. Your father should be home soon," she acknowledged. "Ken will be staying with David in his room. Paul's sisters are coming in some time tonight."

"Mom, you didn't tell me we were having a lot of people for dinner." Jewel said annoyed.

"It's not a lot of people dear, it's just your father's sisters."

"Who have ten kids a piece."

"Jewel! That's not true." Theresa said, in a scolding way.

"Maybe not, but it seems like they do, with all the noise they make. Those little brats are so out of control. If I knew they were coming, I'd skip coming home."

"I know," Theresa said looking at Jewel with a smile.

"Alright, just don't get mad if Ken and I up and leave in the middle of dinner tomorrow."

"You wouldn't dare," said Theresa.

"Don't be so sure that I wouldn't Mother," Jewel said as she picked up her bags and headed out of the kitchen as Ken followed.

"I like big families," Ken commented.

"Good," said Jewel "then I'll just leave you here with them when I leave tomorrow. David! David! Tessa where is David?"

"I'm right here girl," David entered the room with one headphone in his ears and another out.

"Can you show Ken to your room please? Ken, this is David," Jewel introduced.

"So you're Ken," David said, inspecting Ken, "right this way."

Paul spent the entire meal talking to Ken, asking him questions about school, what it was like where he lived, his goals, etc. Jewel could see that her father liked Ken immediately, but she was annoyed at some of the questions he was asking him.

He was acting like Ken was his future son-in-law and he had to know all the little details about his life. All in all dinner went well. Everyone liked Ken and Ken was enjoying being a part of Jewel's family.

Paul's sisters got in late that night, but they were up early the next day. Jewel went into her bathroom to wash her face and throw on her robe. She was not ready to get up, but the noise woke her up. She went straight to the kitchen, where she knew her mother would be.

"Hi, sleepy head," Her aunt Judy said, as she grabbed her and gave her a kiss.

Judy was Paul's eldest sister. Judy had a lot going for her, according to Paul, but she just couldn't keep a husband. She was divorced twice and decided that marriage was just not for her. She had a boy and a girl. Her daughter, Melissa, was a rebellious sixteen year-old. Her son, Matt, from her last marriage was five years old and he could do no wrong.

Jewel liked Judy and Denise, Paul's younger sister. Paul adored Denise. She was married to Mark and they had three children, Georgia, Christy and MJ. Paul also had two brothers, James and Joe. Jewel wasn't sure whether they were coming or not, but she knew that her Grandma Lynnie and Gran and Papa would be there also.

As Jewel was assessing her surroundings, Denise came up behind her and said, "so, here is the college girl. You couldn't stay awake long enough last night to greet us?"

"Sorry, but I was really tired," Jewel explained.

"I'm just kidding with you, sweetie," said Denise. "Your Dad told us you drove up yesterday right after your last class, with a handsome young man I hear."

Jewel felt her face heated up. How embarrassing, she thought, wondering what else her father was telling everyone about her and Ken.

"Yes, and we have met him," said Judy.

"You have?" asked Jewel.

"Yes, apparently he is not a late sleeper like you," Denise said.

Jewel looked up at the clock. It was eight in the morning. She hardly considered that sleeping in late. She couldn't believe that Ken was up already. She was wondering where he was.

"He went with your father to the store to pick up some things that I needed," Theresa said seeing the puzzled look on Jewel's face.

"And when they get back, it will be game time. They've already placed their bets on the games," said Denise. "Welcome to the world of having a man in your life."

"hmm, hmm, that's why I don't have one today," said Judy.

"He's not my man," said Jewel. "We're just friends."

"If you say so dear," Denise said.

"Jewel I need you to get dress so that you can help me," Theresa said.

"Oh, let her enjoy her, 'friend,' said Judy putting up her hands and giving the quotation sign.

"That's right," added Denise, "besides we're here. What do you want us to do?"

Jewel left the kitchen unnoticed, as Judy and Denise gathered around her mother to help out. Jewel decided to go to her room to get dress. There was going to be no sleeping late today. She heard the kids in the playroom and David was out back with some of his friends from the neighborhood shooting hoops with Mark.

"All dressed and nowhere to go," Jewel said to herself as she flopped backwards onto her bed.

She looked over to her nightstand and grabbed her address book, wondering if any of her old school friends were still around, or home for the holidays. Her mind went to Lois. It would be great, she thought, to see Lois. She called the number, but the number was disconnected. That was strange. A couple of things went through her mind. Lois' family was always struggling to meet their bill, maybe the phone was cut off. People usually didn't change their number. She looked through her book again and dialed another number.

"Hello, may I speak to Ashley?" Jewel heard someone yell out for Ashley.

Ashley and Jewel talked on the phone for about fifteen minutes making plans for later. She also called Jarod, who was also home from college. They all planned to meet later on that night.

The day went well. Paul dominated Ken, even though Mark was there. Jewel helped set the table and spent some time with Tessa and Melissa, who just wanted to watch music videos all day.

She played some pool with Ken and David, until Paul and Mark came in, making it a foursome and insinuated that she should help the women in the kitchen.

Gran and Papa finally came and Jewel spent time with them talking about college and trying to convince them that she and Ken were just friends; she finally gave up and let them believe what they wanted.

By the time Grandma Lynnie arrived, it was time for dinner.

"This food is really good," Ken whispered to Jewel, "you sure you can't cook like this, because if you could, girl I'd marry you right now on the spot. Your father has practically given me his blessings."

"You male chauvinist," Jewel whispered to Ken, "I bet you like your women bare foot and pregnant."

"Actually, just barefoot and naked would be just fine," said Ken.

"ha, ha," said Jewel.

"What are you two whispering about over there?" Paul asked.

"Just table talk, Daddy," said Jewel.

"We apologize for whispering Mr. Stone. Didn't mean to be rude."

Jewel looked at Ken and asked, "why are you sucking up to my dad?"

"I'm not sucking up. Who knows, I just might marry you some day, ya know," said Ken. "You can't cook, but you have a rich family and they can cook."

"Dream on." said Jewel deciding to ignore Ken and talk to David, who was sitting next to her.

After dinner, Jewel found quietness in her room while she took a nap. Ken was watching football with her Father, David and Mark. She was going to try to find where Lois' parents were staying. She told her Mother about the disconnected number and was told that they moved out of the projects into a nicer neighborhood. Theresa didn't have their new number, but she knew someone from the church who might know it. Jewel called and the woman gave her Lois' parents new address, but said that she didn't have their new number.

Everyone was winding down. Grandma Lynnie's driver took her home. Jewel wished she had spent more time with her. She felt obligated to make an effort to communicate with her, especially since she gave her the money to buy a car for her graduation present, but the timing never seemed right, but then it never was with the two of them. She told her other grandparents that she was going to try to stop by before she left to go back on Sunday and then later in the kitchen, Theresa inquired whether or not she would stop by Grandma Lynnie's as well. She half-heartedly committed to do so, hoping that she would get around to it.

"You ready?" Jewel asked Ken as he looked up from the comfortable chair he had made his own for the afternoon.

"Ready for what?" Theresa asked.

"We're going to hang out with some of my old friends."

"But its late dear," Theresa said.

"Mom it's only eight thirty."

"Go ahead and have fun," Paul cut in.

Ken got up and they left.

"I'm concern that Jewel can find time to hang out, but cannot find time to find a church to attend," Theresa said with concern.

"The child is young and has her entire life ahead of her. Let her have some fun and enjoy herself. She's a good kid and she has her head on right," Paul said.

"I don't want her to forget the values that we've instilled in her," Theresa replied.

"It doesn't look like she has forgotten any values," Denise said, butting in as usually, Theresa was thinking.

"Theresa dear, not going to church doesn't make you lose your values, nor does it make you a Christian."

"I understand that, but going to church services will constantly remind you of those values, so that you don't forget them and it will allow her to meet good Christian friends."

"Ken seems to be a nice guy," Judy said.

Theresa was not getting into this debate with Denise. She never wins. They all seem to join in together and gang up on her. Theresa knew that was an over assessment, but they did it to her all the time and it annoyed her. She got up to go to the kitchen to finish cleaning up. She had quietly decided to call it a night. It was times like these that she missed her sister, Mae, even though she and Mae wasn't that close, a product of her mother's doing, nonetheless, Mae was her only sister and she missed her. The thought of not having any living siblings always made her lonely, when Paul's families were around.

"I'm so glad that you invited me this weekend." Ken was saying, as he shook Paul's hand.

"You sure you guys don't want to stay and attend service with us?" Theresa asked.

"That's up to the driver," Ken said looking at Jewel, as she glared at him and turned to her mother and said.

"Mom, you know how long service can be. I just want to get on the road, so we both can get some rest. We both have early morning classes tomorrow and Mr. 'Whatever Jewel wants,' Jewel said looking at Ken, who was showing all of his gleaming white teeth, "has a paper he has to finish." Ken suddenly stopped smiling.

"My God, you right girl. I forgot about that."

"Yeah, I know you did." Jewel said, as she hugged everyone before leaving the house.

"I had a great time, Jewel." Ken said as they finally made all the turns that got them on the Interstate.

"I actually did too," Jewel said, "despite the crowd."

"You call that a crowd woman?" Ken said, "man, back home when we have family get together, we have to rent a room as big as an auditorium."

Jewel laughed knowing that he was exaggerating. They made small talk the rest of the way, both realizing that whether they wanted to admit it or not, they had grown closer over the holiday weekend. They both knew this weekend changed their relationship for good.

Dawn was back before Jewel. Jewel dragged herself into the Dorm room and threw herself onto her bed, putting one arm over her eyes to block out the light.

"I'm so tired. I think I might actually cut my morning class." She waited for a sarcastic reply from Dawn, when she didn't get one, she took her arm from over her eyes and look across the room to where Dawn was sitting on her bed. Dawn's eyes were red and puffy.

Jewel jumped up off of her bed and went to sit down next to Dawn on her bed. "What's the matter?" Jewel asked comforting.

"I look that bad?" Dawn asked.

Jewel didn't answer. Dawn got up and grabbed a box of tissue and blew her nose.

"Well," she said, as she threw both her hands up and tears began to welled up in her eyes, "this is my last semester. When I come back, or if I come back, I'll be paying for it on my own," she said trying to smile through the tears.

Jewel was totally confused, wondering what happened this weekend. Did Dawn's parent disapprove of Robert that much?

"What happened Dawn, Robert couldn't behave himself for two days?" Jewel asked, trying to make Dawn's smile turn into something genuine, but all it brought was tears flowing down her face, as she tried to tell Jewel everything in one breath.

"I'm pregnant and my dad is furious. He says he isn't paying for me to have a baby in college, so I might as well pack up and come home, until the baby is born. Robert acted stunned, like he doesn't know how it happened and practically didn't speak to me the rest of the weekend. How dare I tell him something like this while meeting my parent's for the first time. Well, I didn't plan on telling him this weekend. I didn't plan on telling anyone this weekend. I just wanted them to meet and get to know one another, but I couldn't hide the morning sickness from my mother and she demanded that I tell her right then and there, so I did, asking her not to tell dad yet. That I wanted to be the one to tell him, but no sooner than she could get out of my room, she tells him right in front of Robert, on Thanksgiving Day. He was so embarrassed that he wanted to leave immediately and I couldn't blame him. I would've done the same thing," as she finished her last sentence, she just began to cry and Jewel moved next to her and put her arms around her and began to rock her, running her hand over her hair and telling her that it was going to be all right.

Dawn didn't have an early morning class, so Jewel decided to cut her morning class to be with her.

Dawn came over to her bed and shook her, "Jewel, you have about fifteen minutes before your class."

Jewel turned over, "I'm not asleep. I was just waiting for you to wake up. I didn't want to wake you up. You probably need the sleep."

"I did need the sleep," Dawn said, "but not at the expense of you missing your class."

"I wasn't planning on going anyway. You want some breakfast?" Jewel asked, "I'm starving."

"Me too, but I have not been able to keep anything down lately, except some dry toast and a cup of black tea or coffee."

"How about the smell of food?" Jewel asked.

"That's even worst," said Dawn.

"Well then, I guess it's toast and tea for you and a bagel and coffee for me," Jewel said, as she went into the bathroom to wash her face and put on some clothe to go down to the corner deli for their breakfast.

Dawn was on the phone when Jewel came back with breakfast.

"I thought you loved me?"... "I don't want to talk about something so important to us over the phone."... "There is a lot to talk about."...

"I didn't get pregnant by myself."… "We have to discuss our plans."… "I know you're still hurting about the way you found out about the baby but…Robert? Robert!"

Dawn looked up at Jewel with a disappointed look on her face trying to strain a smile, "he hung up."

Jewel gave Dawn a small bag.

"Thanks," Dawn said taking out the tea and toast.

"So what did he say?" Jewel asked as she sat in an Indians squat on her bed across from Dawn.

"Basically, that he's not ready for this and since I've already made the decision not to have an abortion, then I'm on my own. His plan for his future doesn't include a baby, not right now anyway."

"What!" Jewel couldn't believe she was hearing this. "What World does Robert think he's living in? He can't actually think that because he's not ready this baby isn't his responsibility, as well?"

"I don't know what he's thinking," Dawn said lamely, "I think he's still hurt. I'll give him some more time."

Jewel and Dawn spent the rest of the morning talking about what Dawn was going to do. Her plan was to have the baby. She wanted to continue to go to school, but her father was not going to pay for her to go to school next semester and it was too late to apply for any type of grant or loan, not that she would get either with her parent's income. She would have to file independently, which meant she had to probably take on another job, but she knew the chances were slim that anyone would hire her in her condition. She decided to finish the semester and go home and have the baby. It was obvious that she was not looking for Robert to propose marriage, but she was hoping for his support. After a long discussion, Jewel and Dawn decided to go to their afternoon classes.

Robert avoided Dawn over the next few days. He walked in the opposite direction, when he saw her heading his way and he wouldn't answer any of her calls.

"Can't you talk to him? He's your friend," Jewel was pleading with Ken to talk to Robert.

"Why do you say it like that?" Ken asked.

"I didn't know I said it any kind of way, it was just a statement. He is your friend, correct."

"He is an acquaintance, someone I know from school," Ken corrected.

He'd already talked to Robert and wasn't pleased with the way he was handling the situation. In his country, a real man took care of his own.

"Okay, I stand corrected, but still, can you talk some sense into him?"

"I'll talk to him," Ken said as he reached over to Jewel and gave her a kiss on the lips, which made Jewel warm all over.

Neither one of them could figure out, or wanted to figure out, how their relation got to where they began to kiss goodbyes and hold hands and talk on the phone until wee hours of the night, but they both were delighted that it did.

It was the last day of school, before winter break. Dawn was packing her things when Jewel came back from her last class. Jewel was dreading the tears, but she didn't want to miss the opportunity to be there if Dawn needed her.

However, tears were not what Jewel witnessed when she walked into the dorm room. Dawn was humming and smiling.

"So, are you that happy to be rid of me?" Jewel asked, teasingly, which made tears well up in Dawn's eye, as she stopped her packing and went to Jewel and hugged her.

"I'm so going to miss you."

"Me too," said Jewel, "but I didn't intend to make you cry again. I haven't seen you smile since I came back from Thanksgiving and here you are humming a tune and smiling. What's going on?"

Dawn sat Jewel down in a chair and moved some clothes into a pile on her bed and sat down facing Jewel.

"Robert took me to lunch today. We had a long talk. He is driving me home. He said that he loves me and that he wants to work something out. He doesn't know what yet, but he says that the baby is just as much his responsibility as mine and no man in his family has ever ran from their responsibility."

Jewel had a few things to say about what Robert put Dawn through while getting to this decision, but she decided to keep it to herself. She did not want to ruin Dawn's joy.

She got up and hugged Dawn.

"That's great news. I'm so happy for you. I told you everything was going to be alright."

Dawn got up and went back to her packing, "yes you did, and thanks for putting up with me these last several weeks. You are a true friend Jewel."

"You too," Jewel said.

"You'll be graduating this June," Dawn said to Jewel, "please send me an invitation."

"You know I will," Jewel said.

"So what about you and Ken?" Dawn asked.

"What about me and Ken? We're just friends."

They both laughed, knowing Jewel could no longer say that with a straight face.

"I don't know," Jewel answered honestly, "but he's taking me out to a special place tonight and I guess we'll discuss where our relationship is headed. He still has two more years and I'll be here in law school for at least three or more years, so we have time to take things slow."

The girls hugged again, as they both express their happiness for each other.

Jewel was not prepared for what was about to take place at dinner. The waiter sat wine glasses in front of them and began to fill them.

Jewel looked up at him puzzled and he said, "It's not alcoholic Miss."

Jewel smiled at Ken, who thanked the waiter.

"Jewel, I'm so nervous about this, so I want us to talk before we order, okay."

"That's fine Ken," Jewel said, puzzled at what he could be nervous about. It's not like they haven't talked about everything.

"Jewel," Ken said, as he took Jewel's hands and held them in his, "I've been offered a position on the Olympic field and track team."

"Wow!" Jewel exclaimed excitedly, "this is great! When did you hear this?"

"About a week now," Ken said.

"Will there be a try out, or something?" Jewel asked.

"No," replied Ken, "They have seen me run and want me."

Jewel heart began to beat fast. Was this the end of their relationship? Had they spend so much time pursuing their goals and not pursuing a relationship and now the relationship they had come to know and love was going to end just like that.

Ken was still holding her hand.

"Jewel, will you marry me and come with me?"

That question not only cut into Jewel's thought, but it cut into her heart.

"Ken?" Jewel said puzzled. "I graduate next summer and then I'm going to law school, remember. When will I have time to marry you and go be with you, as you run in the Olympics?"

"Jewel I love you, and these last few weeks has been the most wonderful times of my life. I called your father and ask him for his blessing and he has given us his blessings."

"You did what?" Jewel was now hurt and confused.

"I'm not getting married to you Ken. I know I feel something deeply for you. It may be love, but I am not ready to give up my life for feelings that I can't even identify."

Now it was Ken's time to be hurt. He let go of Jewel's hand and Jewel willingly pulled her hand away.

"I thought we felt the same way," Ken said with his eyes looking down.

"Ken, we feel something, but how can you say that it's love. In order for me to make a commitment like that and put my dreams on hold, it has to be love.

"Jewel my dreams are your dreams. We want the same things, a nice house, cars, children, but now you don't have to work to get them. I'm going to be able to give you all those things as my wife."

"Excuse me," Jewel said, "I never told you I wanted children and it's not about getting things. It's about my life. I want a career as a lawyer. I've always wanted to be a lawyer. You want a wife to take care of your big beautiful home and your children. Ken," Jewel said with care, "that person isn't me. It will never be me. Not for you, or for anyone else for that matter."

Ken shook his head.

"I see. I guess I let my emotions run wild with my mind."

"I hope we can still be friends," Jewel said.

"Always," Ken said disappointed, because they both new their relationship had taken another unexpected turn and they would never be as close as they once were.

Jewel went back to the dorm saddened. Dawn had left. They wanted it that way. They did not want to say any more goodbyes. Ken was leaving in two days and would not be back. Jewel never felt so lonely in her life. She picked up the phone and call home.

"Hi Mom."… "I'm calling to let you know I'm going to be home sometime tomorrow."… "No Mom, Ken and I are not engaged."… "I'm okay."… "Really."

She hung up the phone and began to cry. It seemed like everyone that she met and love kept leaving, Lois, Dawn and now Ken. She would never let her guard down again and get close to anyone. Her goal was to finish law school and become a lawyer, not just another lawyer, but one who would make a difference, but for now she was longing to be home with her family.

She got up and packed her suitcase and took her things to the car. She decided to leave right away. She would be home in a couple of hours. She couldn't wait to be home where she knew she was loved and the people there would never leave her.

The Intercessor

...And the Intercessor prays, in our vulnerable state Lord, we fail to see our fate, and the enemy lies lurking at our gate. With deep emotional groaning from within, the next phase has begun. What's this I see Lord, is it a vision or a dream; this child, this child, so precious in your sight.

Chapter Eleven
Lucifer

"It's time to move forward!" The little imp's eyes, bulging as they were, seemed to be popping out of the slimy little imp's head, as the command came from Swathteke, the demon that was given charge to aid him in his plan.

He jumped up and down clapping his hands.

"Fun and games are over," he announced. "It's time to pull out all stops."

The demon was annoyed at the little imp's joy. He was doing all the work and if he wasn't careful this little nothing of an imp could get all the credit. He was not going to have that, but now was not the time to deal with the little imp. He still needed the little imp to follow through with things already set in motion.

Satan had shown great interest in the lives of these two young women, but still had not given them any more demons to work with, so he had to use what he had. It didn't help that Bedeekle constantly reminded him that this was his idea. Left alone to it, he would sure botch it up and Satan was the one he had to answer to not this little imp.

"Yes, it is time. Are all players in position?" The older demon inquired of Bedeekle.

"Yes Sir!" came the reply, as he tried to stand to his full diminutive size to salute the bigger demon.

The demon just eyed him with contempt and said, "then let's put things in motion. You two, Queens, New York, you two, Atlanta, Ga."

The big demon commanded. He gave the little demons instruction and off they went.

"What about me? What about me?" Bedeekle inquired of the bigger demon.

"Just sit tight and wait. I'll let you know when and where."

Bedeekle wasn't happy with this assignment, but he did what he was told. He didn't want to mess up anything and feel the wrath of Lucifer.

Ever since the Pastor of the Ekklesia Church began to get involve with issues outside of the church, Lucifer was on a rampage. He let out all kinds of forces on the church and many of their members were under severe demonic attack.

Satan was constantly back and forth in the heavenlies trying to get the Most Holy One to allow him to loose the death angel on some of the members, but the One who sits on the right hand of his Father was constantly against any such attack.

Satan was given a season to render his attacks and only if one of the saints gave up would he be allow to send out the death angel.

Bedeekle had hopes of becoming a death angel some day, but he was far from that now. If the death angel was ever sent out on one of his assignment, he could watch them work. He had never had the pleasure of seeing the Death angels at work.

"One day, one day," he whispered.

"What?" the big demon screamed at him.

"Oh nothing sir."

The big demon looked at Bedeekle with his one eye and said, "Do not call me sir and please be quiet. I am thinking."

Chapter Twelve
Lois

Lois walked in on Kelly and Steve arguing and he left as soon as he saw her. Kelly was lying across her bed crying.

"Why do you let him do this to you, Kelly?"

"I'll be alright."

Kelly got up and went into the kitchen to put ice on her eyes.

"That never works," Lois said, "you're still going to wake up in the morning with a black eye."

"I know," Kelly replied, "but it cools the pain."

Lois got another cloth and wrapped ice in it and put it on another spot that was bruised.

Kelly looked at Lois and said, "not tonight, Lois. I do not want a lecture."

"Fine," said Lois, "then I'll leave this ice pack to comfort you, goodnight."

"Goodnight," Kelly said taking the other ice pack and holding it on the other side of her face.

Kelly hated that Lois took her and Steve's fights so personal, if she didn't, maybe she could talk to her about it, but Kelly knew Lois couldn't be objective when it came to Steve.

Kelly and Steve's fights got worst and Lois began to spend a lot of time at Deb's. She confided in Deb once about it, but Deb gave her a lecture on moving out, or getting Kelly some help and calling the cops the next time it happen. Lois was not going to do any of those things, so she never brought the subject up again.

"Are you going to go with us to church this Sunday?"

Deb was going to add, you hadn't been in awhile, but Lois cut her off and said, "I think I will."

"You could stay over the entire weekend," Deb said.

"That would be great," Lois said, "matter of fact, why don't we plan to do something Saturday."

"Like what?" Deb asked.

"I don't know, something the kids would like, maybe a movie, the zoo, something, it doesn't really matter."

Deb hollered at the Kids, "Hey you guys would y'all like to go to the Zoo, or to a movie on Saturday?"

"The Zoo!" All three replied simultaneously.

"The Zoo it is," said Deb.

"The Zoo it is," Lois confirmed.

Lois was feeling really lighthearted for the first time in a long time, since she broke up with Troy. His girlfriend, or whatever she was to him, was harassing her at first, but then she realized Lois was not her problem.

Saturday was a great day. The children enjoyed the zoo. The adults did as well. They ate at McDonalds and when the children were asleep, Lois helped Deb prepare her Sunday dinner.

After service was over, Lois took Bridgett and went in the vestibule to wait for Deb outside, as Deb made her rounds greeting everyone in the church. Kevy and Mickey came running to Lois grinning. Lois grabbed the two of them and scolded them for running in the sanctuary.

"Mom wants you," Kevy announced.

"Yeah, Mom wants you," Mickey confirmed as the two boys starting laughing again.

"Oh God," Lois thought, "I hope she's not trying to get me to join anything again."

Deb was always trying to get Lois to join some auxiliary, hoping that it would keep her connected to the church.

As Lois approached Deb, she couldn't help but notice that she was talking to the good-looking organist. Lois was sure that he was new to the church. This was her first time seeing him there. It was hard not noticing someone who was that good looking and playing the church organ in front of the church.

"Lois, come here," Deb called out. She reached out and grabbed Lois' arm and pulled her next to her. "Matthew, this is my niece Lois. Lois, this is Matthew, our new organist."

"Hi," Lois said awkwardly.

Matthew held out his hand and Lois took it and shook it.

"Just call me Matt."

"Hi Matt," Lois said again.

Deb looked around the church and began to wave at Karen, "I'll be right back," Deb said, "I'm going to see if Karen has room for all of us in her car. I really don't feel like taking the train home today."

Lois felt even more awkward, as Deb ran off leaving her with Matt. She didn't know what to say, finally she said, "You're good."

"Thanks," Matt said. "Your aunt tells me you're from Tennessee and don't know very many people."

"Well, that's not entirely true," Lois said. "I've been here for over two years now and I do know some people. I live with my best friend, Kelly, and of course she knows people and have introduced me to a few."

"Great," said Matt, "so how do you like New York, so far?"

"It's okay," Lois said, "actually it's more than okay, I really like it here."

"Well, you know what they say," Matt said, you either hate it or love it."

"I definitely love it," said Lois.

"So what do you do for fun?" Lois wasn't sure how to answer, but she didn't have to because Deb came back just at that time.

"Karen has a load. I guess we have to train it."

"I could give you guys a ride home, if you want."

"Oh no, we don't want to put you out of your way, besides my kids can be little terrors."

"They're not," said Lois in their defense.

"I'm sure they're not," said Matt.

"I know what," Deb said, "we'll ride with Karen and Lois can ride with you."

Lois was truly put out by Deb's suggestion.

"Aunt Deb, I'll take the train. I don't mind."

"Why?" ask Matt, "you don't want to ride with me?"

"I don't want to put you out," said Lois.

"It'll be my pleasure."

"If you're sure," said Lois, as she gave Deb a look that said, "I'll get you for this."

Deb just smiled and left. Lois was sure Deb had planned the entire thing.

"Matt, why don't you just come on over for dinner," Deb said walking away, as if it was a settled issued.

Matt saw Lois' embarrassment. He didn't want the ride home to be uncomfortable for either of them, so he turned to the choir director, Nate, and yelled, "hey Nate! you still need a ride home." Nate looked kind of confused, not remembering whether or not he had asked Matt for a ride or not.

He still had some things that he wanted to finish up before he left, so he yelled back, "It's going to be a bit before I am ready to pack it up, so I'll probably take the train."

"I'll catch you later then," Matt looked at Lois and said, "are you ready?"

"Yes, I am," Lois replied. "Then let's go."

Matt opened the door for Lois, which made her feel even more uncomfortable. She never had anyone to open a car door for her before.

"Matt! Matt!" two of the girls from the choir were running towards Matt's car.

Matt stood at Lois' door as the girls approach.

"Hey, are you going downtown? We want to go to BBQs."

"Wasn't planning on it, I'm headed to the Bronx," Matt replied.

"Well we thought you guys would want to hang out with us," one of the girls said leaning over to make sure that Lois knew that she was included.

"No, I'm already invited to dinner, but I'll drop you guys off."

"You sure, we don't want to inconvenience you."

"It's okay," Matt said looking into the car window for Lois' response. "Your aunt wouldn't mind if we're a little late, would she?"

"Knowing her and Karen they'll probably make a couple of stops before going home anyway," Lois said.

"Great!" said one of the girls as they hopped into the back of the car.

"You guys know each other?" Matt asked.

Matt was the newcomer in the group and he didn't know how often Lois came to the church. He didn't want to assume.

"I don't think that we've been formerly introduce. "I'm Cynthia and this is Janie."

"I'm Lois."

"Oh we know your name, said Janie. We just were never introduced. You're usually trying to knock everyone down to get out of church after service." Everyone laughed, but Lois was sort of embarrassed that she had given that impression.

"She's just kidding," said Cynthia reaching over to pat Lois on her shoulder, "we know how it is. We don't want to be in church any longer than we have to either."

The two girls chatter all the way downtown and Lois was glad. Every now and then they would ask Lois and Matt a question and they would reply, but other than that it was a two-way conversation between Cynthia and Janie.

Lois was glad when they got to the girls destination, but a little nervous about the rest of the ride to Deb's house.

"What kind of music do you listen to?" Matt asked Lois, as he started to go through his tapes to see what he wanted to put into the tape deck.

Lois wanted to say gospel, but she didn't want to lie. She liked some of the gospel artist and she listened to the gospel stations on Sundays, but she didn't want to pretend to be someone she was not.

"I don't have one favorite type of music, I like gospel, rap, R&B, you know."

"Yeah, me too," Matt said.

"Have you ever heard Take 6?"

Lois was glad to be able to say yes to that, being part of her youth group at her old church introduced her to gospel music that a lot of the young people liked to hear and Take 6 was one of those groups.

"Yes, I have."

"You like them?" Matt asked.

"Yes I do," Lois replied.

"Yeah, me too," said Matt.

"I like their ocapella style of music. So what do you do?" Matt asked Lois.

"I work at this company that makes vacuum cleaner bags, but I'm going back to school for business. I want to work in an office."

"Doing what?"

"Whatever," Lois replied. "I just want to be able to go to work and dress like a professional person that makes lots of money."

"How about you?" Lois asked Matt.

"Well, I'm sort of into music. My mom and I worked out a deal with the church. I play the keyboard, sing, assist the choir director and in return the church is going to give me a scholarship to go to a School of the Arts, that is, if I'm accepted."

"Wow," said Lois, "you really are into music, huh?"

"Yep, ever since I could remember, I wanted to be the next Luther Vandross, or something close."

"So you don't want to play gospel music?"

"I want to, and will play anything that will get me into the business." Matt said.

Their conversation continued with Matt sharing his dreams and Lois was glad. Her dreams weren't as thought and planned out as Matt's. It was good listening to him. It made her feel good, but she wasn't sure why listening to someone else's dreams made her feel good, but it did.

By the time they reached the Bronx and Deb's house, they were laughing and feeling a little bit more comfortable with each other. After dinner, Matt took Lois home and made a date to see her again.

Church became a regular occasion with Lois again. Matt picked her up for church and brought her home. They went to the movies together and Matt eventually got Lois to agree to sing on the choir. That way they could spend even more time together, especially since the choir took up so much of Matt's time.

Lois went over to Matt's home a couple of time for dinner, but she didn't think Mrs. Edwards liked her that much. She was beginning to feel self-conscience about it. What about her brought about a negative affect with mothers. Lois saw her staring at her every now and then, with a displeased look on her face.

What Lois didn't know was that Mrs. Edwards had a long conversation with Matt concerning her. Mrs. Edwards was a good Christian woman who was left to raised her children by herself. Her husband left them when her elder son, Craig, was seven. Matt was three and didn't know his father that well and Carla, their sister, a baby at the time, didn't know him at all. Patricia Edwards had a lot of problems with Craig. He couldn't seem to do the right thing, or want to. He dropped out of high school to get a job and ended up selling and using drugs, which ended him in prison. Patricia became very protective of Matt and would do anything she could to keep him on the right track, which included giving advice concerning females that she thought was not right for him. She didn't know much about Lois, except that her aunt had three children out of wedlock. She respected Deb for getting saved and raising her children up in the ways of the Lord, but she also felt that if Deb wasn't promiscuous, she wouldn't be in the predicament that she was in now. So it was no surprise that Patricia wondered if Lois was like her aunt, before she got saved. She felt a little more comfortable when Matt told her that Lois was a virgin.

Her comment was, "for her own good, I hope she stays that way until she's married."

It didn't matter to Patricia that Matt wasn't a virgin, because she didn't feel like Matt could mess up his life by becoming pregnant, so she decided not to come down so hard on him concerning Lois. She just hoped that Matt would soon get tired of her and move on, but that didn't happen.

Matt continued to see Lois and they spent a lot of time at Lois' apartment. Kelly became jealous of Matt and Lois' relationship.

She and Steve were constantly fighting with each other. She knew that if she wanted to make something out of her life, she was going to have to break it off with Steve. He was becoming more verbally and physically abusive anytime she tried to do something other than work at the factory, but she was afraid to break it off with him, because he threatened to kill her if she did.

On Lois' 21st birthday, Matt rented a limousine and took her out to dinner and a musical show on Broadway. He bought her a dozen roses and after the show, they pulled up to one of the ritziest hotels in Manhattan. Matt paid the limousine service and escorted Lois into the hotel.

Lois wasn't sure what he had planned, but the entire evening was so magical; she didn't want it to end, so she asked no questions. She just allowed herself to be caught up in the magic of the night, because as far as she was concerned, Matt had cast a spell over her and she didn't want him to take it off.

The evening could not have been more perfect. She felt like a princess. Matt had bought her a lovely gown for the evening. It was a long sleeveless red gown with an x-strap back and fake studded diamonds around the low cut neckline of the dress, revealing more than Lois ever revealed of her body with any guy. The bodice was cut to her figure and fitted her as if it was made just for her. Matt wore a tuxedo and before dinner he arranged for them to take pictures at the local glamour studio.

As Matt opened the door to the hotel room, there were candles and balloons all around the room. Matt led Lois to the bedroom and there was a lovely gown lying across the bed.

Matt said to Lois, "the bathroom is in there if you want to freshen up."

Lois was new to this, but she had seen so many movies and fantasized so many times about evenings like this that she did not need to be coaxed as to what to do.

She took the gown off the bed, reluctant to change out of her dress, because she felt like she could wear it forever, so the night would never end.

When she came out of the bathroom, Matt was lying on the bed with a rose between his teeth and two glasses of champagne. He gave Lois a glass and took the rose and placed it in her hair.

"Tonight you are old enough to drink, so our first toast should be to that."

Lois took her glass and said, "I'll drink to that," and they did.

They made more toast and when the bottle was empty, Matt took Lois' glass and placed it on the nightstand. He reached on the nightstand and gave Lois a small box. Lois was hoping in her heart that it was an engagement ring. She could hear her heart pounding and her hands were shaking.

Matt took the box from her and opened it. It was not a ring. It was a beautiful necklace with a heart shaped pendant on it.

Matt placed it around Lois' neck and said, "You have become my heart."

He gently kissed Lois as they lay down on the bed together. Lois was feeling light head from the champagne and all reasoning was gone. She was caught up in the fantasy and she loved every moment of it.

She said to Matt, "I love you." And Matt replied the same.

Matt's touch felt like fire all over her body and she knew the only way to make the fire go out was to give herself to Matt completely.

The next morning Lois awoke to a hangover. Matt was standing over her saying something. Finally it registered.

He was saying, "The fantasy is over my princess. We have thirty minutes to vacate the premises, or my next paycheck will go to paying for this room one more night."

He gave Lois some coffee.

"Here, people say this works. It never has for me, but maybe it will for you."

Lois took a sip of the coffee and placed the cup on the nightstand and went straight to the bathroom thinking she may throw up, but she didn't.

Matt came to her side, "are you alright?"

"I think I am." Lois said, not really sure if she was or wasn't. She looked at herself in the mirror and said, "I look a mess."

"Not at all," Matt assured her as he cupped her chin in the palm of her hands and tilted her head upwards, so that he could look into her eyes, "you still look amazingly beautiful." Matt kissed Lois on her forehead, "Get dress, and I'll call us a cab."

Lois took one last look around the room, not really looking for anything that she may have missed, because she only brought what she had on to the hotel room. She wanted to remember the hotel room and that night for the rest of her life.

The cab took them to Lois' apartment. Kelly came bolting out of her bedroom, when they arrived.

"So you couldn't call and tell me you were going to spend all night out."

"I'm sorry," Lois said genuinely, but Kelly went on and on about how worried she was.

Finally Lois said, "get over it Kelly, it's not like you report to me every time you stay out with Steve."

Matt jumped in and said, "I'm sorry Kelly, Lois didn't know she was going to spend the night out. It was part of my birthday surprise to her."

Kelly finally calmed down and said, "Your mother wants you to call her. She wanted to know if you got her birthday gift and I told her you did."

"Thanks," Lois said.

"And here," Kelly said, picking up a wrapped gift off the couch, "Happy birthday from me and Steve."

It was a bottle of champagne with a note that said, "you can drink now."

Lois showed the note to Matt and they both just laugh.

"I'm sorry Kelly, thank you for the gift. It's just that I don't know if being allowed to drink when you turn 21 is a good thing or not, after last night."

Matt looked at Lois and kissed her and said, "Oh, I think it is."

"Thank Steve for us," Lois said, although she knew that Steve probably didn't have anything to do with buying a gift.

"Troy called to wish you a happy birthday." Kelly said.

"That was nice of him," Lois said.

"Who's Troy?" Matt asked.

"A friend of ours." Lois said.

Kelly wanted to say more, but decided not to.

Matt began to spend lots of night over at Lois' apartment. Matt convinced Lois that after the night of her 21st birthday there was no going back. They had to move forward with their relationship. They talked about it and agreed that they were going to be responsible and take the necessary precautions, but sometimes they forgot.

"Do you know what you're doing?" Kelly asked.

"Excuse me?" Lois responded.

"I don't want to get in your business, but you were so protective of your virginity."

"I was waiting for Matt," Lois replied sarcastically with a smile on her face.

"You mean your prince charming?"

"And that he is," said Lois.

"I thought prince charming was supposed to marry you and take you off to a beautiful castle or something."

"Is that what your prince charming has done for you?" Lois snapped, annoyed with Kelly's judgmental tone.

"I never said that Steve was my prince charming, or that I was even looking for a prince charming."

"Well, maybe you should," Lois said, "or at least someone who would treat you like a person."

Kelly backed away with her two hands up in surrender, "I'm sorry. I was just concerned."

"I'm a big girl Kelly. Matt and I love each other and we're talking about getting married. We want a big wedding. Matt went all out for my 21st birthday and we just want to top that with our wedding day. Matt has his music and I'm going to go to that business school, because Matt hates that I work at the factory. We want to do it right."

"I'm glad for you. It seems as though you guys have talked it all out."

"We have, but thanks for your concern and I didn't mean what I said."

"Yes you did, and you're right. I need to find someone who at least treats me like a person."

Lois went up to Kelly took her hands and said, "Break if off Kelly."

"That's easier said than done, but I'm working on it."

"Let me know if there's anything that Matt and I can do?"

"Sure. I'm glad that you've found Matt. He seems like a swell guy."

"He is," said Lois, "he is."

Chapter Thirteen
Jewel

As Jewel sat in her class listening at her law Professor down grading them, calling them everything but total idiots; Jewel knew that in a couple of weeks, this large class of law students would be reduced to half the size. It was like the first day of college all over again, except this time Jewel was not intimidated. She put her hand over her mouth as she smiled at some of the things the professor was saying. She didn't want him to see her smiling. He had already dismissed one boy for laughing.

Jewel entered law school with a whole new sense of confidence. She had graduated in the spring at the top of her class and gave the class valedictory speech. She worked hard in college to keep her grade point average at 4.0, but she was surprised to be the one to give the speech. There were other students that had 4.0 GPA, but nominations were based on other qualifications as well. She had come out of her shell in just enough time to participate in other college activities, which made her the better candidate.

It was an honor to speak for her entire graduation class and of course her parents were extremely proud of her, even people from her church and community came to hear her speak, as well as her relatives, including Grandma Lynnie.

After graduation, Jewel went home for the summer to take a break and get ready for law school. Tessa also graduated that spring. It was touch and go for her for a while. Tessa's grades began to drop her last two year in high school. She had become rebellious, claiming everyone wanted her to follow in Jewel's shoes, her parents, her teachers, even the youth directors. She was determined to be herself and since she really didn't know who that was yet, she made a couple of blunders and almost failed the year of her graduation. Jewel was able to talk to her when she came home for winter break. After that talk, Tessa began to straighten up a little to get her grades back up to be able to graduate.

She was a good student, but her rebellion almost ruin her chances of getting into a good college, but things worked out and she got accepted to a college far away from home, just what she wanted.

That summer turned out to be one of the best. They all spent a week in the Mountains, where the Stones timeshared a log cabin condominium; that was as roughing it as any of them wanted. They went to Florida for a week at Disney World and the rest of the summer were cookouts, weekend trips and family gatherings. Paul and Theresa knew that with Jewel going away to law school and Tessa so far away to college, they may never get another opportunity to do family things with all of their children for a long time, so they planned the entire summer around doing family activities.

Tessa and David had a few objections at first to their planned summer, but soon were caught up in all the family activities. Jewel welcomed the distractions of her family. Going away to college, having friends and then losing friends made her realize the importance her family played in her life. They were the one constant relationship she could count on and right now they were helping to keep her mind off Ken, at least most of the time.

The professor dismissed the class with some comment about waiting to teach the class when more of the students dropped out. Jewel picked up her things and headed for her car.

She was living in a boarding house with some of the other students. This was a lot better than the college dorm. She had to share the bathroom and Kitchen, but she had her own room. She could keep a microwave, hotplate and a small refrigerator in her room, so she did not have to have much contact with the people in the boarding house.

The boarding house was also co-ed. Her college counselor recommended this type of setting, because it would allow her to meet other students and form a nucleus of friends that she could relate to and study with. Her parents were not so happy with the setup. Her other option was an apartment, which was more costly and she would have to work more hours to keep it. Her parents offered to pay for it, because they wanted her to be focused on her studies, but Jewel declined the offer. She wanted to see how the boarding house would work out first.

She also knew that with Tessa going so far away to college, they had to consider the expense for her tuition, as well as David, who had become a senior in high school. She did agree to let them pay for the boarding house room. They all agreed that if things didn't work out at the boarding house, she could reconsider the apartment.

As she reached her car, she began to fumble for her keys and end up dropping all her books, disgusted, she began to pick her things up after retrieving her keys.

"Having some problems?" a guy with a deep voice asked, while bending down to help her pick up her things.

"Thanks," Jewel said.

As she looked up, she was staring into the deepest blue eyes she had ever seen; she almost lost her balance, as he handed her a book.

"You should have your keys always accessible avoiding this, so much can happen on campus."

"You're right," Jewel said, "but I also don't need another lecture right now after the one I just had."

The guy laughed and said, "I know. I just came out of that lecture myself; sorry if I sounded like I was about to lecture you."

Jewel smiled, "it's okay. You're right. I should be more organized and usually I am. I was unprepared for the professor letting us out early."

"I'm Brad," the young man said extending his hands to Jewel.

Jewel threw her books in her car to have a free hand "I'm Jewel."

"First year law student?" Brad asked. "Yes, how about you?"

"First year," he answered.

"Well it's nice meeting you Brad and thanks for your help and your advice. I appreciate both."

"You're welcome," Brad said. "Maybe we'll see each other around some time."

"Maybe," said Jewel as she hopped into her car and drove out of the parking lot.

The class had dropped to about half the size before the first test. Jewel knew most of the students were not dropping out of law school. They just decided that it was going to be hard enough to get through law school without being discouraged their first year. They would have to take the class again, which was probably going to be taught by the same professor, unless something happened and he didn't teach, but this professor had tenure and wasn't going anywhere, which was the case with most of the law professors. As the class got smaller, Jewel saw more of Brad and they would smile at each other in passing.

The boarding house was a good choice. At night before most of them went to bed, they would get together in the common area and talk about their classes and their professors. The talks usually help to shed some light on a topic that someone may have been vague on. The group huddles helped Jewel a lot and she was glad she chose the boarding house to live.

The other students in her boarding house were Olivia Martin, who always had an opposing view on everything; Paula Benjamin was quiet. Jewel knew her mom would characterize Paula, as having a sweet spirit. She was not confrontational. She took it all in and just did away with the things that were not good. Stuart Caldwell, who had an overrated opinion of himself, came across as a rich kid who was in the boarding house as a punishment for not doing better in school and getting into Harvard. He had all the answers, a know-it-all-kind-of-guy. Everyone saw him for what he really was and he intimidated no one. William (Billy) Callahan was easy going, but he wasn't sure that he wanted to be in law school. His father and brother were lawyers and they had their own business, with the expectation that Billy would join them one day.

The ratio between black and white was very poor in law school. There was only one other black in her boarding house. A guy name Eric Bridges. Jewel was always reluctant as to what to do in these situations; she didn't want to be accused of trying to act like she was white by the black students, so she tried to mingle with everyone. Eric was a really nice guy and everyone liked him. He was funny and smart. If there was anyone she would want to form an alliance with, it was Eric, not because he was black, but because he was smart and fun to be around.

The only other black she communicated with a lot was a girl she met in one of her class. Her name was Justine Pierson. She was smart and looked more like a model than a law student. She also didn't want the White students to think she gravitated towards only her race. However, it seemed like people of the same culture and ethnic backgrounds just seem to flock together no matter what the circumstance.

It was easy to lose your identity and forget where you came from in order to fit in and not be different. Of course, times were changing and there were more black students than before, but in comparison the numbers were still small.

On weekends, they would mostly hang out at the local bar and grille in walking distance of the college, so none of them would have to drive back to the dorm, if they were too drunk to do so. Jewel and Justine met there often. Jewel was not that comfortable with the bar and grille, but no one cared that she didn't drink. Matter of fact, a lot of the students didn't drink, as much as Jewel thought they would. Most of them would have one can of beer to fit in and sip on it all night. Justine didn't drink and was certainly not intimidated by anyone who did. Eric and Paula began to join Jewel and Justine at their table.

Jewel became a little uncomfortable with Eric, when Justine commented that she thought Eric was gooey eyed over her, however, Paula seemed to be everywhere Eric was. Without knowing it, Eric and Jewel began to spend a lot of time together, as friends.

"I think Paula likes you." Jewel said to Eric one night when he was going over some notes with her.

"What?" Eric seemed surprised, "you think so?"

"Yeah," said Jewel, "I really do."

"Too bad," said Eric, "I'm not looking to get involved right now.

It's going to be hard enough getting through law school without having to deal with a serious relationship."

His comment put Jewel at ease concerning their relationship. It made her more comfortable and open around him, knowing that he was not looking to get involved, because she wasn't. As it turned out, Justine and Eric became a couple.

"You traitor," said Jewel to Justine, when Justine told her how she felt about Eric and she thought he felt the same way about her.

"I always liked him, but I thought he was attracted to you," Justine admitted.

"Not at all," said Jewel.

"Yeah, I realize that now. That's why I want you to know how I feel. I didn't want you to be surprise or caught off guard. You're okay with it, aren't you?" Justine wanted to know. "Because I wouldn't do anything if I thought you liked him. I mean, it's not like I want to marry him or anything like that. I just want to have a good time. You know?"

"I guess," Jewel responded, although she wasn't sure what Justine meant.

She thought they were having a good time together as a group, but she didn't want to get into it with Justine, so she said, "Justine, it's great. You and Eric make a handsome couple. It couldn't have happened to two nicer people."

Jewel wasn't sure about that though. Eric was a serious kind of guy and he wouldn't enter into a relationship just to have a good time. It would definitely be a commitment. She hoped it worked out for them, whatever it was that they were looking for in a relationship. She also felt a pang of jealousy. She missed her relationship with Ken, but she only wanted to show happiness for Eric and Justine.

One afternoon at the bar and grille, Jewel, Justine, Paula and Olivia were deep in studies when some of the guys came in and interrupted. To Jewel's surprise they had picked up a stray.

"Hi ladies," said Eric, "mind if we joined you?"

"Sure," said Justine, without waiting for anyone else to respond.

As they began to pull up chairs and squeeze around an already small round table, Billy began to introduce their straggler to everyone. When he got to Jewel, she put out her hand and said, "We've already met, Brad, isn't it?"

"Yes, good memory," said Brad.

"Well you have to have a good memory here don't you?"

"You're right" said Brad.

Study time was soon over for the girls, as the conversation went to every topic possible that night. Jewel and Paula finally decided to call it a night and got up to walk back to the house.

"I'll give you guys a ride. I have to go any way," Brad offered.

"We're right around the corner," said Paula.

"I know, but I have to go that way anyway."

Jewel didn't want to stand there arguing the point, so she said, "That'll be great. Thanks."

Brad became a member of their little inner circle and occasionally he would bring his friend, Gordon, who seemed to be taken with Olivia.

Jewel began to feel uncomfortable with Brad around. Every time she looked his way, he would be staring at her. It made her feel strangely uncomfortable.

One night after a big exam everyone agreed to go out dancing, to shake off some of the tension. To Jewels' surprise, Brad asked her to dance.

"Why do you ignore me?" Brad asked.

"Excuse me," said Jewel, confused by the question, "I didn't realize I was doing that."

"Well, you do," said Brad.

"Well, I'll be conscience of it in the future. Can you forgive me?" She said teasingly.

"I can do that," Brad answered with a smile that made Jewel's heart skip a beat.

Jewel thought a lot about that conversation in the weeks ahead, as Brad seemed to make it his business to be in her presence. He would wait until she took her seat in class and he would sit by her. He began to frequent the bar and grill and always try to squeeze into a seat next to her and was attentive to everything she said.

"That white boy has got it bad for you girl," Justine said in Jewels ears one night when Brad got up to get them some drinks and snacks from the bar.

"What are you talking about?" asked Jewel.

"Oh, come on," said Justine, "like you don't know this. I know you're not as naive as you want everyone to think and you know I know. You know all too well that he likes being around you and go out of his way to do so."

Jewel just shrugged Justine's remark off. Of course she knew and it was sort of a nice feeling. It seemed like everyone was pairing off, but she didn't want to get involve with someone because everyone was pairing off.

By the end of their first year of law school, Jewel and Brad's relationship grew. No one was calling them a couple, but they were becoming more comfortable around each other. Brad never asked her out on a date, because he wasn't sure how she felt about interracial dating and wasn't sure how he felt about it. All he knew was that there was something about her that kept drawing him to her from the first day they met in the parking lot.

They ended their first year of law school, as friends.

Jewel went home for her first annual break from Law school. It was a rough year and she needed the break. She also needed time away from her feelings concerning Brad. She was always thinking what it would mean to be in a relationship with someone of the opposite race. She had many white friends, but she didn't have feelings for them like she was having for Brad. She kept trying to be cool about it and not let her mind run away with her, besides it wasn't like they ever went out on a date or anything.

She called up all of her male friends, including Ken, who was doing well. He was getting ready for the Olympics with great expectations. He invited her to come down to visit him for a weekend and she accepted.

The visit didn't go as well as she hoped. She constantly thought of Brad and it was clear that Ken still had his old fashioned ways concerning relationships and her role in his life. They were glad to see each other, but they knew it would never work with the two of them.

Finally Ken asked, "who is it?"

One thing about Ken, he was very perceptive and Jewel knew she could share almost anything with him.

She told Ken about Brad, her fears and her concerns.

"Look Jewel," Ken began, "you're a smart girl. You never do anything without thoroughly thinking it through, but sometimes you think about things too much. Don't think happiness out of your life. I know you have your dreams and your goals, but it's not so bad to have your dreams come true and some happiness along with it."

"I thought happiness was having your dreams come true," said Jewel.

"Like I said, you're a smart lady. You know what I mean."

Jewel didn't know how she was going to handle the situation with Brad. She thought about it all summer long, trying to talk around it with her parents, without giving them details.

She ended up going back to school, with the attitude that she would take it one day at a time. Maybe she wouldn't even see Brad this term, or maybe he became interested in someone else over the summer or something, but none of that happened and she saw more of Brad than she hoped for. Eventually she stopped trying to avoid him to see what would happen. What happened was they became a couple.

The Intercessor

To intercede is not a glamorous job. It is one fill with moanings, groanings and sobs. When call to intercede, there is no time to consider personal needs. Once again my tired soul is called to fight. I understand these battles are won in the wee hours of the night. The warring saint must fight and not faint, or some wondering soul will be lost and cast into a deep dark hole.

Chapter Fourteen
The Demonic Forces

They say, "New York never sleeps," but some do, taking their rest from a busy day. The state where resides the three major forces of the world, religion, economic and foreign affairs is practically home of the demonic world in a nation where there's freedom, liberty and justice for all.

If you walk the streets at night, you can smell the rank, sulfuric scent of demonic activity, but for most New Yorkers nothing is strange and the unusual is ignored.

In an old abandoned property some of the major demons are having a meeting, while many others are controlling the thoughts and minds of those awoke to wreck as much havoc as possible in the city, "that never sleeps."

Chapter Fifteen
Lois

Lois woke up feeling like she had a hangover. The nausea feeling that she was experiencing for the last few days came upon her again and she raced to the bathroom, got on her knees to kneel over the toilet, but there was nothing in her to throw up. She got up ran the cold water, cupped her hands together and threw the cold water on her face. While she was up, she decided to take her shower. After her shower she went to her room, got dress and sat at the kitchen table, half listening to Bryant Gumble on the morning show and staring out the kitchen window at the brick wall of the building across from them.

She decided to make some hot tea and some toast with nothing on it. Kelly came out of the room holding a box in her hand.

"Here," she handed Lois the box.

Lois took the box, read the label and rubbed one hand over her face.

"You think I'm pregnant?"

Kelly was taken back by the childlike way that Lois asked the question.

"I didn't go out and buy this just for you. I keep one handy, just in case. I've had those symptoms before, so I know what it could mean, besides, your period is late by almost a month. You're never that late. Have you and Matt always been careful?" Kelly inquired.

Lois put both of her hand over her face and when she lowered them she said, "No, we haven't. Sometimes when he forgot to bring protection, he would try the other method."

"The other method?" Kelly asked, "what other method?"

"You know," Lois began to shyly explain, "where he stops before it happens."

"For goodness sake Lois, guys don't really do that you know. It's just a lie they tell us, so we can think it's safe. Guys don't have that kind of control."

Lois looked at Kelly in disbelief. Matt wouldn't lie about something so important. She placed her whole face down on the kitchen table and placed both her hands over her head.

"I'll do it after work," came Lois' muffled voice. "I don't want it to ruin my day at work," she said as she got up from the table.

"You can't postponed it forever Lois," Kelly said, as Lois walked back into her room to get her things for work, "it won't just go away."

"I know," Lois said.

Lois regretted not taking the test earlier. It was on her mind all day. She looked despondent and far away.

"Lois, are you okay?" Christine asked.

"No, I'm not feeling well." Everything she ate seemed liked it wanted to come back up, so she didn't eat, because she didn't want to start any rumors by having to go to the bathroom to throw up.

"Maybe you should go home," said Christine.

Lois was glad for the suggestion. She never took a day off from work. She was hardly ever sick. A couple of times she had the bout with the flu, but Deborah clued her in on taking care of herself by drinking a lot of orange juice, dressing in layers and maybe taking some extra vitamin C, during the winter months.

"I think I will," said Lois, "will you be able to find someone to cover for me?"

"Girl, get out of here and go home," said Christine, "I'll pull someone from off the table to finish up for you today.

The table was where workers would go to do miscellaneous work, when their machines were going to be down for a long period of time."

"Bye," Lois said to Christine as she walked to the time clock to punch out, "and thanks a lot."

"Go get you some cold Medicine, or something and get in bed and get a good night rest!" yelled Christine as Lois was walking away.

Lois turned and smiled at her. It was pointless to say anything to her from this far away because the machines were too noisy. Lois only wished that cold medicine could take care of her ailment.

When Kelly came home, Lois was lying across the bed. Kelly thought she was sleeping, so she decided not to say anything. She tiptoed into the bathroom where she saw the pregnancy test carton was empty. She was anxious to know the result, so she went back into Lois' room and whispered Lois' name.

"I'm not sleeping." came the muffled voice, "I heard when you came in."

"Well?" Kelly asked.

"According to the test, I'm positive."

"Wow," Kelly said, not excited or surprised, just matter of fact.

"How accurate are those test?" Lois asked.

"I don't know for sure, but they have always been right for me," Kelly answered.

"What do you mean?" Lois looked up at Kelly puzzled.

"When I wasn't pregnant, it was negative and when I was, it was positive."

Lois stared at Kelly trying to register what she was saying.

"Have you ever been pregnant?" Lois asked.

"Yes, twice," responded Kelly.

"What happened?"

"I had an abortion and I lost one."

Lois was surprised at Kelly's confession.

"The next step is to see a Doctor for confirmation," said Kelly, "or will you tell Matt first?"

"I don't know yet? Maybe I should wait until I'm sure."

"What will you do if you are?" Kelly asked.

"What do you mean?"

"I mean," Kelly answered, annoyed that Lois was acting so naive about the whole thing, "are you going to have the baby, or not?"

"By not, do you mean if I'm going to have an abortion?" Lois asked.

"Yes," Kelly responded.

"I don't think I could do that. I've been preached about how wrong it is by both my parents and my pastor. I just couldn't. Matter of fact, just the other day my mom was telling me about all the things that are going on in the ministry. They are now actively protesting abortions and helping women who are pregnant and alone, by leading them to Jesus, counseling them and helping them prepare for the arrival of their babies"

"That's all fine and good," said Kelly sarcastically, "but it's about what you want to do, not your parents, or your pastor?"

"Me and Matt will work it out. I think Matt feels the same way I do on this."

"I hope so," Kelly said.

Even though Lois saw Matt several times after she took the pregnancy test, she decided to wait to tell him when she was sure.

She made an appointment the next day after taking the home pregnancy test to see a union doctor, because she didn't have one of her own. She got the results back the same day. The nurse sat up another appointment for her at the doctor's request, so that she could be thoroughly examine and begin her prenatal care.

Matt wanted to go to a movie, but Lois told him they needed to talk. He didn't mind, so they ordered pizza and rented a movie.

"So what's up?" Matt asked.

Lois looked at him realizing that he did not have a clue. She wondered how that could be. She would always tell him when she had her period, because they didn't have sex those times and he wanted to have sex every time he came over, yet she didn't mention her period for over a month and he thought nothing of it.

"I thought we would watch the movie first," Lois said, with a mouth full of pizza.

Matt laughed at her because cheese was hanging down from her lips. He took it off and popped it in his mouth and they both laughed.

"No, because you may decide to talk while the movie is on and you know I don't like talking while watching the movie," Matt said.

"I'm pregnant." Lois said it before she realized the words were out of her mouth.

She stared at Matt with a weak smile on her face, as Matt stared back at her in disbelief. "Are you kidding me?" Matt asked.

"I wouldn't kid about something like this," Lois said defensively.

Matt didn't say another word for a long period of time and finally Lois was annoyed and said, "well, say something."

"I don't know what to say," Matt responded.

"Say, okay, we can handle this. This is not a bad thing," Lois said trying to coach Matt into saying what she wanted to hear, but Matt only continued to stare at her in disbelief.

Finally, he put both his hand on his head and said, "Okay, we'll just have to take care of it then."

Lois felt relieved. She didn't know what Matt was going to say, but hearing him say that they would just have to take care of the baby put her at ease, only that wasn't what Matt meant.

"You think we can talk to your doctor about taking care of it, or should we go somewhere else? I don't know how it works? It's legal, so we shouldn't have a problem finding a good doctor to do it, without having to risk something bad happening to you."

"Matt, I don't know what you're talking about," Lois said softly with a puzzled look, but she had a sinking feeling in her stomach that maybe she did know what Matt was talking about.

"The abortion," Matt said aloud. "I'm talking about how we should go about getting it done."

"The abortion?" Lois voice was a mixture of hurt and confusion.

"Yes," Matt said, "the abortion. What did you think I was talking about?"

Lois began to shake her head, as if she was trying to shake out what she was hearing.

"I'm not having an abortion Matt. We are both Christians. How can you even think about something like that?"

"Lois, I never lied to you about the reason I was going to church. I told you I had a deal with the church. You forgot about that. I can't have a baby. I'd lose my scholarship and I can't afford a baby. We can't afford to have a baby. I'm not getting some two-bit job, while you continue to work in a factory to help support us. That's not my dream

Lois. I'm just not ready for this; are you?"

"We were ready to have sex and you even lie to me about being able to stop in time, when we didn't have protection."

"Don't be ridiculous Lois. You know that was a joke."

"A joke?" Lois couldn't believe what she was hearing. Her voice suddenly didn't sound like it was a part of her. "I trusted you. What do you mean a joke?"

"You trusted me to do what?" asked Matt accusingly, "to make sure you didn't get pregnant? Well maybe you should've taken a little more responsibility for that yourself. It's your body."

"But you said…" Lois began as Matt cut in.

"I said that I would stop before it happen, but you knew I wasn't doing that so don't try to make like this is all my fault, because you're the one who's pregnant."

"We're pregnant Matt. We are." Lois said staring at Matt not knowing what else to say.

Matt got up, picked up his coat and said, "I have to go."

"Go where?" Lois said, "You usually sleep over."

"I'm not feeling like it tonight," Matt said.

"What are we going to do about the baby?" Lois asked him with tears now swelling up in her eyes.

As he put his hand on the doorknob, Matt turned and said, "I've said what we should do. If you're thinking about having the baby, then Lois I guess you're on your own."

Matt opened the door and walked out. Lois was in disbelief. She had rehearsed in her mind for days her and Matt's conversation concerning the baby and this was not how it was supposed to happen. She was sure that Matt would suggest that they get marry, so they could be a family. She got up and went to her room and cried herself to sleep.

"He just needs time to let it register in his mind. Matt's a good guy. I'm sure he'll be back and do the right thing."

Kelly words were a light of hope to the heart sickened Lois. She wanted so much to believe them.

"You think so?" Lois asked.

"Yeah, I do," but Kelly really didn't. She hated giving Lois false hope, but it was better than no hope and Lois could use some hope right now.

"Have you told anyone else about the baby?" Kelly asked.

"No," Lois responded.

"If you decide to keep the baby, people will know soon enough."

"I guess there is no need to announce it then, huh," Lois stated. "Kelly, why didn't you keep your baby?"

"I didn't even think to keep it," Kelly responded, "I want more out of life. I didn't want to be saddled down with a baby."

"What did Steve want?" Lois asked.

"I didn't tell him," Kelly answered.

"Why?" Lois asked, surprised.

"Because if I did, he would want to marry me. It would be like he had some power over me and I didn't want to give Steve any power over me."

"Don't you want to marry Steve someday?"

"Are you serious? Do I look sadistic? Why in the world would I want to marry a man who treats me like his property?"

"Then why do you stay with him?"

For the first time since they were living together, Lois saw a vulnerable side to Kelly.

"I'm afraid."

"Then why don't you leave him? Get a warrant out or something?"

"I would if I thought it would keep him away from me, but I think doing something like that would just set him off. You read the paper, Lois, see the news. My best bet is to make it big and get out of here. Get lost in another state where he can't find me."

"Why don't you leave?" Lois asked, "not that I want you to, but I want you to be happy."

"You know what they say," Kelly responded as she began to sing, "If I can make it here, I can make it anywhere, it's up to you New York, New York, dun dun dunna nunt, dun dun dunna nunt." Kelly got up and put both her hand up in the air and sang the verse of the song again, as Lois gave a weak laugh.

Kelly stopped, looked down at Lois and asked, "was that a laugh, a giggle, or I know that was a smile at least, because I saw lips spread and teeth shown," at that Lois did laugh.

"I think we need some lessons on how to pick the right guy," Kelly said as she flopped back down on the couch next to Lois.

Weeks had gone by and Lois could feel her stomach growing. She avoided Deb at work and stopped going to church. She wanted to prolong telling her, as long as possible. She knew that once Deb knew, her mother would know too. She thought about Matt all the time. She called him repeatedly at first, but all she got was, "sorry, he's not here," by either his mother, or his sister. She even thought she heard him say to his sister one night, "Please tell her I'm not here." She stopped calling for awhile.

Kelly changed shift at the factory and began to work nights. She got accepted at a really good modeling school that she was trying to get into for some time. Lois was ecstatic for her. She told Steve she was working another job cleaning an office building. She wasn't sure why she lied to him. He couldn't take her there anyway, because he worked during the day. She believed this school was going to lead to her big break.

"Lois, maybe you should work the night shift. They are always looking for people to work nights, because no one wants to, then you could go back to school during the day like you said you would."

"That's great, but I'm pregnant now, remember. I can't afford to go back to school now. I'll think about it after the baby is born."

"If you keep putting it off Lois, you'll never do it."

Lois knew Kelly was right. She hadn't planned to put it off this long, but here she was pregnant at twenty-two and finding yet another reason not to go back to school.

One night she decided to call Matt again. Mrs. Edwards answered the phone.

"This Lois?" She asked.

"Yes maam," Lois responded.

"Listen dear, I go to church with your aunt and she's a nice Christian and out of respect for her I've tried to bite my tongue, but I just can't anymore. You ain't the first little hussy that has tried to trap my Matt and I'm sure you won't be the last, but you need to stop calling here, or I'm going to file harassment charges against you."

Lois was dumfounded. She wanted to hang up the phone, but she didn't want to disrespect Matt's mother. She was always raised to have respect for older people.

"Listen Lois." Mrs. Edwards went on, not expecting Lois to say anything. "Matt is going to that Art School. He just got accepted and I won't allow you or anyone else to ruin my son's life."

Tears began to pour down Lois' face.

"Now he says, he doesn't know whose baby that is you're carrying, but even if it is his, I'm telling you now; it isn't my son's fault you done gone and get yourself knocked up. I know I can't tell you what to do, but you have family and I'm sure they'll be there for you, so please don't call back here anymore."

The buzzing sound of the dial tone sounded in Lois' ears for about a minute before Lois could bring herself to place the phone back on the hook.

Lois started wearing big shirts over her jeans at work, but she knew that people were beginning to look at her strange and talk, or maybe it was her imagination.

She missed Kelly so much. She began to consider changing shift, just to be with her. Troy, who usually kept his distance now that he had a new girlfriend, began to stop by and talk with her from time to time, but it was quick conversations. He may say something silly to make her laugh, or talk about someone, but he didn't stay around her too long, because his girlfriend knew he and Lois use to be together and she hated Lois.

Lois and Kelly teasingly played with Troy just to make her mad. It worked every time. She was so gullible.

"Troy to Lois. Come in Lois. I know this place is noisy, but didn't you hear me calling you?"

TWO SIDES OF DESTINY

"Sorry," Lois said, "what?"

"What? You usually come back with something smart or sarcastic. You losing your touch?" Lois smiled weakly.

"So what was it about this Matt that made you give it up Lois, when I could barely get to first base?"

Lois looked at Troy and then looked around, as if everyone could hear what Troy had just said.

"What are you talking about?"

"Kelly told Steve you're pregnant?"

Lois held her head down. She did not want to look in Troy's eyes, for fear that tears would begin to flow as they often do, at the thought of Matt.

"I'm sorry Lois. I didn't mean to hurt your feelings."

Troy lightly hit Lois on her upper arm with his fist and said, "You know you're my home girl, Lois."

That made Lois feel a little better. Troy's first remark was so accusational that she felt so ashamed.

"Look, I wish you the best girl," Troy said. "So what now? You and this Matt gonna get married, or something," now tears really welled up in Lois's eyes as she just shook her head and held down her head and wiped her eyes with her sleeves.

She hoped that if anyone were watching, they would think she was just wiping dust off her eyelids.

"Let's just change the subject all together," Troy said.

They just began to talk about silly stuff after that and Troy was able to make Lois laugh a little.

"Lois any time you need a friend, just let me know, okay."

"Sure. Do I have to get permission from, you know who, first."

"You had to go there, huh."

"Yeah I did," said Lois, as Troy walked away smiling back at her.

Early one Saturday morning, while Lois and Kelly were still in bed, Kelly from a hangover and Lois just hiding out from the world, the doorbell rang. It rang and rang and rang. Lois, as well as Kelly tried to pull the pillows over their ears hoping that it was Jehovah witnesses and they would just go away. Then each thought maybe the other one was expecting someone and they would get up and get it. Finally Lois got up, because she knew she never would win this, even if the door was for Kelly, she would not get up to answer it and more than likely it was for her.

"I'm coming, for goodness sake." Lois said, as she grabbed her robe and slide into her slippers.

She looked at her clock again to make sure of the time. It was 9 am. She peeked through the peephole and was shocked to see her aunt standing at the door. She looked down at herself. It was clear to tell that she was either pregnant on gained some weight from what she had on. She quickly went back into her room to throw on her sweat pants and a big pullover shirt.

Deb was about to ring the bell again as Lois opened the door, "Aunt Deb, what are you doing here this early in the morning and where are the kids?"

Deb walked into the apartment without being invited in and said, "The kids are with Mrs. Washington as usual on Saturdays, when I do my errands. You know that, but the question to why I'm all the way down here in Queens at...," she looked at her watch, "9 am on a Saturday morning is yet to be answered."

"Why are you here?" Lois asked.

"Well, since I see that you're about to play some little game with me, I'll just ask out right. Are you pregnant?"

It was a point blank question and there was no way of getting around the answer and Lois was tired of the charade anyhow.

"Yes, I am. Who told you?"

"Well never mind about that, the question is, why didn't you tell me?"

"I was going to." Lois knew that was a lie; she had planned on just letting it become the obvious.

"When?" Deb asked, "when the baby is born?"

"No." Lois said holding down her head just wanting to be honest.

"Honestly Deb, I was hoping that you'd find out when I began to show."

"I see," said Deb.

"How did you find out?"

"Mrs. Edwards pulled me aside last night after service. We were having a week of revival," Deb offered the explanation of why she was at church on a Friday night.

"What did she say?" Lois asked, not really wanting to hear, again, any of the horrible things Mrs. Edwards spoke to her over the phone that night.

"What she said isn't worst repeating. She probably has already said most, if not all of it, to you anyway. According to her, she set you straight." Deb saw that Lois was about to cry.

She grabbed Lois and hugged her, as Lois began to cry out loud uncontrollably, saying over and over again, "I thought he loved me."

Kelly heard her and ran out of her room yelling, "Lois what is it?"

When she saw Deb, she stopped in her tracks suddenly aware that she only had on her bra and panties.

"Oh, I didn't know you were here Deb. Everything alright?"

"Yes, everything's alright," Deb said to Kelly while holding Lois tightly in her arms, "You can go back to bed." Kelly turned and did as she was told.

"It's out of the bag now," Lois said to Kelly the next morning as they were having breakfast at the kitchen table.

"Is that a southern expression?" Kelly asked.

Lois laughed. "I guess it is. It means the secrets out."

"Oh, I see," said Kelly.

"I have to call my mother today, or Aunt Deb will do it for me. I have a mind to let her do it." They both laughed. "I'll call her this afternoon, when I know she's home from church."

"How do you think it'll go?" Kelly asked.

"I don't know. I haven't talked to her for awhile. Aunt Deb was very sympathetic and supportive."

"That's not surprising," said Kelly.

"Why you say that?" Lois asked.

"Well, she has three kids of her own. I just assume that she would understand these things."

"I guess you're right," Lois said, "she probably does."

"Your mom should too, right?" Kelly wasn't sure, but she thought Lois had mentioned once that she didn't really know her real father.

"Yeah, I guess she would." Lois said.

Kelly got up from the table, "I hope it all goes well."

"Oh, by the way," Lois said, "my aunt says that Matt had a choice of going to the school of the arts in New York or LA and he has chosen to go to LA."

"I see," Kelly replied, then as a second thought, she asked, "are you okay?"

"Yeah, I will be," Lois said, "at least now I know where I stand. I can now plan for me and the baby's future."

Kelly left the room and tears began to well up in Lois eyes, but she stretched herself, got up, literally shook herself and said, "enough of that Lois, no more tears," she rubbed her stomach and said, "I'd better save some of those tears for when you come. I can't imagine that it's going to be easy to raise a child by myself."

Beedeekle:

The small imp whispered into Lois' ear, "not in your wildest dream can you imagine, missy, but I will certainly make it as hard as possible to meet your expectations."

Lois:

Lois shook herself again as an eerie feeling suddenly came over her. She looked around the kitchen, as a moment past and she smelled something that she thought was spoiled. She looked in the refrigerator and sniffed a couple of times, but couldn't place the smell.

Beedeekle:

"I won't be found there." he said with a gleeful, playful attitude. As he rubbed his hands together, and said to another little imp, "let's give this little girl a life to remember." The other little imps began to jump up and down suddenly excited that they were in on this.

Lois:

Lois could not stop her mother from coming to New York for the birth of the baby. It was clear that she was shocked and then a little disappointed, but never once did she judge her. To Lois' surprise, she was very supportive and so was Richard.

Lois gave birth to a seven pounds, six ounce boy and she named him Daniel, spelled Danijel from the Hebrew dictionary. The name meant, judge of God. She did a thorough research of the name, because she wanted her son to one day be somebody.

She remembered pastor Fischer always talking about how parents should take more care in naming their children, because names meant so much.

Daniel also meant, "to rule, to strive at law, contend, execute judgment, minister judgment, and plead the cause. She thought that maybe one day Danijel would be a lawyer like her old friend, Jewel.

Her mind suddenly went to Jewel. She wondered if she finished college and was going to law school. She would have to ask her mother about Jewel. If she did, the church would sure be praising Jewel and scorning her. Stephanie was holding the baby and looking at him smiling. Lois was glad that she was there.

Chapter Sixteen
Jewel

"So it's you and Brad now?" Justine inquired. "I guess we all saw that one coming, personally, I didn't think you had the guts to go interracial, even if Brad's sort of cute, for a white boy. So when do you take him home for dinner?"

Jewel was not particularly interested in having this conversation with Justine. She did not want to explain her relationship with Brad.

"Dinner? Get it?" Jewel didn't get it and Justine laughed out, "you know the old movie, look who's coming to dinner."

"Come on Justine, give it a rest. I don't think interracial relationships are that big of a deal anymore," Jewel commented.

"Maybe not in Atlanta," Justine added, "but what about Brickenbrat, Tennessee?"

"My parents are very open about these things Justine."

"Okay, so you say."

"Besides, there's no reason for me to take Brad home for dinner, or any other meal. We're just friends."

"Whatever," Justine said to Jewel flicking her hand and turning her head, "If you want to believe that, that's your prerogative, just tell it to Brad before he falls any deeper."

The girls changed the subject as Eric and Brad came over to their table.

Eric and Justine were history, but they remained friends. Eric began showing an interest in Paula, who was acting like a love stricken teenager. She became all giddy when Eric was around. Eric, on the other hand just wanted an experience, as he put it, "I have no intentions of getting involve with a white girl. I've worked to hard to get where I am today and you never know with these rich white chicks. If their parents don't approve and want you to become history, that could mean your entire career as well. I'm just not willing to take that chance."

Jewel's only goal was to become a successful lawyer, but she was introduced to a whole new world of, casual dating, interracial relationships, and it was rumored that Billy might be gay. Jewel would find herself staring at Billy for signs, but she had never been around a gay person and Billy didn't act like the gays you saw on television. He was quiet, but not feminine. He kept to himself, but with this group, Jewel thought, "he was the smart one for doing so."

Law school had proved to be harder than Jewel thought it would be. When she failed a test, she was devastated, but more determined to do a hundred percent the next time. She wanted to be ranked top of her class and was determined to let nothing stop her.

"No Brad I can't go tonight. You know what I made on the last test."... "That maybe true, but I'm not measuring myself against no one else, just me."... "No you can't come over. I am going to be in my room the rest of the night, for several nights, matter of fact."... "No, I don't need your company. You are too much of a distraction."... "Okay, I'll talk to you later." Jewel hung up the phone and picked up her book.

When Jewel grades picked up, she started spending more time with Brad. They got together with the group sometimes, but mostly it was just the two of them.

"You know what I would like?"

"What would you like Brad?"

"I would like to go home with you for Christmas."

"What?" Jewel got up off the bed where she and Brad were doing some studying and some fooling around. "Brad I don't think we're at that stage in our relationship and we may never get there."

"Jewel, I guess you don't know, but I love you."

"Love you." The words echoed in Jewel head. Did he just say that he loved me? Oh boy, thought Jewel. He was obviously serious, or he wouldn't have said it.

"Brad we haven't gone past kissing." Jewel said.

"Having sex doesn't mean that you love someone Jewel. I respect your decision to wait until you're married. That doesn't stop the way I feel about you. I was raised in a Christian home too. I understand.

Jewel decided to call his bluff, "okay, let's go to your parents for Christmas."

"Jewel, my parents knows that I'm dating a black girl, if that's your point. If you want to do that, we can."

Jewel was taken back. He never said that he told his parents about them before.

"What did they say?"

"Not much. I told them during the summer-break, when you took off to meet your old boyfriend to rekindle a fire, or something."

"I went to visit a close friend, because he asked me to come see him."

"Yeah, right," Brad said. "Anyway, my parents took the opportunity to try to match me up with every blonde female in a thousand mile radius of us. I thank them before I left and told them that it didn't help getting you out of my system, it just made me miss you more. You are so different and refreshing, not to mention stunningly beautiful," Brad said as he reached out to grab Jewel and threw her down on the bed for a big kiss.

"Okay, but I'm not going to tell my parents that you're white. They'll just have to see when we get there. I'll just tell them that I'm bringing home a friend that I want them to meet, someone who's more than a friend."

"Okay, then it's your home for Christmas. I'm already psyche," said Brad.

The trip down was good. Brad was a good driver. Jewel wasn't ready to admit anything to Brad yet, but she really loved being with him. He said he loved her, but she was not ready to make such a bold commitment.

In spite of sending their children to one of the best private school in the area, which was predominantly white, Paul and Theresa were not ready for this.

"You could have warned us, you know," Paul stated.

Jewel decided to play dumb. "Warn you about what?"

Jewel looked up at her parents. They were sitting at the breakfast table. Everyone was still sleeping. Jewel would have been too, but she knew her parents were early risers and would be in the kitchen for their early morning discussions, mainly about them, or bills, or what was going on in the community. This morning Jewel knew the topic of discussion was going to be her and she decided she wanted to be there for it.

"I think you know what your father means Jewel."

"Okay, I'm sorry, and yes I could have told you that Brad was white, but you've always raised us to respect and love people for who they are and not the color of their skin. Pointing out Brad's race to you before you met him, would have seemed just like I was warning you and why would I have to warn you about someone that I was bringing home. I've never done so before."

Paul and Theresa had no words for her reasoning. Paul scratched his head and rubbed at his beard and Theresa just looked at him, waiting for him to say something. When he didn't respond and there was too long of a gap in between the conversation, Theresa asked, "Is he a friend from school, like Justine?"

Jewel looked at her mother smilingly, "yes mother. He is a friend from school, but he's not a friend like Justine. I think we're more than friends."

"You think?" Paul asked.

"Well, right before I decided to invite him over for the holidays, he said that he loved me."

"How do you feel about him?" Theresa asked.

"I'm not sure. I do care for him a great deal, but I haven't gone as far as saying, I love you."

"But he has," Paul acknowledge.

"Okay, let me ease your minds. I'm a big girl. I can take care of myself, I think, but even if I screw up, I have to learn from my own mistakes. I'm still a virgin. I've talk to Brad about my commitment to remain a virgin until I'm married and he completely understands. I do want to say that at one time I was keeping that promise strictly for religious reasons, but now I am committed to it, because I don't want anything or anyone to interfere with my dreams and goals. I'm finding out just how hard law school is. It's hard for women to be the top in their field in a male dominated career, especially a black woman, but I believe if I work hard I can be one of the best. My focus right now isn't a relationship with anyone. I really like Brad and I may even love him, but that's sort of on the back burner for now. If Brad is still around when I arrive at where I'm going, then maybe we'll see what lies ahead for the both of us together. In the meantime," Jewel got up indicating the conversation was over, "I like Brad and I enjoy his company. School is hard enough, but it makes it a little easier with friends like Justine and Brad. I'm grateful for the both of them being in my life. As for the holidays, I say to the both of you, exhale and get to know Brad and let's have a great holiday."

She came around to the side of the table where her mom and dad were sitting and gave them both a big hug and kiss on the cheek, "now I'm going back to sleep. I'll see you guys later."

"Okay sweetheart," Theresa said. "What do you think?"

"I think we have a great daughter. She's smart, beautiful and she has good mind. She knows what she wants out of life and she intends to get it. All we have to do is support her. We've never had any reason to not trust, or believe that she would be anything but honest with us. I think this is going to be a good holiday. A little different, but I intend to get to know Brad and see what happens from there." Paul got up from the table and left Theresa to her own thoughts.

Theresa held her head down and clapped her two hands together in prayer. It was just a whisper of prayer, like she so often do for her family at this very place in the house, "Oh God, I wish my husband could see the bigger picture. Jewel's statement about not remaining a virgin, because of religious reasons is a clear indication that she's going further away from you. God, show me what to say to her, without accusing or nagging her about her walk with you. I don't want my daughter to gain the whole world, but lose her only soul."

Theresa got up and looked out the window.

Beedeekle:

"Oh she won't lose her soul," the little slime lurking near said, "I intend to take it." At his comment, the other little imps drooled with delight.

Jewel:

Theresa was still staring out the window, when Brad entered the Kitchen.

"Excuse me, Mrs. Stone." Theresa turned around abruptly. "I'm sorry. I didn't mean to startle you," Brad said apologetic.

"Oh, you didn't, I was just thinking. Please come in and sit down. You're up early."

Brad looked at the clock. It was 8am, but judging from the quietness of the house, it seemed that everyone was still sleeping.

"Would you like some coffee?" Theresa asked.

"Please don't go to any trouble," Brad said.

"No trouble at all. It's already made."

"Then in that case," Brad responded, "let me get it. Would you like a cup?"

"Yes, thank you."

"What do you take?"

"Cream and sugar," Theresa said.

Brad fumbled around the kitchen without asking where anything was. He saw some cups in the dish drainer and pulled open two drawers before he found the spoons. He got the cream out of the refrigerator and saw a small dish on the kitchen table that he assumed contained sugar. It did. He sat the cup of coffee and creamer in front of Theresa and sat down in the chair across the table from her. Theresa smiled, as she recalled that it was the same chair Jewel sat in earlier.

"You have a nice home," Brad said.

"Thank you," Theresa replied pleasingly.

"Jewel told me that you have other families that are coming for the holidays."

"Yes, Paul's sisters and their families. Are you going to be okay with that?" Theresa asked?

"Yes maam," Brad said. "My parents usually have big gatherings for the holidays as well."

"How many brothers and sisters do you have?"

"I only have one sister, but my mother and father have seven brothers and sisters between them and five of them are married with children. We usually get together for Thanksgiving and Christmas. They all live in Atlanta, except one. She's single and don't have any children, so her presence doesn't make the number much less, or more."

Theresa kept sipping on her coffee.

"What do your parents do for a living Brad?"

Theresa wanted to take the question back. It was so typical.

"My father's a Lawyer and my mother keeps busy with her charity work."

"Pretty demanding work." Theresa said.

"Not as demanding as being a teacher," Brad responded, "especially a good one."

Theresa couldn't disagree with him. Being a good teacher, which she liked to think of herself, was pretty demanding. She had to go the extra mile with each student.

"Did your father inspire you to study law?"

"Yes maam. He's also my example of a good lawyer, as oppose to the money grubbing lawyers that people make jokes about."

"Well, people don't seem to make jokes, when they need one." Theresa said, and Brad smile.

"My father has a strong Christian background. I think that motivates the way he practices law. I hope to follow in his example."

Theresa looked up from her cup and wondered if this was the answer to her prayer.

"What's your religious background, if you don't mind me asking?"

"Oh I don't mind at all," Brad said.

"My parents were raised in a southern Baptist church, but later joined a non-denominational church. Like I said, my mother likes doing charity work and she does most of it through the church. Although, I've let school hinder me from going to church, I don't think I'll ever get away from the teachings."

Theresa felt a light at the end of the tunnel. "That's good to hear."

As Jewel and Brad sat on the couch in her family den, with her family all around, she felt a little uncomfortable at all the attention Brad was giving her. He was holding her hand and being attentive to her every word, which he always did, but it just made her a little uneasy with her family looking on. It was fine when it was just the two of them and their circle of friends, but home was different. She managed to free her hand from out of Brad's hand after he became engrossed in a movie that everyone was watching.

"Where are you going?" Brad asked as she got up.

"On the porch."

"I'll go with you," Brad offered as he began to get up.

"No, stay and finish the movie, please. I just want to get some of this fresh mountain air."

Brad really wanted to see the end of the movie, so he said, "Okay, I'll join you when this goes off. It should end soon."

"Okay," she said, hoping the movie would last a little longer than that.

Jewel sat sideways on the rocking swing with her legs folded up in the chair and began to rock back and forth in the swing. She stared up in the skies thinking about everything and nothing in particular. Judy, Paul's sister came out and sat down in the small space that she left available. Jewel began to straighten up to make more room for her.

"No, don't," said Judy. "I'm fine. Matter of fact, if I'm intruding just say so and I'll find somewhere else to go."

"No, please don't go," Jewel said, sort of glad that Judy came out.

She always liked to spend quiet times with Judy. Judy always intrigued her, because she was the sister her father always talked about. He was always concerned about what Judy was doing with her life. They both just sat in silence watching the stars.

"Brad seems to be a nice guy," Judy started the conversation.

Jewel smiled, glad that Judy's comment about Brad was good.

"I think he is. We haven't been seeing each other that long."

"Must be pretty serious for you to bring him home," Judy stated.

"I don't know Aunt Judy, besides I brought Ken home and look what happened with that."

"Yeah, but you said Ken was just a friend," Judy said smiling at Jewel, "from what I understand you made it clear to your parents that Brad was more than a friend."

"Yes I did," Jewel said. "I'm suddenly having mixed feelings about bringing him here. It's fine when it's just me, him and our friends."

She was verbalizing her thoughts to Judy.

"Why? Paul and Theresa seemed to be taken with him," Judy said.

"Seems so," Jewel said shrugging her shoulders.

"You don't sound too sure."

"Well they have their concerns I'm sure, but we had a really good talk about it and I think I put there mind at ease, at least Dad's. You know Mom. She reads more into everything."

They were quiet for a few more minutes and Judy said, "follow your heart, Jewel. You are one of the most sensible young adult I know. I wouldn't let Melissa hear this, but I often wish Melissa was more like you."

Melissa, Judy's daughter, was truly the opposite of Jewel. They got through her rebellious teenager years, now as a young adult, she made sure that she did the exact opposite of everything her mother wanted, to the point that Judy was almost tempted to tell her to do the wrong things, hoping she would do the right thing, but she knew that was foolish. She couldn't count on reverse psychology with her daughter, for fear it would backfire on her.

"It was Todd."

"Who?" Jewel asked.

Judy looked at her and said, "the love of my life. His name was Todd. He wasn't white, but he was older than me and we really loved each other, but of course everyone was against the relationship. When Todd went off to college, he said that in his second year of college he would get an apartment and we would get married and I could finish high school, where he went to college. That sounded great at fourteen. He did, but my parents declared, over their dead bodies would I move in with him. I didn't need their permission. It wasn't like Todd was asking me to shack up with him. He was asking me to marry him. Of course I didn't go and I became a rebellious teenager and sometimes I think I'm still rebellious of what my parents and family think is best for me, maybe that's why I'm divorced, maybe that's why my daughter is the way she is. I don't know, but one thing I do know, I wished I'd follow my heart and went with Todd. Would it have worked out? I don't know, but now I'll never know."

"Whatever happened to Todd?" Jewel asked.

"He's a successful businessman, father and husband right here in Tennessee."

"What's his last name?" Jewel asked.

"Some things are better not known. That's why I made up a first name."

"Is that why you moved away?" Jewel asked.

"Yes and no I guess. I don't hate my life. I just wished I'd made better choices based on what I wanted and not what others wanted for me."

Judy looked at Jewel with a smile wondering if her story got across, "you understand what I mean, Jewel."

"Yes Auntie, I do. Thanks," said Jewel taking her aunts hands and squeezing it lightly.

Brad came out and Judy, got up.

"Well, I'd better get these older bones back inside before they go stiff on me."

"Don't leave on my account," said Brad.

"Thank you, but I'll leave you two alone."

Judy got up and went inside. Brad sat down by Jewel and she sat up straight in the rocker and slid over by him and threw half of her blanket around him. They sat there for half an hour not saying a word, just staring up in the skies.

As Jewel and Brad sat together on the porch, Jewel announced, "tomorrow you'll meet more of my family."

Brad sat up straight in his seat and said, "I'm not afraid."

"Silly, I didn't say it so you would be afraid. It was just a statement of fact."

"A statement of fact, huh," Brad responded.

"Yeah," said Jewel with a twinkle in her eyes that said, 'believe it if you want.' "Besides, you've met Grandma Lynnie and came out smelling good."

"I did, didn't I," Brad laughed. "She is certainly a character."

"That she is. That she is," said Jewel. "Grandma Lynnie and I have come a long way. I think her acceptance of you 'tends from the fact that she has probably reasoned in her mind that if I can't past for white, then it sure wouldn't hurt to marry someone white."

"Excuse me?" Brad inquired.

"Never mind," Jewel said, "I'll have to tell you the story about me and my Grandma Lynnie one day. Besides the grandparents you should be worrying about, you'll meet tomorrow," Jewel said flashing a winning smile.

Paul's parents were there early that morning. Grandma Lenny arrived around noon.

"Hi Gran. Hi Papa," Jewel said as she came around to both of them to give them a big hug and a kiss. "

"So here is our precious Stone."

It was a play on Jewel's name that she particularly liked. Even though Jewel was their favorite granddaughter; they didn't let the others feel any less special and they made a point to explain to the other children that it was a joke that they played with Jewel's name, even though she was very precious to them.

"How are you?" Gran asked.

"I'm just fine gran."

"We heard that you brought a nice young man home to meet us," said Papa.

Jewel laughed. She thought she was just bringing Brad home to spend Christmas with her family, but they were making it a big event.

"You'll meet him soon enough."

"Good, we can hardly wait," Papa said winking at Gran.

"I see you two," Jewel said, "be nice to my friend."

"Now would we be anything but nice," Papa said.

"No third degrees," Jewel said in a scolding voice to her grandparents. They just smiled at Jewel and threw up there hands in a truce.

Breakfast and dinner was sort of spread out into two rooms, the dining room and the kitchen. The table was joined together where the end met in the doorway of the kitchen, so they would have easy access to the food, if something ran out on the table. Brad sat between Papa and Jewel and Gran sat next to Papa. They planned it that way, so they could be next to Brad to have a conversation with him.

Throughout the day gifts were exchanged. Jewel got many good gifts. Things she could really use, including some computer programs that she wanted to help her with her studies at school.

Brad gave her a beautiful gold bracelet and she gave him a blue, plush Ralph Lauren sweater, because it was the color of his eyes.

They both loved their gifts. Everyone made Brad feel at home. He even survived the inquisition of Gran and Papa. Grandma Lynnie kept calling Brad, Junior, her deceased son.

"Does Brad remind you of Uncle Junior, Mom?" Jewel asked her mom, curiously.

Theresa looked through the kitchen window to where she could see Brad and said, "some."

"Like what?" Jewel wanted to know.

"Well, he's white and Junior tried to be white."

They both looked at each other with a weak smile, knowing how true that statement was almost brought tears to Theresa's eye. Jewel was suddenly sorry she asked.

"I'm sorry Mom, what a thoughtless question."

"Don't be silly. It's not thoughtless. I would ask the same question myself if I brought my boyfriend home and my grandmother kept calling him by her dead son's name."

"Is it still hard for you Mom, the way they died?"

"That's going to always be hard for me sweetie. They were so young, and with so much to give. Holidays are the hardest, especially celebrating the birth of Jesus and all that it means. I often wonder where they are and will I ever see them again in another life."

"Were they Christians?" Jewel asked.

"I can't judge that sweetie. I certainly hope they made it right with the Lord, before they left this earth. We all have to die, then we will be judged. It then comes down to them and God. I think about it a lot. I know I nag you a lot about going to church and all that, but I just want to know that when I'm gone home to be with the Lord that I will see my children up there one day praising God like me."

Theresa shook herself and cupped her hand under Jewel's chin. "On a much lighter note," she said, "Junior had blue black hair like Brad and it was naturally straight."

Jewel and Brad decided to head back to school right after Christmas, because Jewel had some studying that she wanted to get done. They decided to spend New Year's Eve with their friends, since they all had to be back to school the day after the New Year's holiday.

"Thanks for having me, and thanks for your hospitality. I really felt at home with your family," Brad was expressing his appreciation to Paul and Theresa, while Jewel was making sure that she didn't leave anything.

"It was our pleasure to have you here," Theresa said, and Paul shook his head in agreement.

"Well, I think I got everything. If I leave something, I'll get it when I come back unless it is really important, in that case, you can mail it to me."

"Yes your majesty," David said coming up behind her. She turned around and playfully pushed him.

They all hug each other and Jewel and Brad headed out to the car. Jewel was glad that they drove Brad's car. He was driving an older Mercedes past down from his father, and it had more space for their things than Jewel's convertible. Jewel anticipated bringing back lots of gifts and she did. All of it couldn't get in the trunk. They had to put some things in the back seat of the car. One of the things Jewel wanted was a small TV. She didn't need a TV before, but there was this law channel provided by the school and they were tested on many of the cases that were televised. The boarding house had a TV in the common area, but sometimes the debate concerning the law issues got so intense that they would miss some of the most important issues in the case. She wanted a 13 inch color TV, but of course her parents bought a 19 inch. As Jewel and Brad was trying to fit the TV into the car, they realized why Jewel said a 13 inch. They ended up taking it out of the box to make it fit in the back. She looked at them and they both lifted their shoulders and held out their hands, palms up.

"Where is Tessa?" Jewel looked around.

"Still sleeping, I suppose," Paul said.

"Well, tell her I'll talk to her later."

"Okay," Theresa said as she gave Jewel a last hug.

"You kids drive safely," Paul said.

"Yes Dad," Jewel said as Brad drove off slowly, he could see that they were still waving.

Beedeekle:

"Are we going to cause a car wreck Beedeekle?" the little imps asked jumping up and down impatiently. "We like car wrecks, especially all the blood."

"Yeah we like the blood!" The other imp said excited at the very thought of causing a car wreck.

"Be quiet!" Beedeekle yelled as loud as he could in his squeaky little voice, I'm trying to think! There will be no car wreck," he said, although he had to admit the thought excited him.

Car wrecks were one of his specialties, although he could seldom cause a wreck severe enough to produce enough blood to get excited about, without the help of bigger demons.

"Why, Beedeekle, why?"

"Because!" he said, bringing the tone of his voice down, "we don't have permission, but that's a thought. Maybe later, but when and if we do, we will do it right."

"So what are we going to do?" The little imps looked at each other puzzled.

"I thought you said that you were going to use him. Isn't that why you brought them together?"

"It wasn't my idea to bring them together. That was influenced by another force."

The two imps looked around as if they could see the other forces, because they knew that Beedeekle was talking about heavenly forces.

"So what are we going to do?" The little imp asked Beedeekle, suddenly concerned that they may not be doing enough to meet up to Satan's demands and risk destruction as a result.

"Take that sorry look off your faces!" Beedeekle said, "I have a plan and I'm working it as we speak."

The imps looked at each other and both shook their shoulders, indicating they didn't know about this plan.

"What is this plan Beedeekle?"

"Yeah, Beedeekle what is the plan? We have a right to know."

Beedeekle suddenly grew tired of the little imps and said, "You have a right to obey. You have been assigned to assist me. When the time is right, I'll fill you in on all that you need to know. Right now, you don't have a need to know," he rubbed his hands together and his beady little eyes became smaller as he said, "oh, but it is good. I assure you."

Jewel:

"Is that smell coming from your car?" Jewel asked Brad.

Brad sniffed his nose and said, "no, I don't think so."

He looked in his rear view mirror to see if there was any smoke coming from his exhaust and then he looked up front to see if anything was coming from the hood.

"Maybe it's that fresh Tennessee mountain air," Brad smilingly said.

"Funny," Jewel responded.

"So do you want to go to Ritzi, or my parents for New Year's Eve?" Brad asked Jewel.

"Neither," said Jewel, "I wasn't kidding when I told my parents I had to study."

"Jewel, it's one night. If we go to Ritzi, we can get there by ten and leave a little after midnight, when we've wished everyone a happy New Year."

Jewel knew she was not ready to go to Brad's parents, so that was out. Ritzi was a small club fifteen minutes away from the boarding house. On special occasion the club was transformed from a club to a ballroom. New Year's Eve was one of those occasions. Everyone raved about the Place. They told the others they would try to get back soon enough to join them there.

"We'll see Brad. It depends on how much studying I get done."

Brad was annoyed at Jewel's response, but he didn't want to get into an argument with her about it especially since they had such a great time together at her parents. He was often annoyed at how driven Jewel was and wondered if anything else matter to her, even him.

Beedeekle:

Suggesting thoughts into Brad's mind, Beedeekle rubbed his hands together and said, "Let the fun begin."

The other imps began to get excited, but they didn't have a clue as to why.

Chapter Seventeen
Lois

"Please shut that baby up!"

Lois was in her room rocking Danijel back and forth trying to get him back to sleep. She got up and walked him around the room, then sat back down and rocked him some more, but nothing was working and Steve yelling at her to shut him up didn't help.

Lois thought, "he doesn't even have to be here. Why don't he just leave."

"Can I help?" Kelly's voice was sympathetic.

Lois did not hear Kelly come into the room, but if she could help that would be great.

"I don't know what's wrong with him. All he wants to do is cry. I'm sorry about the noise, but if I could help it, I would. I want peace and quiet just like everyone else," Lois said, suddenly feeling defensive.

"Don't pay Steve any attention. He's leaving anyway. Here let me hold him." Kelly took the baby from Lois and began to walk back and forth with him.

He seemed to scream even louder to Lois. Lois knew it wasn't right that Kelly had to suffer sleepless nights too, because of the baby.

In the days following her mother's departure, Lois often wished she'd took her mother's advice and went back home for awhile, but the thought of going back home as a single mother seemed such a failure to her and she didn't come to New York to be a failure. She was determined to make it on her own.

Lois finally just let herself fall backwards on the bed and closed her eyes, but she couldn't close out the baby's screams.

Lois woke up in the middle of the night. The room was dark, so she just lied there looking around until she could access the situation. The baby's cries had ceased. She looked over to the crib and saw him lying fast asleep. She got up and quietly left the room. She peeked into Kelly's room and Kelly was also asleep.

"This was good," Lois thought, yet knowing it was only temporary. He could start to cry again for no reasons. He didn't eat, so he would probably awake for that. She looked into the baby's garbage disposal and saw that Kelly changed him before putting him down. Lois knew she wouldn't have long more to sleep, so without taking a shower, she took off her robe and slipped under the covers to try to get some more sleep.

The baby awoke during the night to be fed and amazingly went right back to sleep, but when the alarm went off, Lois was startled and like every morning lately; she just lied in her bed watching the red numbers on her alarm clock tick away minute by minute. She remembered when she used to awake before the alarm went off, now she had to get up an hour earlier. She had to dress Danijel, prepare his bag with diapers, formulas, change of clothing, then she had to bathe and feed him. She was glad the babysitter lived across the street from her apartment building. It saved a lot of time.

Ms. Bakker was recommended by one of the girls at the factory. Her name was Mona. Lois met Mona when they placed her to work at the table, in her latter months of pregnancy. The machine Mona worked on was always breaking down. Mona had a three-year-old daughter, Kiesha. She said that Mrs. Bakker had to be good, because if she wasn't, her very talkative daughter would have certainly told her by now. The only thing she didn't like about Ms. Bakker was that she had lots of cat. Mona said that Kiesha loved the cats, but she strictly told Ms. Bakker that Kiesha could play with only one of the kittens, but not to go near the cats. The children were in a room separated from the cats, but Jewel wondered about that, because she often found cat's hair on Danijel's clothing.

"Kelly thanks for last night," Lois said as she passed her, while leaving the bathroom to go to her room.

Kelly responded with a grunted sound. Lois hoped that meant she was welcome.

As Lois was getting ready to leave, Kelly stopped her and said, "Lois we have to talk. I should be home early tonight. I'm skipping work tonight. If you can get Danijel to sleep early that would be great."

"I'll try," Lois said, wondering if Kelly thought she had any control over Danijel's sleep habit.

Lois wished she had listened to her mother; after all she did raise seven children. She must know something about babies. She left Lois with a schedule for Danijel, but after two nights, Lois abandoned it. Her mother said it would take time, but if she stuck with it, she would have Danijel on the schedule she wanted him to be on. Lois wondered if it was too late to try.

Lois was already home when Kelly got there. Danijel was fed, bathe and lying quietly in his crib. Kelly welcomed the quietness in the apartment, something she seldom experienced lately, when she got home.

"Lois, we better talk now."

"Don't you want to take a shower and change first?"

"No, I can do that when Danijel wake up screaming."

"I'm sorry about that Kelly."

"Lois, I know you're sorry, but my modeling teacher says that the bags under my eyes are not helping me. He's been hinting that there will be some modeling scouts coming around soon looking for some new girls. He thinks I could be one of them."

"That's great Kelly!" Lois was truly glad for Kelly.

"It is great, Lois. That's why I can't risk anymore-sleepless night. I'm moving out." Lois felt like the bottom had just dropped from under her.

"Moving out?" she asked in disbelief.

"Yes, this weekend. Rinoldo, my agent, says that he knows where I can crash for a couple of weeks until I can find something on my own.

Hopefully by then, I will have landed a modeling contract. It's really beginning to happen for me Lois. It really is."

Lois didn't know what to say. She could hear the excitement in Kelly's voice, even though she tried to sound matter of fact. This was what Kelly always wanted and she wanted to be happy for her. She knew Kelly was down playing it because of her.

"Kelly, I'm so happy for you," Lois heard herself saying, but not feeling it, "I didn't even know you had an agent."

"I know Lois. We haven't had time to talk like we used to. All your time is spent taking care of Danijel and it's hard getting a word in while he's crying."

Lois was beginning to feel hurt. She knew Danijel had his bad nights, but didn't all babies.

"He really is a good baby, Kelly."

"I'm sorry, I didn't mean to make it sound like he wasn't. I'm sure he's only doing what babies do. I didn't mean to criticize. I was only making a point."

Lois didn't know Kelly was dealing with her own demons. After Danijel was born, It was hard watching Lois with him. She began to wish that she didn't, so hastily aborted her own.

"You're my best friend, Kelly. What am I suppose to do without you? I certainly couldn't pay the rent on this apartment alone."

"Oh yeah, about the apartment, we have to give it up when the lease runs out."

"What!" Lois stared at Kelly not sure what to say next.

"Yeah, Teri called and said that it was going to work out with her boyfriend. He asked her to marry him and she said yes. She's giving up the lease when it's up for renewal."

"Kelly, that's three months from now. I can't afford to rent this place. The rent will go up with a new tenant. What will I do?"

"You have time to think about it and I'll help however I can. You know that."

Lois didn't know that. She knew she was on her own.

"Thanks," she said to Kelly, "where will you be staying?"

"Uptown Manhattan."

"Wow," Lois said in a low voice with a weak smile, "you're really moving on up. Do they allow women with children there?"

Lois was only kidding, but Kelly thought she was serious, "No, I'm afraid not, besides it's only for models."

"I was just kidding." The two girls just stared at each other and then Lois looked away and stared around the living room into the kitchen. Her mind was racing like it never did before. She thought for sure she would have to move back home.

"Maybe your new friend could help you out," Kelly suggested. "What's her name?"

"Mona," Lois answered.

"Yeah, Mona."

After an awkward silence, Kelly got up and put her hand on Lois' shoulders and said, "It's going to work out," as she walked away.

Lois wanted to be happy for Kelly, but the feeling of being abandoned overwhelmed her. She sat back on the couch with her legs crossed hugging a throw pillow.

"God, what do I do now?" Lois was not aware of any presence of God, but saying it gave her a sense that may be He was in control of her life and if he was, then he could help her.

She buried her head down in the pillow and many thoughts began to go through her minds. "Where would she live?" Why was everyone she loved leaving her? How would she afford a babysitter and an apartment own her own? Could she even find a place in three months?

Lois was up early Saturday morning and Danijel felt like sleeping in for a change. Lois stood looking over his crib, "It's just you and me little guy. I promise I'm going to do whatever it takes to take care of you. I'll make sure you have food, clothes and a place to live. Maybe one day I'll even be able to provide a really good education for you. Who knows maybe you will be a lawyer, or a judge, but whatever you become I will always be there for you. I will never abandon you."

Lois went to her clothes drawer and pulled out her diary. She looked around the room and then smiled, "some things will never change, I guess." She always spied out the room before she began to write in her diary, for fear that a little brother or sister would pop up from under the bed or behind a door, but right now she didn't even have that. All she had was her diary and Danijel.

Lois came out of her room when she heard Kelly moving things into the living room area.

"You need some help?" Lois asked.

"No, I have been packing since last night."

Kelly didn't have much to pack. They only had to buy their bedroom set, when they moved in. The living room and the kitchenette belonged to Teri.

"Are you taking down your bed today?"

"No, my sister is going to come pick it up next week. I won't need it. The rooms are fully furnished where I'm going."

"That's great," said Lois, "is Steve helping you move?"

Kelly hesitated.

"You didn't tell him you were moving, did you?" said Lois in disbelief.

"I know I should have, but I've told Rinoldo all about Steve. He says that I should make a clean break. There is no way Steve will be able to find me. I'm not even going to leave my new address with you."

"Oh, that's great," said Lois, "so now he can come around here and knock the door down trying to find you. I have a baby to take care of you know, besides he knows where we work."

"He knows where you work," said Kelly, "I quit. Yesterday was my last day."

Lois could not believe what she was hearing.

"I don't understand Kelly, I thought we were friends."

"We are Lois, and Danijel is my godson. That's why I thought it best not to tell you too much of my plans. Steve can't make you tell him what you don't know."

Lois held down her head, shaking it in disbelief.

"Lois, you've always told me that I should just leave Steve, now that I'm doing it, you don't approve. I don't understand."

"It's not that I disapprove. It's just that I know how it feels to find out second hand that someone you love and whom you thought loved you just left your life without any words of explanation or nothing."

"It's for the best," Kelly said.

"What is?" asked Lois, "Matt leaving me without an explanation and a baby to care for by myself, or you leaving Steve without an explanation."

The doorbell rang and Kelly said, "It's not the same Lois. Steve and Matt, are not the same," as she went to open the door, Lois thought about what she said, and she was right. Steve didn't deserve an explanation, in that sense she was happy for Kelly.

"Come on in Rinoldo," Kelly said, "I'm packed and ready to go."

Rinoldo looked over to Lois who was leaning on the wall next to the entrance of the kitchen door. She still had on her robe.

"And who is this lovely lady?" He asked.

"Oh, I apologize," said Kelly. "This is Lois, my roommate."

Rinoldo extended his hand and Lois reluctantly took it, "nice to meet you."

His handshake was weak and Lois wondered what that said about him. She heard Richard say once that you could tell a lot about someone by how they shake your hand but that was all she knew about handshaking.

Lois nodded, "same here," but she was just being nice.

She decided not to like Rinoldo, at first sight. She was quietly blaming him for taking her best friend away. She knew she wasn't being fair, but it was how she felt.

"I know I'm stealing your roommate from you, but it's all to her best interest."

Lois suddenly had the feeling that she would never like this Rinoldo and hope that she would never have to see him again.

"She's more than just a roommate," Lois said. "She's my best friend."

"Let me go and get the rest of my things Rinoldo," Kelly jumped in, "I'll be right back."

When Kelly left the room, Rinoldo asked Lois, "Have you ever considered being a model yourself?"

"No," answered Lois pointedly.

"You would probably make a good model. You have the height and you're very pretty." He looked Lois up and down and Lois suddenly felt chilled, "and beneath that robe, you probably have a great body."

"I have a baby," said Lois.

"Some of the models do," said Rinoldo matter of fact.

"Okay, we can go," Kelly said.

The three of them stood in the living room not sure which one was expected to make the next move, finally Rinoldo said, "Why don't I take these down," he picked up Kelly's overstuffed bags and grunted, "you should've given most of these things away to the salvation army, because I'm sure you'll not be needing most of it."

Rinoldo turned before he left and said to Lois, "It was nice meeting you Lois. You should give my suggestion some thought."

Lois wasn't aware that it was a suggestion. It sounded more like a come on.

"Sure," she responded in disbelief.

Rinoldo bowed his head at that and said, "I'll be waiting for you down stairs in the car. Take your time."

As an afterthought, he placed one of the bags on the floor and took a business card out of his pocket and handed it to Lois, "seriously Lois," he said, "think about it, and if you're ever interested, give me a call first."

Lois took the card and looked it over while Rinoldo picked up the bag, opened the door and let himself out. When he left, she balled it up in her hand.

"What was that all about?" Kelly asked.

"Ask him," Lois said, "he's your friend."

Kelly shrugged and approached Lois. The girls embraced for a while without saying anything, when they separated, Kelly went into Lois' room to Danijel's crib. He was still sleeping. While Lois stood in the door watching, Kelly rubbed Danijel's head and began to speak to him.

"You take care of your mommy little man. I'm going to visit often and when I move to LA and make it big, I'm going to send for you and your mommy. Your mommy is my best friend. She's the only person, besides my family who believes in me and accepts me for who I am. She's never judged, or criticized me and she's always there when I need her the most. I know she thinks I'm abandoning her, but I'm going to pursue my dreams. She'll realize that one day, because I'm doing exactly what she came to New York to do, pursue her dreams and whether she realizes it or not, you're part of that dream."

At those words, tears began to roll down Lois' face. She took her nightgown and wiped her face in it. Kelly's words made Lois think back to the last day she was at her old church. Pastor Fischer spoke a message concerning predestination. Suddenly she wondered if Danijel was part of a predestined plan for her life. She didn't mean to, but she found herself loving him more everyday. She thought she would despise him because of Matt, but she didn't. She loved him so much and he'll love her one-day too, but for now it was okay that he just needed her.

Lois thoughts came back to Kelly as she saw her leaned over to kiss Danijel on his head. When she walked back to Lois, Lois was wiping more tears from her eyes. They embraced again.

"I love you," said Lois.

"I love you," said Kelly.

Lois stood there with tears coming down her face. She didn't want to cry, but she couldn't help it. Kelly didn't say another word to her knowing she would also break into tears. Kelly looked over to where Lois had thrown Rinoldo's business card. It had missed the garbage can and was lying on the floor. She picked it up and gave it back to Lois.

"If you need me, he'll know where I am."

This time Lois embraced the card and said, "thank you," as Kelly walked out the door not looking back.

Mona did help Lois find a place to stay. Mona knew someone personally, who sped up the process for Lois. It was in a low-income apartment where Mona lived in the project.

Lois cried for two nights, but she knew it was the best she could do for now. She kept promising Danijel that it would only be temporary.

They moved the next day after one of the worst blizzards in New York.

"Mom it'll be alright," Lois was saying to Stephanie, who called almost every day after Deb told her what was going on.

She wished Deb would mind her own business, but according to Deb, she and Danijel were her business.

"He's going to be alright Mom. I'm going to bundle him up real good.".... "No, thanks, I don't need any money. I have everything I need for now.".... "Mom you have your hands full. I only have Danijel.".... "I can support and take care of him. We're going to be fine." The rest of the conversation was spent talking about all the cute little things that Danijel was now doing.

"By the way Mom thanks for the advice on that scheduling thing, it's working great. I'm actually getting some sleep now, and so is Danijel. He's such a good little guy. Mom, I got to go. Mona is here to help me move.".... "Today is a good day to move. The city is still recovering from the Blizzard and the factory is close because of power outage." ...."No, I don't get paid when I don't work.".... "Mom, I...".... "Okay, whatever you send I'll make sure that I use it for Danijel.".... "Thanks mom.".... "Love you too."

Mona was sitting in the living room listening to Lois' side of the conversation. When Lois got off the phone, she let out a sigh and wiped the top of her forehead as if she was wiping sweat from her head.

They both laughed and Lois said, "I can't believe I'm actually thanking my Mom for advice. I suddenly feel like an adult."

"When you have a child, you have to grow up quick," said Mona.

"Yeah," Lois said with a quick thought on how true that was, "well let's get this show on the road."

"Let's," said Mona.

Lois had more stuff than Kelly. She smiled at Danijel all bundled up in his stroller smiling back at her and realized he was the reason she had so much stuff.

The women at the factory threw her a baby shower, orchestrated by her aunt. They had it one day during lunch. It wasn't anything fancy. They all brought a dish from home and a gift. Lois got a lot of things. Deb bought her the baby Stroller and her mother and Richard bought the crib. They picked it out when her mother came down for Danijel's birth.

Mona knew a guy with a truck, which was great, because they didn't have to break down the crib.

"That's it," Mona said dusting off her hand as if she was house cleaning, "I'll take Danijel down and you can come down with the rest of the things."

"I'll be right down," Lois said.

After Lois gathered the remainder of her things, she went through each room and cupboard to make sure she had everything. The floor in the living room was hardwood and not carpeted like the bedrooms, but Lois copped an Indian squat right in the middle of it and looked around the room.

"My first apartment. I'll never forget this place."

She sat there for a while, then got up and left. She took the keys downstairs and left them with the Super of the building.

"Sorry to see you ladies leave," he said. "You were good people."

"Thank you," Lois said, then she thought to herself, "yeah we were good, because we never complained when you didn't fix things, when you should."

Lois didn't put Danijel back into the stroller, when she got out of the truck. The walk to the building wasn't long and with near zero degree temperature and the wind chill factor making it feel ten degrees lower than it was, she wanted to hold him close to her, so the wind didn't get in his face.

As she entered the building, the inside was almost as cold as outside, yet there were men and women hanging around in the Lobby trying to hide what they were smoking. Who were they kidding? Lois thought, you could smell the stench of tobacco and reefer. It took the longest for the elevator to arrive. It seems to linger on each floor. The building had ten floors, compared to the six where she used to live. They stood there patiently looking up at the light on the elevator.

"Kids hold the elevator for each other and parents get their children to hold the elevator until they get there," Mona said.

Lois nodded that she understood. When the elevator door opened, the stench of urine came bursting out. Lois wanted to take Danijel and run, but it was too cold to take him back out there, especially since they didn't have anywhere to go.

"I have the keys," Mona said. "I know the Super personally."

Lois was beginning to wonder who Mona didn't know, "personally." The apartment was not as cold as downstairs and the hallways, but it was running close.

"Is the heat on?" Lois asked, but the rattling noise coming from somewhere was an indication that something was on. Lois looked around for the heating elements. "Can we control it?"

"The only thing we can control is our ovens," Mona said, as she went into the kitchen and turned the oven on and open the door.

The guys who Mona got to help them move took everything off the truck and brought them up to the apartment building.

"What's that smell?" asked one of the guys.

Lois and Mona went to the kitchen. The oven had just begun to heat up, but it was so filthy that the smell that was coming out of it was not worth the little heat it was putting out, so Lois turned it off.

"I have two electric heaters," said Mona, "I'll let you use one of mind."

"I thought we couldn't use them," Lois said to Mona.

"I guess you read the rules and bylaws of the building," Mona said, "and that's good, you should read everything before you sign anything, so they say, but now you can trash it. They don't intend to keep their end of that agreement and you'll soon find out that you will have to do what you have to do. The Super practically knows that everyone has heaters, but for a couple of bucks every winter, he keeps his month shut. If he likes you, he keeps his month shut for free."

"I gather he likes you," said Lois.

"There's nothing wrong with being liked," Mona said looking at Lois wondering if she was judging her.

Lois picked up on it and said, "I'm sorry Mona. That didn't come out right. You have Kiesha, of course you have to do what you have to do to take care of her. I really would appreciate it, if you would let me hold one of your heaters, until I can get my own. If I have to pay the

Super, I'll do what it takes. I won't let Danijel freeze to death in this place."

"I'll go get it. By the way, I live in Apartment C, one floor up."

"Great," said Lois.

Lois wasn't sure what to do next. Mona hadn't come back down with the heater, so she didn't want to put Danijel down. She wanted to place him in a place where the heat could be directly on him. Lois walked around checking out the rooms. She only had one bedroom. It was allowed until Danijel got a certain age, then he would have to have his own room.

The rooms were twice as small as the rooms in the other apartment. It was painted, but it had a lot of work to be done before she would be able to call it home. She came back into the living room and sat in the big chair she bought from Teri.

"I won't cry, Danijel. I won't cry," she said as tears came down her face. "I promise you, we will not be here long.

As she said that she was suddenly aware of little roaches crawling all over the floor and as she looked up on the walls, they were crawling around up there too. She saw rat droppings in a corner of the room and a mousetrap in another corner.

This time she began to cry.

"I promise Danijel. We won't be here long. I promise."

Danijel with his little black round eyes, round face and perfect lips stared up in his mother's face, all bundled up in her arms and took his tiny little fingers and began to feel the tears running down her face.

Beedeekle:

The two little imps jumped all around Beedeekle with glee asking him, "what now, Beedeekle, what now?"

"The best is yet to come," said Beedeekle. "In the meantime, let's go check out the place. I think I saw some imps and demons that I may know. Maybe we can get some assistance from them. We're going to need a lot of help with this one. Her mother is a praying woman."

The two little imps suddenly stop cold in their tracks, stared at each others and said, "oh oh."

Chapter Eighteen
Jewel

Brad looked over at Jewel sitting on the passenger side of the car. She had not said a word to him since they left the boarding house. Brad's home was forty-five minutes away from Atlanta. There was nothing else Brad could think of to say to calm Jewel for the visit with his family. It wasn't a special occasion, or a holiday. It was just a day at his parents. They didn't even plan to stay over. They were going to drive up early that morning, spend the day and drive back at night. Although Brad thought Jewel was making too much of this visit, he sympathized with her. It wasn't easy for him to meet her family, but he thought he made a good impression with them, maybe they even liked him.

Jewel and Brad had become much closer over the past year and were spending most of their time together. He didn't want to push Jewel into meeting his family. He wanted it to be her decision just as it was his to meet her parents, but it seemed that Jewel was never going to make the move, so Brad insisted and persisted and she finally gave in.

"We're about ten minutes away from the house," Brad said to Jewel, wanting more to make conversation than to inform her.

"It's gorgeous around here," Jewel said.

Brad lived in an upper class suburban town. It was not too far from the city, but far enough. Most of the houses were old Victorian style homes. The road leading up to Brad's home had willow trees on both sides of the road. The branches of the trees cascaded over the road and met each other forming an arch covering, making the road look like one long aisle.

About a quarter of a mile down the road, a house began to appear. The house was a red brick, three-story home. The yard was immaculate. The grass was green and all the bushes were well trimmed. There was a flower garden on both sides of the house and flowers of yellow, purple, blue and orange were in full bloom.

Brad pulled up behind a small red BMW and a silver gray Mercedes Benz sedan. Brad got out of the car, but Jewel didn't budge. Brad went around to her side of the door and opened it. This was not there custom. Jewel made it clear to Brad that it was nice that he was a gentleman, but she could open her own door. She let Brad know that she didn't need him or any man to open doors for her. She was quite capable of getting them open herself.

Brad stood with his hand out to Jewel and she took it and mumbled underneath her breath, "here we go."

"What?" Brad asked.

"Nothing," she replied.

Brad took his keys out and began to open the door.

"Shouldn't we knock or something?" Jewel asked.

"I have my keys," Brad said.

The door opened to a grand room. Jewel looked up at the steep cathedral ceiling and around the room. Every thing looked antique, the windows, the chandelier, the floors, the chairs and a long staircase that swerved around at the top.

"Hi Brad," came a voice from around a corner somewhere.

The girl was tall with dark hair like Brad's. She came up to Brad and kissed him on the cheek.

Brad took her hand while holding Jewel's and said, "Amy this is Jewel. Jewel this is my younger and only sibling, Amy."

Jewel extended her hand to greet Amy and she responded likewise.

"Nice to meet you Jewel. Brad has said a lot of nice things about you. I hope you can live up to them."

"I hope I can too," Jewel said, "but please don't fault me for your brother's fantasies."

"Where is everyone?" asked Brad.

"By everyone, do you mean Bob and Katie."

Jewel looked at Brad inquisitively. She had never heard Brad talk of a Bob or Katie.

"They would be our parents," said Brad to Jewel's inquiring look. "My dear sister has taken up calling our parents, Robert and Katherine, Bob and Katie to their disapproval, of course."

"Of course," said Amy.

Jewel shook her head in understanding.

"They'll be right in. We all went out for a ride this morning and being the better rider, I made it back home before them," said Amy.

"Can you ride a horse?" Amy asked Jewel.

"I've been on a horse, during summer camp, if that counts as riding," Jewel responded.

"I see," said Amy as she looked Jewel over again. "Anyway," Amy said turning her attention to Brad with a twinkle in her eyes, "I know this was your special day to bring your little friend up to visit with Bob and Katie, so I hope you don't mind that I've asked a friend up as well."

Brad realized Amy was being condescending to Jewel and if he let it continue, he knew she would get even more condescending as the day went on, so he felt the need to correct her, even though he knew Jewel was quite capable of dealing with Amy on her own.

"Amy, my dear sweet sister, I certainly do not have a problem with you inviting one of your friends to spend a day with you, however, for the record, please do not refer to Jewel as my little friend."

Jewel let out a quiet sign of relief, Amy assessment of her did not go unnoticed and if Brad didn't say anything, she had already decided she would. Brad did warn her about Amy. She liked to put on heirs and on any given day she could be downright obnoxious. It seemed that she had chosen today to be just that. Jewel hoped she would get to see the other side of her; the side Brad liked about her. She hoped there was such a side, besides in her brother's big heart.

"Who's your friend?" Brad asked Amy, "Do I know him?"

"Oh did I say it was a him?" Amy asked arching her eyebrows at him.

Brad knew that meant his little sister was up to playing her silly little games. His heart skipped a beat. He prayed she wasn't playing one of her silly little games at Jewel's expense. She could be cruel, when she wanted to be.

"No, I guess you didn't," Brad said, "I guess I just assume."

"Oh, but we mustn't assume dear brother," Amy said with a smile.

"Oh darling, you're here."

Everyone looked towards a door that led down a long hallway. A woman came up to Brad. She was wearing a well-figured riding outfit. Her hair was pepper and short. She gave Brad a kiss on both cheeks and turned to Jewel and said, "You must be Jewel. It's so good to finally meet you."

She extended her hand to Jewel and Jewel said, "same here, Mrs. Conners?" Jewel had seen a picture of Brad's mom, so she knew who she was.

"Why are we standing here in the foyer?" Mrs. Conners asked, and before anyone could respond she said, "let's go into the sitting room."

"Where's Dad?" Brad asked.

"Oh, he was helping Cecelia get off her horse and then he said something about unsaddling them before coming in. He should be right in."

Brad suddenly tense and Jewel made a mental note of it.

Someone brought some tea into the sitting room. Jewel was not sure who she was, Brad never said anything about having servants.

"Molly," Brad said, "this is my girlfriend, Jewel. Jewel this is Molly. She helps out around here."

"Nice to meet you," Jewel said.

"Nice to meet you as well," said Molly.

She placed a jug of tea and glasses down and left the room.

"How tactless Bradley," said Am,. "introducing your girlfriend to the servants."

"Molly is not a servant," Brad said.

"Yes. She is." Amy adamantly said.

"Okay, you two enough," Mr. Conners said as he entered the room.

Amy just rolled her eyes at Brad and shook her head. Brad got up out of his chair and greeted his Dad.

"Dad, this is…"

"Jewel," Mr. Conners said, before Brad could finish the introduction, "of course, who else would it be." He shook Jewel hand and Jewel realized she was probably going to like him better than Brad's mother and sister.

She seemed to assess that Amy's pretentious ways might have been inherited or learned from her mother.

Mr. Conners took a seat next to his wife and they began to get Brad caught up to speed on things that were going on around the home and in the community.

"Brad!" All eyes and heads turned towards a woman, who had just entered the room.

Jewel guessed it was Amy's friend, Cecelia. She was beautiful. She had long blonde hair, a shape like a model, a small round face with thin lips that housed a Colgate smile.

"I'm sorry I took so long to come down, but I just had to get out of that smelly ole horse clothes."

She walked over to Brad and the gentleman that he was; he got up to greet her.

"Hi Cecelia." Brad hugged her and she kissed him on the cheek.

"Jewel," Brad said turning to face her, "this is Cecelia. She's sort of a friend of the family. Her family and our family go way back. I went to school and played with her brothers." Brad made the introduction, but didn't mention the fact Cecelia had always had a crush on him.

"Nice to meet you," Jewel said.

"Yes," Cecelia pause checking Jewel out, then smiled a wryly smile and finished, "same here," and she said it like she actually meant it.

By noon, Jewel began to feel a little agitated. She was ready to go, but willing to stick it out. She had never met a challenge she couldn't handle.

"How're you doing?" Brad asked Jewel at brunch.

Jewel smiled and said, "great. Your parents have an outstanding home and your father makes me feel welcome."

Brad knew that meant she didn't feel welcome by the women of his family.

"Once you get to know my mom and Amy they are pretty harmless," Brad said feeling the need to justify his mother and Amy's behavior, but he knew Jewel was too smart to buy into any excuses that he had to offer.

She intended to keep her guard up with Katherine, Amy and Cecelia. She wasn't fool by the long time friend of the family introduction. It was clear that Cecelia wanted her to know that there was much more between her and Brad than simply family ties.

After brunch everyone agreed to go for a swim. Brad had promised to take Jewel around and show her around. Jewel smiled at the thought. It could take most of the day to tour the huge plantation and then it would be time for them to go. However, something kept coming up and he had to postpone it.

When everyone went to change into their bathing suits, Jewel was left to find her room on her own. She couldn't remember where Brad said Molly put her things. She wandered upstairs drawn down the hallway by voices. She thought she remembered Molly saying that it was in the room next to Amy. Actually she said, "Miss Amy." Jewel thought to herself, "thank God Molly wasn't black." She didn't think she could handle it if they had black "servants," as Miss Amy would say.

As she got closer to the voices she could make them out. It seemed that it was Ms. Conners, Amy and Cecelia.

"What do you think?" Amy asked.

"Think about what?" Mrs. Conners seemed confused by Amy's question.

"Come on Katie. Don't play games with me. The sole purpose of this day is to check out Brad's girlfriend."

"Brad's black girlfriend." Cecelia corrected.

"Yeah, very black girlfriend," Amy said, and the two girls began to laugh. "I think back on the plantation, she would be called a darkie."

The girls laughed again. "You would think Brad could find a lighter one to date."

"Amy! Now, that's enough," Mrs. Connors said, outraged at her daughter's comment, "both of you. Jewel is not here for us to check her out. She's here because Brad wanted us to meet someone he cares a great deal about. It doesn't matter whether she is light, dark, Indian, or Chinese. Brad didn't go out looking for a specific nationality, or color. He says this girl is special to him and she's our guest today and regardless of any prejudices you two may have, you had better keep them to yourselves. I thought you kids were more liberal or something. I thought it didn't matter what the color of people skins were to your generation."

"It doesn't, when you don't have to personally be subjected to them," Amy said.

"What do you mean?" Mrs. Conners asked.

"We know they're everywhere. We have to go to school with them. We have to work with them and we even try to be friendly or sociable with them. All of that's fine and good, as long as you don't have to bring them home and that's what Brad is doing. He's bringing them home with him. It's not just her you know. It's her family and friends too. I heard they're like leeches."

"Amy, stop it now!" Mrs. Conners was appalled. "You are being absolutely ridiculous, besides they're not getting married."

"And I aim to make sure that never happens," Cecelia said.

Mrs. Connors looked at both girls sternly and said, "I don't know what you two have up your sleeves, but you had better behave yourselves."

"Katie come on," Amy said, "I can't believe you and Robert are encouraging this relationship, and since you missed it mommy dear, Brad said he loved her, not care deeply for her. You guys better face reality. This could end up in a marriage. Is that what you want?"

"Amy, stop exaggerating, besides it's not what we want. It's what Brad wants. We just want him to be happy."

"Bull!" said Amy.

"That's enough young lady, maybe you and Cecelia should excuse yourselves for the rest of the day. We'll miss you, but I think it's best."

"Oh, I'll behave Katie," Amy said, "I love Brad too and I only want the best for him. I just don't happen to think that this relationship is the best for him, but!...," she threw both her hands up and shrugged her shoulders in protest to any further comment her mother may have, "but, I promise to behave today."

Mrs. Conners stared at Amy for a while to affirm that she meant what she said, then turned to Cecelia and said, "you're Amy's guest today Cecelia. Brad didn't invite you here, nor did we. Now I don't know what you and Amy think you are doing, but I'm telling you that it will not happen in our home. Do you understand me young lady?"

"Yes maam," Cecelia humbly replied, with a drawn out southern drawl.

As Mrs. Conners turned to leave the room the two girls winked at each other, held their head down and smiled.

Jewel stood frozen. She knew Mrs. Connors was about to leave the room. She didn't know if she wanted to face her and have her know that she heard the conversation, or run and hide and pretend she never heard it.

Jewel saw an open door across the room. She could have sworn it wasn't there before, because if it was she would have entered it and not have eaves dropped on their conversation. Jewel suddenly began to tip toe across the hall. She made it into the room and behind the door just as Mrs. Connors was leaving.

When Mrs. Connors was out of the room, she looked up and down the hall because she thought she heard someone coming. She looked across the room at the open door. She knew that was the room Molly had put Jewel's bags, so she peeked in to see if Jewel was in the room. Jewel stood very still behind the door and Mrs. Connors reached in to close the door. She sniffed around trying to identify a scent.

Beedeekle:
"You see, prejudice is a dangerous thing. It makes people do and say awful things. It also makes people react in strange ways. I wonder

how Jewel will react," Beedeekle said as he took his long green pointed finger and pressed it against the side of his forehead, which was so soft it sunk in from the touch of his finger.

The other two imps stood staring at Beedeekle and at each other, as they tried to figure out Beedeekle's plan.

Jewel:

Unknown to Jewel she now had a constant companion, an unknown accuser. He stood behind her, as tears were streaming down her face, as she stood still behind the door in the dark room. He was a third of Jewel size and she couldn't see him, but she often smelled his sulfuric body. Although small in stature, his voice could be carried far as he whispered many words of discouragement to Jewel.

Jewel felt like lead was holding her feet down. She didn't think she could move, but she did. She made it to the bathroom and pulled down a guest towel from the bathroom rack. She ran cold water on the cloth and placed it on her face. She took a couple of deep breathe and held her face over the sink and cupped her hands and let cold water run into it, then she splashed it on her face and took the towel and wiped her face. She went through her things. She had brought her make-up kit, because Brad told her they may be going horseback riding and swimming, so she needed to be prepared to freshen up afterwards for a semi-formal dinner.

Jewel looked at herself in the mirror and began to speak softly to herself, "You are a beautiful, smart, intelligent black woman. You do not need superficial accolades from a couple of uptight white girls. I'll not let them get the best of me. Now that I know the game, I can play it as well." Jewel took another deep breath and went into the room to put on her bathing suit and a cover-up. She checked the mirror one last time before leaving the room. "Good, no signs of tears."

"Where's Jewel?" Mrs. Conners asked Brad as she took a lounger chair next to her husband.

Amy and Cecelia were already in the pool. The sun was up and beaming down on them. Brad was wearing sunshades as he lie down on a lounger next to his Dad.

"I thought she was with you guys. I guess she'll be down any minute now, if not, I'll go see if she's okay. If she got lost, it's my fault. I have been meaning to show her around the house."

"Oh, there she is now," Mrs. Conners acknowledge. "Did you find everything alright Jewel?" Mr. Conners asked.

"I found everything. I just made a wrong turn, but I finally found the room with my things in it," Jewel explained.

"Good," said Mrs. Conners. "Is this lounger taken?" Jewel asked Brad.

"No, I pulled it here for you." Jewel sat down and put her straw bag next to her.

She pulled out her tanning lotion and handed it to Brad, "do you mind?"

She sat up straight in the chair and Brad began to smooth suntan lotion on her back. Cecelia and Amy got out of the pool and walked towards them.

"You have beautiful skin," Brad said to Jewel as Amy and Cecelia approached.

"And you have strong hands," Jewel repaid the compliment as she turned and look into Brad's eye.

"He does, doesn't he?" commented Cecelia, but neither Brad nor Jewel acknowledge her.

For a brief moment they just stared into each other eyes, Jewel smiled and reflected her eyes downward, when she looked up again, he was still staring at her and for a moment she felt like he was assessing her soul. It made her uncomfortable, so to make him stop, she kissed him. This was a surprise to Brad. Jewel wasn't one to express public affections, if she was changing; he liked it.

"I'm going in for a swim," Jewel said to Brad, while getting up, "coming?"

"I think I will," Brad said.

"Are you sure that you have on enough suntan lotion?" Cecelia asked Jewel, "I'm not familiar with the texture of your people skin and this sun is merciless out here today. I would hate to see you get burn."

Jewel stopped cold, turned to Cecelia and looked her straight in the eyes and responded, "I guess you do have a lot to learn about my people. We're very thick skinned. You wouldn't believe the things we can take and still come out strong and on the top," and without saying another word, Jewel turned and jumped into the pool causing enough splash to wet Cecelia, who scurried annoyingly out of the way.

Jewel made herself inseparable with Brad for the rest of the day. She did not allow Cecelia one minute alone with Brad, but Cecelia kept trying. Brad wasn't sure what he did to deserve so much of Jewel's attention, but he was enjoying every moment of it. At every opportunity that Cecelia got, she shot hot glances at Jewel, but Jewel only smiled back, which annoyed Cecelia even more.

Jewel had brought two dresses for dinner. She didn't know which one she would wear. Justine had gone with her shopping for a dress.

The one she chose received Justine's frowned and disapproval, "Too common, too homey," she said.

Jewel had good taste in clothes, but trying to find the right thing to wear to dinner with your boyfriend's parents was an entirely different thing. Justine finally picked out a rust colored, low cut front and back dress that came a quarter lengths above Jewel's knees. They picked out a pair of nice uncomfortably pumps to go with them.

"The important thing here is to look good," Justine said, "this color brings out the Indian in you. After your day of horseback riding and swimming, the only thing that you're going to be able to do with your hair is wear it up."

Later that afternoon Justine showed her how to pin it up and leave enough out to fall around her face.

"Please, no pony tails with this dress," Justine said, pointing a finger in her face, "I will ask Brad, you know."

She was suddenly glad to have Justine as a friend. She had decided that even though she and Brad may never make it as a couple, she was not leaving today with her tail between her legs.

Brad was sitting with his parents waiting for the girls to come down. Jewel came down first. Brad saw her as she was coming down the stairs and instinctly he arose to meet her at the end of the stairs. He cupped his arm and she put her arm under his and he walked her to a seat next to his, where they were having hor de'erves and drinks.

"You look so beautiful Jewel," Brad said, as if in disbelief.

Mostly, he had only seen Jewel in jeans, sweatshirts with her beautiful black hair in a pony-tail. She did wore slacks to the New Year's Eve party.

"Thank you," Jewel said as she took her seat next to him.

He leaned over and kissed her on the check and whispered, "I really mean that." Jewel knew he did.

Amy and Cecelia came down. Amy was wearing something more casual than semi-formal, but Cecelia was wearing something very revealing and a little distasteful that really didn't do much for her.

Brad made a point to himself not to compliment Cecelia on anything, but when he saw what she was wearing, there was really nothing tasteful to say about it.

Cecelia had been annoyingly rude to Jewel throughout the day. A couple of times Brad was tempted to put her in her place, but Jewel picked up on it and averted his attention. She did not want Brad fighting her battle with Cecelia and for some reason that's what it had become, a battle, but Jewel didn't know why she was being so hostile. Brad never mentioned Cecelia. They talked about their high-school sweethearts and other people they dated, but Cecelia's name was never mentioned.

Dinner was pleasant enough. Everyone was talking and making small talk, except for Cecelia who seemed annoyed. She was seated between Amy and Mrs. Connors.

She and Amy had secretly talked about making sure that she sat next to Brad at dinner. What Cecelia didn't know was that Mrs. Conners told her husband about their conversation earlier. He was very disturbed about it and had a little talk with Amy.

He made it clear that she and Cecelia were to behave themselves for the rest of the day. If they didn't, he would see to it that Cecelia was taken home, even if he had to take her himself.

Amy played her little games with her mother, but she knew not to play them with Mr. Conners, especially when he was serious and he

202

seemed very serious about making sure Jewel was not made uncomfortable in their home in any way.

"So Jewel, what does your parents do? Brad tells us they live in Tennessee, but he hasn't said much beyond that," said Mr. Conners.

"Dad come on, you're not going to do the parent check thing are you?" Brad asked.

"Don't be so defensive Brad, it's only conversation," said Mr. Conners.

"I don't mind talking about my parents," Jewel said, "not that they need my approval, but I'm very proud of what they do. My Mother is a teacher and my Father has a very successful business."

"In what?" Mr. Conners asked.

"Construction. He builds," Jewel laughed and said, "and that's his slogan actually, 'We Build.' My dad's an architect and he created a company that builds homes and businesses, mainly from the ground up, but he does some remodeling and renovations, as well"

"And your mother, what grades does she teach?" Mrs. Conners asked.

"She teaches elementary school. She wants to teach high school, but my dad doesn't want her to take on that kind of stress, especially since he feels there's no need for her to work at all."

"Men," said Mrs. Conners, "they don't understand the need for a woman to feel like she is making a difference in the world."

Mr. Conners put his hand over his wife's hand on the table and looked at her and said to Jewel.

"My wife, the liberal."

"That's not funny dear," said Mrs. Conners.

"I didn't say it to be funny, or to put you down dear, but it's nice to know there are other men out there that feel as I do."

"And it's nice to know that there are other women out there that feel the way I do," said Mrs. Conners.

"You and I should get along very well Mrs. Conners, because I feel the same as you and my mother," said Jewel.

This time it was Brad who placed his hand over Jewel and held it softly.

She smiled at him and Cecelia got up and said, "excuse me."

"Is everything alright Cecelia?" Mrs. Conners asked, "You look a little pale."

"I think I'm going to be sick," Cecelia said glaring at Brad and Jewel.

As she stormed out of the dining room, Amy got up and said, "I'd better go make sure she's okay."

"I hope she's okay," Jewel said to Amy, who just looked at Jewel knowingly.

Somehow Amy knew Jewel was playing her and Cecelia's game, but she didn't know why Jewel felt the need to play it.

"I'm sure she's going to be just fine, but I'll tell her you were concern," Amy said.

"Please do that," Jewel said.

"Dear, maybe you should check on her," Mr. Conners said to his wife.

"I will in a minute, but first we're going to have some desert. If there's an emergency, Amy will call for us, I'm sure."

"Jewel, you are going to love this desert," Mrs. Conners said focusing her attention on Jewel. "I don't have much time to cook," said Mrs. Conners.

"Thank God," Mr. Conners replied jokingly.

"But I know some of the best caterers," Mrs. Conners said while giving her husband a feisty stare, "and this particular caterer makes the best key-lime pie on this side of the Mississippi, as they say."

Every one laughed and the remainder of the dinner was done informally with lots of talking and getting to know each other.

Brad was really pleased with how the day ended, so was Jewel. She decided that Mrs. Conners was nothing like her daughter and Mrs. Conners genuinely liked her.

"Jewel you have to come back soon," Mrs. Conners said as she hugged Jewel, "and bring my son with you."

"Gee thanks, Mother," Brad said, "I'm glad you included me."

"Son," Mr. Conners said, not one for hugging men, gave Brad a slap on his shoulder and said, "call when you get home and drive this lovely lady home safely. We hope to see her again soon."

Despite everything she overheard, Jewel left with a good feeling. Brad parents were, as Brad said, sincere, loving and straightforward.

Beedeekle:

"Beedeekle the plan failed!" said the little imp excitedly.

"How do you know the plan failed, when you don't even know the plan!" screamed Beedeekle, glaring and breathing fumes at the little imp.

The little imp pondered the comment and realized he didn't know the plan. Beedeekle's eyes were gleaming, but he didn't know if that was from accomplishment or disappointment.

Jewel:

"Brad you really need to get your car checked out," said Jewel.

"I know," said Brad, "I keep putting it off. That smell seems stronger than at other times."

"Hmmm," said Jewel.

"So, did you have a good day? How do you like my parents? Aren't they like I said they were?"

"One question at a time, please."

"Sorry," said Brad smiling at Jewel.

"Basically, I had a good day. Your parents are wonderfully good people, and yes you were. however!," she said before Brad could further comment. "We have to talk about Miss Cecelia. You never told me you dated her."

"I didn't," Brad said looking at Jewel defensively, "but I'll tell you about her, but I want to first apologize for my sister."

"There's no need. Everybody has hang-ups and issues. I don't think she and I will be friends, but I'll try to keep it civil with her."

"Jewel, just gave her a chance. She seemed to be mixed up in this high society thing. She's trying to find herself and where she fits in. Granted, she's a little mix up, but she's a good kid."

Jewel looked at Brad. He was really defending his sister. She wondered if she should tell him about the things she overheard. Should she tell him that her sister is a prejudice, uptight witch.

Brad looked at her while she was in her thoughts and tried to reinforce what he said, "she really is a good kid."

She knew that Brad really needed to believe that, so she decided to let it ride but she knew there was probably no hope for her and Amy.

Intercessor

"Oh God keep these soul safe from the pain of sin. Lead them away from the enemies Den. father the danger signs are flashing before their eyes, but they cannot see the enemy of Lies. Loose your supernatural power upon them. Let them be able to resist the enemy's gems.

Pause: (crying and moanings)

Tears are not enough. The fighter must be tough. The enemy is taking no hostage, and he is overtaking every blockage. I will not be hindered by sleep, for I hear the marching of angelic feet. I cheer them on, Go! Go! Go forth!, I command. The Intercessors are making a final stand! The glory of the Lord will prevail and Satan will retreat like a soft-shelled snail. Victory! Victory! Victory! We claim! The end of this matter will be a victorious reign!

Chapter Nineteen
Lucifer

"Where is this place Beedeekle?" One of the slimy little imps asked.

"I'm not sure," replied Beedeekle. All the while his bulging eyes were dashing back and forth.

"It sure doesn't smell all that good either," said the other imp. "And it's getting hotter and hotter with every step we make."

"Quiet!" Beedeekle demanded through clenching green fork-like teeth and made a sudden stop and one of the imps bumped into him and stumbled and the either imp quivered from the sudden smoke that seemed to have appeared out of nowhere and stumbled over the fallen imp.

Beedeekle eyed the two on the ground with contempt. He didn't know why he was given two of the most incompetent imps to help him carry out a job that had become number one on Lucifer's list; seeing Beedeekle's anger the two imps scurried hurriedly to get to their feet.

"Move it!" Beedeekle said to both of them.

"But where to Beedeekle, we can't see anything, because of the smoke."

It was growing increasingly hotter and the sweat poured off the three imps leaving puddles of water that turned into boiling water seconds after hitting the ground.

Suddenly a thunderous voice called out to them. "Stop right there!"

The voice sounded like thunder and it sent shivers up and down the spiny cords of the imps. They turned around to see a fiery red object standing before them. They had never seen Lucifer in this form before.

He walked on two legs, but he had smoke coming out of two horns on his head. As he neared the two imps, there seemed to be voices crying in the background. Lucifer turned sideways from the imps and with one great breath of air, blew away the smoke in front of the imps.

The imps were suddenly shaken like leaves as they saw how close they were standing to a pit that was consumed with fire. The voices they heard seemed to grow louder and louder; cries of anguish and pain.

Beedeekle tried to open his mouth to plead with Lucifer not to destroy him, but his mouth was glued shut, so were the mouths of the two imps.

Lucifer eyed the three imps and said, "This will be your demise, if you don't accomplish your task!"

He began to walk away and he turned quickly and the ground shook and the three imps almost tumbled over into the fire, but Lucifer used his long extending index finger like a rope and wrapped it around them and drew them near to him and said, "And there will be no excuse!"

He then threw the imps into the air. It was a long while before the imps landed and when they did, they landed somewhere outside of the deep dark place.

The imps began to move their mouths to see if they could.

They were about to speak, but Beedeekle held up his hand to silence them, "I think it is clear that we have work to do and it is also clear that we need help to do it."

His green eyes bulged out of his head as he eyeballed the two imps and hollered, "Now let's get to work!"

Chapter Twenty
Lois

It was blistering cold outside, thirty degrees, but the wind chill factor made it felt like ten degrees below. Lois wished she had worn a hat, but that would have messed up the fifty-dollar hair-do she had done just for the interview today. She wore her sneakers and dropped her heels into a carry bag. She had on gloves and her down waist jacket. She now wished she had bought herself a long overcoat. She kept promising herself to buy one, but since Danijel came along everything she wanted became last on the list and after she paid the babysitter and the bills, bought pampers and groceries, there was never enough money for anything else. She was so glad that he was finally out of pampers.

The down jacket was warm enough, but it only cover the upper part of her body and instead of wearing jeans with leg warmers over them, she was wearing a nice two piece business suit, sheer stockings to show of her nice long, sleek, but extremely cold legs. The socks and sneakers helped to keep her feet warm and the gloves helped to keep her hands warm, but the cold air was going up her dress causing her to cramp even more. It just happened to be that time of the month and being out in the cold was not giving her a warm, cozy, comfort feeling.

She thought about canceling the interview, but she was too determined to get out of that rat and roach infested apartment, not to mention how cold it got in the winter and how hot it was in the summer. As far as she was concerned, New York only had two seasons, fall and winter. They had some hot days during the summer, which to Lois only last a couple of weeks at the end of July and the beginning of August.

Lois finally made it to the train station. She didn't realize the walk to the train station was that long. She was looking forward to a seat on a warm train. One of the older subway trains pulled into the station. Lois soon realized there was no heat on the train and the train was already full. The train just sat there for a few minutes and Lois hoped that maybe another car would be better. She quickly ran out and into another car, but it was no better.

"Well, thank God I decided to wear my sneakers," she said to herself.

There were more men sitting than women and not one of them offered their seat to a woman. They kept the paper up to their face, either deep into their reading or pretense of reading, so not to acknowledge that there were women standing over them. She had just missed the last express train of the morning. The train stopped at every stop and people held the doors for others who yelled out for them to "hold the door!"

They probably didn't even know the people they held the door for. The conductor voice was heard over the loud speaker, "Please, do not hold the doors. There is another train right behind this one. Please step in and watch the door!"

People ignored him and held the doors anyway. They seemed not to believe him, when he said there was a train right behind them, because people continued to squeeze in. Some hang half way out of the train, so when the doors close they would be pushed in, crushing against someone else.

Lois was glad that she got on where she did, because although she didn't have a seat, she was hanging onto one of the over hangers, but now there were two other people, one in front of her and one behind her, who were hanging on to the same hanger. At the next stop, a guy who was holding on to a poll behind them decided his poll was too crowded. He reached over and behind Lois and began to hang onto their hanger. He was uncomfortably close to Lois, so she took her bag and held it close to her in the front, hitting a man's newspaper. He looked up at Lois, who apologized, but really wanted to say, 'if you would offer me your seat, then I wouldn't have to stand over you with my bag.'

A lot of people got off at the first stop into the city, just to cross over to catch another train. The next stop was Lois'. Lois was so glad that her connecting train was one of the nicer trains and she even got a seat. She took off her socks and sneakers and put on her black pumps.

The walk from the station to the restaurant was not that far. Lois began to feel butterflies in her stomach. She really wanted this job, even though she never thought of herself as a model. Kelly's friend or agent, Rinoldo, seemed to think she was. She wanted to at least see what it was all about.

Kelly was doing really well. She was living in a really nice apartment, wearing nice clothes and buying her and Danijel nice gifts. She invited them to her apartment one Sunday for a day in the city. She lived in a really nice neighborhood. They went shopping and to lunch and took Dandan, Kelly's nickname for Danijel, to the park.

She sent them home in a limousine car service. It was a really great day. One of the few weekends Kelly had off. She mainly worked on weekends and some time during the week, mainly at night.

Lois didn't ask Kelly much about her modeling career, because she felt Kelly would tell her as much as she wanted her to know. She used to say, the less you know the less you can tell Steve, but according to Troy, Steve had moved on to torment someone else's life, but he was still calling Kelly's family demanding to know where she was. He used to come by the job and demand information from Lois, but Lois' supervisor told the owner of the company. One day he was there when the owner was around and Christine pointed him out. Two of them came over and asked him to leave and told him that they would instruct office personnel to call the police, if he ever came back in the building. Steve never came around after that. He didn't know Lois' new address or phone number and Lois made Troy promise not to tell.

Lois didn't know what Rinoldo would say when she called. She was surprised that he even still remembered her. She didn't tell Kelly what she was doing. She thought if she got hired it would be a nice surprise, but if she didn't maybe she would tell her, maybe not.

Rinoldo asked what Lois thought were normal questions for someone in the modeling business. Questions like what size she was? Did she gain any weight, since he last saw her? How old she was? He seemed pleased with her answers and agreed to meet with her at an upscale restaurant in Manhattan.

Lois was early for the meeting. The waiters and waitresses were very nice to her. She thought to herself they seemed to enjoy their jobs and wondered how much money was in waitressing.

As she was deep in thought looking over the expensive menu, she was suddenly aware of someone standing over her.

"Hi, Lois."

Lois knew it wasn't customary for a woman to stand to greet a man, but she felt at a disadvantage as he stood over her.

As he sat down, Lois said, "Hi."

"So how was your trip to the city?"

Lois wanted to say as awful as could be, but she didn't want to sound whiny, so she said, "It was okay."

"Was the traffic as hectic as usual?" Lois looked at him puzzled.

"Excuse me?" she said.

"Your drive into the city," he clarified, "was it hectic?"

"I took the train."

"Oh, no," said Rinoldo in disbelief. "Had I known that I would have sent a car for you."

Lois wanted to say, "darned!" but she refrained and said, "it wasn't so bad."

"Well don't worry about getting home."

He called to one of the waiter, "Pierre' is it?" He inquired of the waiter's name, as he pulled out his wallet and took out a business card. "Pierre,' do me a favor please and call this company and tell them Mr. Rinoldo is requesting a car here in about an hour." Pierre' took the card and acknowledged Rinoldo politely and left.

Rinoldo turned his attention back to Lois, "I don't intend to keep you any longer than that, but if I do, they'll wait."

"Thank you. Thank you very much," she said gratefully.

"It's not a problem."

Lois hoped he wasn't expecting her to pay for it, because she only had another token to get home and a few dollars for emergency.

Lois had offered to pay the driver of the car that Kelly sent her home in, but Kelly had already paid in advance. When she asked how much it would have cost her, just in case she wanted to use their service again, he said over thirty dollars. Lois knew it would be the train for her the next time she attempted to come to the city.

"Mr. Rinoldo, would you like to order now?" The waiter asked, as he placed drinks in front of them.

"No, not right now. Give us about fifteen minutes to talk business."

Lois didn't recall a waiter asking them what they wanted to drink.

Rinoldo sipped his drink and looked at Lois. "Are you not drinking, or would you prefer water to your seltzer?"

Lois blushed, "I'm sorry, I thought it was alcohol."

"I wouldn't order you alcohol without knowing if you drink."

Lois picked up her glass and sipped a little and placed it back on the table.

"Would you care for something else Lois?" Rinoldo asked.

"If you don't mind, I would really like something hot."

Rinoldo smiled and motioned a waiter who seemed to be just standing around waiting to be called.

"Yes, Mr. Rinoldo."

"Please bring the young lady something hot to drink."

The waiter looked at Lois and said, "we have tea and hot chocolate."

"Tea with lemon," Lois said and looked at Rinoldo and said, "thank you Mr. Rinoldo."

"Now let's get down to business. By the way, just call me Rinoldo. You can drop the mister. Let me tell you a little about what our girls do. They are trained. You would have to stay in a home for several weeks, while you are groomed to sit, talk, eat and drink and it doesn't have to be alcoholic beverages, but if you so choose, we can teach you how to drink modestly. We teach you how to handle yourself with our customers and what to do in a compromising situation. You are taught how to apply make-up, what to wear, what's acceptable and what's not. I run an escort service, while helping the girls pursue their modeling careers. Our girls escort our customers around the city. Most of our customers are from out of town. Our girls escort them to whatever benefit they're in town for, if they so desire. They may just want a dinner or a lunch guest. They pay all the expense. We pay you. You may accept tips. Our girls, like these waitresses, sometimes make more in tips on a good day than their take home pay for the entire week. Once you are groomed, you will be allowed to move out of the training house. All of our girls have apartments in the city. We pay the rent in a building we choose. You buy your own furniture and pay utilities. If you choose to leave the agency, we no longer pay the rent, of course, but if you can afford to pay the rent, you certainly will be allowed to keep the apartment, with some stipulations. We don't own the building, but we sign the lease. All of that will be spelled out in your contract. Raises are contingent on your performance. Everyone makes the same during training, but we rank our girls and the ones that receive the most offers for escort are more valuable to us and we pay them more. Any questions? I know it's a lot to take in, but I'm here to answer all your questions."

"What about the modeling? When do I get to model?" Lois asked.

"The world of modeling is a crazy business and we're not in the modeling business per se. However, we do prepare you for it. Our girls model for different companies every day. These companies are looking for girls to model clothes, underwear, gowns, and swimsuits, whatever. We have contracts with many companies and magazines. This is how our girls get recognition in the modeling world and some have gone on to make it big. Some of our girls may never become a model in that sense, but they will continue to have a job with us, as long as they want."

"It sounds really good, Mr..., I mean Rinoldo, but I can't take the job. I don't have anyone to keep my son, while I stay in the city for several weeks for training. I don't even want to be away from him that long." Lois felt disappointed. He knew she had a son, Lois thought, why would he think she could abandon him for that long and with whom.

"I'm sorry. I just didn't know the terms, had I known, I wouldn't have called you."

"Miss Johnson."

Lois' heart skipped a beat, suddenly he was being formal. Was he going to tell her off and embarrass her in the restaurant?

Before he could finish, Lois stood up, "maybe I'd better go. I apologize for wasting your time, Mr. Rinoldo."

"Miss Johnson," Rinoldo said, "please sit down."

Lois looked around and timidly sat back down. She did not want to make a scene, but she didn't want him yelling at her either.

"I was about to say," Rinoldo continued. "I don't have time to waste. I would not have asked you to lunch, if I didn't think I would hire you. Granted, I had to take a good look at you before I made my decision. That's why you arrived at the restaurant first, while I sat in my car and watch you enter, take off your coat and was seated. If I didn't like what I saw, I would've told the waiter to serve you lunch on me. I would have told him to tell you that something came up and I couldn't make it, but I would call you later, which I never would have. Concerning your son, you will be taking care of your son yourself, while you are in training. We will provide a babysitter for the times you will need one. You and your son will share an adjoining room. We make accommodations for certain situations. After you move out, you'll have to find the proper daycare for your child. I suggest one that is flexible, because you will mostly work in the afternoons and evenings."

Lois could not believe her ears. She wanted to pinch herself. Surely this was one of those dreams that seem so real that you hated having to wake up from it. Lois sat very still, not knowing what to believe. Her mind was racing with thoughts, if this is a dream, please God don't wake me up.

"When can we expect you?" Rinoldo asked.

"I got the job?" Lois asked in disbelief, but Rinoldo only smiled, "just like that."

"Just like that," Rinoldo responded.

"I don't need to give the factory any notice, and I'd just as well be out of my apartment today than tomorrow."

"Good," said Rinoldo. "I'll have someone pick you up next weekend. That should give you enough time to take care of your business. I won't be able to pick you up personally, because I'll be out of town. I'll arrange for someone to move you. Madame Reddan will be there to welcome you and I'll come by to see you, when you are all settled."

"Who is Madame Reddan? Lois looked puzzled.

"Madame Reddan is the woman who will be training you and she likes to be called Madame. She started out with the agency before my time, in search of a modeling career, but she never made it as a model and decided to stay on. When the original owner died, she left the business to Maryann Reddan, aka, Madame Reddan. You ready for lunch? I am, unless you have some more questions."

"I probably do, but I can't think of them now."

"I'll be in the city until Friday morning. Give me a call with any question you may have."

"Thanks. I think I will," said Lois, "and yes I am ready to eat."

Rinoldo smiled. "Oh, another thing, if you're prone to junk food, you'd better eat all of it before you get to the house, because Madame Reddan is very intolerable of bad eating habits, Waiter," Rinoldo call to the waiter, who was just standing around waiting to be called.

Rinoldo didn't talk anymore about the job. He questioned her about her life, her dreams, her family, and her friends. She guessed business was over for him, but Lois heart was racing at this great job she was about to take on. They were not only going to train her, but they were making accommodations for Danijel as well. Lois tried to stay focus and answer all of his questions. She even managed to ask a couple of questions concerning him, but he was very vague with his answer, always focusing back on Lois.

As Lois sat in the warmth of the luxurious gray leather seat limousine, she kept reflecting back over the things Rinoldo said to her. She had her doubts about coming today.

When he came to help Kelly moved, she thought he was a creep, but now she felt that she had misjudged him. She couldn't wait to call Kelly, or should she wait to tell her in person. She thought of all the things she had to do. She would go to work tomorrow and quit. She couldn't afford to work the entire day, because she had lots to do.

Her main thing was to pack up all of Danijel's things. She was told not to bring much of her clothing, because she probably will not need most of them after training. She was going to get an entire new wardrobe and sometimes the models got to keep the things they modeled.

Lois finally closed her eye. She was having a nice warm fuzzy feeling and she wanted to enjoy it.

"I just came in today to tell them I'm quitting. I didn't want anyone to worry about why I didn't show up for work two days in a row."

Deb looked at Lois not knowing what to think. Lois was standing in front of her with a huge grin on her face and Deb didn't know what to make of this sudden announcement.

"Quitting?" She asked.

"Yes maam," Lois said teasingly.

"What are you going to do?" Deb asked curiously.

"I'm going to be a model."

"A model?" Deb asked in disbelief.

"Yes, a model," said Lois offended at Deb's response, "what, you think I don't look good enough to be a model?"

"You can model with the best of them sweetheart. It's just that I'm somewhat surprise. You've never talked about modeling before. I didn't know you had any interest in modeling. I thought you were going to a business school."

"I didn't, but an opportunity of a lifetime has come my way and I'd be stupid not to take it, especially since someone who is in the modeling business thinks that I can make it as a model."

"When did this all come about sweetie," Deb voice took on a concern tone, but she wanted to be careful not to offend Lois.

She wanted to hear the entire story.

"Tell me all about it," Deb said just as the bell went off to start working.

It also meant every machine in the factory that was in working condition would be turned on and everyone had to be at their post ready to work, or the supervisor would make sure they were docked for every minute they weren't, even if they had already clocked in. Deb looked at her watch. It was 7:30 and the mechanic had started her machine.

"Let's talk at lunch time, okay!" Deb had to yell every word for Lois to hear her.

"I can't," Lois yelled back. "I have too much to do today. I start my new job in less than two weeks and I'm moving to the city next weekend!"

"Moving?" Deb yelled the question.

"Yes moving," Lois yelled, "you'd better get to work!"

Lois was now holding her ears. The machines in Deb's section were much louder and Lois was not use to them.

"I'll see you after work!" Deb yelled. Lois just shook her head as she left.

It was pointless talking once the machines started, but she didn't remember telling Deb she was coming over and Deb hardly ever came over to her apartment. Lois disregarded Deb's last statement.

By the time Lois finished all of her outside errands; it was time to pick up Danijel from the babysitter. She was hoping to have finish hours ago, so that she could get home and pack up some of his things before she had to get him. She wasn't planning on sending him to the babysitter the rest of the week, in order to save some money, but she thought she might have to tomorrow, so she could get some more things done.

As she was getting off the bus at her apartment building, she saw Deb waiting for her in the lobby.

"My favorite grandnephew," Deb said, as she scooped Danijel out of his stroller.

He was all smiles, with his deep dimples, as Deb kissed all over him.

Lois looked at Deb, suddenly engrossed with Danijel and wondered what it was about him; he seemed to make you forget all about your troubles. His big round black eyes twinkled as he laughed at you and now with a full mouth of baby teeth accompanied with two of the deepest dimples; his smile and laughter sucked you into his world of care freeness.

"He's getting too big to carry," said Lois to Deb, as Deb positioned Danijel in her arms.

"No, he's not," Deb said looking into Danijel big eyes, "at least not today."

When they got to the apartment, Deb took a seat with Danijel still in her hands. She sat him on her lap and began to cuddle him and talk to him. Lois went to put down his things and then she came back for him.

"Come on sweetie," she reached out her hands to him. He was reluctant to go.

"Does he have to go now?"

"Yes Deb," Lois said sternly, "its our routine. You of all people should know the importance of keeping routines."

"Yeah, if you have three children, thank God you only have one."

"I thank God for Danijel everyday," Lois said, as she reached down to pick Danijel out of Deb's arm.

Deb splattered him with bye bye kisses as he giggled.

With Danijel in his playpen, Lois began to make his dinner. "We can talk in the kitchen," yell Lois to Deb, "the sooner he eats, the sooner he sleeps and I need him to sleep as early as possible tonight. I have a lot to do."

"So you really are moving," Deb said as she got up to go to the kitchen looking at the boxes stacked up in the corner of the living room.

"Is your heat on?" Deb asked hugging herself to keep warm.

"It's on," said Lois "and that's part of the reason why I'm not thinking twice about leaving. The rat traps in the corner and the roach motels in every cupboard are some of the other reasons."

"Everyone has rats and roaches. It's New York," said Deb.

"No Deb, everyone does not. That's the problem. Everyone that lives in the projects thinks everyone does, but they don't. When I lived home we didn't have much, but there were no rats and we kept our roach problem under control. I don't want my son to be raised like this. I'm tired of freaking out every time I see him pick something up off the floor, because I think it's a roach or mice dropping." Lois was near tear before she was finished.

Deb knew she couldn't argue with that. If she had the opportunity she wouldn't stay in the projects either.

"So," Deb said, "tell me all about this new job and where you're moving to."

"You can not be serious," Deb finally said after listening to Lois' plans for about fifteen minutes with her mouth half open.

Lois looked at Deb wondering what she meant by the statement.

"That sounds so unbelievable. What job would offer something like that without a catch? If it's too good to be true, it usually is."

"It's not too good to be true. It's the same agency that Kelly is working for."

"So, Kelly got you the job?" Deb asked trying to understand this elaborate arrangement that Lois just described to her.

"No, matter of fact, I haven't even talk to Kelly about it yet. She doesn't know I had an interview with Rinoldo."

"Rinoldo?" Deb tried to register the name. "Is that the guy who help Kelly moved out?"

"Yes," Lois said.

"The creep?" asked Deb, "as you so described him."

I didn't say he was a creep. I said that he made me feel creepy, but I was wrong about him," Lois added quickly before Deb jumped on that statement.

"You should never judge someone that you don't know anything about, besides I wasn't being fair. I was just jealous because Kelly was leaving and finally realizing her dreams."

"I see," said Deb arching her eyebrows, but she didn't really see it at all.

She sensed within herself that she needed to do, or say something to stop Lois from making a big mistake. For some strange reason, Deb felt like it was going to be the biggest mistake Lois ever make, but how was she to tell her that. How was she going to get that across to her without sounding jealous, or crazy? She thought, this guy must have painted a glorious picture for Lois and she didn't know how to bring shades of gray to the picture.

"Why don't you let Dandan stay with me until the training is done and you get your own place."

"I couldn't impose on you like that, besides why would I? Dandan is going to be right there with me. I'll be taking care of him, right through the training. This is better than what we had. I couldn't ask for more than that, but thanks for offering and I'm sure Kelly will be spending time with him while I'm in training."

"Have you told your parents yet?"

"That's one of the things I plan on doing tonight. You want to stay for dinner?" Lois asked.

She didn't cook enough for someone else, but she asked knowing Deb would decline. Lois wasn't sure who the kids were with, but Deb wasn't going to let them stay there for long.

"No thanks, I told Mrs. Washington I wouldn't be long, so I better head home, before the boys gets restless and hungry."

"I'm going to try to get by there," Lois pause to think, "hopefully by Friday afternoon. I'm just moving to the city, but I don't know when I'll get to see them again, so I want to come by and let Dandan spend some time with them, if that's okay with you."

"Yes, that's fine." Deb turn to leave the kitchen and Lois followed her to the door.

Deb stopped and looked at Lois a long time. All the while praying within herself that God would suddenly give her the words to say to stop Lois from making this move, but it seemed like her tongue was tied.

Lois grabbed Deb's hand "Aunt Deb," she said using the title aunt, because she could see the concern of her mother on Deb's face, "It's going to be okay, I promise. I'll call and be in touch, but if I don't do this, I'm always going to wonder what if. There are already too many things in my life that I am wondering, what ifs about and I'm only twenty-five."

Deb squeezed Lois hands and said, "You know where I am, if you need me please don't hesitate to call. Always remember you have people that love."

"I will," said Lois with a big smile as she hugged Deb.

Stephanie's reaction to her daughter's good news was worst than Deb. She began to cry and gave the phone to Richard. Richard had tried not to meddle in Lois' life since she left on her own, but he comforted his wife many nights, even to the point of getting up with her and praying with her for Lois. He didn't know what was going on now, but it seemed to have made Stephanie very upset.

"What's going on Lois?" He asked as he placed the phone to his ears. "Is everything alright? Are you all right? What about Dandan?"

"I'm fine, Dandan's fine, aunt Deb and the Kids are fine. Mom's just overreacting."

"To what?" Richard asked trying to find out some more information, but Lois was being very vague.

"Richard, she'll tell you all about it. I can't repeat it all now. I don't want to run this phone bill up."

It wasn't the phone bill she was worried about; she just didn't want to have to explain her life to Richard.

"Okay, I'll talk to your mother and try to get her to calm down. We'll talk to you later then."

"Yeah, later," said Lois, "and Richard tell Mom I love her and that we're going to be just fine."

"I will, and we love you too." Lois paused, when Richard said "we."

She knew she was being cold to him, but she still couldn't forgive Richard whole-heartedly like her mother, after all the things that he put them through. She quietly hung up the phone without saying another word.

The Johnsons:

"Baby what's the matter?" Richard said, sitting next to Stephanie and taking her in his arms as her body shook from crying.

"I don't know." She finally stopped crying to tell him about Lois' job and the move.

"Sounds too good to be true," Richard said.

"It is," Stephanie said, "it is. I don't know what, but I know that it is."

"All we can do is pray baby," said Richard, "It's her life and she plans to do what she thinks is best for her."

"I know," said Stephanie, as she buried her face into Richard's chest and muffled another, "I know."

Lois:

Lois couldn't believe the reaction she received from her family. She knew they were going to be a little skeptical about all of it, but she never imagined this to be their response, but what really hurt Lois was Kelly's response.

Kelly practically begged her not to take the job. She accused Kelly of being jealous and afraid that she would make it big as a model before her. After all, modeling was her dream, not Lois.' Before Kelly hung up the phone, she told her that she was going to do whatever she could to get Rinoldo to withdraw his offer. Lois didn't know if to be concerned, or not. She suddenly wondered what Kelly and Rinoldo's relationship was. Rinoldo did come to help Kelly moved, whereas he was just sending someone to help her. He said that he had other plans, but now Lois wondered how much clout Kelly had with him.

She picked up the phone several times within the next two days to call him, but she finally decided not to. If he was going to take back his offer, he would have to call her.

Lois didn't get around to Deb's before she left. She called her on the phone early that Saturday morning. They always got up early for a big breakfast on Saturday. She told Danijel she was going to take him to see them, so every hour on the hour, he would get his coat and stand by the door and say, "go see Icky, Kavy."

She concluded there was something new to learn about parenting everyday and today she learned that she wouldn't tell him they were going anywhere in the future, until they were actually walking out the door. She tried to explain to him that they were not going to go again, but was going to call them on the phone and he could talk to them on the phone. When he finally understood what she was saying, he ran to the phone, picked it up and began to punch the buttons, saying "ello!, ello! Icky, Kavy."

She was so proud of him. His words grew clearer everyday and it was clear when he said, "love you too, Yannie Aab."

It was still hard for him to make his consonant sounds. Lois took the phone from him and he ran off to go search for another toy to pull out of his packed toy box, as Lois kept an eye on him.

"Did you speak to your sister?" Lois asked Deb, who responded that she had spoken to Stephanie.

"She's pretty upset. I've asked Richard to try to make her understand. There's no reason for her to be all upset about what I'm doing. Everything is going to be fine," Lois said. "I'll keep calling her. Matter of fact, I think I'll make it my business to call her at least once a week, until I feel she's comfortable knowing we're okay." Lois laughed. … "You're right Aunt Deb. The minute I stop calling, she's going to think that something is wrong. I can't win with my mom, just the same, I have to keep in touch, so she'll know that we're okay."… "Love you too."… "I will."

She hung up the phone and looked over at Danijel, who she had stopped watching for a while. He had once again managed to dump all of the toys out of the box onto the floor. She had packed that box seven times if not ten, but she just smiled at him and opened her arms and he ran into them.

"I guess I'll have to pack them one more time," she said as she gave him a big hug and tickled his stomach as she slowly laid him down on the floor while he wiggled and giggled.

The doorbell rang. She stopped tickling Danijel and looked into his eyes. He got serious, as he knew she was.

"It's time Danijel. Today is the first day of the rest of our lives and it's going to be great."

Beedeekle:
The slimy imp went around the project building thanking all the imps for helping them to move their plan to the next level.

"You should come with us and celebrate," said Drakel, the head demon of the project building.

He stood ten feet tall, fat and puffy with slime pouring off him. "There will be lots happening tonight. Two brothers will come head on with each other and one will kill the other tonight over some drug money that one tried to swindle from the other."

"Yeah we staged the whole thing," said another smelly demon that lived in the building.

The two little imps, with Beedeekle, eyes grew wide at the prospect of being in the presence of a death demon. Beedeekle stared at them motioning them to calm themselves down. They couldn't be side tracked by other demon's activities. He was learning the importance of being focus. These demons had it easy. There were many death demons assigned to this project building and all these demons had to do was set the stage and influence the mind of a few gullible humans.

They, on the other hand were dealing with something more powerful, even more powerful than the death demon. They were dealing with interceding Believers of The Most High God and there was no time to goof off.

Lois:

'The House,' as it was call, was a split-level brownstone on the East Side. The downstairs was a mixture of modern antique furniture with hardwood flooring throughout. Each room of the house was painted a different color with furniture that accented that room. Lois could see a room off to the right painted mango with a decorative lime splash, with leather sectionals that were mango and lime.

She stood in the foyer looking around not knowing where to go. The guy, who moved her, Owen, was outside taking her things off the truck. A young Mexican girl suddenly appeared from one of the rooms.

"You must be Lois," she said as she took a bag out of Lois' hand. She took her other hand and squeeze Danijel cheeks, "and you must be Danny." Lois wanted to correct the girl's pronunciation of Danijel's name, but decided not to.

"I'm Penny, the maid. I'm to show you to your room, then someone will be up to see you and show you around the house. Follow me please." Penny proceeded upstairs, as Lois followed carrying Danijel in her arms.

Danijel kept turning his head from side to side as they walked up the stairs watching the exotic and historical pictures mounted on the walls.

"This will be your room," the girl said as she stopped and held out her hands so that Lois could enter first.

Lois looked around the room, as Penny clicked on the light switch by the door. The room was a good size room, not too big and not too small. All of the furnishings were done in cherry wood. The lush shag carpet beneath her feet was rose and cream. The room was painted cream with rose borders around the mid-section of the room and at the top near the ceiling. Every painting that hung on the wall blended into the color scheme and decor of the room. Penny went through a pair of swinging doors.

"This," she said looking back at Lois "is where Danny will sleep."

Lois followed her into the adjoining room. The room was painted blue and beige. The colors of blue range from sky blue to midnight blue and it was amazing how the colors blended in one with the other as if the painter used one brush that would go from one color of blue to another with one stroke of the brush.

There were lots of toys in the room and a big toy chest. Lois opened the chest. It was empty.

"It's for his toys," Penny explained.

Lois thought, you couldn't ask for much more than that.

The room had a rocking horse, a child's rocking chair, stuffed animals and little train sets. "Did they do this just for us?" Lois asked.

"We keep a room made up just for a little girl, or boy. If you had a girl, she would be staying in the pink and Rose room. Does Danny like dogs?" Penny asked.

"I'm not sure, he's never really been around any. Why?" inquired Lois.

"Madame has a dog, a brown cocker spaniel named lady CeCe."

Lois looked at Danijel and said, "you here that Dandan, a dog," she looked at Penny and asked, "what about cats?"

"Sorry, Madame can't stand cats. Too finicky, she says."

"Oh, don't apologize," Lois, said, "I'm not partial to them myself. It's just that Danijel's babysitter had lots of them. She said she kept them away from the children, but everyday I had to wash his clothes in Lysol. There were cat's hairs all over them."

"Yuuck," said Penny frowning.

"Yeah that's what I said to," Lois said smiling at Danijel, who was pointing at the rocking horse and wanting to get down.

"Alright, but you be good, okay."

Danijel jumped down and he was true to form of child in a toy store. He did not know what toy he wanted to play with first. Finally he settled for a big stuffed bear that was almost bigger than him and began to roll over on the floor with it.

"Come, I'll help you unpack."

Lois wasn't sure she wanted to leave Danijel alone, but Penny did something with the door that made them stay open on both sides.

"See, I'll show you," she said, as she showed Lois how to make the adjoining doors stay open, "this way you can keep an eye on him whenever you want."

"Thanks," said Lois.

They had just about finished unpacking, when Penny announced that she had to go and start lunch.

"What does he eat?" Penny asked referring to Danijel.

"Not much," Lois said, "but he loves hot dog."

"Typical American child," said Penny. "I'm not Americana," Penny said, "but I think you got that from my accent. I'm Mexican." Lois nodded in acknowledgement with a smile, as Penny left the room.

Danijel had run out of energy. Lois picked him up off the floor and pried a toy out of his little fingers. He stirred and Lois sat with him in the rocking chair in his room until he was sound asleep.

Lois noticed the crib that he was going to sleep in also converted to a bed. "Convenient," said Lois as Danijel went off to sleep.

Lois was out on the balcony of her room taking in the view. She wondered what it would look like during the night. It certainly was not another brick wall like the view from her apartment in Queens. She actually could see trees and people on the ground. Far away there was a view of a river and a bridge, but she wasn't sure which river or what bridge it was. She would have to ask.

She was startled at a knock on the glass balcony door of her room. She looked around and saw a really beautiful woman waving and smiling at her to come in side.

"I'm sorry if I startled you. I knocked at the door, but I remembered Penny saying that your son might be sleeping. The door wasn't lock, so I came in to see if you were sleeping as well. Then I saw you on the balcony, so I knocked on the window to get your attention, because as you can see I don't have on a jacket. Now that I have babbled on," the woman kept talking, "let me introduce myself. I'm Lydia Amerson. Everyone calls me Lady Lydia. I ask them not to, but Madame Reddan insist that they do, so they do, and I've gotten use to it. I came to help you get ready for dinner. Everything here is training. Every meal and get together is an opportunity for training."

She walked over to the closet and started looking through some clothes.

"Here," she said taking a beige floral knee length dress out of the closet and giving it to Lois, "why don't you wear this. It's going to be a light lunch, so you should feel comfortable in this. First lesson," she said, "always remember as an escort, appearance is everything. Penny will come for you in about thirty minutes."

"What about my son?" Lois asked.

"Whatever you think is appropriate for him to wear, will be fine I'm sure."

"I'm sorry," said Lois, "I meant does he come down for lunch also?"

"Why of course, he can come down to any meal unless otherwise specified and then we will provide a babysitter for him."

Penny knocked on Lois' door exactly thirty minutes later. Lois picked up Danijel who was rubbing his red eyes. She hated to wake him up out of his nap, but she didn't want to be late, or give the impression that Danijel would be a problem.

He was a little fussy, but she managed to calm him down and get him ready, as well as herself. She was use to getting them both ready in a few minutes, especially when she woke up late in the morning after turning off the alarm for another five minutes of sleep that sometimes turned into thirty or more minutes. When Lois opened the door, she had Danijel in her arms and was ready to go.

"Follow me," Penny instructed.

They followed Penny downstairs into a room right off from the dining room. The room looked like a den, but there was no TV. There were big bookshelves built into the walls and lined with books. The furniture was traditional wood. There was no couch, but several reclining chairs. Soft music played in the background.

An eloquently looking older woman got up and walked over to Lois. Her hair was black with white streaks. She wore a two-piece well-tailored suit that said she had style. It made her size ten look like a size eight.

"Hello dear," she addressed Lois with an extended hand "I'm Madame Reddan."

She looked around at the others sitting in chairs around the room.

"You've met Lady Lydia."

As she swayed her hands slightly to each person, they rose out of their seat and greeted Lois.

"This is Sue Ann and this is Marilyn. Ladies this is Lois and her handsome son Danijel. Lois will be in training with you for this session. Welcome to Madame Reddan's school of Escort. When you leave here, you will know how to speak, eat, walk and dress like the richest of women. You may not have a dime to your name, but you will look and act like you are from royalty."

Every word she spoke was meticulous and well chosen. Her voice was a low sonant sounding voice. She wasn't loud, but she spoke with an air about herself demanding acknowledgement of every word spoken.

"Ladies," she turned, and it was a precise turn as if she counted one, two, three, turn, "let's go have lunch."

"Watch your step," Lady Lydia said to the girls.

There were three-tier half round brick steps downward that led out of the huge sitting room into a big dining area. Everything in the dining room looked antique. The table was a long oblong table that seated at least ten people, four on each side and one each at the head. The table was well decorated with everything matching in an array of wintry colors.

"Ladies please find your place card for seating."

Lois didn't need a place card to see where she was going to be seated. There was a high chair for Danijel next to her chair.

Marilyn began to pull her chair out and Lady Lydia motion her, "Remember ladies, Madame Reddan always sits first, then you may sit."

Madame Reddan did a slight bow at Lady Lydia and sat down. Everyone wasn't sure if they should wait for Lady Lydia to sit, so they stood until she sat down and then she motioned them to sit.

"Since this will not be a full course meal," Lady Lydia began to instruct, "we will begin with the fork on your left for our salad."

The entire meal was like that. Lois was so nervous that Danijel would make a mess, because he was not table trained, especially since they never ate at a table. She always ate with him sitting on the couch in the living room, while watching TV.

Danijel sat between her and Madame Reddan, who was very good with him. In between the instructions from Lady Lydia, Madame Reddan would exact information from each girl about their background.

Before they left the table, Lady Lydia announced they were having guest for dinner in the evening and she would be up to assist everyone with what they should wear.

Lois took Danijel downstairs later to make something for him to eat. She wanted him fed and in bed before she went down for dinner. She cleaned up everything she messed up and hoped no one noticed she was there.

The house was so immaculate. No little fingerprints spotting up the nice shine on the coffee table.

Lady Lydia came up while she was downstairs and laid out a dress for her. She was ready at seven forty-five and decided to go downstairs and wait in the sitting room.

She heard talking, as she approached the entrance of the room, then she heard the dog barking. Lady CeCe must be joining them for dinner Lois thought, as she laughed at the thought of a dog having a seat at the formal dinner table.

Lois paused at the entrance of the door suddenly feeling a little intimidated. From what she could see it was a room full of beautiful women and she felt out of place.

"Come Lois," said Lady Lydia, motioning to her.

"For the next three nights we will be having dinner with our Ladies from each building. This will give you an opportunity to meet each other and to meet some of the women, who will probably be your neighbors after training. Tonight we have the ladies from the Gardenia building. Mae, Starr, Francesca, meet Sue Ann, Marilyn and Lois."

The girls shook hands.

"Kelly Caldera is also in this building, but she couldn't make it tonight. She's out of town on some business."

Lois wondered if she was with Rinoldo, who was also out of town on business.

"Where is that handsome son of yours Lois?" Madame Reddan inquired of Lois.

"He's in bed for the night."

"I'm sorry to hear that. I brought Lady CeCe down to play with him."

Madame Raddan was holding Lady CeCe in her arms.

Lois walked over to Madame Reddan and rubbed her hand on the back of the dog's neck, "Hi Lady CeCe. My son is going to be excited to meet you."

"I hope so," said Madame Reddan, "it's good that you have him on a schedule. You will find that scheduling is important around here," she said as she looked around the room making sure that all the girls heard the comment.

Lois was learning that everything Madame Reddan and Lady Lydia spoke was part of their training and one had better take heed to hear what was being said.

Dinner was great. It was much better than lunch. The ladies from the Gardenia Building were very nice and helpful.

The next two nights they met the other ladies from The Rose and Pandora buildings. Lois particular liked Adrienne from the Rose building. She seemed more down to earth than the other ladies. She wasn't too pretentious. Lois hoped they would become friends.

They didn't do much the first week. They learned some basic routines, but no training seemed basic to Lois.

Danijel fell in love with Lady CeCe. It was too much for him to call her Lady CeCe, so Madame Reddan allowed him to call her just CeCe, which Lois started to call him also, so Danijel wouldn't get confuse.

At the end of the week, Lois called her mother. Stephanie was still pretty upset, but was glad Lois agreed to call her once a week during the training. When she got her own apartment, she would give them her new number, so they could call her whenever they wanted to.

Rinoldo did come by to see her on Tuesday, but she still hadn't heard from Kelly.

A couple of nights into the next week, they had another dinner guest. It was Kelly.

It was awkward for both of them. Rinoldo came with her. They acknowledge to the others Kelly and Lois' relationship. It was also told that Kelly was given a promotion in the agency. She was accepting escort appointments out of state. Only a couple of the girls were allowed that privilege. They were thinking of starting an agency in Los Angeles and they were considering Kelly to head it up. Her job would be identical to Lady Lydia, who trained and only escorted customers who had at least seven digit numbers behind their names.

"I'm so happy for you," Lois said to Kelly later when they were in the sitting room and she was finally able to talk to her alone.

Although it seemed like it was arranged that way.

"Thank you," Kelly replied, "but if you're wondering if I talked to Rinoldo about withdrawing his offer, I did. He didn't listen to me. He believes you will be an asset to the Agency, but Lois, this is wrong for you and Danijel," Kelly began to speak in a low whisper with a voice of urgency. "You don't want to be here. You don't want to commit to this. If you don't get out now, you won't be able to."

"Kelly please," Lois slightly raised her hand to stop Kelly from going on, "I'm here, and I'm staying. This is an opportunity of a lifetime and I'm not going to let it pass me by. I promised Danijel a better life and I aim to keep that promise."

"Maybe Danijel only wants your love," Kelly pleaded.

"I'm sure he does, but he's going to need more. Just be happy for me Kelly, like I am for you."

Kelly gave up feeling a little helpless. She knew Lois was sold and there was nothing she could say to discourage her enough to make her pack up and leave.

Kelly hugged Lois and said, "Don't lose hold of the morals that you came here with Lois."

"Kelly, I had a baby outside of marriage. I've already broken moral codes."

"You made a mistake, Lois. Everyone does. You don't have to ruin your entire life because of one mistake, remember that."

"I'm doing what you're doing Kelly. How is that ruining my life?" Lois asked sensing there was more that Kelly wanted to tell her.

When training was over, Lois moved into the Gardenia building with Mae, Starr, Francesca and Kelly. Kelly and Lois' strained relationship got better. Kelly began to love the idea that she could visit Danijel, as often as she wished.

Every time Lois saw them together; she knew Kelly regretted the abortion she had. Kelly loved being around her family and Lois and Danijel had become a part of her family. Lois hoped that one day Kelly would have a family of her own.

During training, they did runway practices, but nothing prepared Lois for her first real modeling job. Everyone was in the dressing room. There were professional people helping them with their make-up, their hair and to help with the changing of outfits. Madame Reddan and Lady Lydia were not there, but Rinoldo showed up.

Adrienne came just in time to put on her first outfit.

"Your hair looks really great," Lois complimented.

"I know," Adrienne replied.

Lois was too nervous to smile or care whether or not Adrienne was being conceited.

"Lighten up girl," Adrienne said to Lois. "Look," Adrienne said, "take a deep breath and let it out."

Lois took a few deep breaths and then shook herself.

"A little better?" Adrienne asked.

"A little."

"Remember to give eye contact, but choose the good-looking guys. You don't want to get stuck with some old cigar smoking mafia grandfather."

"What?" Lois asked puzzled and then she and Adrienne burst out into laughter.

"You're kidding right?" Lois asked.

"Not really." Adrienne pulled back the curtain and peeked out. She looked through the audience for a few seconds then pulled Lois over.

"See, there," she said "the one with the light gray wool suit. He's cute enough, or that one over there."

"Where?" asked Lois.

"There, with the three piece, pin-stripe, black and white suit."

They shut the curtain.

"I just want to get on the stage and off."

"No sweetie," said Adrienne. "You want to get customers, if you don't, you don't get paid. I mean really paid. I'm up," said Adrienne as she heard her name being called out.

"You did well. Was this your first?" Francesca asked Lois.

"Well, we did some during training and a couple after training, but nothing this big."

"Everything before this was training sweetie." Adrienne said, "but Francesca is right, you did good."

"Now what?" Lois asked.

"Now we go back to the office and see if there is any one requesting our presence for the night, if not, our time is our own," said Adrienne, "want a ride?"

"I don't want to put you out of your way," Lois said.

"Believe me if it was out of my way, I wouldn't ask."

"In that case, I certainly would like a ride," Francesca said.

"I wasn't offering you," Adrienne said.

"Doesn't matter," said Francesca "I just saved you the trouble of asking."

Adrienne shook her head and the two girls laughed.

Francesca and Adrienne could actually go for sisters. They were both tall and beautiful with almost the same light chocolate cream complexion and black hair. Adrienne was African American and Francesca was Italian.

Adrienne drove a black two door, stick shift Ferrari, with leather interior.

"Be careful with that umbrella. Try putting it down before you get into the car," Francesca said to Lois as she was getting in the car.

It had started to rain and she was trying to close the umbrella and get into the car simultaneously without getting wet.

"Adrienne doesn't love anything more than she loves this car."

"That's right," said Adrienne, "so Francesca if you know that, then you should know to take your filthy shoes off and stick them in your pocket or purse or something."

"Yeah right," said Francesca.

Lois stood, back up out of the car and let the umbrella down, getting herself wet, while Adrienne and Francesca giggled under their breath at her. Before Lois got into the car, she began to take off her shoes.

"Girl, what are you doing?" ask Adrienne while Francesca began to laugh aloud. Lois looked at her puzzled. "Get in the car and close the door. You're letting the rain in. Don't pay any attention to us. Francesca and I are at it like this all the time" Adrienne said to Lois.

"Yeah she's right," said Francesca, "but Adrienne really loves this car, and probably wants us to take our shoes off."

"If I wanted you too," Adrienne said as she put the car in first, "I would have made you."

"Oooo, scared of you," Francesca said as Adrienne sped off.

Some of the other girls were already back at the office.

"Adrienne took the scenic route again?" One of the girls yelled.

Everyone laughed.

"Ha, ha," said Adrienne smiling.

Lois followed her as she walked up to the desk and asked, "anything for us, Joe?"

Joe, short for Josephine was the Agency Girl Friday. She gave out escorting appointments and paychecks.

"You know you do," said Joe.

"Same?" asked Adrienne.

"Same," replied Joe, "but I don't have them prepared yet, so if you guys can wait around for a few, I'll have them for you."

Lois was nervous as she opened her envelope. It was a formal invitation and it read: "You are cordially invited to attend the Opera for the viewing of the Pirates of Penzance. It gave the time, date, and where she would be picked up. Mr. Harry Garrett will escort you.

"It's so formal." Lois said.

"Oh, that's Joe's idea, before she came it was written on a card and placed in our box. Now it doesn't matter if we're invited to a ball game, Joe types up all the invitation in a formal manner," said Adrienne.

"It's a nice touch," said Francesca, "we like it."

"You like it," said Adrienne, "I frankly don't care how I get my assignments, as long as I get them."

"Where are you going, and with whom?" Kelly asked Lois, as she came from out of one of the offices.

"The opera with Mr. Harry Garrett," Lois said, reading the name again.

Kelly looked at Joe, who just shook her shoulder.

"He insisted," said Joe.

"What?" said Lois.

"You know him?" Kelly just shook her shoulder.

"We all know Mr. Garrett," said Adrienne, "he has lots of hands, but he knows to be nice to all his first time escorts."

The latter part of her sentence was for Kelly more than Lois.

"I know," Kelly said, "still," she said as she walked off.

She turned around and asked, "when is it?"

"When is what?" Lois asked.

"When are you going to the Opera?"

"Oh," Lois said looking at her invitation again. "Tomorrow at seven."

"Great! You and Dandan want to come over tonight for dinner?" As Lois was thinking about it Kelly added, "it's spaghetti."

"Then you know we will be there," said Lois.

Danijel loved spaghetti; especially the way Kelly cooked it.

"Hey what about us?" Asked Adrienne.

"If you're free tonight, you're invited."

"I'm not," said Francesca.

"Your lost," said Adrienne matter of fact.

"That's so cold," Francesca said as she shook her head.

"You got the numbers to get in touch with me, if you need to, right?" Lois asked Alexis the babysitter. Alexis babysat for Lois at the House during Lois' training, so she knew Lois was a little overprotective, but she had been babysitting for a while and she was concerned when the parents weren't a little overprotective.

"I got the numbers. I got the emergency number at the House, if I can't reach you. I know how to dial 911. I know the number to the fire department and the child protection agency."

"What?" Lois asked looking at Alexis suddenly.

Alexis began to laugh.

"Funny," said Lois, "you can't be too careful you know."

"No you can't," said Alexis, "but you have everything covered."

Lois went over to Danijel who was playing with one of his favorite toys and picked him up, "you are getting too big for me to pick up. You be good for Miss Alexis, okay."

"Kay mommy," said Danijel looking into Lois eyes with his big mooneyes, "you look pretty mommy," he said.

"Oooh, and you are such a sweetheart," said Lois as she planted a big kiss on his puffy pinchable little cheek.

"You got everything right?" She turned once again to Alexis while putting Danijel down.

"Yep, I have your aunt's number in the Bronx, your mother's number in…"

"Okay, Okay," Lois said, "I guess you got it."

"Yes I do," said Alexis.

As Lois picked up her purse and headed for the door, Alexis said, "Dandan is right, you sure do look good. Enjoy."

Lois really enjoyed the opera. They went out for a late dinner afterwards, and she managed to sip on one glass of wine through the meal. She didn't want to be lightheaded on her first job, so she kept her drink to one.

Despite Kelly's concern, Mr. Garrett, who wanted to be call Harry was very nice. He was old enough to be Lois's father, so Lois just thought of it as a date with her father. She could envision spending a night like this with her father, if she knew him. Mr. Garrett politely asked Lois to his hotel room for a nightcap and when Lois declined politely, he just said, "next time then."

Next time with Mr. Garrett never came. Peter Long, a self made billionaire met Lois one night at a banquet where she was escorting Christopher Madison, and was totally fixated with her.

Mr. Madison, who really liked Lois, was disappointed when he was told at the escort service that Lois' calendar was already booked through the month.

Peter Long was in town on a big corporate takeover deal. He had told the Agency that he was going to be in the city for an indefinite period of time and wanted to be escorted by Miss Johnson only.

Lois got a lot of cold shoulders from a lot of the girls, even Adrienne, who finally came around and said, "All's fair in love and war. I got a Ferrari out of him. All paid up. Have fun. He knows how to treat a woman and when he likes you, he likes you and doesn't have any problem showering you with gifts and money and he's one of the few agency clients that's not married, so there's no guilty feeling, you know." Lois shook her head, but she really didn't know.

"Is that why the girls are all giving me the cold shoulders? Have all the girls been his escort?"

"Most of them have," said Adrienne, "and the others wish. A lot of the girls have broken friendship because of him. They believe their friends flirted with Peter, until Peter dropped them, but that's not how it is. Peter doesn't work like that. He simply got bored and move on, period. Anyway, you'll like him."

And Lois did. There wasn't anything to dislike about Peter. He wasn't that good looking, but he must have gone to charm school to make up in manners for what he didn't have in looks. He was ever so attentive. He treated her like she mattered, sometimes placing what she said above what his colleagues had to say at the time.

Before each date, he presented Lois with expensive outfits that had to be taken back after she worn most of them, but if he really liked her in one, she got to keep it.

Lois was busy with him night and day. She even had her picture taken with him, which appeared in the society section of the paper the next day with the caption, "Texas Billionaire Tycoon back in town to swallow up million dollar conglomerate with beautiful model at his side."

"Beautiful model," Lois said to Dandan while trying to read the paper and eat breakfast at the same time.

Francesca had rung her doorbell earlier to give her the paper as she was headed out the door.

"They are calling mommy a beautiful model."

"Mommy beauful," Danijel said.

"Thank you sweetheart," Lois said leaning over to kiss him, who said it again and gave Lois his other little cheek to kiss.

"You little stinker," Lois said kissing him again, "who taught you how to get kisses from women."

"Lexy, kiss two time all time," Danijel said.

"Alexis, huh, I'll have to talk to her about that," she said as she pinched both his cheeks and tickled his stomach, until he began to giggle and swarm around in his chair.

"Okay, enough, before you choke on your food."

They settled down and finished their breakfast, as Lois thought that she might cut the article out and frame it or something.

"So what do you want to do today Dandan?" Lois asked an excited Danijel.

He was excited because his mother was going to spend the day with him. Lois had not spent an entire day with Danijel in months. Her schedule with the agency was keeping her busy. Since Peter had become her number one customer, she was spending most of her time with him. When she went by the office Friday after her lunch date with Peter, Joe said that she had nothing plan for Saturday and an invite for Sunday evening.

"What about furniture shopping? We sure need some furniture sweetheart."

Lois found out quickly why the agency paid the rent on their apartments. For one, they wanted them in the city, because they got lots of last minute request from clients.

Lois once went out with a guy who was nominated for an award. His long time girlfriend called it quits the night of the event and he needed an escort.

"Of all nights," he complained all the way to the affair, "she broke up with me tonight over something stupid. This is one of the most important, if not the biggest event of my career and she breaks up with me, go figure."

Lois just sat quietly and listened. It was her worst job to date. No wonder his girlfriend broke up with him. All he did was talked about himself.

The agency didn't pay enough for them to afford to live in the city. The utilities took up most of Lois' check and the rest went to daycare and babysitters for Danijel, but since she was seeing a lot of Peter, her paycheck had tripled, because of his tips.

She didn't want to spend it all, because she knew Peter had to go back to Texas someday, so she wanted to keep a little savings for when that happen, but today she felt like going to look at some furniture, at least look.

The other girl's apartments were furnished so lavishly, she wouldn't dare buy any old thing, so she decided to buy one, or two things at a time, until she had the apartment furnished the way she wanted it.

"The dor, the dor mommy," Danijel yelled while shaking Lois. Lois had turned the television on in the living room for Danijel to watch cartoon and she fell asleep.

She awoke to Danijel's yelling and pointing at the door.

"The door?" she asked him groggily.

He just shook his head while pointing at the door.

"Who is it?" Lois asked. She wasn't expecting anyone and none of the girls knew that she was off today.

She peeked through the peephole and saw Peter standing in front of her door with roses in his hand. "One minute, please," she said.

She looked around the room and then down at herself and pulled her robe tightly and tied it.

"Peter," she said as she opened the door a little, "what are you doing here?"

"Did I wake you?" he asked, "It's ten o'clock. I thought you would be up. I didn't take you for a late sleeper."

"Well, I am," said Lois, "however I was up with my son."

"Son?" said Peter as he pushed his way into the apartment uninvited. Lois didn't know what to do.

"I didn't know that you had a son."

"And I didn't know the Agency gave out our addresses," Lois said a little sarcastic.

"They don't," said Peter, "but that never stopped me from finding out information before. Hey there little fellow," he said to Danijel, who ran to Lois and wrapped his face in her robe. "Shy now, is he?"

"Actually, he isn't," said Lois, "but he is a little leery of people he meets for the first time, especially those who barge in on you unannounced at ten o'clock on a Saturday morning."

Peter just laughed and said, "Are you offended? Here," he said giving her the roses, "these, little Lady, are for you."

Lois reluctantly took the flowers, smelled them and laid them on the kitchen counter.

"I would ask you to sit, but as you can see there is no chair," Lois said unapologetic.

"Where do you sit? Do you have one of those little chair as well?" Peter asked pointing at Danijel beanbag chair that Kelly gave him to sit and watch TV on.

"No, I don't." Lois was getting tired of Peter's questions.

"I'm sorry Mr. Long. I don't mean to be disrespectful, but…"

"but you are annoyed with me," Peter said. "I'm sorry. I would have called, but I didn't know your number."

Lois wasn't buying that, "you could find out my address, but not my telephone number."

"Touché," said Peter. "I didn't want to risk being told no. You see, I found myself in a sort of a predicament. I thought I was tired and needed a day to rest, but with this deal accelerating, my mind is racing with all the things that I need to do. I got up and started to write them down, but the more I wrote them down, the more information kept bombarding my mind," Peter said holding his head, "so, I realized I needed a diversion. I called the Agency to arrange something for us, but they said you had other plans for the day. What were your plans?"

Now Lois was really upset and she annoyingly responded, "My plans are, Mr. Long, is to spend the day with my son."

"Can I tag along?" he asked.

Lois just looked at him and looked down at Danijel, who seemed somewhat frightened of Peter and said, "I don't think that's a good idea."

"I tell you what," said Peter, "why don't you go and get dress and leave me with the little one. What's his name?"

"Danijel, we call him Dandan," Lois said.

"Dandan," Peter said looking around the room and finding one of his hot wheel toys on the floor.

Peter took off his jacket and threw it on the floor. He picked up the toy and looked around the room again. He walked over to the kitchen and kneeled down on the tile floor. He began to make revving up sound with the hot wheels and then he let it go crashing into the refrigerator.

"Oh my God, call 911," he began to say, "there's been a crash and I think people are hurt."

Danijel began to laugh and before Lois knew what was happening, Danijel ran over to the phone and picked it up and began to say, "911, peeple hurt, come fast."

Peter looked up at Lois and said, "we'll be playing while you get dress."

"I have to dress him too."

"Throw his clothes out, I'll be glad to help him put on his duds."

Lois was a little skeptical and still a little annoyed, but seeing Danijel warm up to Peter was putting her at ease.

"Okay," said Lois, "but we're only going to do what he wants to do today, got it," she said. It was a statement, not a question.

"I can live with that. And what do you want to do little Dandan?"

Lois heard him asking Danijel, as she went into her room to dress. She heard Danijel responded but she wasn't sure what he said.

When she came out of the room, Danijel was dress and ready to go.

"Good job," she said to Peter. "Do you have children?"

"I don't and I don't plan to, but I enjoy others bundle of joy," he said.

Lois wondered why a self-made billionaire didn't want children to pass on his inheritance. She would have to ask him that one day.

"You ready?" Peter was asking her.

Lois looked at him and wanted to remind him of their deal for the day, but before she could, he looked over to Danijel and said, "so where are we going first sport?"

"Buy furnsure," he said. Peter looked puzzled. He wasn't sure he understood Danijel.

"Did he say, buy furniture?"

Lois was a little embarrassed.

"Uh, yeah, that's what I said we would do today, but it can wait."

She looked at Danijel and stooped down to put on his jacket and asked him, "Dandan, what do you want to do? Go to the zoo? The museum? McDonalds?"

"Buy furnsure," Danijel repeated louder as if they didn't hear him the first time.

"Then it's buying furniture we go." Peter said.

"I'm sorry," Lois said wondering why she was apologizing to someone who had barged in on her and Danijel's day.

"Oh, that's quite alright," he said, "this should be fun. We'll take my car, if that's alright with you two?"

"Let me see," Lois said placing her finger to her head, "the bus? The train? or Mr. Long's nice comfortable limousine?" She said looking at Peter sarcastically.

"The Limousine it is," said Peter.

"I think I speak for Dandan and myself when I say," she pauses as if on a game show and said, "the Limousine!" Peter laughed at her silly little game as they walked out the door.

Peter took charge of the day. Their first stop was to the most expensive furniture store, Lois thought, in the city. They had a few pieces of furniture in their showcase that was on sale, but you had to order out of a book. The salesperson knew Peter right off.

"We usually come to your house and help you choose the right pieces from our catalog to fit your home style, but with a little description from you, I'm sure we'll help you choose pieces that you will enjoy for a long time, if not a lifetime," the woman stated.

"Actually, I'm just looking," Lois said nervously. She didn't even want to hint that she might be interested in anything in the store, because she couldn't afford it.

"Don't be silly," Peter said, "you're sitting on a bean bag on the floor. You need furniture. We might as well look and see what they have to offer. You might be interested."

Peter didn't intend on spending the entire day going from store to store. This was the reason he bought Lois to the store where they knew him. He knew they would make sure she got everything she needed and some.

Lois felt embarrassed. She didn't want to say she couldn't afford to shop in the store, so she went along with Peter and the woman. Soon she was caught up in her own fantasy and decided to pick some things out that would look really nice in her apartment.

They were almost finished when Peter and the woman stepped off and talked amongst themselves, while she and Danijel looked at furniture for his room.

"We can have your things delivered in a week Miss Johnson," the woman said.

Lois suddenly came back to reality and said, "Oh no, I'm not through looking yet. I want to go to some other stores, before I make my final decisions."

"Nonsense," Peter said, "deliver everything next week and put it on my account."

"There's no way I can let you do this Peter."

Peter looked at her puzzled, "you're not letting me do anything. I want to do this."

Lois began to protest some more, but the saleswoman leaned over to her and said, "you're not going to win."

Lois was furious, but she didn't want to argue with Peter in the store, or in front of Danijel, especially since he seemed to like Peter. She decided she would just send everything back when it came. There was a sign in the store that said, "no sale is final, until customer is completely satisfied."

Peter picked Danijel up in his arms and had him choose the furniture he liked for his room. Lois wanted to insist that he not buy everything Danijel picked out, since he was only two and a half years old and didn't really know what he liked, but it was pointless to try to reason with Peter. She would just send it all back.

After the furniture store, they went to the Museum of Natural History and Danijel loved seeing the huge life-liked animals. Lois just hoped that he didn't have nightmares later from the stories Peter was telling him about how they killed the animals and what the animals use to do to people. Lois was almost frightened by some of his story. It seemed Peter had a very vivid imagination. Lois guessed that was probably why he was a billionaire.

They decided not to go to the zoo, since it was a getting late and a bit colder. They took Danijel to McDonald and watched as he played in the inside play area.

"Are you ever going to get marry and have kids?" Lois asked.

"Marry?" He thought about it for a while and then replied, "maybe I'll try it one day, but children, no."

"Why not?" Lois asked, "you seem so great with Dandan."

Peter smiled at Lois. "I don't intend to bring any children into the world, so they can inherit what I've built and then waste it away, because they didn't work hard for it."

"That seems selfish to me," Lois said, "suppose your wife wanted to have children."

"My wife will know before we get marry that I can't have children and if that's her heart's desire then she'd be better off finding some other poor sucker to fill that need."

"How do you know that you can't?" Lois asked.

"Because I had a nice little operation and if I do, I'm going to own the doctor that perform the operation."

"Would you marry a woman that already has children?"

Lois wanted to take the question back the moment the words came out of her mouth. She thought surely he would think she was fishing.

"I don't know," Peter said, "I honestly have never thought about it."

He looked at Lois to see if she was going to try to get him to think about it now, but Lois was already kicking herself for asking the question in the first place, so she went silent, sipping her milk shake while watching Danijel play.

"Is the interrogation over?" he asked.

Lois looked at him annoyed, "I'm sorry you felt like I was interrogating you, I just wanted to know more about you, that's all," Lois said a little offended.

"You're offended easily," Peter said.

"Not really," Lois said in her defense.

Peter wasn't going to argue with her about it.

"If you want to know me, then ask me about me, my work, how I became a billionaire."

"Tell me about you," Lois said quite intrigue that he would even consider volunteering any information.

One of their lessons was to never ask a client about his business and very little about his personal life, unless he wanted to share it and share Peter did.

Lois left McDonald feeling like she knew Peter a little better. No wonder the girls hated her right now. Peter Long was quite an interesting man to know and to be with.

By the time they got home that evening, Peter was carrying a sleepy Danijel in his arms up to their apartment on the fifth floor. Lois was dragging behind tired and exhausted. Peter seemed to still have more energy to go the rest of the night, which he was trying to convince Lois to do; to call a baby sitter and join him for a late dinner.

Lois was so tired she felt she could fall on top of her bed and sleep the rest of the night. She reminded Peter of their date the next day. She thought he was still going to try to convince her to go out with him, but surprisingly he didn't. He took Danijel to his room took off his coat and shoes and even pulled his clothe off, so that he was lying comfortably in his tee shirt and underpants.

He pulled the cover over Danijel and kissed Danijel on his forehead and said, "goodnight little Dandan. It was nice being with you today. You kept my mind off of business. I don't think I've ever met anyone who could do that." Lois stood in the door smiling.

It melted her heart seeing his care of her child. It made Lois sad to think that he would never have any of his own, but that's what he wanted.

Peter walked back to Lois and kissed her on the forehead and said, "goodnight, don't let the bed bugs bite and I'll see you tomorrow."

He opened the door and left. Lois was a little sad that the day with him had ended, but glad that she could now do what she was feeling. She took off most of her clothes, got under the comforter and slept more soundly than Danijel.

By the end of the following week, Lois had an apartment filled with beautiful, expensive furniture and the store person was right. She couldn't get the deliverers to take anything back. She didn't even remember ordering some of the things that was delivered.

"Furnsure! Furnsure!" Danijel jumped up and down on the couch with delight.

Peter's business was coming to a close and Lois began to feel the distance between them. She told herself that it was just because he was so occupied with the takeover, especially since it was almost finished. He was working in the adjoining room to the bedroom in his hotel suite. It was early in the morning and Lois regretted once again not going home to Danijel.

She had called him as soon as she awoke, but Alexis said that he was still sleeping. She promised to call back later. She picked up the phone and order their usual for breakfast.

There was an envelope next to the bed with her name on it. She was getting use to Peter leaving her little gifts lying on the night stand every time she spent the night over, earrings, necklace, but never a ring, not even a friendship ring. She smiled thinking they had time.

She opened the envelope and inside was money. She took it out of the envelope and flip through it. It was all one hundred dollar bills. She put the money back into the envelope and placed it back on the table.

The bellhop came with their breakfast. Lois wrapped her robe around her and opened the door. Peter gave her authorization to sign the tickets and tip the bellhops, so he wouldn't have to be bothered with that.

She poured two glasses of orange juice and was about to take it in to him, when he suddenly appeared all dress in his business suit, briefcase in his hand and ready to go.

"You're going to work now?" Lois asked.

"Yes, I have to wrap things up this morning," Peter said, "I have a two o'clock plane to catch. I need to be back in Texas by dusk."

"When will you be back?" Lois asked.

"I won't be back in these neck of the woods for sometime, if I can help it," Peter said.

Lois was puzzled. "I don't understand." Peter grabbed her in his arms and sat down with her on his lap.

"Let me see if I can explain it to you. I really had a good time being with you. I was hoping to leave before you woke up and leave a message for you with your agency, because I don't like goodbyes. I wanted to get you something really nice, but things got rushed and the best I could do was to leave you some money, that way you can buy whatever you want and something for little Dandan."

"What about Danijel?" Lois asked, "are you not even going to say goodbye to him?"

Lois loosened Peter's arms from around her, and stood looking down at him.

Peter stood up and his six foot three inches Texan frame towered over her.

"This is why I don't like goodbyes," said Peter, "they get too emotional and messy."

"Emotional and messy?" Lois asked dismayed. "You come into me and my son's life and you just walk out like that and…and… leave money behind like I was some kind of prostitute."

Peter cup Lois' face in his hand and raised it so that she was looking in his eyes, "You are Lois, a very expensive one and one that I have enjoyed very much and if you don't make a fuss now, maybe when I'm back in town, we can get together."

"Oh, thank you very much, Mr. Long," Lois began very sarcastically, "I'm glad that I was of good service to you. I am much obliged to you. My son and I are so happy to have met your acquaintances," Lois said as she bowed on her knees in front of Peter.

"Stop it!" Peter demanded, as he yanked Lois up off of her knees. "I've never treated you like that and you know it. Don't try to make me responsible for your son. I'm not the one that knocked you up and went off and left the kid without a father. What did you think we were doing here? Rehearsing for our life together? It's over. I don't need any emotional ties. This is why I got a vasectomy. I travel a lot and meet a lot of wide eye girls like you, looking for the catch of the day, or at least hoping to make the catch of the day pay for something stupid the rest of his life."

"My son is not something stupid," Lois was openly crying now.

Peter looked down at his watch, realizing he needed to go.

"Lois, I left five grand for your kid and ten for you. Take it and do something good with it, but here is a bit of advice. If you're looking for a lifetime mate, you're in the wrong business kiddo." He leaned over and kissed Lois on the forehead and said, "I'm sorry it had to end like this. I really liked you and your kid. You can stay here until you get yourself together, but the hotel services will be here to pack my things and send them to the airport."

Peter picked up his hat, put his hand on the doorknob, looked at Lois and said, "Have a good life Kid," and he was gone.

Lois took the money and flung it across the room and then she threw herself across the bed and cried. She cried for almost thirty minutes, when she got up and looked into the mirror her eyes were red and puffy and white from wiping them with tissue. She sat on the bed and began to slowly get dressed.

She was walking out the door when she looked over into the corner and saw the money that she had thrown in the corner. She walked over and picked it up and said, "I deserve every penny." She straightened up herself, held her head up and walked out of the room.

Lois began to give Adrienne, Kelly and Francesca the cold shoulder. She was always too busy to hang out, or was just about to leave when one of them wanted to come over.

She found an unlikely ally in Starr Beroire. The girls asked Starr to try to talk to her, befriend her, but every time Starr tried she would brush her off.

One evening Starr invited herself over and Lois let her guard down. She really wanted someone to talk to, but not one of her friends. She bore her soul to Starr, who told her that she would get her something that would take the edge off.

"Here," Star said to Lois looking around to make sure that no one saw her.

"When you're with a customer, just take one of these. This will make everything null and void."

"Is it drugs?" Lois asked, "because if it is, I'm not interested."

"It's not addictive," said Starr, "it just help you forget who you're with and why you are with them. In about thirty minutes it's over and so is everything else," Starr said smiling, "if you get my drift."

"I don't know," said Lois, "if we get caught taking drugs, we're out of here."

"I see you read the manual," Starr smiled, "that manual says a lot of things, that fictitious. Here just try one. If it's not for you, then fine, nothing lost. You certainly can't get addictive by taking just one."

Lois took the pill from Starr and put it in her purse. She would never use it, she told herself. She would just let Starr think she did and then she would never ask for another. She would simply tell Starr it didn't work for her.

Lois looked around the room to get a grasp of where she was. The room spun for a while, but she soon was able to focus.

She saw Christopher Madison getting dress and talking to her. All of a sudden she began to laugh. Starr was right she didn't remember anything. For some reason, Lois thought that was the funniest thing. What a trick to play on a trick, she thought as she began to laugh again at her choice of words. She rolled over on her side and began to laugh until tears came to her eyes.

"I know the girls have thought a lot of things of me Miss Johnson, but never funny."

Lois was holding her stomach as she said, "I'm sorry," but she couldn't make herself stop laughing.

"Maybe it's the side affects of the drugs you're taking." Lois stopped laughing, as his words registered. She got up and became sober.

"I truly am sorry, Mr. Madison."

"It's okay Lois, but you should be careful of what you're taking. Some of these street drugs can do you much harm."

"I'm not on drugs," Lois said.

Christopher Madison was just getting to know Lois before Peter Long came along. He remembered Lois as a picture of sweet innocence. He knew that after Peter she would probably become cold and unfeeling and he was right, but he still wanted to be with her. He was infatuated with her. He was not Peter Long, but he could make Lois happy.

Christopher Madison was a millionaire. He inherited it all from his father who died young. Peter Long couldn't stand the likes of

Christopher Madison, because he was the very image of what Peter wanted to avoid. A son inheriting his father's wealth only to waste it away and waste away was all Chris Madison knew to do.

He spent a lot of his time working out in the gym and had a good physique to show for it. He was what women wanted in a man, someone who was tall, dark and handsome, if he was tall, or handsome. He was almost a little shorter than Lois. He wasn't handsome, but he wasn't ugly either. He was just an average kind of guy.

"If you give me a chance Lois, I can make you forget about Peter Long."

Lois sat on the edge of the bed puffing on a cigarette and looking at Chris, whom she thought was worthless. She snuffed out the cigarette and asked him, "you got the stuff, because I'm not doing anything if you don't have nothing."

"For once Lois, can't you be with me in your right mind. I want you to enjoy our time together, not try to snuff it out with drugs."

Lois looked at him, got up and snatched a bag that he had placed on the table and went into the bathroom. When she came out, she was in another world.

Beedeekle:
The green-eyed imp looked at his other two companions and with delight for the first time said, "We got her! We got her! One down, one to go, and go we shall, back to Atlanta."

The three imps took off and minutes later they were in Atlanta to make havoc in someone else' life.

Chapter Twenty-One
Jewel

Jewel pulled the letter out of her mailbox. It was the letter she was waiting for from her counselor, Professor Saunders. She ran up to her room and threw her books on the bed, ripped open the envelope and sat at her desk to read it. It read:

Dear Miss Stone:

After reviewing your request, I propose that you pursue a more pliant course of the law. I recommend business law. Your knowledge, understanding and sense of detail of the law will be a great asset in your success as a lawyer. I know of many organizations that would profit greatly from having an individual like yourself on staff as a resident lawyer, however, I do not recommend that you pursue a career in criminal litigation, because you are too timid of the law. To be a good litigator one must possess an edge and you do not have this quality. You are a very bright student and will probably graduate as one of the top law student of your class. I would hate to see you burn yourself out by trying to become something that you neither have the talent or nerves to do.

I wish you much success in your pursuit of a law field that is correct for you. I think based upon my assessment; you will make the wise and necessary choice.

Sincerely, Professor Saunders.

Jewel sat shell shocked at her desk after reading professor Saunder's letter. She neatly folded the letter into more parts than it was originally folded, as she sat staring at the walls of her room.

She tried recalling her actions and participation in his class that would make him come to such an assessment of her. He always complimented her on her assignments. The other students considered her the teacher's pet. Some of the students even said to her that she could probably write her on ticket where he was concern. He was over the criminal law curriculum at the school. Jewel had always wanted to be in criminal law. A trial lawyer was her dream. She couldn't imagine herself going to a nine to five job everyday giving heads of corporations, who made more than her, advice on legal matters. She began law school with her focus on criminal law, but was advised to be versatile and to take courses in all aspect of the law, before making her decision as to which field of law would be best for her.

She couldn't think of what would make him come to such a conclusion. She wondered if she would ever know, as she continued to stare at the bare walls thinking of what she would do now.

"Hi babe," Brad said as he freely came into her room unannounced.

"You should knock," she said to him after he leaned down to kiss her on the lips.

"Sorry, I thought we had an understanding," Brad said staring at the disappointment in her eyes and hoping it was not because of him, "I thought if the door is open, I can come in. If it isn't, I knock."

Jewel got up and went to her kitchenette. Brad followed her and put his arms around her waist.

"You all right babe?" he whispered the question in her ears.

She pulled away, "I'm just fine. I just had a reality check." Brad stood listening. "I just receive my recommendation from Professor Saunders and he has assessed that I am a wimp and should pursue a career in law that will keep me out of court."

Brad laughed, "you're kidding. Professor Saunders is one of your favorite professors and you're probably one of his best, if not favorite, student."

"Now there lies the irony," Jewel said, mimicking Professor Saunders, "here is a bright young law student full of ambition and very smart. Will probably be one of the top law students of her class. I, personally like her, but she has this one flaw, you see; she is a wimp. A total idiot who wouldn't know her way into court let alone around the court system."

"Come on Jewel," Brad said reaching out to her, as tears began to fill her eyes.

When Brad touched her, she jerked back and wiped her eyes with the back of her sleeves and then looked up at Brad and asked, "Why are you here?"

Brad didn't know that he had to have a reason. He never did before.

"One, I wanted to see you, and two, I wanted to know if you wanted to go and hang out with the guys before everyone head home for the holidays."

"No, I don't feel like doing anything right now and I really don't feel like going to your parents for the holiday either." Brad was suddenly taken back.

It took him awhile to convince her to come home with him for the holidays, especially since it involved staying over.

Brad came over and sat next to Jewel on the bed and placed his arms around her, "I understand you not wanting to hang out with the guys, but…"

"I will not be good company for the holidays, Brad," Jewel cut in, "I just want to be alone."

"Okay, so we'll just find a nice restaurant here and spend some quality time together."

"I want to be alone Brad, by myself."

"Oh come on Jewel," Brad said agitated. He paused for her to change her mind, but she didn't.

"Okay, if that's what you want, then I'll just stay here and make sure you're okay. If by chance you decide that you really don't want to be alone, then I'll be here. I'll see you around," Brad said as he got up to head for the door.

"Hey," Jewel called out before he got to the door. "I'm sorry. I shouldn't take it out on you. Let's keep our plans for the holidays. I just need to be alone right now."

"Okay," Brad said, as he came back to give her a hug and a kiss, "I'll pick you up around eight."

"Sounds good," she agreed.

Brad decided to go hang out with the guys, without Jewel. He picked Gordon up and they arrived at the bar and grille after everyone else.

He saw Justine sitting by herself and decided to go over and see if he could get her to call, or drop in on Jewel later.

Gordon went over to shoot some pool with Eric and Brad was glad for the opportunity to talk to Justine alone.

"You have got to be kidding!" Justine said as Brad was telling her about Jewel's recommendation letter from Professor Saunders.

"Shhh," said Brad. "She doesn't want everyone to know."

"I can't believe that little bald head, bony…"

"Easy Justine," Brad said as Justine was searching for more profane words to describe Professor Saunders. "She must really be hurt. I'm going to go over there right now," Justine said reaching for her jacket. Brad grabbed her arm.

"Hey, I didn't send you and we didn't have this conversation. All I need is for her to be mad with me and cancel our holiday together."

"Don't worry. I won't tell her you told me anything," Justine said, "If I don't get back tonight, tell the guys I said to have a safe and happy Thanksgiving."

"You too," Brad said.

"Thanks. I think we all could use a break from this place right about now."

"I agree," Brad responded.

Brad tried the doorknob to Jewel room and it was unlock, but as a second thought, he knocked.

"Who is it?" Jewel yelled.

"It's me, Brad."

Jewel placed her hand over the phone receiver, "the door's open."

As Brad entered, she pointed to her bags, "my things are over there. I'm talking to my parents."

"I'll take these down stairs," Brad whispered.

Jewel shook her head and took her hand from the receiver to reply to her mother.

"Yes Mom, I'm going to miss you guys for Thanksgiving too."... "Yes, it is the first Thanksgiving that I have not been home."... "I'm sure I'm going to have a good time at Brad's parents, don't worry. I'm fine."

She really wasn't fine, but her talk with Justine had put her in a better mood. Justine had a way of making her see things differently. She made Jewel realized that it was only a recommendation and the final decision was hers.

"I'll call you when I get back and let you know how it went. Brad's on his way back up Mom, I gotta go, tell dad bye, love you both and give everyone my love." She hung up the phone and took a deep breath.

"So, does everyone have somewhere to go for the holiday?" Jewel asked.

Brad looked over at her puzzled, as she smiled and said, "I know you went to the bar and grille last night. Why else would Justine show up unexpectantly with rehearsed words of encouragements?"

"Caught," Brad admitted. "You're not mad with me are you? I was really concerned about you. You seemed pretty upset and out of it when I left."

"I was, but it's just something I have to deal with. I can't let Professor Saunders' recommendation ruin my entire law career. I'll take what he said under advisement and go from there."

Jewel wanted to sound more in control than she was last night or even felt at the moment. She hoped Brad was buying it, because she didn't want to get into the dynamics of her true feelings.

She respected and trusted Professor Saunders, in spite of his ornery ways. She defended him with the other students, thus landing her the right to be called his little pet. He always called upon her when he was out of options, as to who to call on for a correct answer in class; to say she was upset about his recommendations would be a little too mild; she was devastated.

For the first time in her life, she had a panic attack in the middle of the night and thought she was having a heart attack. She got up, took several deep breaths and was able to calm herself. She feared his recommendations would be the end of her future as the lawyer she dreamed of being. She wondered how much influence he had with the other professors and would he give them advice concerning her. Too many thoughts were going through her mind and she hoped that this weekend would allow a diversion, where she could find some time to refocus, but now she didn't want to discuss it anymore with Brad, who was eyeing her more than the road.

She looked over at him and placed her hand on his shoulder and said, "I'm fine."

He looked at her for more reassurance than that. "I am."

"Okay," Brad decided to let it drop for now, "but if at anytime this weekend you want to discuss it, we can."

"Thanks Brad. That means a lot."

"I think everyone is going home except Paula. She's going to Olivia's and Billy is taking his friend home."

"Art?" Jewel seemed shocked.

"Yes, he's going to tell his parents that he's gay and that Art is his lover. I think he may even tell them that he's dropping out of law school. His grades are so low and he's already on academic probation. He doesn't think he should waste any more of his parent's money, or his time. He wants to focus on photography. Art showed some of his work to some people he knows and it seems they may be interested in his work."

"Wow!" Jewel exclaimed. "That seems like a lot to drop on your parents all at once."

"It's his life, Jewel. He has to live it his way, or be miserable trying to live up to everyone else' expectations and standards."

"Then you approve of his lifestyle?" Jewel asked.

"It's not for me to approve or disapprove," Brad responded.

"But the bible says…" Jewel pause, realizing she really didn't know what the bible said about it. She thought she did, or at least she once knew, but now she wasn't sure.

"What does the bible say, Jewel?"

"That it's wrong. It's unnatural," Jewel answered.

"Did you read that for yourself, or are you just repeating what you've been programmed to believe?" Jewel was offended at Brad's question, but then she really never took the time to read the bible for herself.

"I wasn't programmed, but I do know that when it was taught in our church, we always turned to the scriptures that the Pastor, or teacher were referring to," Jewel defended.

"Me too," Brad said.

"Then why are you trying to make me out to be the bad guy? I like Billy and want the best for him too. There isn't a better person I know," Jewel stated.

"I guess the one thing that we have to understand is that we still have to love Billy," said Brad.

"Yes, that's the important thing," Jewel agreed, "should we have told Billy what we believe, Brad?"

"I don't know. I'm not a bible scholar and who are we to judge Billy, when we don't do the things that the bible require us to do."

"What does it require us to do?" Jewel asked.

Brad looked at Jewel unknowingly, "maybe we both need to revisit church."

"You're probably right," said Jewel, "but we know it requires us to love one another and do good."

"I guess that's part of it," Brad agreed.

Jewel looked away, "I hope it works out for Billy."

"Me too," said Brad. Jewel reached over to cut the radio up, "I like this song." They drove the rest of the way listening to the music and not talking much.

They arrived at Brad's parents home at 10:20 in the morning. Leroy, the Conner's butler, driver and handyman, whom Jewel hadn't met before helped them out of the car and grab their bags.

"I didn't know you had a butler too." Jewel said.

"Leroy is part of our family. Why do you seem surprise? Is it because he's black? You never said anything when I introduced you to Molly."

"You're pulling the race card a little too early in our relationship, aren't you?"

Brad was offended by Jewel's remark. He always felt uncomfortable with having servants in their home, especially when he brought his friends over.

"I'm not sure what you mean by that Jewel, but you didn't and I was just wondering if you were mentioning it now because Leroy is black and Molly is white."

"Molly's not white. She's Hispanic," Jewel corrected, "and all I said was, I didn't know you had a butler. I didn't realize you were that rich."

"I wouldn't call us rich," Brad defended, "my parents just thought spending quality time with their children was much more important than doing house chores."

"My parents did both," said Jewel, "and my mother work outside the home."

"Your point is…," Brad said annoyed.

"I'm just making some observations and for some reason, you're taking it personal," Jewel said shrugging her shoulders.

"Can we just drop it?" Brad asked.

"Sure," Jewel replied.

"Thanks."

"You're welcome." Brad took Jewel's hand as they walked through the door. He looked at her, shook his head and smiled. She smiled back, hoping she didn't offend him.

"Hi dear," Mrs. Conners greeted Brad and Jewel and embraced them with a hug.

"We are just about to have brunch. You must be hungry. Did you stop for something to eat?"

"No, we didn't," Brad replied.

"Then why don't you go get freshen up and come join us. Jewel you're in the same room as before. Do you remember how to get there? I think Leroy has already taken your things up."

"I'll see that she finds the right room Mother, besides I still owe her a tour," Brad offered.

"Please don't do a tour now darling," Mrs. Conners pleaded, looking at the big grandfather clock in the foyer.

"No Mother, we'll probably get around to it tomorrow."

"Good," said Mrs. Conners relieved. "Now run along, so you can hurry back," she said before she turned and hurried away.

Brad and Jewel looked at each other and laughed, as Mrs. Conners was gone as fast as she appeared.

Jewel never saw Mrs. Conners so occupied before. It seemed like she was checking to make sure that every little thing was perfect.

"Who else is coming to dinner?" Jewel asked Brad.

"I don't know. Why do you ask?"

"Your mother seems so preoccupied with making sure everything is just right."

"You're right," Brad acknowledge, as Amy came down stairs.

"Oh brother dear, you're here," she grabbed both of Brad's arms and gave him a kiss on both cheeks, "and Jewel," she said weakly as she gave Jewel a weak hug and no kiss.

"Glad to see you again too Amy," Jewel said sarcastically knowing she was the last person Amy wanted to see her brother bring to dinner.

"What's going on, Amy? Mom seems so preoccupied. Who else is coming to dinner?"

"Who isn't," Amy laughed.

"I didn't realize we were having a big dinner."

"It's a dinner party Brad."

"Why?"

"It's a surprise dear. You're going to have to wait and see."

Brad looked at Jewel sympathetically, "I'm sorry, I didn't know. If you want to get out of here, we can leave now. We can have dinner at a nice restaurant in town, get two rooms at a hotel and stay until the morning."

"Don't be silly," said Jewel, "I'm fine, besides I welcome the distraction. It could be fun."

Brad arched his eyebrows at Jewel as he put his arms around her waist, "you're definitely special Miss Stone."

As Jewel gave Brad a kiss, she kept one eye open to see Amy's reaction. Amy turned in disgust and said, "I hope you brought something appropriate to wear Jewel."

Brad turned to look at Amy and back at Jewel and asked, "Did you?" Jewel just smiled at him and gave him another kiss.

Guests started to arrive at six o'clock. Cecelia was one of the first to arrive. She wore a royal blue long straight dress, low cut front and back with gold trim around the bust line. It highlighted the evenly brown tan she was sporting.

Winter was a few more weeks away, but it had already arrived in Atlanta, so Jewel wondered how Cecelia managed to look so tan. Jewel felt a pang of jealousy, as Brad took a second look at Cecelia. She was holding the hand of a handsome man, who Jewel hoped was a love interest.

"Brad and Jewel," Cecilia said as she spotted them.

She was looking for them the minute she walked through the door.

"So glad to see you," she hugged Brad and kissed him on the cheek and acknowledged Jewel with a headshake.

She turned to her date, "oh I'm sorry. I must've forgotten my manners. Brad, Jewel, this is Felipe. Felipe this is Brad and Jewel. Felipe's my date for the night."

"So you're Jewel," Felipe said reaching for Jewel's hand. He placed a slight kiss on it and let it go. "I've heard so much about you, so it's certainly a pleasure to finally meet you." He turned to Brad and said, "It's nice to meet you too Brad. I must compliment you on having such a lovely companion."

"Thank you," said Brad, "and have you heard nothing of me from Cecelia."

"Oh, but of course," said Felipe, "in my line of work, I hear a lot of things about a lot of people, so it is quite interesting when I get to meet some of them."

"And what line of work is that?" Brad asked. Before Felipe could answer, he was whisked away by Cecilia.

"Oh come Felipe, we must find Amy."

"Oh, but of course," agreed Felipe.

"Hairdresser," said Jewel.

"Huh?" Brad asked.

"Hairdresser," Jewel repeated, "Felipe is Cecilia's hairdresser."

"You think?"

"People gossip a lot in beauty salons, trust me, I know."

"She wouldn't be so tacky as to bring her hairdresser here in disguise as her date."

"Desperate, may be the word you're looking for," Jewel commented, "but then again maybe she likes him."

"Right," Brad said rolling his eyes, "do you know something I don't?"

"No I don't."

"I guess anything is possible with Cecelia. Was she really trying to fake a French accent?" Brad asked.

They both laughed at how ridiculous Cecelia sounded.

"Like I said Brad, this evening may just turn out to be fun." Brad only rolled his eyes at Jewel. "Promise me one thing," Jewel said.

"What's that?" Brad asked.

"Don't leave me alone for one second tonight."

"Only if you promise the same."

They both shook hands and said, "promise." They burst into laughter, as Cecelia stood across the room fuming and wondering, if they were laughing at her.

Amy came into the room with a handsome looking gentleman on her arms.

She was introducing him around, when Jewel and Brad walked up behind them.

"Where have you been keeping your friend Sis?" Brad asked as he touched Amy on her shoulder and she turned to smile at him.

"I was getting over to you. John," she said grabbing the young man's hand "this is my favorite brother, Brad. Brad this is John."

"I'm her only brother," Brad corrected, "so I guess I'm the favorite by default." Brad reached out his hand and shook John's hand.

"Glad to meet you," John said, "Amy talks so much about you."

"Does she now," Brad said, "well she has managed to keep you a secret," Brad was caught up with the intrigued he saw in Amy's eyes that he forgot to introduce Jewel and Amy deliberately failed to do so.

Brad knew Amy made a point of not talking about her family to her men friends, nor did she give out information to her family about them.

There were many men in Amy's life, but they were never around long enough to matter, so Brad could tell there was something more; something Amy wasn't telling.

"I'm Jewel." Jewel said reaching around Brad, as Brad continued to eye Amy who was deliberately avoiding eye contact.

"I'm sorry," Brad said, "please forgive my manners. This is Jewel, my girlfriend."

John looked stunned and didn't bother to reach out to shake Jewel's hand. He gave Amy a puzzling look. Amy turned red and Jewel withdrew her hands.

Brad placed his arms around Jewel quickly and drew her close to him.

"Excuse us Brad," John said, "but we must find your father. Perhaps we will talk later."

Brad wanted to say, perhaps not, but instead he just nodded and said, "perhaps."

As they walked away Brad wasn't aware of how tight he was holding Jewel.

"Brad," she said, "if I was Amy, you would see how red I am right now."

Brad looked at Jewel puzzled and she added, "you're stopping my circulation."

"I'm sorry sweetheart," Brad said. "Are you okay?" He asked referring to John's behavior.

"I'm just fine now that I can breathe," Jewel responded knowing he was not referring to how tight he was holding her.

"I meant…," Brad was about to explain his concern, but Jewel cut in.

"Let's not talk about it right now, please."

Brad saw tears welled up in her eyes and he knew she just might cry if he pursued it, so he noddingly agreed. Brad wanted to take her away at that very moment. He knew she was trying to be brave about it by keeping her composure. He didn't want to further embarrass her by making a scene.

John pulled Amy into the Library as Amy tried to smile at everyone they pass. John was not smiling when he closed the door behind them.

"What was that?" John asked.

"Excuse me?" Amy decided to play dumb.

"Your brother and that… that…colored girl."

"I think they prefer being called black, John," Amy tried a weak smile.

"Are you funning with me Amy?" John asked, "because if you are, let me assure you this is not the time, or the place."

"I'm sorry dear," Amy said as she reached out her hands to caress John's face.

He knocked her hands away and said, "and don't pacify me either."

"What is the matter with you John?" Amy asked tiring of John's behavior.

"Your brother's girlfriend is the matter? What is that all about? You never said anything about your brother dating a colored girl."

"Dating? Who said anything about dating? My brother said she was his girlfriend. In other words, she's a friend of my brothers from law school. That's all. There's nothing romantic going on between them."

John seemed to calm down at Amy's explanation of Brad and Jewel's relationship.

"You had better be right Amy, because there is no way my parents will consent to a marriage where there may be a hint of colored people mixed up into the family."

"So, what are you saying John?"

"You know what I'm saying Amy."

"Are you saying that if my brother is in love with Jewel, you wouldn't marry me?"

"Oh, I could still marry you without my parents consent. We would be penniless that's all."

"Oh, that's all," Amy smiled as she tried once again to caress John's face with the palm of her hand.

"Amy I don't intend to lose my inheritance because of you, or anyone else."

"So, are you saying that you don't love me that much, John."

"I love you very much Amy, but I can love you much better with my inheritance."

"John, you're being silly. Don't worry about my brother and that little black girl. My brother will probably end up marrying his long time love, Cecelia."

"I don't wish that on him, but the latter is the better of the two evils."

"Oh, John," Amy said, as she cupped John's face in the palm of her hands and kissed him, "let's go find my Father, shall we?"

Amy pulled John by the hand leading him out of the room. John hoped Amy's assessment of Brad and Jewel's relationship was correct, otherwise the rest of the evening was going to be a waste of everyone's time.

Jewel sat in between Brad and Mr. Conners at the dinner table and she was truly glad for that. The dinner was great. Molly didn't prepare the meal this evening. Caterers were hired as Molly assisted in helping them find things around the kitchen.

"How's law school coming along Jewel?"

"Great, Mr. Conners, thanks for asking."

"And your family, are they all well?"

"My grandma Lynnie isn't doing so well, but other than that everyone is fine, thank you."

Every chance Brad got he took Jewel's hand and kissed the back of it, he rubbed the back of her neck and was totally attentive to everything she was saying, whether she was talking to him or his father.

Felipe sat in between Brad and Cecelia and Brad made it clear that he was not interested in anything Cecelia was saying or asking him. His answers and responses were cut and dry, as he hurriedly turned his attention back to Jewel every time.

He could almost feel the eyes that were on them. Jewel was the only black at the table. Despite her composure, Brad knew she must have felt somewhat uncomfortable, especially after the incident with John.

John, on the other hand wasn't hearing anything Amy or anyone else was saying to him, because he kept his eyes focused on Jewel and Brad, which drew the attention of others to them, including his parents.

At one point, Brad just looked into Jewel's eye as he smiled and said through clinched teeth, "If you make it through this dinner, I promise I will get you out of here."

Jewel smiled back and said. "I'm alright." Brad was not convinced.

"So, you go to law school with Brad, dear?" John's mother asked Jewel from across the table.

"Jewel," replied Jewel, as John's Mother looked confused, "my name is Jewel, and that is correct. I do attend the same law school as Brad."

"That's so nice. I guess it's true what we hear concerning the advancement of your people."

Brad suddenly pulled on Jewel hand and she had to avert her attention to Brad, who coyingly whispered, "Please don't honor that with a response."

Jewel smiled at Brad and indeed ignored the comment.

Mr. Conners started a conversation concerning social events and things that were happening in the news.

Dinner was over and Jewel got up from the table and let out a big sigh.

"I know baby," Brad said to her while rubbing her back, "I know."

Jewel looked at Brad and responded, "No you don't and you never will."

Brad felt small at her response, but he knew she was right. He couldn't believe the ignorance of his parent's friend, yet these were people he had known all his life.

"I'm sorry Jewels," Brad said putting an 's' at the end of her name as he sometimes did, making it sound like Jules.

"I can't believe that I went to school with some of these people and played with some of their kids."

"What school did you go to?" Jewel suddenly wanted to know.

"Huh?" Brad asked with a puzzled look on his face. "What school did you attend, Brad?"

"What?" Brad asked confused, "Preschool? Kindergarten? Elementary? High School?"

He stopped knowing that Jewel knew what college he went to.

"Did you go to private schools?" Jewel clarified.

"Yes, but what's your point? You went to private schools."

"Were they all white private schools?"

"I don't remember," Brad lied, something he never did with Jewel.

"Were there any blacks that attended any of the schools that you went to?" Jewel persisted with her question.

"I don't recall. I mean… I'm not sure, but I'm sure there were blacks that attended."

"But you can't associate one name with one face, can you?" Jewel further inquired.

Brad helplessly tried to search his memory for a face and a name.

"Jewel, I'm sure there were blacks that went to the schools that I attended."

"But you are not sure, which means there probably wasn't any, or you and your friends made it your business not to associate with any of them."

Brad was lost for a response.

"There lies the problem Brad. You nor your friends have ever been exposed to blacks and their culture, therefore, you know nothing about us, which means you know nothing about me."

Jewel was about to leave as Brad grabbed her arm and said, "I know you Jewel and I know I love you," he drew Jewel close to him and they stared in each other eyes.

As Brad leaned over to kiss Jewel, his father tapped on a wine class with a spoon trying to get everyone's attention. Jewel and Brad was lost in each other for a moment, but Mr. Conners kept tapping his glass, until he was sure that he had their full attention as well.

They stood holding hands, as they gave Mr. Conners their full attention.

"Ladies and gentlemen," Mr. Conners said, when he was assured that he had everyone's attention, "I want to make an announcement. John and Amy please come up here."

As Amy walked up, Jewel and Brad noticed a huge diamond ring on her finger. They gave each other a quick look, because they knew they hadn't seen it earlier.

"I want to announce the engagement of my daughter, Amy Conners, to Mr. John West. The waiters are passing around champagne and I want everyone to grab one, so we can officially toast the engaged couple."

Everyone began to clap and grab champagne glasses as they talk gaily among themselves about the surprised announcement.

"Does everyone have a glass?" Mr. Conners asked, "if you don't, please raise your hand and the waiters will see to you."

A few people in the corner of the room had not received a glass yet, as soon as they did, Mr. Conners finish the toast, "To John and Amy."

Everyone began to raise their glasses as they repeated, "to John and Amy."

Brad finally made it around to congratulating his sister without Jewel, who excused herself and went upstairs to her room. She told Brad that she really didn't feel like she should be sharing this moment with his family and friends, especially since John nor Amy would care for any well wishes from her.

Brad knocked lightly on Jewel's door. His room was on the other side of the house, but he wanted to check on her before he went to bed.

"Who is it?"

"It's me Jewel, can I come in?"

"I'm already in bed Brad," Jewel lied, "I'll see you in the morning."

"I just want to make sure that you're okay."

"I'm okay."

"Goodnight then," Brad said reluctantly.

He felt he should have insisted that she let him come in, but they both had a long day, so he resolved to let her rest. He hoped the rest of the weekend would go better for her. He would have to see to it.

Jewel heard talking as she came downstairs for breakfast. She wasn't sure if she should have waited on Brad to escort her down, or go down on her own. It was quite early, she thought, maybe no one would be up. She wanted something other than water to drink and she knew Brad was not an early riser, neither was she, but she couldn't sleep.

As Jewel came closer to the sitting room, she recognized Mr. Conners' voice. She paused wondering if she should tip toe by and go straight to the kitchen, or stop in to say good morning, but she stood frozen as she heard her name.

"Mr. and Mrs. West, you are making way too much of this. We certainly cannot assure you that my son will never marry Jewel."

"He wouldn't if you forbid it," replied Mr. West.

"That's nonsense. My son is free to make his own choices in life. If your son, choose not to marry our daughter then it will certainly be his lost."

"Father!" Amy cut in, "you know that Brad will listen to you, if you speak to him about this."

"It's just scandalous to have colored people in your family!" Mrs. West injected, "we are from a long line of pure white blood. We are not about to settle for anything different now."

"If my son should ever decide to marry Jewel, how does that contaminate your pure white bloodline? And do anyone of us know for sure that our ancestors never cohabitated with negro slaves?"

"I will not sit here and be insulted, Mr. Conners," said Mr. West.

"I apologize if I have insulted you. That was not my intention. I am trying to make sure that we maintain an open mind about this."

"If it's assurance that you want Mr. and Mrs. West, then I guess I'm the only one that can do that." All eyes were suddenly fixed on Jewel.

She stood in the entrance with tears in her eyes, but she held her head up high.

"I will assure you that Brad and I will never marry. I would never want to be the one to taint your pure white blood with my black blood, even though my people have come a long way and have shown much advancement in your white world," Jewel said, the latter as she looked at Mrs. West.

"We don't mean any harm dear, but we would certainly like to have that in writing," Mr. West requested, "we would pay a good sum to have you sign something to that extent."

"I'm sorry Mr. West, but I would not take any sum of money from you. I don't need your money. I'm afraid my word will just have to do." Jewel looked towards Brad's father," Mr. Conners, would it be okay if Leroy took me back to Atlanta, right now?"

"I'm afraid Leroy has the day off, but I'll wake Bradley and he can take you back, although I wish you wouldn't leave like this," Mr. Conners said apologetic. I can't say how sorry I am that you had to hear this and I don't think you should make any promises that you can't keep. I know how my son feels about you."

Jewel knew if she blinked, tears would come down like a flood. She stared wide eyed at everyone in the room and saw Cecelia standing by Amy and they were trying desperately to hide their delight at what was taking place, but the smirks were evident on their face. Jewel drew strength from that as she drew in a deep breath and stuck her chest out which made her diminutive figure seem taller than it was.

"I assure you Mr. Conners this is a promise I will keep and I would rather not wait for Brad. He will probably want to leave with me and I'm sure you would rather him spend the rest of the holidays with his family. I would appreciate it very much, if you could give me a ride to the nearest bus stop. I'll get back from there."

"I'm not sure the buses run out here on the holidays, Jewel," Mrs. Conners spoke for the first time.

Mr. Conners decided to do the noble thing and help Jewel leave with the dignity that he saw she was desperately trying to maintain.

"Why don't you get your things. I'll drive you back to Atlanta."

"Thank you. I'll be down in about fifteen minutes." Jewel was about to leave as she turned around and said, "by the way, my name is Jewel, not dear."

It was less than fifteen minutes when Jewel came back down with her bags. She stuffed all her things in her bag, not caring if she left anything behind. She didn't want to waste time checking the room or looking back.

"I'm ready to go," Jewel said as she found Mr. Conners in the Library.

"Jewel you don't have to go. This is my home and I want you to stay."

"I think only you and Brad share those sentiments Mr. Conners, but thank you for offering, but you know as well as I do that I can't stay here any longer. If it was you, would you stay under the circumstances?"

"I guess not, but I did mean what I said earlier. You are not obligated to keep any promises you made to those people."

"Thank you again Mr. Conners, but you and I know that it's probably for the best."

"I'm not going to lie to you Jewel. I believe life holds many trials in itself without inviting trouble. I can't say that I don't believe you and Brad would be inviting trouble, if you decide to take your relationship any further, but I want you, as well as Brad, to know that I support whatever decision the two of you make. Love happens to the best of us and I say, thank God for it. It's a cliché', but it does make the world go 'round, or at least it makes it better."

"Thank you for your honesty Mr. Conners. I appreciate that."

"I hope you realize Bradley isn't going to let you just walk out of his life. If I know my son, he won't give up on you that easy."

"I know," Jewel said.

The drive back to Atlanta was pleasant enough, but awkward. Mr. Conners kept the conversation light and even was able to make Jewel laugh a time or two.

"Is there anything you want me to tell Brad?" Mr. Conners asked Jewel as she was getting out of the car.

"I'm going to go upstairs, freshen up and head home to spend the rest of the weekend with my family. Tell him to enjoy the rest of the weekend with his family and I'll see him when we get back to Atlanta. I have a couple of days off before I have another class, so I may not be back by Monday."

"I'll tell him."

"Thanks again Mr. Conners. I really appreciate you taking the time from your family to drive me back to Atlanta."

"You're welcome. Take care Jewel and drive home safely."

"Thanks, Mr. Conners, I will."

Brad was sipping on coffee and reading a magazine in the breakfast nook. This was his favorite place in the mornings. He checked his watch again. It was eleven thirty. He wanted to share this moment with Jewel, but it looked like she was going to sleep until noon.

He stared through the windows. He could see the stables and the wooded area behind. It seemed quiet and peaceful.

They hired a service that came around and fed the horses and groomed them. He could see that they were finishing up and heading out.

If he sat in the bay window of the breakfast nook from the other angle, he could see the pool. It was cold, so no one would be out there today. They were probably in the sauna room where they kept two hot tubs, or in the game room. He wasn't sure, but he didn't see anyone stirring. He wondered if everyone was still asleep. He knew his mother and father was up somewhere in the house, because they were always early risers. Matter of fact they probably had coffee right at this table, Brad thought, before they went off to do whatever it was they had planned for the day.

Brad was going over in his mind what he and Jewel would do today. He knew his parents had planned on a family-riding day early Saturday morning, so he didn't want to do that today. He would find out from her when she woke up, he thought, maybe she just wanted to go shopping. It was what she would be doing if she had gone home to her parents. It was her mother's favorite thing, to shop early in the morning the day after Thanksgiving.

They had some pretty nice malls, he thought, and there was this one mall that had a movie theatre and restaurant all in one. That would be great, to go shopping with her, help her buy presents for her family and she could help him and then they could see a movie later and get something to eat.

Now that he had their day planned, he couldn't wait for Jewel to wake up any longer. He was looking forward to spending this weekend with her and he wasn't going to let her sleep the rest of the day away.

At school, he had to compete with her books and paper writing, but he wasn't going to compete with a bed.

Brad took the last sip of his now warm coffee, which made his face squint and then he got up to go wake Jewel.

"Jewel," Brad said quietly while knocking lightly at the door.

He paused to hear any signs of her moving around, but he didn't here anything. He knocked a little louder this time and called her name a little louder. He never known Jewel to be a hard sleeper, at least she never said she was. He could almost remember her saying the opposite. Brad knocked again getting a little agitated.

"If you're looking for your girlfriend, she's probably back in Atlanta by now," said Cecelia, who was on her way back to her room to get something.

"What?" Brad asked puzzled.

"See for yourself," Cecelia said as she brushed pass Brad and opened the door to Jewel's room. "See," she said waving her hand across the dark room.

Brad turned on the light and looked around for Jewel's thing, but they were not there.

"How? Why? When?" He asked, too upset and disappointed to form a real question.

"Your father took her early this morning while you were sleeping. Matter of fact, he isn't back yet. They left around nine-is. The 'why' you'd better ask your parents." Cecelia wanted to act snotty, but she saw the hurt in Brad's eye and decided to capitalize on his pain. "I mean...I sort of know, but I think your parents would want to be the ones to talk to you about it. She had a run in with the Wests and wanted to leave."

"A run in with the Wests?" Brad's confusion was causing him a sudden headache, as he began to massage the temple of his forehead.

"Yes, but like I said you should talk to your parents about it." Cecelia put her hand on Brad's arm, "I'm sorry Brad. I think the Wests may have said something to hurt her feelings, but I'm here for you if you need to talk."

Brad looked at Cecelia with scorn in his eyes, "I don't think I'll be needing any comfort from you Cecelia," Brad said as he took his hand and moved her hand from off of his arm. He turned the light off and left the room leaving Cecelia standing in the dark, with a smirk on her face.

Brad went all through the house looking for his mother. Amy and John were in the game room.

"I'll get you this time John West."

"You may try Miss Conners, but I think I have somewhat of an advantage over you."

Amy stopped playing on the pen ball machine and stood in front of John and placed her arms around his neck, "and what may that advantage be sir?"

Brad burst into the room. "What happened this morning with Jewel, Amy?"

Amy still had her arms around John, who said, "well, good morning to you too Brad."

Brad shot John a deadly look and Amy took her arms from around John's neck.

"Could you leave me and my brother alone for a few minutes John?"

"Actually, I would not," said John, "I'm going to be a part of this family soon and since the incident in question involves me and my parents, I think I should be here in defense of my family's good name."

Brad was staring John down, but he didn't let it faze him.

"John's parents had a conversation with bob and Katie this morning concerning your relationship with Jewel. The Wests had a problem with approving John marrying me, if there was a chance that you might marry Jewel. Jewel eaves dropped on the conversation and heard much of it. She assured the Wests that they did not have to worry about approving our marriage, because she never had any intentions of marrying you." Amy looked at John and asked, "does that about sums it up sweetie?"

"I think so, except for the part where she demanded that your father leave his guests and take her back to Atlanta."

"Oh yes, I forgot that."

Brad was becoming incensed and he imagined his hands around his sister's neck until he had choked the life out of her, but instead he turned to John and landed his fist right across his cheek and nose. Blood came gushing out of John's nose as Amy began to scream for help. John held his head up and pinched his nose to stop the blood from dripping on the floor. Brad was about to walk away, but he turned and planted his right fist into John's abdomen and John went down sprawled out on the floor, as Amy knelt over him screaming.

"For the record," Brad said, "let it be understood that anything Jewel agreed to this morning was said out of hurt and distress and should not be held against us."

Brad was walking out of the room when the Wests and his mother came running into the room.

"My God, what is going on here?" Mr. West asked looking at Brad as the women ran over to John.

John laid ball into a fetus position crying, "my nose, my nose, I think it's broken."

Brad looked at Mr. West and pushed his way past him and went up to his room to pack his things.

"Brad, what on earth are you doing? The ambulance is on the way to take John to the hospital. You may have broken his nose."

"Be thankful that's all I may have done Mother."

"Where are you going Bradley?" Asked Mrs. Conners, as she noticed Brads bag on the bed stuffed with his thing hanging out.

"If Jewel isn't welcome here Mother, then I don't want to be here either."

"Brad you're just upset. Please wait until your father returns."

"For what Mother, so he can explain to me why the two of you sat there and entertain such a conversation with those people? Are those the kind of people we want to associate ourselves with?" Mrs. Conners had no answer.

She was truly ashamed about what happened, but Amy was her daughter and she wanted her to be happy. How could she admit to Brad that she was somewhat relieve that Jewel said they would never marry. She and her husband spent hours at night discussing Brad's relationship with Jewel. Mr. Conners seemed more tolerant than she, but they both agreed they would support whatever decision Brad made, even if it meant a marriage they were not a hundred percent in approval of.

"Brad, Amy loves John. We had to hear them out for her sake, even if we didn't agree with them. It was unfortunate that Jewel had to hear any of that. I would give anything to be able to erase this morning's event. You and Jewel's decision to marry, or not to marry should have never been a topic for such prejudices in our home, but it is the world we live in. It's the world she lives in. I'm not trying to justify what happened this morning, but I'm sure Jewel has been faced with this before and will again."

Brad sat in the chaise lounge chair with his legs crossed. His mother sat down on the bed next to him.

"Mother you're right. You shouldn't try to justify what happened this morning, because there is no justice for it, but you know what bothers me the most, the fact that my sister is marrying someone like that. I thought I knew Amy, but I don't. Do I?" Brad asked not expecting an answer from his Mother. It was a realization to him, "to think that she would even consider marrying someone like that and raise children to think like he thinks. That to me Mother is really shocking." Brad held his head down. "Obviously, she's of the same opinion as he, yet I can't remember you and dad raising us to be like that."

Mrs. Conners looked at the hurt in Brad's eye and put her hand on his shoulder and said, "we didn't, but in an attempt to give the two of you the best life possible, we may have made some wrong choices. I think sending Amy to an all white girl private school may have help formed the way she thinks now."

Brad looked at his mom remembering the conversation he and Jewel had the other night, and said, "I don't think sending me to an all white private school helped me that much either mom. Academically, yes, but what about the rest of the world and how to relate to other people of other culture and background. It was never even discussed. We lived as if we rule. I lied to Jewel the other night about not remembering whether or not there were any blacks that went to the schools I attend.

I was too embarrassed and hurt at the truth that we never made any attempt to know about other ethnics. I'm in love with a beautiful woman that I can't even identify with. How am I supposed to win her back? We were raised in an excluded world, Mother. How do we compensate for that now?"

"You start by getting to know her Bradley. You can't change the past, but you can change." Mrs. Conners advised her son.

Jewel arrived home at about two thirty in the afternoon, but it felt like two thirty in the morning. She had a long day. It felt like the longest day of her life and it still wasn't over. There were cars in the driveway with out of state license plate. Jewel knew her mom went out early in the morning to shop, but maybe she was back by now depending on how good the sales were.

Jewel didn't know what she was feeling. Did she want her mother to be home, so she could have her put her arms around her while she cried her eyes out, or did she just want solitude.

She grabbed her bags and got out the car. She used her keys to open the door, as she began to call out, "Mom! Dad! Tessa! David! Aunt Judy! Aunt Denise! Anybody!" The house was quiet. Jewel looked around the house some more. She looked upstairs, quietly knocking on closed doors just in case someone was sleeping; she didn't want to startle anyone. She checked her parent's room. She checked the garage. The van was gone. The Mercedes was in the garage, but there was no sign of her Dad's work truck. She checked Tessa and David's room. Then she went into her room. Someone was staying in her room. She didn't know who, but she saw bags and clothes thrown around the room, but the bed was made.

"Well, they're not here now," Jewel said to herself.

She took off her jeans and put on a long T-shirt and lay across the bed. She was asleep before her mind could begin to recap the events of the day. She had already rehearsed it over and over in her mind on the way home. Sleep was a nice reprieve.

"Isn't that Jewel's car?" Tessa asked Theresa.

"Where?" Theresa looked around

"There, on that side of the street."

"I think it is, but what is she doing here?" Theresa pulled the van onto the grass besides Denise's van.

All the women had car pooled and decided to go shopping together this year. Melissa and her one year old son, Akeem, took her mother's car and went off on their own, since there was not enough room in the van for the baby's car seat. Denise's husband Mark, and James, one of Paul's brothers took the boys to the fun park. David was hanging out with his friends and Paul went to the office to take care of some urgent business.

Tessa jumped out of the almost parked van and ran into the house yelling Jewel's name. She went into Jewel's room and jumped on the bed next to Jewel, as a groggy Jewel could barely turn her head and focus on the person that had just disturbed her now, short nap.

It seemed like hours to Jewel, who glanced out the window and squinted at the sun beaming through, "jeeze Tessa what are you doing?"

"What am I doing? What are you doing here? You're supposed to be somewhere in Georgia with your boyfriend and his family, remember."

"I remember. We had a change of plans," Jewel groggily replied.

"Did Brad come with you?"

"No, he stayed at his parents."

"Did you two have a fight?"

"Come on Tess, you jump on the bed and wake me up out of a sound, much needed sleep to ask a million and one question. Can you let me get my bearings first?"

"Sorry," Tessa apologized looking hurt.

Jewel turned over and stared at the girl on the bed next to her wondering if this was her sister. For the first time in years, Tessa wasn't making a fashion statement. There was no obscene color in her hair, no rag tag jeans or dress, or funky jewelry around her neck and wrist. Instead, she was sporting a bob hair cut. Her hair was dyed jet black. She was wearing a sweat shirt with her college name on the upper left shoulder and some regular blue jeans and sneakers, which Jewel knocked off of her bed causing Tessa to sit up straight on the edge of the bed staring down at Jewel.

"What?" Jewel asked.

"I'm waiting for you to get your bearings so you can tell me what happened."

That was another thing Jewel didn't recognize about Tess. When did she ever want to know what was going on with her.

"Well, you're going to have to wait. Since you woke me up, I think I'll take a shower and change."

"Jewel what on earth are you doing here?" Theresa said as she walked through the door.

Tessa stood and said, "You're going to have to wait until she gets her bearings, or whatever. In the meantime, I'm going to my room. If I can get in it, as it is now occupied with a couple of brats," she said rolling her eyes at her mother, speaking of Christy and Georgia, Denise's two daughters.

"Some things never change," Jewel said, speaking of Tessa's complaints of having her two cousin stay with her in her room, which they did on every visit.

"Well?" Theresa asked looking at Jewel and ignoring Tessa's comment.

"Mom I was in a deep sleep when Tessa came and jump up and down on the bed to wake me up."

"I didn't jump up and down!" yell Tessa as she was just stepping out of the room.

"Well, you might as well," Jewel yelled back.

"I'm going to take a shower, change and I'll come out later and we'll talk, but I don't want to talk around everyone, so don't ask me about it in the presence of anyone, other than Dad. By the way, who's staying in my room?"

"Melissa and her son."

"Her son?" Jewel asked shocked.

"Yes, her son. They kept it a secret."

"I see," Jewel said as she got up and walked out of her room into the bathroom that she and Tessa shared by adjoining doors.

"Is that Jewel's car parked on the other side of the street?"

"Yes, it is," Theresa said answering her husband's question.

She was standing at the kitchen sink rinsing out dishes to place in the dishwasher.

Paul came up behind her and reached over her for a glass.

"What is she doing here? Is everything all right? Did she and Brad have a fight?"

"I don't know. I don't know, and I don't know," respond Theresa as she turned holding a dripping dish with a towel placed underneath it so the water wouldn't drip on the floor.

Both of them stood staring at each other and finally Theresa said, "She is in her room taking a shower. She will tell us all about it later, but she doesn't want to be asked any questions if anyone else happens to be in the room. She was here sleeping when we got back from shopping and that my dear is all I know."

They stared at each other a little longer, then Paul scratched his head and said, "I think I'll go take me a shower."

"You do that dear," said Theresa smilingly.

Everyone was surprised to see Jewel. Melissa seemed embarrassed and put out. She had begged Judy not to tell anyone that she was pregnant and the only reason her mother was able to convince her to come with them was that she told her Jewel wasn't going to be there.

Melissa looked up to Jewel and felt that her mother and everyone else were always setting a standard for everyone else based on what Jewel did, so when she got pregnant she felt like the black sheep of the family. She was convinced that Jewel would never have made such a mistake. She didn't intentionally get pregnant, but she didn't think of Akeem as being a mistake.

Jewel didn't know what to say to Melissa. She was too occupied with her own problems, but she made Melissa feel better by arranging with David to stay in his room on a pull out cot, so that Melissa and her baby didn't have to find somewhere else to sleep.

It was late and after Jewel convinced Tessa that she would talk to her tomorrow, Tessa finally went to bed. Paul and Theresa were not going to be put off that easy. They were not intending to go to bed until they hear what happened at the Conners. Jewel was dreading it, but she knew she needed to give them an explanation.

Both Theresa and Paul were shocked at what Jewel told them. Paul wanted to call the Conners, then he said he was going to go to their home. Theresa and Jewel convinced him that there was no sense in doing anything like that. They agreed that it was hard to change people's prejudices unless they wanted to be change and any confrontation with the Wests didn't make any sense, especially since it wasn't Brad's parent's integrity that was in question.

"It doesn't say much about Brad's sister now, does it?" said Theresa.

"No Mom it doesn't and the sad thing is that Brad will now have to see the truth. He's going to see the true side of his sister. The side he's been denying exists."

"What about his parents?" asked Paul. "Children aren't born with these prejudices. They learn them from their parents."

"I don't know Dad. I know Brad isn't like that, not to say that he is perfect and don't have any prejudices, because we all do, but he's not like that and his parents have never said anything to make me feel unwelcome, or made any prejudicially remarks to me, or innuendos 'black jokes.' I mean it was just that one incident, but it wasn't Mrs. Conners. It was Amy and Cecelia."

"What incident?" Paul asked.

Jewel looked up realizing she had never mentioned that incident to her parents.

"And whose Cecelia?" ask Theresa.

"Why on earth would you want to be around people like that?"

"I'm not around them Dad. Brad and I attend the same law school. Don't make it sound like I hang around these people all the time and subject myself to their prejudices," Jewel was getting defensive. "Don't forget. I've lived with prejudices like this all my life. My own grandmother never thought I was good enough because my skin wasn't as light as hers."

Theresa was heartbroken at Jewel's word, yet she knew them to be true. Paul glanced at Theresa, who held her head down and put her head in her hands.

"I'm sorry Mom, I didn't mean that." Jewel got up, "I don't want to talk about this anymore. It's over between Brad and I. We'll probably remain friends, if he wants. I don't have any ill feelings towards him. I hated leaving without letting him know I was going, but just the same, I really don't want to talk to him right now. He'll want to talk it through, but I'd rather wait until I can see him face to face. I have other things on my mind. This has been the worst weekend of my life." Jewel laughed weakly, "and it's not even over yet."

"What other things?" Paul asked.

"I don't want to get into it right now. I'm probably going to be here until Tuesday, so we'll have plenty of time to talk. I'm tired. I'm going to bed. Goodnight."

"Goodnight, sweetheart," Paul said.

Jewel went over to her mom, who was still holding her head in her hand and kneeled down beside her and placed her arm around her.

"Mom I love you. You are the best Mother anyone could ask for. Just like Grandma Lynnie's prejudices didn't rub off on you, I guess that's the same way with Brad." Jewel hugged her Mom and kissed her on the cheek.

She did the same to her father and said goodnight again and went off to bed.

The rest of the weekend wasn't as bad as Jewel thought it would be. Brad kept calling all day, but she alerted everyone that she was not taking any calls. Everyone suspect that they had a fight and honored her request, no questions asked, for which she was grateful.

Jewel let herself get caught up in Tessa and David's life. David was going to the University of Tennessee, while Tessa had decided to quit college and go to fashion school.

She sent some of her drawings to a fashion school and they accepted her. She would start the next year in the fall. She had a couple more weeks to finish up this semester and decided not to register for the spring.

"What's the point in wasting dad and mom's money."

"I agree," said Jewel, "but when are you planning on telling them?"

"When I come home for winter break."

"You think you can make it in the fashion industry?"

"I think so. What do you think? You've seen my drawings."

"I think they're really good."

Tess looked at Jewel hoping she wasn't just being kind.

"Seriously," Jewel assured her and to Jewel's surprise Tessa leaned over and hugged her.

"But I'm confused," Jewel said, "it seemed that now should be the time that you make your fashion statement, but it looks like you've turned into Miss Conservative."

"I'm into a more sophisticated style, not the fads. That was my way of trying to let everyone see that I am not you and that I'm my own person. I'm beginning to know who I am now. I also realize that mom and dad are not really trying to make me into you."

"That's a good thing," said Jewel, "because I'm not quite sure who I am right now, but I know who I am not, if that makes any sense."

"That makes perfect sense."

It was Jewel time to hug her little sister, "I'm really proud of you, not that you need my approval."

"I'm glad you approve, that means a lot to me," then she stood with one hand on her hip and the other hand waving in the air, "not that I need your approval."

They both laughed and continued to talk. They promise to call each other more and to keep up with what's going on in each other's life. They decided to call David more as well. He was becoming a loner and an outsider.

"I think he has a girlfriend that he's really serious about," said Tessa.

"Really, so why don't he bring her over for us to meet her?"

"I don't know. Who knows why David does what he does."

"We should make it our business to know," Jewel said and Tess nodded in agreement.

Jewel felt good about renewing her relationship with Tessa. David still was being a little aloof, but he agreed to keep in touch with them and let them know what was going on with him. He did admit to being interested in a girl he met at college, but he said it was new and they were just getting to know each other.

"Jewel, that professor doesn't know anything about you," Paul was saying to Jewel after she told him about the letter of recommendation from Professor Saunders.

She waited until she had her father all to herself.

I mean, who am I? Am I really timid? Is that why I allowed the Wests to coerced me into a promise to end my relationship with Brad? I know you and Mom think that I've handled Grandma's Lynnie's rejection of me well for a child, but have I? Do you really want to know how it made me feel, or how insecure she made me feel around her?"

Paul was speechless. He was as guilty as Theresa for letting Jewel be subjected to Linda's insecurities.

"Jewel, I know we were wrong…"

"No Dad," Jewel cut her father off, "I'm not trying to place blame. I just want to take an honest assessment of myself and see what changes I need to make in order to accomplish what I want to accomplish with my life. As much as I was hurt by Professor Saunder's recommendations, I have to wonder how much of it is true and to do something to make the necessary changes."

"I know I may not be objective," said Paul, "but I do know that you're going to do what you need to do to get where you want to go."

"You're right Dad. You are absolutely right."

Tessa left Sunday afternoon, so did everyone else, except Jewel. She stayed until Tuesday morning and decided to get a head start and leave the same time her parents left for work.

Theresa and Jewel managed to have some time alone to themselves, but Jewel stayed away from emotional conversation, even though Theresa wanted her to talk more about her feelings.

Jewel got some final words of encouragement from her Dad on changing those things about herself that she didn't like, if it was going to get her to her goals.

The drive back was one of reflection. Jewel knew Brad would confront her, but that was the least of her concerns right now. She had a renewed vigor to change whatever it was about herself that needed to be change.

Theresa gave her a name of a psychiatrist that she might want to talk to. She told Jewel to make the arrangements and have the bill sent to them. Paul wasn't too keen on the idea, but after talking to Theresa one night about what they had allowed to happen to Jewel, he agreed that it was a wise thing to do.

They always believed that if they did not make a big deal of Grandma's Lynnie's prejudices, then Jewel wouldn't think it an issue, but hearing Jewel's assessment of it open up new wounds for Theresa. It brought back memories of Mae. She didn't want Jewel to end up like her sister. After discussing it with Paul, they agreed to call their friend who knew a psychiatrist in Atlanta. They gave Jewel the information and left the decision up to her, whether or not she wanted to see a counselor. Jewel was thinking that she might. Her new motivation now was, whatever it was going to take.

Jewel was unwinding from her ride back to Atlanta, when she heard the knock at the door.

"Who is it?"

She called out, knowing it would be Brad. She was not ready for a confrontation with him, but it was inevitable. She didn't accept any of his calls while at her parents.

"Brad."

Jewel took a deep breath and opened the door. Jewel felt her heart skipped a beat, as she saw the hurt in his eyes. She stepped sideways and motioned with her hand for him to come inside.

"I tried to call you at your parents," Brad said, stating the obvious, but he was not sure where to begin.

"I know," Jewel responded uneasy.

She rehearsed what she was going to say to him over and over on her way back to Atlanta, but now she was lost for words. She tried to avert her eyes from his shimmering blue eyes that were trying to hold back tears, but they bored into her soul. Jewel tried to turn away, but he grabbed her by the shoulder with both hands forcing her to look into his eyes.

"Jewel, we can't let what we have end like this. We can't let people dictate our future and our happiness with their bigotry and their misinformation."

"I know Brad. I don't intend to let that happen. All my life I've been motivated by what others thought or expected of me. Now, I'm going to be motivated by what I want and I don't want us to end like this either."

The words were coming out of Jewel's mouth, but she couldn't believe it was she who was speaking them. This was not what she rehearsed alone in the car. She was prepared to end their relationship. She convinced herself that she didn't love him enough to have to go through the changes, but seeing him in person made things different. His very presence made her stomach feel queasy.

Brad could not believe what he was hearing. He too had rehearsed what would happen when he saw Jewel. He was determined and prepared to put up a good argument concerning why they should try to make their relationship work.

Brad drew Jewel close to him and hugged her tightly and she responded.

Brad and Jewel spent another thirty minutes sharing how the rest of their weekend went without the other. Then he left so Jewel could get some rest, for her early class the next day.

Despite the conversation they had that night, they didn't spend as much time together as Brad hoped. Jewel decided to move out of the boarding house and get her own apartment. She found one about fifteen minutes away from the school and thirty minutes away from the boarding house.

It was in the basement of an elderly couple home. The previous tenant was a law student, who got an internship outside of the state. Jewel saw the ad on the information bulletin at the school. She moved in the following week.

She also requested a change in academic advisor. She was determined to pursue her studies in criminal law and since Professor Saunders was not going to approve it, she got assigned to another advisor. She was learning how to play the game.

She knew she was going to be in for a lot of work. It was pretty close to graduation and her new counselor gave her a hard time about being able to fulfill all her requirements before then, but she stood her grounds pointing out her excellent academic record as her defense. The counselor gave in citing that her academic record, entrance scores and her determination showed that she was capable of doing the work, even if it meant spending more time in school, but she had no intentions of being in law school one more day than she planned.

She started seeing Dr. Brink, the psychiatrist that her parents recommended and she was extremely glad she did, even though she kept it a secret from her friends. She decided to stay in Atlanta during the winter break and only went home for Christmas Eve and Christmas day and returned the day after.

Brad managed to get her to spend enough time with him so they could exchange their presents, but other than that Jewel spent her break doing research and writing papers for her classes. She was glad for the three days she had with her family, but she was itching to get back to her studies.

Jewel thought her parents would've been upset with Tessa's announcement that she was dropping out of college, because she was accepted into a fashion school in New York. Instead, they were very supportive of her decision. David had Christmas dinner with his girlfriend's family and they came over later that evening for desert. From the look of things, they seemed pretty close. Jewel found herself envying them and wishing she was with Brad, but she had convinced him that it would be best for them to spend Christmas with their own families.

For the first time in many years, this was the smallest Christmas gathering they ever had. Judy invited everyone to her home for Christmas, but her parents didn't go because neither, Jewel nor Tessa's had the extra time. The only other person at their home for the holidays was grandma Lynnie.

Jewel felt more energized than she had ever been during any of her visits, since she left home for college. When her parents asked her what was behind the change, she told them she was seeing the psychiatrist and a lot of emotions that she kept inside were being revealed and she was finally finding out who she was.

Later she sat down with her parents and they talked about some of the changes that were taking place in her life.

"I really want to thank you guys for recommending and paying for me to see Dr. Brink. I certainly couldn't afford her myself."

"Jewel, we're just glad that you took us up on the opportunity," said Theresa.

"Thanks Mom. I'm really unlocking some things that could have held me back for a long time."

"While I'm glad that you're getting the help you need, I don't want you to substitute it for what we all need, and that is Jesus."

"Mom, please don't start."

"What? Do you think that I'll ever stop telling you about the one most important thing in life, a personal relationship with the Lord."

"Don't start with that now Theresa. Give her a break. She knows right from wrong. She will make the right decision, when the time comes," said Paul.

"I don't doubt that, but tomorrow is not promised to us."

"I hear you loud and clear Mother," Jewel said, as she got up indicating the end of the conversation.

Jewel did not want to tell her mother that one of her breakthroughs was realizing that she did not have to believe like her parents, that it was okay to have a different point of view of God. She knew her mother would be outraged. Somehow she thought Jewel was seeing a Christian psychiatrist, but Dr. Brink did not confess to being a born again Christian.

The winter break was over and Jewel was back to her grueling routine. She distanced herself from her friends and Brad. She reasoned that they would understand. After all, they were all in this together with one goal, to get out of law school at the top of their class and with honors.

One night while studying for a major exam, she had her answering machine turned on to pick up her calls. The phone rang so much that she finally turned off the ringer. She did not return anyone's call, not even an urgent call from Brad and Justine. They were all studying for the same exam and she was convinced they were trying to get her into a group study and she knew they always ended up having more fun than studying.

She couldn't believe it when someone knocked at her door. It sounded like Brad and Justine and maybe one of the other guys from the group. She wasn't sure whom. She just kept quiet and refused to open the door. That wasn't hard to do, because she never studied with anything on. She was not going to be sucked into a group study tonight. She was going to study early and call it quits early, so that she could get a good night sleep. She would make it up to them later she reasoned.

The next day in the hallway next to the exam room, she ran into Justine who gave her the cold shoulder. She just made a mental note to herself to talk to her later. She usually finished her exam before Justine, so she would wait for her outside the exam room, so she wouldn't miss her.

As she prepared herself to take the exam, she looked around for her friends. She spotted all of them except Billy, but they all seem to deliberately avoid eye contact with her.

Brad arrived right before the professor began his speech, as usual. He never got to exams earlier than he had to. He hated the waiting and people dragging him into last minute discussion about something that might be on the test, always trying to persuade him to see it their way.

He sat next to Jewel in his usual seat, but he too avoided looking at her.

She reached out to touch his arm and mouthed to him, "Are you mad with me too?"

Brad didn't get to respond, as the professor monitoring the exam began to speak, so he just shook his head saying, "no."

"Good morning class. I know this is a major exam for all of you and it would be foolish to tell you not to take it seriously. For some of you, you feel like your entire future is base on doing well, but I want to say to you today that this is not all there is to life. You have to learn to stay focus and set priorities, or you too could end up like our fellow student, William Callahan."

At the mention of Billy's name, Jewel froze and turned again to see if he was in his usually seating. He wasn't.

Jewel looked to her friends for an answer, but they all looked strained, even Brad, who turned to look at her, as she mouthed, "What?" but Brad just let the professor continue.

"Let's show our respect by bowing our heads for a moment of silence."

Jewel didn't hold down her head as she looked to her friends for an answer. Brad slipped her a piece of paper and as she read it, her head became dizzy.

The note read: He killed himself.

Brad did not want her to find out about Billy like this, but she did not return his calls, even the urgent ones. She either wasn't in her apartment, or refused to open the door for him and Justine.

Brad mouthed to her, "Are you going to be okay?"

She nodded a weak, "yes," with eyes brimming with tears.

Jewel was very upset and taken back over the news. What a way to find out about a friend's death, but she knew she had only herself to blame for the way she found out. She should have at least answered the door when Brad and Justine came over. She decided there was nothing she could do now, except focus on the exam.

The Professor announced a memorial service in the school's chapel for friends and fellow students who wanted to attend and then announced that his remains was taken home and the funeral service would be held in his home town on the next day. He gave a number for anyone who wanted more information and a number for those students who may need counseling.

Jewel had hoped to finish the exam before all of her friends, so she could be with them, but Olivia and Stuart had finished and left. She stood outside in the hallway waiting on the others.

"Eric," Jewel called out as Eric was walking towards the exit. Eric turned to see that it was Jewel. He looked down at the floor and then back at Jewel and said, "look Jewel, I really don't want to talk right now."

"You don't want to talk, or you don't want to talk to me?"

"Both."

"Look Eric."

"No, you look Jewel. A friend of ours killed himself. Someone we all knew. We all just wanted to be together. Yeah, we all had to study and we did, but we grieved too. He was our friend."

"I didn't know about Billy."

"And why was that Jewel?"

"Yeah why was that Jewel?" Paula asked as she walked up behind Jewel.

"I'm sorry," Jewel said.

"Are you?" Paula asked as she and Eric walked away.

Justine came out next and even though she wasn't as cold as the others, she clearly let Jewel know she was not happy at the way she was acting.

"I thought of all people who would understand it would be you Justine." Jewel tried to reason.

"Understand what Jewel? That you are self-absorbed and have no time for the people who care about you? No Jewel, I don't understand that."

"It's not my fault Billy killed himself."

"No it isn't Jewel, and I don't think anyone is accusing you of that," Justine said as she too walked away.

"Are you mad at me too?" Jewel asked Brad who had just walked out of the exam room and walked past her, not seeing her standing with her back against the wall.

"I'm not mad with you, nor are the others. They're just upset and disappointed, that's all."

"Upset with me? What did I do?"

"You didn't do anything Jewel. That's the point, not even pick up the phone."

"Why didn't you say something on the answering machine?"

"Telling you Billy killed himself on the answering machine, just didn't seem the thing to do."

"You think it was better to hear it from the professor right before a major exam. I probably failed the entire exam."

Brad looked at Jewel and said sadly, "I'm sure you did well."

"Are you going to the memorial service and the funeral services?"

"Yes, I'm going to the memorial, but I'm going to pass on the funeral. I didn't know him as well as the rest of you did."

"I don't think anyone of us knew him that well. I don't think we know each other as well as we think we do."

"Well Jewel, these are the times when people find out how well they know each other."

"Do you mind if I go with you to the memorial service? I don't want to go alone, especially the way everyone is feeling about me right now."

Brad walked closer to Jewel and put his arms around her neck and she buried her face into his chest.

"No, I don't mind. Afterwards, I think we're all meeting at the sports bar. I'll pick you up, if you if you want to come."

"Yes, I want to," Jewel said.

"I'll pick you up around six thirty. See you then," Brad said as he began to leave.

"You mind walking me to my car?" Jewel asked.

Brad held out his hand she took it and said, "I'm sorry I've not been available," Jewel said apologetic.

Brad wanted to believe her. He missed her, but it was she who had begun to shut him out. Brad walked Jewel to her car kissed her on her forehead and watched her drive off before walking over to his own car and leaving the parking lot.

There were a lot of people at the memorial service. Billy was a very likeable person. There weren't many people that he met that he didn't befriend.

Out of all in the group, Jewel liked studying with Billy, because he was always serious about studying and made the group refocused when they strayed away from their studies or a topic.

Jewel wondered what happened during the Thanksgiving break. He was going to tell his parents he was gay and introduce them to his friend, but Jewel never asked Billy or anyone else how it went, because she was too occupied with her own life to concern herself with what was going on with others around her.

Stuart and Eric spoke on behalf of the study group and other students who knew Billy spoke. Art, Billy's friend, spoke of his love for Billy and what a waste it was for him to end his life the way he did, because he couldn't please the people he loved.

Jewel suspect he was talking about Billy's parents. The Chaplain finish the service by speaking some of the same things that the Professor had said early that morning, about being focus and knowing what is priority.

Everyone's mood was very somber. No one knew what to say.

"I can't believe that Billy would do something like this?" Jewel spoke first.

"Believe it Jewel, you don't even have a clue as to what Billy was going through." Olivia spoke with tears welling up in her eyes, "You have been so self-absorbed. You don't even know what any of us have been going through. What happened to, we're all in this together?" Olivia lashed out at Jewel.

"Come on guys, I think we've been hard enough on Jewel. It isn't her fault that Billy killed himself," Paula said feeling sorry for the way everyone was treating Jewel. "It's none of our fault, so we need to stop condemning ourselves."

"He was just so tormented. We all saw it, but we were all too caught up in our own world to reach out to him," Eric added.

"Did he ever get around to telling his parents about him and Art?" Jewel asked.

"Yes," Stuart replied, and his parents lost it, disowned him and all that."

"He just wasn't prepared for that," Paula said.

"He should have been," Justine said.

"What do you mean?" Stuart asked.

"I mean, Billy should have known. We may live in a world where gays are out of the closet and blacks and whites are dating and getting married," Justine said looking to Brad and Jewel, "but let's face it, not everyone is so accepting. We accepted Billy because he was a good person and a good friend, not because of his lifestyle, but let's have a reality check, how many of us can say that our parents would welcome us telling them something like that with open arms and acceptance. I know mines would not. The little help that I'm getting from them would be gone."

"I guess you're right," Olivia said, "My parents would probably freak out. However, I do believe that after they've had time to adjust, they would accept me and love me for who I am."

"Well Billy didn't wait to see whether or not his parents would have a change of heart, now did he?" Stuart said, "everything that he ever did in his life was to please them."

"That's why we have to do what's best for us, no matter what others think," Jewel said.

Everyone thought she was talking about her and Brad, even Brad did as he held her hand tightly to show his support of what she was saying.

"I can understand what Billy must have been going through, trying to please everyone. I just thank God that I realize now, before it's too late that I need to do what is best for me and maybe you guys will never understand that, but Billy's death has made me realize just how important that is."

"Is that at the expense of friends and people who love you and care about you Jewel?" Paula asked.

"Friends should understand and people who care for you should care enough to support you in your dreams and goals, no matter what it takes. It may mean losing a friend on the way, but those who are your true friend will be there for you. No, I wasn't there for Billy, but none of us were, because we are all pursuing our own personal goals. Does that mean we didn't care about Billy? I hope not. Each one of us will need to search our hearts for that answer." Jewel finished her soda and got up to leave.

"If you're not ready Brad, I'll catch a cab."

Brad didn't have much to say about Billy. He was there for the moral support and he felt that Jewel needed his support right now, so he got up and said goodnight to the others, as he prepared to leave with her.

"Hey Jewel," Justine got up and walked over to her; she hugged her and said, "I hope you reach those dreams and goals."

She turned to the group and said, "I hope we all reach our goals, but let's keep things in perspective, and if we need help, let's get it."

Everyone held up their drinks and said, "hear, hear."

Stuart lifted up his glass again and said, "to Billy."

And everyone replied, "to Billy."

They got up and embraced each other as they left the bar one by one.

They never met as a group after that night and most of them never went back to the sports bar. Billy's suicide changed each of their lives forever.

Chapter Twenty-Two
Bedeekle

"What's next boss?" The little imp inquired of Bedeekle.

Bedeekle was relaxing with his slimly green vine like arms around his distorted head. His beady blood shot eyes were gleaming red and his mouth was open with a wiry grin showing all of his blackened teeth.

"Now, little one, we just sit back and watch. Everything has been put into motion in Atlanta and New York and there is nothing else for us to do, except sit back and watch these two destroy themselves. This will be the beginning of the downfall of the Ekklesia church."

The two imps stared at each other in confusion, "we don't get it boss."

Bedeekle jumped up in a fury, "of course you don't, you stupid little imps, if you did you would be in charge and not me!"

The two imps shrugged their little shoulders as they looked at each other and back at Bedeekle.

"Do I have to spell it out to you?" Bedeekle yelled.

"Yes boss, because we don't know what connection these two have with that church."

"There are people there who will lose faith and hope because of what's going to happen to these two and then they will practically destroy themselves and their Pastor."

"Ahhh, we see." The two little imps said, not really seeing at all, but were too afraid to continue to question Bedeekle.

"Well, it doesn't matter if you see it or not," Bedeekle said, knowing that he didn't quite see the big picture himself, "all we have to do is our part and if everyone else does their part, then everything will come together. It's about confusion! Now, do you get it?"

"Ah yes, boss, confusion. We like confusion." the two imps said empathically shaking their loose wirily necks that spun around, when moved too abruptly.

Chapter Twenty-Three
Lois

"Is she in there?" Francesca asked.

"I can hear Dandan," Adrienne said, as she continued to pound on the door while Francesca rang the doorbell.

"Lois, Open the door! We know you're in there!"

"Should we call the Landlord or something?" Asked Francesca.

"Wait a minute," said Adrienne, Kelly or Alexis might have a key. I don't have Alexis' number. Go call Kelly."

Francesca race down the hall to her apartment, while Adrienne continued to knock on the door; she came back about three minutes later, "she's on her way."

"Let's keep knocking in the meantime."

"You think…" Francesca began.

"I don't think anything," Adrienne said cutting Francesca's question off.

She didn't want to think that the situation was that out of control, even though the thought kept crossing her mind.

Lois had been depressed for months now and heavily on drugs. They all covered for her one time or another, hoping they could get through to her to pull it together, before someone from the house found out. She tried to hide her addiction by telling the other girls that it was cold medicine or something she was taking to help her sleep.

"What is going on?" Kelly asked as she walked up to Lois' apartment door, with her keys in her hands, "Is she in there?"

"We don't know," Adrienne said, "but Dandan is, we can hear him."

Kelly took the key Lois gave her for emergencies and opened the door. The three women race to the room where they immediately heard Danijel's voice, upon entering the apartment. Their hearts were racing not knowing what they would find. They entered Lois' room where she was lying across her bed fully clothes. Danijel was sitting in an Indian squat tapping her on the shoulder trying to wake her.

"Oh my God, I'll call 911," said Francesca.

"Wait!" Adrienne yelled, as Francesca stood motionless with the phone to her ear.

Adrienne checked Lois' pulse and said, "she has a good pulse. Help me get her up and to the shower."

"Shouldn't we call 911?" a shaking Francesca asked.

"No!" said Kelly, "they'll take Dandan, if they think she tried to overdose or something."

Kelly helped Adrienne dragged Lois into the bathroom.

"Take Dandan into the next room Francesca, if you need something to do," Kelly said after observing Francesca still holding the phone.

Kelly and Adrienne managed to drag Lois into the shower and they turned the cold water on her. It took a second before Lois began to grasp for breath and swinging her arms, as if she was drowning, lashing out at Kelly and Adrienne

"You think she's awake?" Kelly asked Adrienne, sarcastically.

"I think so."

Adrienne turned the cold water off and Lois furiously asked, "What do y'all think y'all are doing?"

"Saving your butt," said Adrienne.

"My butt doesn't need saving."

"Maybe not," said Kelly, "but you sure do."

"Where's my child?"

"The child you left alone while past out on whatever it is that you're own," Kelly said clearly annoyed at Lois' attitude.

"Mind your own business Kelly."

"You made Dandan my business, when you ask me to be his godmother and gave me a key to check on him in case of emergencies.

If Dandan wasn't in this apartment with you, I would've let Francesca called 911."

"I guess you want me to thank you?"

"I want you to get it together."

"I need to get out of these wet clothes and I can do that by myself."

"We'll be in the living room waiting for you, with your child," Kelly said with the emphasis on "your child."

"Hey Dandan, have you eaten?"

"Yes maam Auntie Kell," he said pointing at a very messy kitchen, "I eat corn flakes, milk and sugar."

The girls laughed.

"You sure you got to eat any of it?" Adrienne teased, after viewing the mess on the floor.

"I eat."

"Then why don't we get you cleaned up and out of these clothes?" Kelly said taking his hands.

"I wear blue jean and big bird shir."

"Blue jeans and big bird shirt it is."

That was easier said than done. It didn't look like Dandan had anything clean to put on judging from the pile of dirty clothes in his room.

"He can put these on," Lois said as she entered the door with clothes in her hands. "Here Dandan put these on for mommy."

"I wan big bird shir and jean."

"Big bird shirt is dirty, just put these on please." Lois said through clenched teeth.

"Big bird shir mommy, big bird shir," Danijel began to whine.

Lois began to rub her forehead as she grabbed Danijel by his little arm and squeezed it and said in a very low intimidating voice, "I said, big bird shirt is dirty, now put these on," she said shoving the clothes in Danijel hands.

Danijel began to cry and Kelly reached out to help him, "Why don't Aunt Kell give you a hand?"

"I do it," Danijel said between stifles, "I put own clothes on."

"Yes, he can do it himself," Lois said to Kelly, insinuating that she had overstepped her boundary, "and since you have done your good deed for the day, you all are free to leave."

Kelly stepped out of the room, "I'll wait for you out here," she said to Lois.

"What are you doing?" Kelly asked when Lois came out of the room.

Lois slightly pulled Danijel room door close and said to him, "why don't you watch TV for a little sweetie, I'll be right back."

"It is one thing to get high with your customers, but when you begin to past out on your four year old child Lois, it's time to get help."

"I wasn't passed out. I had a headache when I got in early this morning. I must have taken too many aspirin."

"If we had to call 911, they would've taken Dandan away and have you in some hospital on the psyche ward."

"Don't be dramatic."

"I'm not. What you've done is serious.

"Whatever."

"The neighbor called the cops on you, because they suspected you were leaving Dandan alone," Francesca said, passing on a rumor she had heard in the building not knowing if it was true or not.

"That was a misunderstanding," Lois said, "I only went downstairs for a minute, or so to get something from someone and those old busy bodies across the hall, who can never mind their own business called the cops. They're just miserable about their own boring life that they always try to keep something going."

"That may be true Lois, but if the cops already have a record of you leaving your child in the apartment by himself, you can believe they're not going to take a second offense for granted," Adrienne said.

"What record? Like you know this."

"I do. I know people who've had their kids taken away from them Lois."

"You would," Lois said as an insult to Adrienne, "but no one is taking my child anywhere, okay, and as for those nosey old busy bodies, I've told them to mind their own business."

"You think that's going to make your problems go away, because you've told everyone to mind their business?" asked Kelly.

"Thank you for what you've think y'all have done, but I got it from here," Lois said ungratefully.

"We have to get back to work anyway," Adrienne said, picking up her coat and motioning to Francesca.

Lois began to laugh with a high pitch and said, "I wish you guys would stop acting like we do some real work, or like we are making some difference in the World. We are part of the problem, not the solution. We break up marriages and wreck homes. We are your modern day prostitutes. What we do is not a job!" Lois yelled behind Adrienne and Francesca as they were leaving.

Kelly stayed around to talk to Lois, but she did not have much success in reasoning with Lois to get help.

"Lois you can choose to ignore what we've tried to say to you today, but you'll only be hurting yourself. I'm concern about Dandan and what may happen to him, if you don't pull yourself together. If you hate this business so much, why don't you just get out? You're right. We are modern day prostitutes, but we don't have pimps and no one will hunt us down, if we choose to get out. We can walk away anytime we want. I tried to warn you not to get into this business. You didn't want to listen. You blindly walked right into it, despite any warning from me and I suspect you won't listen to me now. I don't know what to do to help you, but I fear that if you don't do something you are going to regret it in a big way."

"It's not so easy as all that Kelly. If it were, you would have been out. I want the same things that you want, a good life for me and my son. I don't want to go back living in the projects, where it's too cold in the winter and too hot in the summer. I refuse to live in a place where I have to continue to check on my child for fear the rats and the roaches will eat him up at night."

"That's fine Lois, then get clean and face reality. If this is for Dandan, then make it work for him. I doubt that you have one dime saved up, because you're putting it up your nose."

"You don't know anything."

"Maybe I don't, but I have a good idea of what's happening." Kelly picked up her coat and walked to the door. She turned before walking out the door and said to Lois, "get help Lois."

Christopher Madison grabbed Lois' wrist and squeezed it really tight, "Have I ever denied you anything Lois?"

Lois began to squirm as she took her free hand and tried to pry his tight grip on her wrist loose.

"Let me go!" she said raising her voice.

Christopher let her wrist go and pushed her on the bed, "what did you do with it, put it all up your nose?"

"I don't know what you're talking about?"

"Oh, I think you do," said Chris, who once vied for Lois' company, now he looked on her with disdain.

"I'm sorry, but this will be the last time I request your service."

Christopher had become Lois' main source of income, for which she was able to keep her hundred dollar a day cocaine habit. She was suddenly frantic. She got up from the bed and began to apologize.

"I'm sorry Chris for whatever it is that you think I've done."

"I don't think. I know you have been taking money from me for weeks now. I refuse to be nothing more to you than your cocaine fund. I want a Lady. The Lady you use to be, before, before…this," he said as he began to go through her purse for her stash.

Lois grabbed at her purse, but he held her back with one hand until he found what he was looking for.

"What are you doing?" Lois asked as he walked towards the bathroom with the vile of cocaine.

"I'm helping you get started with your rehab program."

"I don't need a rehab program!" Lois screamed trying to snatch the vile out of his hand. "I just need a little help now and then, that's all," she said yelling.

"Lois, I'm going to do something I've never done before. Here, this is my card. You can reach me at anyone of those numbers. When you've gotten help for your habit, give me a call."

As Christopher was walking towards the door, Lois grabbed his arm. "What are you going to do?"

"I'm not going to do anything Lois. Your secret is safe with me, although I know your Agency has a zero tolerance for drugs."

"I thought the Agency had zero tolerance for escorts sleeping with customers. Don't fool yourself Mr. Madison concerning the credibility of this Agency."

"I was under the impression that what the Escorts do after they were off duty were their own business. I think you're off duty now. What we had was off the clock. It was because both of us wanted it, or at least I wanted you and you wanted my money. We both got what we wanted."

"Then what's with your holier than thou attitude all of a sudden?" Asked Lois.

"I don't like drugs, but I would've tolerated anything to be with you. What I won't tolerate is you stealing from me."

"You're worth millions and you're worried about a few dollars."

"A few hundred dollars Lois, and no I'm not worried about it. What I am worried about is you and what you would do to get a fix. My brother died of a cocaine overdose Lois. I know what it can do to you. You will never get enough. You will go from a hundred to a five hundred dollar a day habit."

"That's ridiculous."

"Is it now? I remember when you use to settle for the twenty dollar vile I use to bring you and I hated myself every time I did it. I tried to detach myself from it, just like I did my brother, lying to myself that it was okay. I did a little myself. It's not going to hurt him, I said to myself. I stood by and watched my brother self destruct."

Christopher turned and cupped Lois' face in his hands, "you don't have to go this way Lois. I'll pay for you to get the best help, if you want it."

Lois slapped his hands from her face, "If and when I need your help, I'll call one of these numbers that you have given me," Lois said flicking the card in his face.

Christopher was not moved by her sarcasm, "don't wait until it's too late, before you use the number," he said before he left the room.

"Hi Kelly," Lois said rocking back and forth on the couch with the phone covering her face instead of the usual ear to mouth position.

"I need a favor. Can you watch Danijel for me? I need to go out."…"Thanks Kelly. I'll bring him right over."…"No, I won't be long."

Lois was gone for five hours and Kelly had to get one of the other girls to meet her customer at a Broadway show. Lois finally showed up after midnight.

"I don't believe you Lois. Where have you been? You knew I had to work tonight. I had a very important client tonight."

"So my son isn't more important than one of your johns?"

"Mr. Fein is not a john. He's a widower, who is well respected in his circle. Don't try to put no guilt trip on me concerning Dandan, because he is your responsibility Lois not mine."

"Excuse me then, I will just take my responsibility and leave you alone to see your Mr. Fein. Where is he?"

"It's after midnight. He's sleeping. You should just leave him here until the morning."

"I don't think so. My son will not stay where he is not wanted."

"Lois, I'm tired and you are too stone for me to get into this with you tonight, so if that's what you want to do, go ahead. Go home and sleep it off."

Lois stormed into the bedroom, picked up Danijel and left.

"Lois, I really need to be out of here before six in the morning. I have an early morning exam and I can't be late. I know I need the money, but I can't afford to fail a class because I'm late. I plan to graduate this fall and that doesn't include making up any classes," Alexis was hoping she was getting through to Lois. If it weren't for Danijel, she would have quit babysitting for Lois a long time ago

"You're a sweetheart Alexis," Lois said pinching Alexis on her cheek.

Alexis jerked her face away, "I'm serious Lois. Don't make me late."

Alexis woke startled at a faint sound. The TV was turned down low, so that she could get some studying done. She had put Danijel to bed at eight o'clock. It was now one o'clock in the morning and Lois was not home. Alexis began to panic. She couldn't miss this test in the morning. She still had time. Lois said she was only going to a fundraising affair and was going to come straight home.

Alexis decided not to panic. She would give her a little more time. Alexis tried to study some more, but her eyes were heavy and she soon fell asleep.

She awoke in another panic. She had a dream that she missed her exam and her professor was going to make an example of her and not give her a make up test. She got an "F," failed the class, didn't graduated and decided to drop out of college.

She looked at the time and it was four o'clock in the morning. She ran to Lois' bedroom, but she wasn't there. Sometime she would come in so high and go right to bed and reluctantly Alexis would leave, hoping and praying that Lois would wake up before Danijel. She was unaware of how many times that didn't happen. She called Kelly.

"Alexis calm down."…"Yeah, okay,"…"I'll come over and watch him until Lois come home."…"I know, I know."…"Give me a minute."…"You're welcome."

"How could she do this to me? I practically begged her to come home on time, so that I don't miss my exam this morning. She doesn't seem to care about anyone except herself anymore. I don't think she even cares about her own son," Alexis said, crying to Kelly.

"She cares Alexis. She is just going through a rough time now, just be patient."

"Patient? I don't think so. I don't think I can work for her anymore. I mean it this time."

"Alexis calm down. You still have plenty of time to get home, shower and get ready for your class."

"I know. I guess I just don't understand her, but I care so much for Danijel."

"I know how you feel. You go ahead now and do good on your exam."

"Thanks Kelly," Alexis said as she ran out of the apartment with one hand in the sleeve of her coat and her book bag on that shoulder as well.

Kelly called Adrienne by one in the afternoon when Lois hadn't showed up yet. "What do you think I should do?" Kelly asked.

"What can we do except wait?" respond Adrienne, "The Agency doesn't have any information except the initial meeting place. I know that much. She was meeting a customer at the Ritz for a Gala fund raising affair. That was over at midnight. Where they went from there is the question."

The phone rang about two thirty in the afternoon. "Who is this?"…"Yes, I know her."…"A motel?"…"Which one and where?"…"Okay, thank you. I appreciate the information. By the way, what's your name?"…"Okay, I'll ask for you when we get there."

"Who was that?" Adrienne asked as Kelly place the phone on the hook.

"I have no idea. Some cleaning women at the Hole Motel a block away from the Bowery."

"What! How did she get down there?"

"I don't know, but the maid said she looks like she's passed out and if we don't come get her soon, she'll have to tell the building manager and he'll call the cops."

"Great!" Adrienne said in disgust.

"I'll go get her. You stay here with Dandan."

"No way am I letting you go down there by yourself."

"It's daylight. No one will bother me."

"No way. I'll call Francesca to watch Dandan. We'll take my car and be in and out of there before the natives can get restless."

Francesca came right over.

The building stank of urine. Kelly was about to ask the woman at the front desk about the girl who called her, when someone said in a soft voice with a heavy accent, "You Kelly?"

"Yes, I am."

"I called you."

"Where is she?"

"Come, I show you."

Kelly and Adrienne followed behind the girl, hoping that they weren't being set up. They had taken off all their jewelries and brought only the money they were going to tip the girl, who called them. They prayed that no one took Adrienne's car before they got back.

"How did you know to call me?"

"Find you name in purse. Says call fo mergencies, see."

"Thanks," Kelly said.

"No problem. She in here."

The girl took out a key and opened the door to the room. It was dark, stuffy and smell of vomit inside.

"Thanks again," Kelly said, reaching into her breast and pulling out a hundred dollar bill.

"Tank you, tank you very much," said the girl backing out of the door.

"Should we put her in the shower to wake her up?" Adrienne asked

"No, she'll catch a death of cold going out in the air. We're going to have to wake her, as much as possible, then walk her to the car. Open that window, while I put on her coat."

Kelly looked around the room for Lois' black mink coat, but didn't see it.

"I don't see her coat."

"You're surprised?" Asked Adrienne, "that little maid got a hundred dollar, a mink coat and whatever else Lois had in her purse."

"You're probably right. Come on help me get her to the window, so the cold air can blow in her face. Lois wake up," Kelly started to shake and lightly slap Lois on the face.

"Wake up!" Adrienne said with a loud hard slap to Lois face. Lois made a moaning sound and opened her eyes.

"What are you trying to do?" asked Kelly.

"Get her, and us out of here as soon as possible and maybe slap some sense into her while doing it."

They got Lois to the window and stuck her head out of it. The cold air hit Lois harder than Adrienne's slap.

"What? What?" Lois tried to mumble.

"You are not asking the questions here sweetheart, we are, and all we want to know is, can you walk to the car?" Adrienne asked.

"I can walk," Lois said as she pushed the two girls away and tried to stand up on her own, but her legs buckled underneath her as soon as she didn't have the support of Kelly and Adrienne.

"Okay, Okay, we got you," Kelly said, grabbing Lois right before she reached the floor, "grab an arm Adrienne and let's get out of here."

Lois was sandwiched between the two girls with her arms over each shoulder. She half walked and was dragged the other half, as they managed to get her in the car and out of the Bowery.

Kelly took Danijel to her place for the rest of the day, so that he wouldn't see his mom in her condition. Adrienne stayed to keep an eye on her. Lois finally was awake and alert about five thirty that afternoon. Adrienne was sitting on the couch flicking the channels on the TV and reading the TV guide.

"You wake?" Adrienne asked, staring at Lois wobbling her way into the living room.

"Barely, where is Dandan?"

"With Kelly at her apartment."

"I'll go get him."

"All you have to do is call and Kelly will bring him right over. She didn't want Dandan to see you in the condition you were in." Lois picked up the phone and called Kelly. Kelly wasn't home, but she left a message to let her know she was awake and she could bring Danijel home anytime.

"I got to go. I have to work tonight," Adrienne said getting up to leave.

"Adrienne, where was I?"

"In some rat hole motel in the Bowery, half naked," Adrienne exaggerated the naked part.

"How did I get there?"

"Girl, if you don't know, I sure couldn't tell you, but I'll tell you this. That should be your wake up call."

"Thanks Adrienne," Lois said in a weak girl-like voice that made Adrienne's heart go out to her.

"You're welcome Lois," Adrienne wanted to say more, but thought, now was not the time.

Lois sat on the couch crying the rest of the afternoon. Kelly brought Dandan home around his bedtime. Lois was sitting in the dark when Kelly let herself into the apartment at seven thirty.

"Mommy! Mommy!" Dandan yelled out, as Kelly flick on the light switch near the door.

Lois turned and opened her arms so that he could run into them. He planted wet kisses all over Lois' face, which made a flood of tears stream from her eyes. Kelly pulled a paper towel from the kitchen and gave it to her.

"Where have you been?" Lois said in a hoarse voice.

"Auntie Kell took me to get some ice-cream."

"What kind did you get?"

"I had choco chip and Aunt Kell had pictasto."

"Hmmm sounds good. Did you eat it all?"

"Yep, I eat it all up," Danijel said rubbing his stomach. Lois laughed and squeezed him tightly.

"Alexis?" Lois inquiringly asked Kelly.

"She's okay. She made her exam, but you may have lost a baby sitter."

"Why don't you go and get into your jammies, sweetie," Lois said to Danijel.

"I wash first?"

"Let me smell you," Lois sniffed under his arms and his bottom, tickling him as she went down, as he buckled over in laughter, "I think you won't kill the bed if you skip it tonight." He laughed harder at that.

"I can't kill the bed Mommy. You being silly."

"I know," Lois said, "now why don't you gave me and Aunt Kell a big hug, and get in bed. I'll come tuck you in, okie dokie," she said saluting him.

312

He saluted back and said, "okie dokie."

"Kelly I really appreciate what you and Adrienne did," Lois began, "I know you're not going to believe what I'm saying, but I really mean it when I say that I'm not doing drugs anymore. Someone once told me that after my escort service is finished, it's my choice what I do with my time. I'm going to change what I do with my time. I may not make as much money as everyone else, but I'll have my dignity and the respect and love of my child," Lois said in tears.

"You need some place to go?" Kelly asked

"I'll be okay, I'm not as bad as you think."

"Maybe not Lois, but I've never heard of too many people quitting cold turkey."

"I'm not sure what that means, but I can do this, because I want to," Lois said, as Kelly took her hands and squeezed them.

"I'm here for you, okay."

"This is a nice surprise," Kelly said as Rinoldo took off her coat and handed it to the maitre'd. "We haven't been out to a nice restaurant in ages."

"You've been a busy lady."

"Oh, it's me who've been busy, huh, and not you?"

"Well, we've both been busy."

"Thank you," Kelly said. As usually Rinoldo ordered for the both of them. It was something that used to irked her about him, but eventually it wasn't such a big deal. His choices were always good, but she would jump in and order something else every now and then, just to let him know that she had a mind of her own and could make her own choices.

Rinoldo didn't waste any time getting to the real reason for such an extravagant dinner, "I heard your friend is having some problems?"

Kelly wondered when they were going to have this talk.

"Yes, she's had a rough time lately, but with the help of her friends, she is getting it together."

"You sure about that, because that's not what I heard."

"Then why don't you say what you've heard and we won't have to play this little game of trying to see how much you can get out of me."

Rinoldo straighten up in his chair, "I heard that Lois is strung out on drugs."

"Strung out is a bit harsh. She was doing a little drug, but she's realized that it isn't the way she wants to go."

"You sure about that?"

"I'm sure," Kelly said adamantly looking into Rinoldo's eye, "has Madam, or Lady heard anything yet?"

"I'm not sure. They haven't said anything to me about it yet."

"Then how did you hear?"

"Joe. She said she got a call from Mr. Mullin. He said that he had his driver dropped her off in a place that was a little shady and if that was the kind of escort that we were going to provide him with, he may take his business somewhere else.

I called him to find out the details. I told him she knew someone down there, and the good hearted person she was, she was always trying to take him something to him, a little money, whatever she could. Just the same he said he'd rather his driver not risk taking her down there. I told him that it would never happen again," Rinoldo look squarely at Kelly and ask, "can you assure me that it will never happen again?"

"Never is a long time."

"Don't play word games with me Kelly," Rinoldo said leaning over the table to Kelly.

"It will not happen again."

"You want to put your job on the line for her?"

"You want me to? I would if I had to."

"I know you would. No. I don't want you to put your job on the line, but she'll be out faster than Satan's fall from heaven, if she tries something like that again. She's your friend. I thought I'd let you handle it."

"I'll handle it."

"Good. Now we can enjoy our meal."

It took Lois awhile to convince Alexis to give her another chance. Alexis wouldn't bulge, until she put Danijel on the phone to ask Alexis to come over and play with him.

Lois was true to her word and got back home, when she said she would.

"Thank you," Alexis said.

"No, thank you," Lois said, "I don't know what I would do without you."

"Here," she said reaching in her purse to pay Alexis.

Alexis counted her money. She felt uncomfortable doing it in front of Lois, but Lois had shorted her before, but because she didn't count her pay before she left, Lois denied underpaying her, saying she must've misplaced the money. Lois had become such a good liar.

When she looked up Lois was smiling, "I think you paid me too much."

Lois had given her two hundred dollars more.

"It's for all the times that I was short, or couldn't pay you at all. You've been a real trooper about it.

"Gee thanks," Alexis said, as she hugged Lois, "I'm glad to see you like this again," Alexis said realizing Lois wasn't as uptight, as she had been lately.

Alexis hoped everything was getting back to normal for her. She felt more comfortable leaving Danijel with Lois, knowing she was her old self again.

Lois spent the next couple of days with Danijel, but she wasn't feeling well. She knew her body was reacting to the drugs. She had gone an entire day without using, but not three days. She convinced herself that she was able to do this on her own, without going through a program.

Kelly came by one afternoon, at Lois' request and watched Danijel, while Lois went through withdrawals.

"Lois you don't have to do this by yourself. There are places."

"I'm going to be all right, Kelly. Thanks for coming over. My head was spinning out of control."

"Is there anything else I can do?"

"No, I appreciate everything you've done."

"Not a problem. I just want you to get better."

"That I can do," Lois said giving Kelly a big hug.

"It's good to have my best friend back."

"It's good to be back."

Lois had made it through five days, but she had wasted all of her savings, and hadn't paid Danijel's daycare in over a month. She received a letter from the Daycare, stating it was his last week, unless she paid in full. Lois considered her choices. Since she worked mostly at night, she could easily just let him stay at home and only pay Alexis to watch him at night.

Lois decided that she wanted to start back attending church services, but there wasn't many in the area, so she began to go with Francesca to a catholic church.

Francesca came over early one Sunday morning bringing breakfast for Lois and Danijel, "Lois, I was wondering if you wanted to go to confession with me this morning?"

"I'm not actually Catholic Francesca."

"You know what they say, confession is good for the soul."

"Is it? What? You confess your sins today and go back the next day and do the same thing. I don't think I could do that. Does it work for you? Do you feel good about yourself after you confess?"

"Yes, it does. My father is dying of cancer. My mother tries to take care of five children by cleaning rich people homes. The money I make help pays my father's bill and helps two of my brother and sister to go to college without having to worry about getting a part time job to help support the family. I'm doing what I have to do Lois, and my check from the Agency alone barely pays the utility bills.

"I see."

"No you don't Lois. You want to sit there and judge me, but you don't know anything about me."

"I can't judge you without judging myself Francesca. I'm sorry I didn't mean to offend you."

Lois stopped going to church with Francesca, because it made her feel like a hypocrite. She had clean up her act, but it wasn't enough. She started toying with the idea of leaving the Agency, but she wanted to have something lined up before she did that.

Lois was diligently looking in the want ads, going on interviews and looking into schools, while accepting less invitation from the Agency.

Her bills were getting behind and every time she talked to one of the other girls, they were always talking about something new they were buying.

In spite of everything, Danijel had a good Christmas because Lois' parents and her friends bought him all kinds of things. She was mostly glad for the clothes they bought him, because he was growing out of everything.

Lois decided that come January, if she didn't have another job, she was going to start business school. The school would last for five to six months. She could qualify for a loan. She could go during the day and work during the night. She was getting more work at night now that the word was out that she had clean up her act. She was working every night trying to get money to pay off the Daycare, so she could put Danijel back in.

She considered waiting until the following fall when Danijel would be able to go to Kindergarten, but she would still have to pay for daycare for part of the day. She didn't want to entertain the thought of putting school off again.

"You have a special invitation today Lois," Joe said as she handed Lois her paycheck and her next assignment. Lois took both and walked away while the other girls were making silly sounds and looking over her shoulder to see what the special invite was all about.

After reading it, Lois stomped back to Joe's desk and threw the invitation on the desk, "I won't take this assignment," she said to Joe.

Joe looked up at her. Joe knew it was her right to refuse an invitation with good reason. She also knew it ended badly for Lois and Mr. Long before, but she couldn't imagine anyone ever refusing a second opportunity with him.

"You realize this is The Peter Long," said Joe.

The other girls stood by to see what Lois would do, but Kelly walked up to the desk and said, "Joe, you know she has every right to refuse an assignment.

"I'm aware of the rules," Joe responded, "but, there has to be documentation of a complaint, before she can refuse an invitation, you know that. I can tell Mr. Long that you have a previous engagement; however, if he insists and he may, you'll have to take it up with Rinoldo or even Madame.

"Please decline the invitation for me," Lois said not intimidated by the mention of Rinoldo's, or Madame's name.

No one said anything about it until they got into Adrienne's car.

"Maybe he'll ask for me," Adrienne said looking up in the mirror to see Lois' response.

Lois stared blankly out of the window.

Most girls were in the business for a while, before they fell for one of their customers, but for Lois it was almost immediately. No one could blame her considering who it was.

Peter Long made every woman he was with felt like his Queen. He never treated them any other way. It was a characteristic not expected from someone as rich as him. He had an overall respect for women, something many of the women in the Agency never experienced, so it was hard not to fall for someone like that, even Adrienne wondered if anything more could come of their relationship.

Because of Rinoldo's obsession with Kelly, he made it so that Kelly never escorted Peter. Francesca had only gone out with him once and he never invited her out again. In some ways, she was relieved, but she dreamed of the money she could make escorting him.

Despite Peter's debonair, he was a very sensitive man and if he remotely sensed that any of the escorts accepted his invitation because of money, he wouldn't use her again.

"Would you mind, if I accept his invitation if he ask?" Adrienne decided to take a more direct approach.

Lois looked into the mirror and said, "You are more than welcome," and turned her attention back to staring out of the window.

Lois hated herself for how she let Peter get to her. She had promised herself that it would never happen like that for her again after Matt, who never called, or inquired concerning their son. Tears were welling up in her eyes, but she kept her eyes wide open until they dried up, she would not let them see her crying. She didn't want anyone thinking she was still hung up on Peter.

The following day Lois got a visit from Rinoldo. It was early in the morning and she was still in her robe.

"Rinoldo, what are you doing here this time of the morning?"

"Well it can't be that early. I see you and the little one are already up and having breakfast."

Lois looked toward Danijel who was engrossed in his Saturday morning cartoons, cold cereal and laughing in between.

"Can I come in?"

"Sure," Lois said tightening up her robe and opening the door so he could enter.

"Hey there little fellow," Rinoldo said squeezing Danijel's shoulder.

"My names Danijel," Danijel said with his mouth full of cereal and never taking his eyes off the TV. He had turned to see who it was when Lois first opened the door, but he was not particular fond of Rinoldo.

"Please sit down," Lois said, "I'll go put something on."

"Oh, don't bother. I'll get right to the point, so that you can continue your Saturday morning family time with your little one there."

"Danijel," Danijel said, again without looking at Rinoldo.

"Feisty, just like his mother."

"Well his name is Danijel and not little one," Lois said.

"My apologies," said Rinoldo tipping a make believe hat.

"I heard you turned down an invite from Mr. Long."

"Yes, I did. Is there a problem?'

"No, no. There is no problem. I just need you to do me a favor."

"And that is."

"I need you to accept the invitation," Rinoldo put up his hand before Lois could protest, "now I could get into how I personally hired you and what this Agency has done for you, but I won't. I'm just asking you to do this one little favor for me. Mr. Long is one of our well respected customers and I want to do this for him, because we want to keep his business for a long time."

"Sounds personal."

"So, what did he do to you? Did he force himself on you?"

"I think you know the answer to that question."

"Then give me one good reason, why you're refusing to see this client. I'll need an answer to give to Madame."

"I don't have one," Lois stated.

Rinoldo got up, "well I would say to you to really give his invite further consideration. You got a day or two." He walked out of the door.

Lois put her head in her hand.

"Mommy you okay?" Danijel got up and put his arms around Lois.

She looked into his big black eyes and gave him a big hug, "I'm just fine. Why don't we go get dress and go out today."

"Oh boy, Mickey D, Mom, Mickey D," Danijel excitedly jumped up and down at the thought of going to his favorite place.

"We'll see sweetie, we'll see. Now come on let's get dress."

"Race ya," he said and took off with Lois racing behind him.

Lois was getting ready for her Monday afternoon escort, when the phone rang.

"Lois."..."Hi Joe, what's up?"..."Cancelled? The event, or my service?"..."My service, I see."..."Well thank you for calling."..."Excuse me?"..."I heard you before, so I have nothing line up for this week?"..."What about during the day? I can find a babysitter, if necessary."..."Thanks, I appreciate it Joe."

Lois began to undress. She knew this was no coincident that all her appointments were cancelled for the week. She would only get the bare minimum pay this week. Maybe Joe could find her something during the day.

Joe wasted no time calling Lois back.

"I see."…"Did you try, or did you call Rinoldo to confirm that I shouldn't get any work this week?"…"I think you do, but that's okay. I'll get by."

Lois hung up the phone this time by not saying goodbye or thanks. She knew it wasn't Joe's decision. She was just the girl at the desk, but she couldn't help being angry with everyone involved.

"Mommy look, no milk," Danijel said as he held the milk jug upside down proving that there was no milk in the jug.

"I know sweet pea. Mommy has to go to the store."

"I go to," Danijel said excited about the opportunity to push the shopping cart around, or at least the thought that he was pushing.

"Maybe not to day," Lois said, not wanting him to get his hopes up.

"When?" he said coming close to Lois, who was searching her purse for how much money they had left.

The event with Peter was on Thursday evening. He would tip enough for her to buy grocery.

"No, no," she said to herself shaking the thought out of her head.

"No, no," Danijel repeated shaking his head in imitation.

"You silly little thing you," Lois said pushing in his belly button.

He giggled and said, "you silly little thing you," and pushed into Lois' belly button.

Lois looked at him and laughed. This was his favorite game, mocking everything she said or did. This would last for a while until something else caught his attention. Lois looked around the room to find something that would catch his attention quicker. She sat staring at him, while he stared back barely able to contain his laughter. He knew all to well that this game annoyed Lois.

The doorbell rang and Lois jumped up and said, "save by the bell."

He jumped up too and said, "save by the bell."

Lois turned suddenly and almost knocked him over, "Dandan quit it and let me answer the door. Go sit over there until I see who's at the door," he was about to repeat what she said, but she put a finger to his mouth and said, "sit. Mommy means it, now go do it now."

He looked into Lois eyes trying to read how serious she was. He knew the look she would give him when she was serious. He decided this was the look and went to sit down in front of the TV.

Lois turned and smile, "never fails," she said under her breath, as she looked back at him once more before peeping through the peephole. It was Kelly.

"Hi girl, what's up?" Kelly asked.

"Not much," Lois responded as Danijel jumped up at the sound of Kelly's voice.

"Aunt Kell, Aunt Kell," he said running right into Kelly's open arms as she squatted to greet him.

"What's up man?"

"Not much, just watching TV. Me and Mommy going to store lately."

"Later," Lois corrected.

He covered his mouth and said with a big grin as if he realized his goof, "I mean later."

"And I didn't say that we were going later, did I?"

He just walked away and smile and went back to watching TV, "although I need to go," she said to Kelly, who had sat down on a stool.

Lois wondered what it was that Kelly wanted. She didn't need a reason to visit, but it seemed like something was on her mind. She kept talking about the oddest things. This wasn't Kelly. She never talked idly.

"Is something going on that I should no about Kelly?"

"No, I,…no, there isn't."

"What is it, Kelly? You're such a bad liar. Did Rinoldo talked to you?"

"He sort of mentioned something to me the other night about the fact that you may not have any work for awhile."

Kelly never told Lois about her first talk with Rinoldo, because there was no reason to, but she knew Lois needed to work. The way the rent thing worked was that they did not have to pay anything as long as their work for the Agency covered it, based on the hours they work and they had to work a minimum of twenty-five hours a week, if they didn't, they had to pay half of the rent and if they didn't work at all, they had to pay all of it. At fifteen hundred dollars a month, Lois couldn't even pay a fourth of it.

"I got some hours in this month, Kelly," Lois said knowing that Kelly was concerned about her financial situation. Two month in a row, she had to come up with half of the rent, leaving almost nothing for grocery and the rest of her bills.

"Did he say how long he would not let me work? Is this some kind of probation or something?"

"I guess it's something like that. You can stay on probation as long as you want provided you can pay the rent."

"You know I can't afford this rent Kelly."

"Want to hear my suggestion?"

"Maybe not," Lois said, but that didn't stop Kelly from saying it.

"I think you should go out with him. What's it going to hurt, except maybe your pride. The way I see it, you can have your pride, or a roof over your head and food on your table for you and Dandan"

"You're probably right."

"Who knows, maybe he'll see just how much he disgusts you and never ask for you again."

"Or, maybe I can take him for everything I can get."

"What are you talking about?" a puzzled Kelly asked.

"Well, just think. If I go out with him for as long as he wants, I'll easily make enough to payoff what I owe on Dandan's Daycare and enough that I won't have to borrow a loan to go to school."

"I don't understand. I thought you didn't want anything to do with that part of the business again?"

"I don't, but maybe this time I'll make it work for me."

"I think you're playing with fire, Lois."

"Maybe, but I already was burned."

Kelly got up to go, "well I think you should escort him once and let it go at that. I don't think you should play any games with this guy. I've never escorted him, but from what I hear, he didn't become a billionaire because he was book smart, but rather because he is street smart."

"And why is that?"

"Why is what?"

"Why have you never escorted Peter. I can't think of anyone in this Agency more prettier than you Kell."

"It was Rinoldo's decision."

"Rinoldo is no better than Steve, Kell. He has more money and he has promises of a lot of good things, but he's still controlling." Kelly didn't want to get into it with Lois, so she got up to go.

"I got to go. I'll see you later. Just think before you do anything stupid," Kelly said,

Before leaving. She went over to kiss Danijel on the top of his head, "I'll see you later, okay."

"Okay, Auntie Kell, lately."

Lois was about to correct him, but she and Kelly looked at each other and laughed instead.

Lois went over to put a glass up that Kelly used to drink water and underneath the glass was a fifty-dollar bill. She started to run to the door to stop Kelly and give it back, but who was she kidding, she needed the money.

"Thank you," Lois said taking the gown from the deliverer, "I'm sorry I don't have a tip."

"Oh, that okay, Missur Long take care of tip," the Chinese man said.

"Then why are you still standing at my door," Lois thought staring at the guy.

She made a little shaking motion with her head indicating that he should tell her what else he needed.

"Oh me sorry, habit," he said as he bowed and left.

"Right," Lois said closing the door.

Lois took the gown out of its plastic garment bag. It came with shoes, purse, necklace, earring and his favorite perfumed for her, which became her favorite perfumed as well, only she couldn't afford to buy it for herself. It all came with a note that read, 'I think this color matches your skin perfectly. Can't wait to see you in it. Pick you up at seven.'

The gown was satin, rust colored with green beads slashed diagonally from the left shoulder strap, which was the only shoulder strap and came down all the way to the end of the gown. The pearls were Ivory with matching dangling earrings. Lois tried on everything quickly to see if he still remembered her size. He did. It annoyed her, but she was not going to let it bother her and she was going to do her best to not let him see her disgust for him.

Disgust was not Lois' feeling that night. Peter wore her on his arms like a valuable piece of Jewelry.

"Why hello Peter," a distinguished looking man approached them with pepper hair and a pepper mustache.

Peter extended his hand "Larry," he said, simply acknowledging the man.

"And who is the lovely vixen," Larry asked.

"Vixen," Lois thought to herself. She wondered at the term. They were found in many dime store romance novels, but Lois thought only women read them.

"This is Ms. Johnson," Peter said, ignoring the man's term to describe her, "Is the governor here?" Peter inquired of the man, looking around the room.

"Not yet," the man answered.

Peter arched his eyebrow at the man and asked, "He will be here tonight, won't he? Because you know I accepted this invitation strictly as a guise to talk to him about my upcoming deal."

"Yes of course, Peter, and he will be here. Come on let's find your table, so you can get seated and enjoy the evening." The man motioned to a waiter, "Show Mr. Long and this lovely vixen to their seats."

"Miss Johnson," Peter sternly corrected.

"My apologies Miss Johnson, my intentions were not to be insulting."

"That's quite alright," Lois finally spoke.

"It's not alright," Peter firmly stated, as they were escorted to their table.

The night was coming to an end and Peter was clearly irritated that the governor had not showed up, but he did not take any of his frustration out on Lois. He was focused on her and her every move and need. It was hard for Lois not to feel special when she was with him, because he seemed to go out of his way to make her feel that way.

"We're leaving," Peter said to Lois, "unless you'd rather stay a little longer."

"I'm with you," Lois responded.

He got up and pulled back her chair and said goodnight to everyone at the table. Larry saw them leaving and almost broke his neck trying to reach them before they reach the door.

"I'm sorry the governor didn't show, Peter."

Peter stared in contempt at the man, "I think you knew the governor wouldn't be here tonight."

"You know how these things are Peter. The governor is a busy man and things come up."

Peter was not one for words. He lightly took Lois' by the elbow and turned to leave.

"Peter," the man called out as they were walking to the door, "I hope this doesn't affect our future transactions." Peter didn't acknowledge his statement.

Peter was quiet in the car on the way back to Lois' apartment building. He was deep in thought and so was Lois. The evening was nice, but Peter didn't get something he wanted and that always put him in a sour mood. Peter looked inquiringly at the driver as he stopped in front of the building,

"Miss Johnson's building sir," the driver announced.

The driver got out the car to open Lois' door.

"Lois, I know we had a bad ending the last time I was here and I know you were reluctant to go out with me tonight. Matter of fact, you probably wouldn't have if I didn't pull some strings, but regardless of all that, I'm going to be in town for a few months and I hope I'll get to see you again."

Lois listened and without a word got out of the car. When she was out, she put her head back into the car and said, "goodnight."

Peter responded likewise and the driver closed the door, but waited outside of the door until Lois was safely in her apartment building.

Lois forgot all about her personal vendetta against Peter and let herself be swept away once again, by his charm. No matter what she thought of him, he was unlike anyone she had ever met. She was just drawn to his charisma, power and intellect. He became her only customer and a there was a fine line between what business was and what was personal. The only time it was clearly defined was when Peter included Danijel in their plans. He was as good with him, as he was with his mother.

Lois totally lost focus. When the time began to approach for Peter's departure, Lois was highly strung out in anticipation of what may happen. Peter called and invited her, personally, to a special night out.

"Dandan how would you like it if Mommy was to marry Mr. Peter," Danijel looked up at his Mommy while she prepared for her evening out, not quite understanding what she was referring to. She looked at the puzzled look in his eyes and sat down on the bed next to him and sat him in her lap.

"How would you like it if we went to live with Mr. Peter and he became your daddy," Lois tried again in terms he might understand.

"I like Mr. Petee Mommy. He's nice," Danijel replied.

"Yes, he is a very nice man Danijel," Lois said using the correct pronunciation of his name, which she did when she wanted him to know that she was serious.

Danijel picked up on the change and said, "you like Mr. Petee."

"Yes, I do," Lois said placing Danijel back on the bed as she got up to finish dress. "He may ask me tonight. He may. He might not, but I'm not going to assume anything. He can be pretty unpredictable about things like that."

"umpedicabul,' Danijel tried to repeat.

"Close enough," Lois laughed and rubbed him on his head, "it means that you can't really tell what someone is going to say, or do, like little children, you never know what's going to come out of their little mouths," she said tickling Danijel until he was giggling and curled up on the bed.

The doorbell rang.

"That must be Alexis," Lois said and Danijel jumped off the bed and headed for the door, with Lois walking in stride behind him.

Danijel stayed in the living room talking with Alexis while Lois finished dressing.

"How do I look?" she asked emerging from the room.

"Wow!" said Alexis and Danijel repeated.

"Wow!"

"You look fabulous. You really do."

"Yeah, fablous, Mommy, and you look real pretty too."

"Thank you," Lois said to Alexis, and she grabbed Danijel's cheeks and said, "thank you sweetie," and kissed him on the cheek.

"I hope everything goes as you hope." Alexis said.

Danijel had been sharing with Alexis the talk he and Lois had right before she came. "hmm," Lois said looking at Danijel, "I think a little bird has been telling you some fantasy. This is no more than a nice dinner to rap up our business with Mr. Long at the Agency, during his stay in the city."

"Oh, I'm sorry. That's what I get for listening to a four year old fantasize." Alexis said truly apologetic and a little embarrassed.

"That's okay," Lois said, "you know kids, they say the darnest things."

Alexis laughed and the doorbell ring.

"That's Peter. Could you get that Alexis, while I get my purse?"

"Sure."

Alexis invited Peter in and when Lois came into the room, He was sitting next to Danijel whispering something in his ear and they both began to laugh. Lois cleared her throat to let him know she was ready.

"Ahh," Peter said, "breath-taken. You are absolutely breath-taken my dear."

"Thank you," Lois said blushing. She went over to Danijel and kissed him on the cheek and said, "bed on time tonight, okay."

"Okay Mommy."

"See you soon," Lois said to Alexis, who smiled and responded.

"Please, enjoy your night and stay out as late as you wish. I don't have school tomorrow."

"Thank you," Lois replied, as they walked out the door.

When they left the apartment, Danijel pulled on Alexis' pants and as she looked down at him, he asked, "what's fanasy?"

Alexis laughed, "Well let me see if I can explain this," she said leading him to the couch where she sat down besides him. "It's like making up a story, that you would like to happen, but it's not really true. Do you understand that?"

"I think so, Mommy told me a fantasy." Alexis looked puzzled and suddenly wondered what Lois really told Danijel.

The evening was perfect. At the end of the dinner, Peter pulled out a small black box and gave it to Lois. Lois was nervous with anticipation as she looked up at Peter for a clue to what it was.

"Open it," he said.

As she was about to open it, he stopped her and said, "wait. I just want to say this first. I've known and been with a lot of women, but I've finally found someone who has changed my heart concerning marriage. I've decided to settle down and be in a relationship with one woman," he paused, saw the anticipation on Lois' face and said, "but enough of that go ahead, open it."

Lois began to open the box, once opened; Lois stared at the box with tears in her eyes, as she vaguely heard the rest of Peter's statement.

"When I get back to Texas, I'm going to ask her to marry me, but I wanted you to have something that would always remind you of me. I believe in the sanctity of marriage and I intend to be faithful to my wife, so this is really goodbye. I will not be using the services of your Agency any longer. I guess I'll be bringing my wife on future trips, when I need an escort. Oh, by the way, Here is something for your son," he pulled an envelope out his inside coat pocket and presented it to Lois.

It was a ten thousand dollar government bond with Danijel's name written on it. I really like that little boy of yours. I hope to have one of my own someday. I just wanted to give you something to help you with his future. I know you have big plans for him and so you should. Lois put the card in her purse and Peter picked up the box and took out a gold bracelet with her birthstone in the center of a gold medallion.

329

"Here, let me put it on for you," he said, reaching for her arm, which Lois freely allowed him to retrieve and place the bracelet on. "Did you read the back of it?" He asked, as he turned it over to read it to a totally dazed Lois. "It says, you are the best, PL. "There," he said, as he latched the bracelet securely on her arm.

Peter asked the waiter for the check and asked Lois, "Are you ready?"

"Yes, I am," Lois said fighting back tears.

She was determined not to make a scene and not let him see she was hurt.

As Peter was pulling out Lois' chair, he said, "I've arranged for a car to take you back to your apartment. I'm going straight to the airport. My private plane is waiting there for me. I'm leaving tonight." He kissed Lois on the top of her head and said, "I wish you the best and I hope that everything I've done for you in the last couple of months will help you to reach some of your goals."

Lois told Peter about going back to school, not so he would give her any money, but he did. She received some large tips from him during the weeks they were together. A lot of things were going through Lois' mind, but Lois knew she wouldn't be able to ask any question, or she would totally lose it, but Peter knew this.

He remembered the scene Lois made the last time he left New York, so he deliberately arranged to tell her in a public place. He could have easily just left, but it was not his style; to him that would have cheapened how he felt about her and he did have feelings for her, just not the feelings Lois were hoping for.

He walked Lois to the restaurant door and gave the maitre'd a tip and said, "Could you please see Miss Johnson to her car?"

"Yes sir. Miss Johnson," the maitre'd said extending his arm towards the door.

Lois slowly, as if in slow motion, turned to look at Peter with disbelief and hurt in her eyes and he simply said, "this is the best way Lois."

Lois turned and walked out with the maitre'd.

When the driver let her out to her apartment building she said, "here."

"That's not necessary," the driver said thinking Lois was offering a tip, "Mr. Long has taken care of everything."

"I know he has, but I want you to have this anyway."

The Driver took it and looked down at what Lois had placed in his hand. It was the gold bracelet. He looked up, but Lois was gone, but not to her apartment. She was walking down the street. "Miss Johnson," the driver called out, "Are you going to be okay?" Lois waved a hand to let the driver know that he was dismissed from his duties.

Lois walked around her apartment building twice before going in.

Alexis didn't need to ask how it went; black mascara was running down her face and she looked tired, not exuberated, as a woman would, who just received a proposal. This was definitely a look of rejection. Alexis knew the look too well.

"Are you okay?" She asked. Lois looked up at Alexis and responded, "I'm not sure. Everything seems to be, what's the word? Surreal." Lois laughed at herself while digging in her purse for money to pay Alexis.

"I can stay a little longer, if you need me to. It's still early," Alexis offered.

"It is, but no thank you Alexis. Go home. I'm going to be alright, once I can get back to reality."

Alexis left and Lois sat on the couch and began to cry.

Lois was in a dazed for weeks afterwards, going through the motions. She played the scene over and over in her mind, sometimes laughing hysterically or crying uncontrollable. She feared she was losing her mind. She was becoming paranoid of everyone talking behind her back. At every laugh, giggle or soft whisper, Lois looked. She began to have headaches that seem never to go away. The only time she felt any reprieved was when she was with Danijel, but that wasn't long. She had placed him back in Daycare. Peter had paid the outstanding balance and a few months in advance and told her to put him back in, so they could spend more time together during the day.

At night, sleep eluded her. She lay awake wondering, when he decided to marry this woman, whoever she was. Did he say he wanted children? How could he? She thought he couldn't. Was everything a lie? Did he come back to have one last fling with her? How could someone be so kind and then so cruel at the same time? The thoughts never stopped and her headaches intensified.

She began to take every over the counter medication she could get her hands on. She took something for the headaches, something to make her sleep, and something to wake her up to a new headache everyday.

Both Kelly and Adrienne were becoming increasingly concern over her behavior. They didn't see any signs of drugs, but feared that it would come to that if Lois couldn't pull it together.

Kelly hated herself for whatever part she played in Lois' seeing Peter Long again. She should've stood her ground with Rinoldo. When they asked Lois how she was doing, she just smiled and said, "I'm fine guys, just fine."

One day Kelly offered to take Danijel for the day, so Lois could have a real break. Lois wondered around the apartment for most of the morning taking one medication after another for her headaches; finally, she put on her coat and left the apartment. She took a cab about ten blocks from where she really wanted to go. She pretended to window shop, stopping for a second to look in every window. She was finally close to the place where she wanted to be. As cold as it was, her hands were sweating. She took off her gloves, wiped them on the leg of her jeans and put them back in her gloves. She was constantly looking over her shoulder, as she picked up her speed and soon she spotted them.

They were on the corner for all to see. The cops could even see them. They just didn't have the time to bust every nickel and dime drug dealer in the city. Lois approached one, who began to advertise what he had, "I got reds, greens, purples. It'll do you good and make you fine, five, ten, twenty dollar bags." He got up in Lois' face with his breath smelling of cheap whiskey and said, "Maam," he said opening his coat, while looking over his shoulder, "It'll wash away your problems."

Lois gave the drug dealer a twenty and he asked, "what'd you want lady?"

"A variety," Lois said, and he pulled out a little bag tied together with a garbage bag tie and said, "It'll give your tired soul some rest, enjoy."

Lois took her bag and ran most of the way back uptown. She was glad she had worn her sneakers. She then hailed a cab and went home.

When Kelly arrived with Danijel, Lois was feeling good. "Kelly, I really want to thank you for taking him today. You don't know how much I needed the rest."

"I sort of figure you did," Kelly replied.

"Can you stay for a little visit?"

"No, I have to work tonight. Don't you?"

"Actually, I don't, for the first weekend this month."

"Oh, this is your free weekend."

"Yes, and I'm going to spend the rest of it with my son," she said grabbing Danijel from behind.

"Great. I'd better run, I'll talk to you later."

"Sorry, you can't stay. Later then."

"Yeah, lately then," Danijel said as they both laughed and Kelly left.

Lois' stop each day, before picking up Danijel from the Daycare, was the Bowery. Christopher had said once that she was playing Russian roulette with her life when she bought her stuff from down there. That was why he began to supply her with the best, but she couldn't call Christopher anymore. The stuff from the Bowery did the job sometime and sometime it didn't. Most of the time it didn't, and Lois was getting tired of wasting her money.

Lois called Jay Moon. Jay Moon worked with the agency, but she was also a seller. Everyone knew she was, but no one admitted it, most of all Jay Moon, "I'm sorry, I don't know who this is," answered Jay Moon.

"I work at the agency," Lois tried to identify herself.

"And?"

"And I'm a friend of Mr. Madison," Lois gave it a shot. She wasn't sure where Christopher was getting his drugs from and she thought she might have blown it, when Jay Moon paused.

"What you need?" Jay asked.

Jay Moon pushed hard and Lois' drug habit went to five hundred dollars a week quick.

When Lois complained about the price, she said, "hey, you can go back to the Bowery, if you want crap, but if you want the best, then you pay. You think that stuff Chris was supplying you was free. I don't think so."

"What connection do you have with Chris?" Lois asked.

Jay Moon looked at Lois, "you the cop or something? Mr. Madison is a customer of the Agency. Someone special to him was doing drugs and although he didn't approve of it, he wanted to make sure she got the best. Every girl in the Agency has her niche'. You do men and I'm a seller. You're no better than me and I'm not judging you, if you have a problem with this set up let me know, you can take your business elsewhere."

"I don't have a problem," Lois said.

"Then we're good. Look I'll tell you what Lois. I like you. I'll let you have the amount you need on credit," she smile, "I know where you work, and I know someone with a body like yours bring in good money."

Danijel's daycare got behind again and Lois didn't apply to the business school.

"When do you start the business school?" Kelly asked.

"I had to put it off again. Story of our lives huh, putting off the thing that's going to get us out of this business. That is, those of us who want out."

"I want out Lois, I still think I can make it as a model, if not, then I'll get the job in California as Lady Caldera."

"So you'll be the pimp."

"Excuse me?" Kelly asked insulted.

"I said, you would trade your dreams to become a pimp."

"That's not what the agency does and you know it."

"Do I Kelly?"

Both girls were silent for a while. Kelly sensed a change in Lois, but she wasn't sure if it was drugs, or she had just become cynical and hard.

"Can I borrow a hundred bucks?"

"Why do you need it?"

"Excuse me?" Lois stood back with her hand on her hip, as she looked Kelly up and down.

"I have to tell you why I need to borrow money from you now?"

"No you don't, but you're working day and night when you can, and you don't have any money? I don't understand that."

"I'm not working day and night. Danijel isn't going to Daycare anymore, so I'm home with him during the day."

"Why?"

"Because I got behind on the fees. I'll catch up and he'll be back in by the end of the month."

Kelly hated to say what she was going to say, but she needed to see where Lois was coming from, "What happened to all the money you saved up, when Peter was here?"

"I gave it away. I don't need him or his charity."

"You earned that money. It wasn't charity."

Lois began to laugh, "you're right. I wish I'd thought of that before I gave the money to those bums down at the Bowery," Lois laughed, because the bums she was referring to were the drug dealers.

Kelly wanted to ask Lois if she was on drugs, but she knew Lois would deny it, so she didn't bother. What Kelly didn't know was that Lois had mastered the game. The game was to be high all the time. It was when she came down from her high that people could tell she was on something. She decided not to make that mistake again. She was taking drugs like it was a prescribed medication, morning, noon and night, highs and lows, spending over a thousand dollar a week for her habit.

"Are you going to lend me the money or not?"

"I have to go back to my apartment and get it."

"Thank you."

Mr. Neiman had promised Lois a lot over dinner. He invited her back to his hotel room for a nightcap. He said the driver would be waiting down stairs for her and she could leave anytime she wanted.

He called ahead for room service, so champagne was waiting for them as they arrived back to the room. Lois became fidgety. Mr. Neiman was new to the Agency. He had money, but Lois didn't know how much. She was running out of drugs and just wanted to get the money and get out of there.

"Let me just change out of these things," he said, "then you can do the same, if you want. I think there is a woman's robe in the bathroom."

He went into the bathroom and came back with a white terry cloth robe.

"Here, if you want, you could put this on."

Lois smiled at him and waited until he went into the room. She began to fumble through his things looking for money. She found a picture of his wife and kids.

"What are you doing?" Mr. Neiman asked Lois as he came out of the bathroom in his robe.

"What am I doing? What are you doing?" Lois returned the question.

"Excuse me?" Mr. Neiman asked upset.

"Who are these people?" Lois asked holding up a picture she found in his things.

Mr. Neiman came around the bed and snatched the photograph out of her hand.

"You have no right to go through my things? What were you looking for anyway?"

"Money."

"Excuse me?"

"You heard me right. I want your money without having to give you anything, you sleazy old man."

"Who do you think you are?"

"The question is, what does your wife think you're doing?"

"My personal life is none of your business."

"You think so, huh, why don't I call her and let her tell me that."

"Why you little tramp! Get out of my room now!" He yelled.

Lois looked around the room and grabbed his wallet and ran out yelling, "Not before you pay up, you scum bag."

"Stop, or I'll call the cops," Mr. Neiman yelled down the hallway, as Lois open the door to the stairways.

She threw his wallet back at him and yelled, "you do that, call the cops," Lois laughed as she ran down the stairs. "Figures," she said, as she looked around for the car that brought her to the hotel. "I'll take the train."

She took the train to Jay Moon's apartment first, then walked home from there.

Lois took whatever extra money she had and used it to put coke up her nose. She could not afford to buy from Jay Moon all the time, so she began to hit the streets. One day she was picked up by a police officer for drug solicitation and Rinoldo had to bail her out.

She claimed she was innocent and that it was a mistake, "I was just going for a walk. I saw a bum asking for money and I wanted to help, so I gave him some money. He tried to give me something in return and I refused, but I remembered what my mother use to always say, if someone wants to give you something in return for your charity, you should take it, because it's their blessing and if you don't, you'll rob them of their blessing. I didn't know what it was that he was giving me. I just assumed he didn't want me to think he was a charity case and wanted to give me something in return for the money I gave him."

Rinoldo squeezed the bridge of his nose, shook his head and said "tell it to Madame. You have a meeting with her Monday morning at nine o'clock sharp missy."

Lois entered the foyer of the house with an air of arrogance. She went straight into the room, where she knew Madame Reddan would meet her, sat down and picked a book off the shelf to fan through.

"Good morning Lois." Lois got up and hugged Madame Reddan.

"Good morning to you Mother Reddan. It's been so long since I've seen you. I wish we all could get together more often."

Madame Reddan rubbed her neck and motioned for Lois to sit down, as she took a seat across from her. The term mother was not lost on Madame Reddan and she was wondering what little scheme Lois had up her sleeves. It didn't matter. She had dealt with a lot of drug addicts in her days and they were all pathological liars, who believed their own lies.

"Lois do you know why I have called this meeting?"

"I'm not sure Madame. I know I've been doing really well at the agency. I want you to know that I certainly have appreciated this opportunity that you have given me and my son. I don't know where we would be without you and this job." Lois reached into her purse and gave, Madame Reddan a picture.

"This is Dandan. He's grown so big, and…"

Madame Reddan put up her hand indicating to Lois to stop her shatter.

"I'm sorry Madame. It's you, who have called this meeting and here I am rambling on."

"Yes Lois, it is I, who have called this meeting and I intend to get to the point. This last incident is of course, without excuse. We have a zero tolerance for drugs here at the Agency and you very well know that. So you have left me no other option, but to terminate your employment with this Agency. You will receive enough money for two months rent on an apartment. You have thirty days to find one. You will also receive two months allowance and it's because of your son that I am being so generous."

"Generous?" Lois stood up, "you call that generous! How am I going to find an apartment in thirty days time? Why can't you just put me on probation and give me another chance?"

"Lois, you had probation…"

"You just can't kick me out. I'll report your little prostitution ring to the cops."

"I run a well organized and respectful organization."

"Yeah, I know, you pay your taxes and file your returns. What a crock!" Lois didn't see Madame Reddan reached under the table, where she pushed a silent alarm.

"Lois, we will do everything we can to help you find a job and an apartment. If we need to, we will extend your time in the apartment, but you will have to be actively looking for a place."

"Is that my severance pay?"

"Yes, you can call it that."

"I don't!" Lois screamed. "It's nothing! You haven't even heard my side of the story!"

"Your actions right now tell me there is no point in that."

"You think you're something. You, you, you witch!" Lois looked toward the door as the doorbell began to ring.

"That would be police officer Jeters. He's a good friend of mind. He usually comes around for coffee and donuts," Madam Reddan laughed, "I guess some things they say about cops are true. Why don't you let him in on your way out dear."

"We're not through!" Lois steamed.

"I think we are dear, good day," Madame Reddan said as she slowly, but cautiously walked out of the sitting room. The doorbell rang again and Lois had second thoughts about going after Madame Reddan to make her see her point. Instead she stormed out of the room, intentionally knocking over a glass ornament on to the floor.

"Good morning." The officer said, as Lois opened the door.

"If you're looking for the witch, she's in there." Lois said as she brushed past the officer and headed for the train station. The officer waited until she was out of sight, closed the door and went back to his squad car, took another look in the direction Lois went and pulled off.

After Lois bought food for Danijel with the money she got from the agency, she went to buy drugs. She didn't look for a job, or an apartment. The Agency sat up job interviews for her and she constantly came up with excuses why the jobs were not for her. She distanced herself from her friends. She pretended not to be home when they came by, or simply not answer the telephone.

She lay around all day in her pajamas and Danijel was left to defend for himself. He mimicked what he saw his mother had done, as he tried to clean up the apartment, although sometimes he made more of a mess. Wherever he fell asleep, he stayed until the next morning. He couldn't remember everything he needed to do, so he forgot to give himself a bath many nights.

One morning he woke up after sleeping on the floor all night and made himself some cereal and a bowl for Lois.

They were out of sugar, so he went into his mother's room where he remembered seeing her put her cocaine, which he thought was sugar. He opened the drawer, pulled out the bag and fingered with it until he punctured it, spilling some on the floor and pouring the rest into the bowls of cereal.

"Mommy, Mommy," he called to Lois, who was buried under the cover for almost two days, "breaffist Mommy, I made you breaffist."

Lois peeked out from under the covers and saw a dirty face little boy with uncombed hair, "did you wash up sweetie?"

Danijel's big eyes widened as he said, "oh, oh, I forgot."

"Then get to it," Lois demanded.

When Danijel left the room, Lois opened her nightstand drawer and reached for her bag of cocaine. When she couldn't put her hand on it, she sat up in the bed and frantically began to look through the drawer. She noticed the white substance around the cereal bowls and down on the floor, as well.

"Danijel!" She yelled, "Danijel, get in here now!"

Danijel shook as his mother called him in an angry voice. He was so scared he didn't know what to do. He didn't intend to make his Mother mad at him. He only wanted to help. Not knowing what to do, he ran and hid under his bed.

When he didn't come out of the room, Lois went looking for him.

"I know you're in here and if you don't show yourself right now, you are going to get it!"

Lois was never abusive with Danijel, until she lost her job. She became more agitated and depressed and began to slap him across the face, swing him across the room, or whatever else she could do to take her anger out on him.

Danijel began to whimper and sniffle. Lois reached for him under the bed and dragged him out.

"Were you in my drawer?" Danijel just stood there, eyes wide and bracing himself for the unknown, "you had better tell me little boy, or I will hurt you!"

Danijel just stood there with tears streaming down his little face trying to hold back the sniffles, for fear he would make Lois even angrier with him.

Lois became irritated with his stance and began to shake him uncontrollably.

"We had no sugar," Danijel finally said, "we had no sugar."

Lois stopped shaking him realizing what he had done.

"You put my medicine in the cereal?"

At the word, medicine, Danijel's eye grew wider. He was really afraid now; he didn't realize the white stuff was his mother's medicine.

"Do you realize that I have no money to buy anymore?" Danijel began to grow stiff with fear.

Lois let him go and began to walk around running her hand through her hair while she paced back and forth trying to register what he had done.

"Did you eat any of the cereal?"

"No Mommy, I came to wash up, just like you said."

Lois breathe a little sign of relief. She went back to the cereal and began to eat her cereal like a ravenous animal, with milk dripping from the corners of her lips. She took the remainder of the milk and put the bowl up to her mouth and drank the milk. She looked at the other bowl of cereal wondering what to do with it. She wondered would it be any good, if she put it in the refrigerator.

Danijel stood in his mother's room door watching and crying, too afraid to think what was going to happen to him.

Lois took the remainder of the cereal and placed it in the refrigerator. She sat on the living room couch until she fell asleep again forgetting all about Danijel, who finally went into his room and closed the door. He turned on his television and fell asleep, forgetting his hunger.

For the next few days, Lois slept and Danijel tried to keep the apartment clean. He made himself hot-dogs and peanut butter and jelly sandwiches when he got hungry.

Lois finally ran out of money and drugs. When she tried to borrow money from Kelly and Adrienne, they wanted to know why she needed the money. If she said food, they offered to buy it and bring it to her apartment; if she said a bill, they asked which one, so they could go pay it.

"How long should we keep this up?" Adrienne asked.

"As long as we have to," answered Kelly.

"What about Danijel?"

"What about him?"

"We don't know if he's okay, or not."

"We have to stand our grounds," said Kelly firmly, sensing Adrienne wanting to back out, "besides, we'll just buy food that he can prepare for himself."

"He's four years old for petesake. What does a four year old knows about preparing food?"

"What do you suggest we do Adrienne? Call social services, or something?"

"No, they'll just take him away. There must be something else we can do that will jolt her back to reality."

"I don't know Adrienne. Are we protecting Lois and neglecting to report what may be child neglect, yet if we do, it may destroy her."

"It may be the thing that will bring her back into reality."

Kelly and Adrienne discussed different scenarios over the next couple of days.

Lois finally stopped asking them for money, so they called her and left a message on her answering machine saying they were going to bring some food over. They rang the doorbell, but Lois never came to the door, so they left the food by the door. Lois peeped through the keyhole and when she was sure no one was there, she opened the door and grabbed the bag of food.

Lois needed drugs and she realized Kelly and Adrienne were not going to lend her any money. She began to borrow from anyone she could sell her lies to. She finally ran out of people she could borrow money from.

She decided to take some of her valuables things to the street and see if she could sell, or trade them for drugs, but she couldn't find a babysitter for Danijel. Everyone she knew was working and Alexis refused to work for her anymore, because she had become rude and didn't pay.

Alexis told her mother about it and she advised her not to baby-sit for Lois anymore.

"Fine!" Lois said slamming down the phone onto the receiver after she tried, without success to get Alexis to baby-sit.

Lois played all kinds of exhilarating games with Danijel for the rest of the afternoon. When he fell asleep exhausted, she put on her clothes and left the apartment.

Lois went straight to the Bowery. She wore her new mink coat that Peter bought her the last time he was in town. She had every drug dealer off their corner trying to sell her their goods. When they found out she wanted to make an exchange, they were not interested.

"Go pick up a john, whore, I aint got time for this. Get out my face," one drug dealer yelled at her.

Some of the girls on the street heard him and alerted their pimp.

"Whose girl is she?" the pimp asked.

"We're not sure. She's been around. I remember the coat and the red hair. Usually she's here buying drugs, but it looks like she might have something else on her mind," one girl said.

"Maybe she's just a druggy looking to get money for a quick fix," said another girl.

"Not on my block," said the pimp, as he pulled out a pocketknife and began walking towards Lois.

As he got closer to her, he flicked the knife and it opened into a sharp stiletto. A car pulled up towards Lois and opened the door. He saw the shiny object in the pimp's hand but wasn't sure what it was, but he knew the pimp had the look of trouble in his eyes.

He opened his door and said, "I'm sorry I took so long honey, got tied up on the bridge."

The pimp snooped over to see who was in the car and kept on walking. Lois looked around not sure who the man was talking to.

"I'm talking to you red. You don't look like you belong on these streets. Maybe you should get in and let me take you somewhere else."

Lois looked around again and saw a line of girls staring at her and some of their pimps as well. She got into the car.

"Thanks," she said.

"Well here goes the old cliché," the man said, "what's a nice girl like you doing in place like this?"

"You want the truth?" Lois asked.

"Straight up."

"I'm looking to score. I need a fix and I need it bad."

The man looked at Lois and asked, "what would you do for a fix?"

"Anything," Lois replied, looking back at the man.

The man reached over to the passenger side and opened the glove compartment. It was packed with drugs and a shiny handgun.

"Take what you need. You can have as much as you can handle tonight, but you can't leave this car with any of it." Lois looked at the man and without any more questions began to help herself to the drugs.

"It's pure stuff baby, the best."

Lois woke up the next morning and looked around the room. She didn't recognize anything. It was not the dump that Kelly and Adrienne had found her in one afternoon, but it was far from being the Marriott, or Trump Tower. She began to remember the night before and looked around for the man that bought her there. Next to her on the bed was a fifty-dollar bill and a small bag of cocaine and a note that read: 'take it, you earned it.'

Lois sat up suddenly in the bed remembering the rest of the night. She looked at the clock. It was one o'clock in the afternoon. She jumped up, heart racing and began to put on her clothes.

"Oh my God! Oh my God! What have I done? What have I done?"

Lois looked for a cab, but there was no cab in sight. She began to run. As soon as she reached the nearest train station, she got on a train to take her back uptown. She was trembling and shaking all the way uptown, looking around the train like a scared trapped animal.

It was not the train she normally would take home, so she began to focus on which stop would place her closest to her apartment building. Finally it was her stop and she ran off the train, bumping into people who were getting on the train.

One guy called out, "Lady you can get kill around here for less than that," but Lois didn't hear him, she ran up the stairs and out of the train station.

Once out she looked around to get a feel of where she was, once she figured it out, she began to run again. Lois slowed her pace as she approached her apartment building. Her heart hurt and her head was pounding, or was it her head hurt and her heart was pounding, she wasn't sure she could tell the difference, but she knew she didn't have time to figure it out.

When she entered the Lobby of the apartment building, her heart sank. The lobby was filled with furniture she recognized as her own. Her clothes were thrown over a desk here and there. Her knees buckled, but she knew she had to make it up to her floor. Her child was still there, or was he?

She pounded on the elevator button, looking up as if that would make it come any faster. It seemed to have stuck on her floor, or someone was holding the door. She gave up waiting for the elevator and took the stairs. As she came to her floor, she was out of breath. She opened the door and quickly closed it back again.

There were cops, Kelly and Adrienne and some other guys moving things out of her apartment. She was afraid to go, but she had to know how Danijel was. Did he hurt himself, "Oh God!" she involuntarily let out.

As Lois was thinking the unthinkable, Kelly heard a movement down the hall. A police officer was questioning her, Adrienne and Francesca about Lois' whereabouts.

"I'm sorry Officer but that's all I know. Like we've said, we haven't seen her in days. She wouldn't return any of our calls, or answer the door."

"Okay, you ladies can go, but we may need to ask you some further questions, so why don't all three of you give me your full names and phone numbers."

He gave Kelly a pad and pencil and she began to write down their names and phone number.

"What's going to happen to her son?" Kelly asked out loud.

345

When the other girls looked at her strange, she tried to give them a clue that someone was standing in the stairway.

"He's probably already in child protective custody. We don't keep children down at the precinct, unless we know someone is going to pick them up, and obviously this is not the case."

"Will I be able to see him? Kelly asked. "I'm his godmother."

"I'm not sure of social services' rule," said the officer, "sometimes it's just immediate family."

"I'm like immediate family," Kelly said passing the pad back to the officer.

"Like I said, I don't know the rules on such matters. You will have to call social services on Monday."

He tip his hat to the girls and said, "thanks for all your help, if you hear from your friend, tell her the smart thing to do is to come down to the precinct as soon as possible."

"Is she in trouble?" Adrienne asked.

"Yes maam, she's in a lot of trouble. This is child neglect and we have previous complaints of child neglect on her."

Lois tried to hear as much as possible. From what she could make out, she was in trouble and Danijel was in social service's care.

"Hold that elevator," the police officers yelled at the guys who were moving the things out of Lois' apartment.

They had finally loaded up enough in the elevator and were taking more things down.

"Are you finished in here?" Kelly asked one of the guys. "No, we have one more load and then we'll be through, but you ladies don't have to wait around. We'll lock up the place when we're finished."

"Thank you," Kelly said. "Why don't we take the stairs up to my apartment?"

The girls didn't question Kelly, because her apartment was only one flight up. They all began to walk toward the stair exit. Kelly stopped them before they entered the stairs and placed her index finger to her mouth, indicating they should be quiet. She looked down the hallway again to make sure that the police officers and the moving guys had gone down before she opened the door to the stairs.

"Lois!" Francesca almost screamed.

"Do you know what the sign for shush means?" Adrienne asked Francesca annoyed at her outburst.

Kelly quickly opened the stair door again and peeked out, "We're good."

Lois was crawled on the floor in deep groans and sobs, trying not to be heard.

"Come on Lois, let's go to my place." Kelly and Adrienne helped a weak Lois to her feet and helped her into Kelly's apartment.

"We should call the cops immediately!" said Francesca, "we all could get fired if we are arrested for harboring a criminal!"

Kelly was livid with Francesca, "look Francesca if you don't want to be here then go, but Lois is not a criminal and we're not giving her up to the cops in this condition. You understand."

Francesca went to sit at the bar.

"I'll make her something hot," Adrienne said.

Kelly sat hugging Lois tightly on the couch, as she cried uncontrollable, when she finally stopped, Adrienne gave her the coffee.

"What am I going to do?" a confused Lois asked.

"You have to turn yourself in," Kelly said, "but first you have to get a lawyer and let them advise you on what you need to do."

"I need to get Danijel back home."

"That's not going to happen tonight Lois, and quite honestly right now, you don't have a home to bring him to."

"Kelly is right Lois, for once listen." Adrienne said.

"I will," said Lois sounding defeated, "are they going to leave my things downstairs in the lobby?"

"No, they will put a note on the door for you where it will be stored, compliments of the Agency. You will be able to pick it up, when you can afford to pay the Agency back ever dime it took them to move it out and store it for however long they have to."

"At some point, I think they sell the stuff to get some of their money back, if you don't show up to claim it." Francesca said.

"What happened?" Lois asked.

"We should be asking you that Lois." Kelly said.

"I just went out to buy something for breakfast."

"Lois as far as we know, you were gone all morning, maybe even all night. Danijel opened the door and was crying in the hallway looking for you. He thought something happened to you. The neighbors heard him and you know what happened from there. Danijel said the last time he saw you were before he went to bed last night."

"Yes, I put him to bed, then this morning I thought I could run out and get something for him to eat before he woke up."

Kelly held up her hand not believing Lois' story, "save it for the lawyer Lois."

"You don't believe me?"

"It doesn't matter what we believe. You have to get a judge to believe it."

"Why did they take my stuff?"

"You were evicted," Kelly continued to fill her in, "The police officer called the landlord, who called the Agency. They already had an eviction notice from a court date you missed, so they call the moving guys, told them to take everything out, store it and change the lock."

Lois got up, "where are you going?" Kelly asked.

"I'm going to see where they took my things."

"No, you need to stay put girl," Adrienne said, "you think they're not going to watch your apartment? They don't know you know they took your son and moved your furniture. They're looking for you to come back."

"If they're not watching, you can be sure that your neighbors will be." Francesca said.

"That's right Lois," said Kelly. "You need to stay put until we can talk to a lawyer and figure this thing out."

Kelly walked Lois through what they were going to do in the next few days. In the meantime, she would stay with Kelly and find a drug rehab program to get herself clean up. Lois agreed to everything. She kept saying over and over that she would do anything to get her son back. Kelly hoped she meant it, because it wasn't going to be as easy as that. She may even do some time in jail, if they couldn't find a good lawyer to get the child neglect charges drop.

Kelly knew she was breaking rules by calling an old customer for favors, but in the business they were in, she learned you never throw away a good business card, because you never knew when you would need it. She was referred to some good lawyers, most of them too big and too busy to take on a small time child neglect case. One lawyer did agree to see them. She specialized in family court, especially helping mothers reunite with their children.

"I will give your friend a free consultation, because you come highly recommended. If I agree to take on the case, it's because I know I can get the mother into a good rehab and reunited with the child, without doing any jail time. My fee is reasonable and I'll need one third up front, but we'll go over all of that when you and your friend come to my office," the lawyer pause, "you are coming with her, aren't you?"

"I can if I need to," Kelly said never thinking she would need to.

"Miss Johnson is good to have a friend like you, and it would do her good if you were there to support her all the way to court. That will give the judge the idea that she has a good support system, which is a good thing to have in these situations," the lawyer further explained.

"Then I'll be there," Kelly said.

"Good. Is Wednesday morning at nine good enough?"

"That's good, but should we go to the cops in the meantime?"

"Absolutely not. I can't see you before then, because I'm in court today and tomorrow, so I don't want you seeing the cops before I prep you on what to say and what to expect. We can go down to police headquarters together."

"What if the cops pick her up before then?"

"I don't think the cops have an APB out on your friend. They have her son, so she is no harm to no one except herself right now, but in the event that something does happen, take down this number." Kelly wrote the number on a piece of paper.

"If you need me, call it and let my service know what's going on. They will call me and I'll get right back with you."

"Okay."

"So we're set for Wednesday then."

"Yes."

"See you then."

Kelly went to tell Lois that she had found her a lawyer. Lois was in the bathroom, with the door slightly ajar, so Kelly walked in.

"I know you don't think you're going to do that in here?" Kelly asked Lois as she walked in on Lois in the bathroom.

"Whatever happened to knocking and privacy?"

"If you wanted privacy, you should've locked the door. Lois I don't want you doing drugs in my home. Don't you think you have enough problems as it is? You think you're going to get Dandan back by being an addict."

"I'm not an addict. I just need something to help me get through this. You can't imagine what it's like to have your son taken away, lose your home and your job."

"No I don't know Lois, but you brought all this on yourself. You had options, but you chose the wrong ones."

"So is this how it's gonna be? This is your apartment and I must abide by your rules. You forgot we use to live together."

"That was another time and another place. I can't go back and neither can you. A lot has happened to change things and we have to move forward."

"Fine!" Lois said gathering up her things as she left the bathroom. Kelly stared at herself in the mirror a long time trying to figure out how things got to be the way they were.

Kelly and Lois did not say much to each other the next two days. When Kelly went into Lois' room to wake her up on Wednesday morning for their appointment with the lawyer, Lois was gone.

There was a note on the bed folded with Kelly's name on it that read:

"Thank you. You have been a good friend, but if we are to remain friends, then I can't stay here. I appreciate all you have done with the lawyer and everything, but if I get my son back, what do I have to offer him? I don't have a job or a place for us to stay. Ever since I held Danijel in my arms in the hospital, I knew I only wanted the best for him. I never thought I would not be the one to give him that. I'm going to pray he gets a good home, and hopefully one day I'll see him again, and my friend, love, Lois."

Kelly crumbled up the note and held it close to her bosom, "Lois what are you doing? Where will you go?" She asked staring at the walls.

Lois went down to the Bowery. She needed something and she still had fifty bucks. The girls on the streets spotted her right away. She saw one of girls leaving the group to make a phone call. Lois hurriedly bought what she needed and took off. She thought the girl called her pimp.

Lois sat on a park bench and when night came, for the first time Lois did not have a place called home to go to. She slept on a park bench one night and in front of an old abandoned building the next. She was too high to think straight. Her only concern was to get a fix during the day and find a place to sleep at night.

When she ran out of money, she was back to hustling the nickel and dime dealers for a fix. Sometimes it worked and sometimes it didn't.

"Hey, you're going to get hurt around here," one girl came up to her and said, "The pimps have stakes on these streets and they don't take kindly to no lone star sweetie."

"I just want a fix," Lois said, looking around to see if there were any pimps around watching.

"Well, maybe you need to go back uptown and hustle some rich man out of their money, or you can call Max."

"Max?" Lois asked puzzled. "I don't know any Max."

"Well he knows you and he's been asking about you."

The girl looked around to see if anyone was looking and gave Lois a number and some change.

"He's the guy that gave you a ride in his bad Benz."

The girl walked away and Lois stared at the piece of paper in her hand and the change to make the call.

"Hello. ...Max? ... I heard you've been looking for me. ...One of the girls gave me your number. ...I'll be here. ...Okay." Lois saw a pimp talking to some girls and she decided to stay in a dark corner waiting for Max.

Lois saw Max's car and she started to walk towards it, but he stop suddenly and got out. All the drug dealers left their spots and met Max at his car. They began to exchange packages. When they were through, Max looked around for the girl who he asked to look out for Lois.

Lois didn't want to suddenly appear out of nowhere after seeing Max making exchanges with the drug dealers, so she stayed in the dark corner watching. The girl nervously approached Max. They talked and the girl pointed in the direction that Lois had went to make the call.

Lois took the cue and went to wait for Max at the phone booth, but not before she saw Max give the girl some money. She nervously looked around and then placed the money in her breast.

Lois was in the phone booth when Max pulled up.

"Hey Red," he said through his window, "I heard you need a ride out of here."

"It depends on where you're going," Lois said.

"How 'bout any where, but here."

"Sounds like where I want to go," said Lois.

Max reached over and opened the car door and Lois got in.

Max took Lois to a nice ranch style home on Long Island.

"Is this better than there?"

Lois looked around, "It sure is." Lois said.

"Then make yourself at home," Max offered.

Max only requirements were for Lois to do a little house chores and be there for him when he got home.

"Don't talk to the neighbors and don't ask any question. You think you can handle that?"

"I think so," Lois said.

"No Red, I need you to know so."

"I can handle it," said Lois.

"Good," Max said walking into another room, "and by the way, never answer my phone. The answering machine will pick it up. You can make calls, but don't give anyone my number and I promise not to bore you with my business, if you don't bore me with your problems."

Lois had a place to stay and all the drugs she wanted, with no questions asked.

"Has she even called?" Adrienne asked Kelly.

"No, and it's been almost a month and those people at the social service agency won't even let me see Dandan. That poor baby must be so confused and scared, in a strange place with strange people. Maybe I should call Lois' aunt. I think I still have her number, if I don't I could probably call the factory or go to her house or something."

"You think they would let her see Dandan?"

"She's family. I don't know, maybe."

"Then you should do it."

"Maybe they'll let her have him. At least we can do something to try to help Dandan."

Kelly and Adrienne went to the Bronx to see Deb.

"Kelly? Where is Lois?" Deb asked puzzled, when she opened the door and saw Kelly without Lois and Danijel.

"I, I, can we come in please?" Kelly finally asked.

"I'm sorry, come in, please. It's just that my sister is out of her mind with worry. She has been calling Lois' number for days and only getting a disconnect number with no forwarding number. She was calling Lois at least once every two weeks, but she said Lois sounded a little down lately, so she started calling once a week to check on her. Did she move? Is her phone cut off?"

"I don't know where she is Miss Deb."

"What? What do you mean you don't know where she is? You're her friend and you're the one who got her that job and..."

"Miss Johnson," Adrienne cut Deb off.

"It's Halls, and who are you? Deb asked.

"I'm Adrienne. I'm a good friend of Lois."

Deb was annoyed that Kelly and Adrienne were standing before her confessing to be Lois' friends, but didn't have a clue to where she was.

"I'm sorry, Miss Hall. I know this is hard for you. It's even harder for us to say it, but I don't think you should blame Kelly for..."

"For not being the friend she pretends to be to," it was Deb's time to cut Adrienne off.

"Miss Deb, I'm sorry. I don't know what to say," Kelly said apologetic.

"Just say that my niece and nephew are okay and you can be on your way."

"I don't know that they are, but if you would like us to leave, we will." Deb was fuming, but she did not want them to leave until she found out all they knew.

Kelly and Adrienne told Deb all about the drugs, Lois being out of a job, the apartment and Danijel being taken in protective custody.

"Oh my God, Oh my God. Not Lois. Not our little Lois," Deb began to cry, "and you don't have any idea as to where she could be."

"I'm sorry," Kelly said.

They sat quietly for a long time and then Deb asked, "Are you girls selling your bodies?"

"That is not what we do!" Adrienne answered the question defiantly, "and that is not what the Agency is all about."

Adrienne knew they had to keep the Agency out of this as much as possible, or she and Kelly could lose their jobs.

"I can't think of anything else that would make my niece turn to drugs."

"I'm sorry," Kelly said again.

"So you've said," Deb said coldly. "I thank you girls for coming down here to tell me this, now if you'll excuse me, I have to call her parents."

Deb didn't call her sister right away. Instead she got on the phone and tried to find Danijel. She called the social service agency in Manhattan to arrange a meeting. She found out the name of Danijel's guardian Ad litem.

They were usually lawyers representing the best interest of the child. She called the lawyer and she agreed to meet Deb at the social services Agency.

Deb met with Peggy Bekow first, Danijel's guardian Ad Litem, before she met with the social workers.

"Miss Hall? Is it?" The social worker asked Deb, extending her hand.

"Yes it is," Deb said as she took her hand and shook it.

"I'm Patricia Hartley and this is Diane Farland. She is Danijel's social worker."

She turned to the lawyer and extended her hand "Peggy, haven't seen you in awhile."

"Is that a good thing?" Peggy asked.

"Depends," said Patricia.

"I see you know each other," Deb said hoping this was good.

"Yes, we do know Ms. Bekow," Ms. Hartley said, "she is the guardian Ad-litem for some of our other children as well. Let's all have a seat."

When everyone was seated in Ms. Hartley's small office, Ms Hartley asked Diane to update everyone on Danijel.

"Well, he's staying with a good family. He's a little withdrawn and scared, but he's doing okay, no problems or concerns. It's his first time in foster care, so like most children his age, he's trying to register what's happening to him and what has happened to his mother."

"And what have you told him?" Deb asked.

"Not much, seeing that the mother has not come forward to claim him."

"What relations are you to Danijel, Ms. Halls?" Ms. Hartley asked.

"I'm his aunt. His mother is my niece."

"And do you know where his mother is?"

"No, I don't," Deb began to cry, "I'm sorry, I just don't know what to think. She hasn't call or nothing and this is just not like her."

Peggy put her arm around Deb and patted her on the back.

Deb regained her composure, and said, "I was hoping to see Danijel and maybe take him home with me."

"Well, I think we can arrange for you to see Danijel Ms. Hall," said Ms. Hartley, "but as far as taking him home, that's a judge's decision."

"How do I go about doing that?"

"You have to file a petition with the court. Ms. Bekow can give you all the paperwork that will take you through the process. In the meantime, we will arrange for you to have a visit with your nephew. I think he needs to see someone he knows."

"Thank you," Deb said, "thank you very much."

A couple of days later, Deb was back at the social service agency. She was going to get a visit with Danijel. She had already filled out the necessary papers to petition the court for custody of him. She didn't know how long it was going to take. She hoped it wasn't long. She was going to call Theresa tonight after seeing Danijel. She wanted to have something good to tell them when she told them every thing else.

"Auntie, Auntie, auntie!," Danijel said as he came running to hug his aunt. His little face lighted up as he hugged her tightly.

"Dandan!" Deb said, excited to see him and hugging him just as tight.

"Where is my mommy? I want to go home."

"I know you do precious." Deb was not prepared for any questions about Lois, so she didn't know how to answer.

"Well, Danijel, you know your Mother hasn't been doing well. Did you know that?" Deb was trying to feel Danijel out to see how much he knew and understood.

"huh huh, that's why she always took the white medicine to get better. Is she better yet?"

"No Dandan, she is not better yet. She had to go away to get better," Deb hated lying, but what else could she say. It was certainly what she was hoping. "That's why you had to come and stay with these nice people. Do you like it there?"

"No!" Danijel said emphatically.

"How would you like coming to stay with me and your cousins?"

"I want to! I want to!" Danijel began to get excited.

Deb knew she shouldn't make him any promises, but she didn't know what to tell her impressionable nephew.

"Now, it's not going to be right away. You're going to have to go back and stay with those nice people, but I'm going to see someone who makes these decision and I'm going to try to make him understand just how much we love you and want you to come and stay with us."

"I love you too Auntie."

"I know baby, I know."

It hurt Deb's heart to leave him, but there was nothing she could do, now for the hard part, telling her sister.

Stephanie was devastated. Deb had to finish talking to Richard. She told Richard everything she knew. She had even gone down to the police station to see what they knew, but they knew nothing and they were not really looking for her. They were satisfied that the child was with social services and they would notify her, if Lois contacted them about Danijel.

Stephanie got back on the phone and said to Deb before she hung up, "Please get my grandchild and find my daughter."

"I'll do everything I can Sis."

"I'll be there as soon as I can."

"Stephanie what's the point in that?"

"What's the point?" Stephanie asked in disbelief.

"I'm sorry, but why don't you wait until I have a date from the judge concerning custody of Danijel."

"Okay, I'll wait to hear from you, but it better be soon."

"It's time for you to move on Lois dear. Get your things and be out by this afternoon," Max said.

"What did I do?"

"You didn't do anything. I'm just tired of you. It was fun while it lasted, but it's time to move on."

"But I don't have anywhere to go."

"That's your problem. Remember the deal was that I don't bore you with my business and you don't bore me with your problems. You're a resourceful girl. You'll figure out something, or find someone else to fulfill your desires."

"You low life! You think you're better than me?"

"Look Lois, I'm not into scenes babe. I've never insinuated that I was better than you. Some people think I'm worse than you. I don't know why. Selling drugs is my business. People choose to use, like you. Let's not go through this whole scene thing. I'd prefer to just skip it."

Lois walked into the room to get her things, which wasn't much. She decided not to make a scene. She'd been here before.

"If you need a ride, I can drop you anywhere you want to go."

Lois came back with a bag with her things in and said, "don't bother, just give me a ride to the train station and I'll find my way."

Max took Lois down to the train station. He counted out five hundred dollars in hundred dollar bills and gave it to Lois and said, "don't put it all up your nose and try to find a place to stay."

Max reached in his glove compartment and pulled out a bag of cocaine and gave it to Lois, "here this should last you a couple of days, if you don't be greedy. That's your problem. You put more up your nose than I can sell."

Lois took the drugs and put it in her bag, slammed the door and didn't look back when Max yelled, "hey, don't slam the door!"

It was the last Lois ever saw of Max.

Lois did find a little room she rented by the week in Harlem. She was out of the drugs Max gave her within a week, so she tried to ration her money for rent and drugs, eating very little. Lois had become thin and drawn. She was only twenty-six, but she looked twenty years older. When she ran out of the money Max gave her, she went back on the streets.

Lois met Owen in the back of a restaurant one day looking for scraps of foods the restaurant threw out. Owen began to follow Lois around.

"What do you want?" Lois yelled at him one day.

"The question is what do you want?" Owen asked.

"I want you to stop following me around."

"Oh, I thought you might want a place to stay."

He got Lois' attention.

"I won't sleep with you for a place to stay."

"That doesn't interest me none, but I can propose a deal for you and me." Lois listened intently to Owen's proposal.

The next day Lois was on the street hustling for Owen. Owen became Lois' protector from the pimps, as Lois would think of him, but Owen saw himself as Lois' pimp.

At night Lois hustle to get them money for drugs, so that they could spend their day in crack houses getting high.

The Intervention

"Oh, El Roi," the Son of the most high stepped down from his throne and bowed before his Father's throne, "I care not to interrupt you, Oh El Shaddai, but I know your eyes goes throughout the earth searching for someone whose heart is perfect towards you, that you may show yourself strong on their behalf."

Immediately the Son had the Father's utmost attention. He didn't speak a word, but the Son knew that he was listening intently.

"I hear a cry," the Son went on to say, "a cry of deep sorrow and pain, a cry of deep moaning and groaning, a cry uttered in a language that is only meant for the ears of Elohim. The cry comes from one whom heart I have found to be perfect towards you. It's a prayer of intercession on behalf of a loved one," the Son lifted up his bowed down head and looked into the eyes of the Father, "Jehovah Sabbaoth it is a cry for battle. I beseech you to allow me to send out the warring angels to take their place in this battle and rescue this tortured soul of one whose heart is perfect towards you."

Tears began to come down the face of the Son and the Father was moved with compassion and he held up both of his arms signaling a host of heavenly beings dressed, equipped, armed and ready for battle.

As they stood before the throne of the Most High, the Father uttered one command in a thunderous voice, "Go and conquer!"

Chapter Twenty-Four
Jewel

Lucifer:

Lucifer quickly began to communicate words to all his host of a special meeting. He was not sure what region the Almighty loosed a host of warring angels, but he wanted to make sure that his demonic host knew this meant war.

The word got around fast and all who heard came, including Bedeekle. The room smelled of many dead animals decaying in one small confinement.

"The smell of fear amongst you all has reached my nostrils!" Lucifer belched, "and you fear with reason, because some of you will be destroyed either by one of the heavenly host, or by me!"

Outside hovering over the meeting was a swarm of heavenly hosts staking out the meeting.

"Do you know what's going on outside! Do you?" Lucifer screamed. "We are being put on notice. A prayer has gone up to the throne room and those heavenly angels out there hovering over us are not here to have a cordial visit. I want you to know that if anyone of you allows one of your charges to get away, if the heavenly angels don't destroy you, I will!" He roared and the demonic beings heard a roar as a lion, but the warring angels heard the sound of an alley cat.

"Now get your whiny, slimly behinds out there and steal, kill and destroy, or be killed!" Lucifer screamed at the top of his squeaky voice.

Jewel:

Brad accompanied Jewel home for her brother's wedding. He had a surprise of his own; a solitaire diamond ring in a little black box was burning a hole in his pocket. He was going to ask Jewel to marry him. They had not spent as much time together in the past several months as Brad wanted, because he wanted to give her the space she needed. Jewel also had news that she couldn't wait to share with everyone.

They arrived three days before the wedding. Jewel and Tessa were two of seven bridesmaids. Jewel really didn't know Saida, her soon to be sister-in-law that well, but what she knew of her she liked.

Jewel met her on Christmas and really didn't get to spend much time with her, but when she personally called to ask Jewel to be one of her bridesmaid, Jewel was taken by her genuine gratitude when she accepted.

She called Jewel many times after that to inform her about the wedding plans. She also wanted Jewel's advice on how to politely tell Theresa that she was doing more than was required, without hurting her feelings. "In other words," Jewel said, "you want my mom to butt out."

When Saida called her one night near tears, Jewel decided to give her mother a call.

"You'll have plenty of opportunity to fuss and stress out over a wedding, when Tessa and I get marry," Jewel said after trying to explain to Theresa why she should let Saida and her mom do all the planning for the wedding and let them come to her when they needed her input.

Later, Saida called Jewel and thank her profusely.

Tessa had landed a job at Saks Fifth Avenue as a counter clerk, but her aspiration was to one day be one of their top buyers, if she could suffer the city that long. She had become home sick and began to keep in touch regularly with Jewel. As a result, Jewel and Tessa had become closer than they ever were.

"My little sister a Saks fifth Avenue fashion buyer, wow!" Jewel exclaimed when Tessa told her of her plans.

She asked Tessa to look up Lois, when she got some time. Tessa agreed, but she didn't know when that would be. School and work were taking up most of her time.

"Alone at last," Brad said as he stuck up behind Jewel and place his arms around her waist. She smiled, turned around and said, "I'm sorry if I've been neglecting you."

"I understand. This is a special time for your family."

"It is. I can't believe my little brother is getting married," she said gleefully.

"I know. I couldn't believe it when Amy got married."

Amy and John were married last spring and Jewel did not attend the wedding. Amy came right out and told Brad that she knew he was still seeing Jewel, even after Jewel promised the Wests that she wouldn't see Brad again, which Brad pointed out wasn't quite accurate. What Jewel said was that she and Brad would never marry and Brad certainly hoped that was a promise Jewel would break. Brad threatened Amy that if Jewel wasn't invited, then he would not come to the wedding either. He was very adamant about it. He didn't even bulge when his parents talked to him about family loyalties and being there for each other. It was Jewel who had to convince Brad that he would regret it big time if he did not go to Amy's wedding.

It wasn't Amy that Brad was upset with. He saw his little sister as hostage to other people's prejudice. It didn't occur to Brad that there were some characteristics that you couldn't ignore when choosing a mate, unless you became tolerable to them, as well.

"How are they doing by the way?" Jewel asked.

"I would elaborate on my sister's life as a wife, if I thought you were interested or cared, but I don't think you do."

"You are a smart man Bradley Conners," Jewel said smiling. Amy was the last person she wanted to think about or talk about this weekend.

"Did you ever get to look up Lois?" Jewel asked Tessa, one night while they were up having girl talk.

"Who?" Tessa asked.

"My best friend Lois; you remember from church. She went to New York right after high school." When Tessa continued to look confused, Jewel elaborated, "the light skinned girl with the red hair, who spent the night with me sometimes. I told you to look her up in New York."

"Ooooh that Lois," Tessa said, as if a light just went off in her head.

"I guess that answered my question."

"I guess so, besides if she was your best friend how come you've never contacted her, or she you?"

"I don't know. I guess we just got caught up pursuing our dreams. Maybe I'll look up her parents, while I'm home and get her number or address."

"Speaking of dreams. What's in store for you now that law school is over?"

"I take the law exam and then I practice law."

"Okay. That much I could guess," Tessa laughed. "I mean, are you and Brad going to get married?"

"Are you kidding? His parents would kill me before they let me marry their son."

"I thought they were the nice ones."

"Oh, they got a good pretense around me and Brad, but I don't buy it. How else could they produce a child who could be so uninformed and prejudice?"

"Brad isn't."

"Exceptions. There are always exceptions to the rule."

"I thought you had to do an internship or something."

"Or something."

"Well you do, or you don't."

"Enough about me, I want to hear all about New York and what you do up there for fun. We don't talk long enough on the phone to get into details. Now I want detail. Start talking and don't leave anything out."

Tessa reached for the pillow and placed it behind Jewel, "so when you fall down from boredom, your head will hit this pillow and not the base board of the bed."

"You think I'm doing the right thing Sis?"

Jewel looked up at David, "you don't think it's too late to ask that now? Your wedding is in two days."

"I know."

"I guess it's okay to be a little scared. This is one of the biggest steps you'll ever make in your life."

"I sure feel better now," David said sarcastically.

"You're going to make a great husband and Saida a good little wife."

"What a sexists comment sis."

"Whaaat?"

"A good little wife? Who says that any more?"

"I'm sorry. I mean Saida is a great girl and I think that you are so lucky to have her."

"Bless is what I am."

Jewel looked at David. His term of being 'bless' to her 'lucky' was a contrast. She never heard David used spiritual terms before.

"I'm curious David. Why now, and not later?"

"Why now, and not later what?"

"Why did you and Saida decide to get married now? You both are young and haven't even finished college yet. What's the hurry? Is she pregnant?"

"No. We haven't even done anything yet?"

"You got to be kidding me."

"No, I'm not. I signed one of those papers too, you know, to be a virgin until I'm married."

"Really, but still, don't you think it's a little outdated."

"No, both Saida and I are saved and we want to do the right thing, and we're not just marrying for sex. We really love each other. After college I'm going into the seminary."

"Get out of here!" Jewel exclaimed, giving David a good shove.

"Yes, didn't mama tell you?"

"No she didn't, and I would think that something like that would make her proud to tell."

"I think she is, but dad doesn't think I can make a living as a minister and that we're going to live a life of poverty."

"I didn't know you bought into all that."

"Wow, I didn't know you didn't," David said surprised.

"I can't believe you guys never mentioned David's decisions," Jewel said to her parents.

"Which one," Paul asked, "he keeps coming up with these outrageous decisions."

"I don't think getting married to someone you love, or wanting to go into the seminary is outrageous," Theresa said.

"I'm sure you don't. I hope you're still living when he comes knocking on your door with his wife and five or more kids, because I'm sure he'll make the decision not to use any form of birth control. I hope you're glad, now that you have one child where you want him."

"And where's that Paul?"

"A religious fanatic."

"I see. Being born again is being a fanatic. I once thought you were saved. I once thought all of my children were saved, but you've let me know that I've been wrong."

"My idea of being saved and yours are two different thing," Paul defended himself.

"That's so utterly ridiculous, either you are, or you're not." Theresa said turning to stare down at Paul, who was sitting in a chair at the kitchen table trying or pretending to read a paper.

"I didn't mean to start a civil war," Jewel said, "I simply asked a question, but I see that you differ on the matter, so I think I'll stay out of it until you two have resolved the issue."

"It isn't our issue to resolve," Theresa said. "It's David's life and David's choice. We've supported all of our children's decision, even if we didn't fully agree with them. We are not about to start treating one child differently," she said still staring down at Paul.

Paul looked up and saw the fire in Theresa's eye and averted his eyes back to his paper and muttered some words under his breath.

"What was that dear?" Theresa asked.

Paul looked up again and said, "nothing, I said nothing."

"I thought so," Theresa said as she turned back to the sink to finish the dishes.

"I think this is where I came in and this is my cue to leave," Jewel announced.

"Wow, I don't think I've ever seen my parents on opposite sides, when it came to us like this before," Jewel was telling Brad what happened.

"How about you Brad? Where do you stand on the whole save issue?"

Brad took a while to answer, as he sat back and gave it some thought.

"I never really gave it much thought, but since Billy died, I've been re-evaluating my life. I want to start going back to church and really become involve. I've been thinking about rededicating my life to God and maybe create a law practice that will do some good, make changes in people lives. I don't want my career to be based upon how much money I can earn, or establishing some pretentious status."

"That sounds good for you to say. You can live off of your parent's fortune," Jewel said.

"But I won't," Brad responded. "You always talk about how much money my family has, but you were not raised a pauper Jewel. You had the best schools, a upper middle class home in a very respectable neighborhood, with some very respectable and known people in your community, so I wish you would stop acting like you're the little poor girl who've had it hard all of her life and had to work to get through college, but" Brad added before Jewel could cut in, "I'm not going to argue with you about this. We'll just have to agree to disagree on this issue. What about you?"

"What about me?"

"Are you saved?"

"No. I thought I was, but I'm not, and I don't see anything wrong with that. I don't have to believe what my parents believes, or you for that matter, to be happy or to live happily with someone. Happiness is what you make of your life, not controlled by some unknown force."

"You think God is an unknown force? Is that what your shrink told you?"

"My doctor's name is Brink, Dr. Brink, and I'm sorry I told you about her."

"I didn't mean to insult you, but I just wondered. I apologize for using the term shrink."

"You know what's so ironic?"

"What?"

"People calling psychiatrist's shrinks. They don't shrink your mind. They help you to expand your mind, to get you out of your little pea brain thinking. They make you think big, expand your horizons beyond what you were raised to believe."

"I sort of think the way I was raised was pretty good."

"And I'm sure you were raised very well on the Plantation."

"Okay, okay, obviously you are going to continue to refer to my family's money, so let's just end this conversation."

"Fine with me."

At the rehearsal dinner, Jewel finally shared her plans with everyone.

"So Jewel what now?" David asked. "I've told you all of my plans and you're keeping all of yours a secret." David said winking at Brad.

Brad was so excited and nervous about his plan to propose to Jewel that he wanted to share it with someone, so he did with David. He just hoped David didn't put him on the spot. He certainly didn't want to have to propose at a table full of people. He was hoping for anything a little more romantic.

"Well, I was going to wait, but since you asked, I guess now's as good a time as any," Jewel said. "I've decided to do my internship in London."

"London! Are you kidding?" Tessa hollered out.

"No, I'm very serious. I went to the school's fair and met with some of the headhunters out there. I talked to three in particular. They got my school scores and I got an offer from all three of them, but I decided on London."

Brad was stunned at hearing this for the first time.

"Where were the other offers?" Brad asked.

"Atlanta and LA," Lois said.

"Whaaat!" Tessa screamed out again, "how could you choose?"

"Tessa, London is an offer of a lifetime. It wasn't that difficult."

"I guess it wasn't," Brad said, obviously hurt, "especially when you make all of your decisions on your own, regardless of any other commitments."

"What commitments?" Jewel asked shaking her head bewildered.

"Hmm," Brad uttered as he got up, "I guess if you have to ask, it must not have been any commitment after all."

Jewel shook her head as she looked around the table a little embarrassed and upset that Brad had rained on her huge surprise. She got up and went after him. She found him outside taking deep breaths of fresh air.

"What was that about?"

"That was about us. How can you make such a big decision and not ask me what I thought about it?"

"Excuse me, but when did I start having to consult you on decisions that concerns my life and future. Did I miss something?"

"Yes, I guess you did Jewel. You miss that I love you and that I want to spend the rest of my life with you, only you. You missed that."

"That's a dream that's never going to happen Brad. You know that, as well as I do. You know your 'elite' family will never accept me and will disown you, if you do."

"I thought we were not going to let other people dictate our lives."

"No, we're not, but if I had to choose someone over my family, I really think that in the long run I would resent them for it, and I don't want you to resent me."

"I would never resent you."

"You say that now, because you're looking at a dream, a fantasy."

"What's wrong with dreaming?"

"Nothing. It's the fantasy that I'm more concerned about."

Paul and Theresa were just as surprise at Jewel's announcement as Brad was, but they decided to wait until the following day to talk to her about it.

As they sat in their favorite spot in the kitchen where they've had countless heart to heart talks, Paul looked up after taking a sip of his coffee, and asked Jewel, "when are you leaving to go to London?"

"In two to three months, depending on how fast I can get my paperwork done."

"This is a big move Jewel, so far away," Theresa said.

"Yes, I know, and I'm glad that I have you as parents, because I know that you're going to support my every decision." Jewel said kissing both her parents on the cheek.

She knew it was not fair of her to use her mother's line at this instance, but she did not want another confrontation about her decision.

"Will you come home before you leave?" Theresa asked.

"Yes, I'll be back about a week before I leave."

Jewel tried not to talk about London the rest of the weekend. Even though Brad was upset and hurt over the news, he decided to stay for the wedding, but he was not going to ask her to marry him again, despite advice from David that it may change her mind about going to London. The fact that Jewel could make such a decision without discussing it with him was too devastating.

He went through the emotions of the weekend, because he didn't want to put a cloud over the wedding, but Jewel just went on as if nothing had expired between them. Brad knew it was over between them, but what hurt him the most was that Jewel knew long before he did that it was over and never bothered to tell him.

It was weeks before Brad brought up the topic again and a few days before they would be out of school. He wanted to see if there was anything he could say to change her mind.

"I'm sorry you feel this way Brad, but maybe it's for the best. I don't know how long I'll be in London," Jewel said as Brad shared his feeling concerning a long distance romance, "I certainly don't expect you, or want you to wait around for me to come back, because I may not, and you're bent on making a career in Atlanta."

"We both talked about staying and working in Atlanta after law school. We both received good offers from law firms. You, yourself said that Atlanta was listed as one of the top metropolitan city for black women to succeed. What about London?"

"I don't know about London, but I aim to find out. I want to expand my horizon and…"

"Oh yeah, I forgot about the expanding of your horizon and increasing your brain," Brad said being sarcastic.

"Okay, let's end this conversation, Brad. I don't want to leave you on bad terms. We had some interesting times together, some good and some bad. I don't want us to end bad."

"So you're saying we're ending."

"Isn't that what you're saying?" Jewel asked.

"I guess we both know it's over, but we're beating around the bushes trying to get the other person to admit it first. Okay, if that's what you want, then it's over. I wish you all the happiness and success that you so desire in London."

He kissed Jewel, a long, passionate kiss on the lips and Jewel felt that funny feeling in the pit of her stomached, but she was not going to base her life on passing moments of feelings.

"Goodbye," Brad said and without waiting for Jewel to say anything he left her apartment.

His kiss left Jewel confused and wanting him, but she was not going to give in to feelings and miss an opportunity of a lifetime.

"Ladies and gentlemen we are beginning our arrival at the London's Heathrow Airport. Please fasten your seat belts and prepare for landing," the pilot voice over the loud speaker jolted Jewel as she sat up straight in her seat after sleeping, on and off for most of her trip.

"Heathrow Airport is one of the world's busiest International Airports," the pilot continued his landing speech, "the hub of the aviation world with over ninety airlines based here. It's the second busiest cargo port. The climate today is mild. It's drizzling rain with some fog. The temperature is sixty four degree."

Jewel looked at her sleeveless top and began to look for a sweater that she threw in her carry on bag as an after thought. It was almost ninety degree when she left Tennessee yesterday and she didn't think it could be that cool anywhere this time of the year

The firm sent a driver to pick Jewel up from the airport, and he took it upon himself to give Jewel a mini tour. Jewel was glad and found the places fascinating. At such names as Edward the Confessor, Karl Marx and William Shakespeare, Jewel was overwhelmed with excitement.

"Farther west is the monarchy's permanent residence, Buckingham Palace. We will not be passing by there today unfortunately."

Jewel was sort of disappointed, but then she didn't know the driver would give her a short tour; that was certainly kind of him and was indeed above the call of duty.

Jewel knew she was staying with the family of a woman that worked for the law firm, but she knew nothing about her. All she knew was that they lived in Knotting Hill.

"Are we close to where I'm going to be staying," Jewel inquired as they past through a dark and dreary area.

"London has many of it's slum areas right outside of some of it's most prestigious community," the driver said sensing Jewel's concern, "Knotting Hill was once considered one of the West End's most run-down areas, but now it is considered one of the trendiest. You will like it here."

Jewel breathed easier.

"When it's foggy and rainy most of London looks dark and dreary, but it's really one of the best places to live," the driver added, as Jewel only nodded.

They pulled into a section of town where the houses were almost uniform in appearances, two stories red brick homes. The landscaping was nice and the streets were cleaned. There were some children playing outside despite the rain.

"Don't mind us Londoners," the driver said, "A day like today is like another sunny day to us compared to where you probably come from. Where is that by the way?"

"Tennessee," Jewel said.

"Here we are," the driver said as he pulled into a driveway.

He got out the car and without coming to open Jewel's door, he went up to the house and rang the doorbell. Jewel wasn't sure what to do, so she decided to stay put until told otherwise.

She watched the driver as the door opened and he began to talk to a woman that looked the age of her mother. She went back in for a moment, but soon reappeared with a yellow rain coat and walked with the man to the car. A boy also came out with her. He looked to be in his late teens.

The woman came around to Jewel side of the car while the driver and the boy went to the back of the car and began to take Jewel's luggage out.

The woman opened Jewel's door and stuck her head inside the car and said, "Jewel, welcome," as she reached for Jewel's hand. Jewel shook her hand.

"Come on, get out," she said.

Jewel got out and almost had to look up at the tall, elegant looking woman.

"I'm Beebe Jamison. Everyone calls me Beebes."

The last name sounded familiar.

"I'm the office administrator for Prescott and Associates. I made all the arrangements for your trip here today."

"Thank you," Jewel said.

"How was your flight?"

"It was good."

"Great, come on let's go inside. I'm still not use to London's nasty weather."

They walked into a small doorway. "Take Jewel's things to Kelva's room Percy. That's Percy, my son. He's seventeen. Did Kendall introduce himself?" Beebe asked referring to the driver who turned and showed a full set of white teeth.

"You know me Beebes, I still forget those formalities," the driver said.

"That's Kendall. He does much of the driving for the firm. Come let me show you around."

They walked through a formal dining room, stepping up to enter a spacey kitchen that looked right into the den. Down the hall from the kitchen were the rooms. The last room down the hall was where Percy had placed her luggage.

"I'm going to leave you to get settled in. It's almost dinnertime, but you have time to take a nap. We'll just have dinner a little late tonight."

"Oh please don't change your schedule for me. I can eat anytime you're ready," said Jewel.

"It's not a problem, besides my husband isn't home yet. Do you need to make a call home to your family?"

"I'm not sure," Jewel thought looking at her watch and becoming a little confused. Her watch seemed wrong. "I don't think my watch is correct," Jewel said, looking around for a clock and then finally asking, "I'm sorry, but what time is it?" she asked feeling kind of embarrassed for not knowing.

Beebe picked up on what was puzzling Jewel.

"It's five thirty." Jewel tried to count in her mind what time that would be in the States.

"I think it's nine thirty in the morning where you're from."

Jewel smile, "I think so. I guess I have to get use to figuring that out."

"It'll take sometime to get use to. That's probably why your watch isn't correct. Did you reset it for the different time?"

Jewel smiled embarrassingly again, "No, I didn't," she said, as she took her watch off and began to set it for the correct time in London.

"You may want to buy you one of those watches that give you the different time zones, that way you'll always know what time it is where you live."

"That sounds like a great idea."

"I'll leave you to get settled in. We'll have dinner at six thirty and if you are sleeping, I'll just put something up for you to eat later tonight."

"Thank you," Jewel said, glad for the offer, but she couldn't figure out if she was too tired or too hungry, so she decided to take a shower, change and put up some of her things, because she was sure that if she laid down for a nap, she wasn't going to wake up until the morning.

At six thirty Jewel came out of her room.

"Hi," Beebes said as she walked into the kitchen, "dinner is almost served. I hope you like pasta. I tried to make something that I thought you would like, so it's pasta and shrimp. I think that's a universal dish. I'm not so worldly, so forgive me if I get some things wrong. My daughter, Kelva, is in the States studying medicine. She's twenty-five.

It's her room that you're staying in." Jewel just nodded allowing Beebes to tell her a little bit about herself. "So you're a lawyer." Beebes stated.

"Not yet, Jewel said. I still have to past the bar exam. I'm just doing my internship here while I study for the exam."

"Oh, okay. You'll like Prescott. Everyone there is so nice. It's mostly a family firm; founded by Oswald Prescott in 1958 and past down to his sons Miles and Haddon and his daughter, Reed Handley.

"Are they all lawyers?"

"The best in London, but I'm a little prejudice. They're good people, especially as far as lawyers are concern. So you haven't met any of them?"

"No, I spoke to a Mr. Porter."

"Oh yes, Nicholas Porter. He is an associate of the firm. He goes out and looks for new talents. In other words, he's the law firm personal head hunter." Beebes opened up a window and yelled out, "Percy! Time for dinner! Put the dog in his house and come in!"

"Dinner? I here," a man's voice came from behind Jewel. He grabbed Beebes around the waist, while looking over her shoulder into the pot.

"This is Benton, my dear beloved husband. Benton meet our house guest, Jewel."

Benton let go of Beebes and held out his hand to Jewel., "nice to meet you, and welcome to our home. Please make yourself at home."

"Thank you," Jewel said.

"Here," Beebes said to Benton giving him a pot, "make yourself useful and take this to the table."

Jewel got up off the stool, "May I help?"

"Not today," Beebes said. Jewel wished she would let her do something, because she felt awkward just standing around.

"Did you call your family yet?" Beebes asked as she came back into the kitchen for something else.

"No, I haven't."

"Well do so after dinner. Like I said, we have a daughter in the States and if she travel half way across the world and didn't call me when she arrived, I would be out of my mind with worry."

"Yes maam," Jewel said. "Oh please don't address me as maam. I know you could be my daughter, but you also have to work with me and I will not have you yes maaming me around the office."

Jewel smiled and said, "yes maam," and then suddenly corrected herself, as Beebes stopped and stared at her, "I mean yes."

"Thank you," Beebes said.

Jewel felt at home with the Jamisons. Their home was nice with lots of nice things, but it had a homey feel to it, or was that them. Jewel wasn't sure. She called home before she went to sleep and gave her parents her number. They called her back, because they didn't want Jewel to have to worry about running up the Jamison's phone bill.

The next day was Friday and Jewel didn't have to report to the office until Monday. The Jamison's went off to work and Percy left as well, but Jewel wasn't sure where he went. She wasn't sure if he was still in school, or out, but he wasn't there and Jewel had the entire house to herself. Beebe's left her a note telling her to just eat whatever appeared edible.

Jewel tried to watch some TV, but TV was foreign to her, she never had time to watch it while she was going to school, so she just settled for the London's news, which was just as foreign.

She walked outside and got acquainted with Roxy, the Jamison's golden Retriever. He was a big dog, but quite friendly. It was a mild day. It wasn't raining, but it was a little foggy. Jewel was still experiencing jet lag, so she went back to her room and slept until Beebes came home. This time Jewel insisted that she help with dinner and Beebes gave in.

On the weekend, they showed Jewel around. They took her to Oxford Street, one of London's busiest shopping areas. Beebes filled Jewel in on the law firm and what would be some of her duties. Jewel looked forward to beginning work that Monday.

Jewel's work at Prescott consisted of research. She became the firm's paralegal. She enjoyed the work and was thoroughly immersed in all aspect of the law, even though her major was criminal. She worked on some criminal cases and even got to go into the courtroom with some of the lawyers. The US laws were adapted from the England laws, so it didn't take relearning a lot.

She moved into her own apartment a month after working at the law firm. It was a studio apartment. Jewel didn't make a lot and most of it went into paying long distance calls to the US. She was in constant contact with Tessa who was taking New York by storm. She had become one of Saks youngest buyer. She didn't call David as much, because when she did he preached salvation to her.

Jewel was adapting to London better than she thought and was looking forward to a long stay with the firm. When she passed the bar exam, the firm immediately made her an associate.

Jewel knew she would get the exposure in the UK that she wouldn't in the US, but she was caught off guard when her first case was a case in which a rich aristocrat's son was accused of shoplifting. The child was fifteen and guilty as charged. She was assigned to the case with Elgin, one of the law firm's oldest associates.

Elgin was arrogant and his motto was to win; he plea bargained the case and got the youth off with no criminal record and fifty hours of community service. Jewel was disappointed; she wanted to see Elgin at his best, but it was obviously in the best interest of the child not to go to trial.

When one of the firm's clients was accused of attempted murder of his wife. Jewel was assigned as the number two lawyer on the case and the district attorney was not interested in plea-bargaining. Jewel was going to get her first day in court.

They went with temporary insanity as their defense although the man clearly intended to kill his wife, because she was cheating on him. Jewel thought it was going to be hard for them to defend someone they knew was guilty, but after preparing their defense, she came to realized that it didn't matter whether her client was guilty or not, their job was to do whatever they could to keep him out of jail.

Because the courts and society frowned on the act of adultery, they were able to convince the jurors that their client did indeed went into a rage when he found out his wife was having an affair. There was only circumstantial evidence to the contrary, so the Juror brought back a verdict in the favor of the defendant. Jewel was excited about her first court experience that resulted in a win.

Jewel proved to be one of the law firm biggest assets. She was eager, ambitious and wanted only to win. She didn't try hard to stay out of court. She pushed for most of her cases to go to court, thus making a name for herself.

She had no time for a social life and eluded all the advances from the other lawyers in the firm. She was forewarned about how badly past relationships between associates in the firm ended, usually with the women being dismissed or forced to leave the firm. She was determined not to make that mistake.

It wasn't easy making friends at the firm, because everyone was so competitive, but she seemed to get along well with Ebba and Chad, two other associates of the law firm. They began to hang out together after work.

Jewel became the envy of all the other associates of the firm. There were even talk about making her a junior law partner.

"Some of us will make good lawyers and some of us will remain good law gofers," Ebba said.

Ebba knew she would never be considered for partner. Her work wasn't glamorous. She did a lot of corporate law for the firm's prestigious corporate client, and their objective was to always settle out of court.

"You can only be exposed if you go to trial and I've been working with the law firm for five years, and have been to trial once and then it was a lost. You, on the other hand have been with the law firm for less than a year, not counting before you past the bar, and you've been to trial how many times?"

"I'm not counting," Jewel answered.

"Which means you have more than one to count, and I rest my case," said Ebba, as they both laughed.

"What are you doing this weekend?" Ebba asked.

"Nothing," replied Jewel.

"This guy, Edmund, which I might be interested in has four tickets to a show. Would you be interested?"

"What show?" Jewel asked.

"Does it matter? It's an opportunity to get out and meet people. You need that. He has a friend that's going to use the other ticket."

"No thank you. No blind date for me," Jewel said emphatically.

"Come on Jewel. You have no social life. Wouldn't it be great just to get out and do something, besides flicking the TV channel trying to find something on to watch," Ebba pleaded.

"Ask Chad," Jewel said smirking.

Chad almost choked on his drink.

"If his friend isn't of the female persuasion, then I don't think so. I know I hang out with you ladies, but I don't go that way. I hang out with you, because I like the company of the opposite sex."

They all laugh.

"besides I don't think Sasha would like it."

Sasha was Chad's girlfriend, whom both Ebba and Jewel had met on several occasions and really liked.

"You should go Jewel. What could it hurt? All work and no play makes for a dull, lonely life."

"Okay," Jewel said surprising both Ebba and Chad.

"Jewel this is Tyler Gustav and Edmunde Hopkins," Ebba made the introductions. "Tyler, Edmunde, this is Jewel."

Tyler was about six foot two. He had hazel brown eyes. His hair was clean cut with a wavy texture. He looked like he weighted about two hundred twenty, most of which were muscles and Jewel had to admit to herself that she was relieved he was Black.

Ebba was white and she didn't want to ask, if her blind date was white or black. She didn't want to make an issue of it, especially since she was only doing a favor for Ebba.

Tyler was an engineer. He was on assignment from his company in the States. He had been in London for six month and was here until his project was complete. He was twenty-nine and handsome by most standards. He had a radiant milk chocolate complexion and star smile. Jewel was truly pleased with her date for the evening.

"Well what do you think?" Ebba asked Jewel when they went to the
ladies room after the main course and while the guys ordered desert.

"He's fine!" Jewel said. "I'm definitely impressed."

"Really, because I think he likes you."

"You think."

"Yes."

After dinner, Edmunde suggested they go somewhere for a nightcap,
but Jewel didn't want to seem eager and besides she had an early
appointment the next day.

Tyler offered to drive Jewel home. When they got to her apartment
building, he walked her to her door.

"I hope that we can get together again," Tyler said.

"I would like that," Jewel said.

"I'll get your number from Ebba and give you a call." Tyler stated.

Jewel wasn't sure why he just didn't ask for her number right there.
Maybe he was just trying to be polite and didn't intend to call. They
said goodnight. Tyler waited until Jewel was inside and heard the click
of the lock, before he walked away. Jewel didn't think she would hear
from Tyler again, which she thought would be disappointing, but not
devastating. She had her work.

Jewel could have used a friend today. It was one of her worst day at
the firm. She refused the advice of a colleague and ended up looking
like a fool. When the client asked to have her pulled off the case, she
had to eat dirt and apologize to the client.

The partners reviewed the case to see if she was going to be the best
associate to continue with the case. It was humiliating to say the least,
especially since she felt most of the associates at the firm envied her
and were probably talking about it behind her back, but they had to put
on the one big happy family smile and support her, because that was
the way Preston run their company, yet she knew they were waiting for
her to fall on her face.

Jewel was flicking the television channel, when the phone rang. In
disgust at not finding anything on to watch, she clicked it off and went
to answer the phone. It was Tyler.

380

"Your timing couldn't be any better," Jewel said. "Yes, I would love to."..."Tonight?" Jewel looked at the black out TV and said, "Tonight is good."... "I can meet you in an hour."... "No, just give me the address."

Tyler gave Jewel the address and she excitedly hung up the phone and went straight to the shower. After she dressed and inspected herself in her full-length mirror, she changed. She didn't like what she had on the second time, but when she looked at the clock, she realized she was running late and she still needed to call a cab.

Jewel decided not to purchase a car, until she decided whether, or not her stay in London was going to be prolonged. In the meantime, she was using cabs, public transportation and Beebs, who picked her up most mornings, unless she wanted to get to the office before the regular nine to five crowd, which was more often than not.

Despite the humiliation of the day's event, she began to feel good inside. She had given up hearing from Tyler. Ebba didn't even tell her he asked for her number, but then she hadn't talked to Ebba in awhile. She and Edmunde were spending a lot of time getting to know each other and things were hectic at work; she barely had time for lunch and usually ate dinner at her desk, while going over a brief for the next day.

Jewel walked into the lounge, went up to the bar and gave the Bartender her name. The bartender looked up once and then pointed, "Upstairs." Jewel walked upstairs and Tyler was sitting on a couch. There was a live band playing jazz. He got up when he saw Jewel.

"I'm glad you came."

"I'm glad you called. You thought I wouldn't come?" Jewel asked surprised.

"Maybe," he said with a shy smile, "please sit," he motioned to Jewel to sit on the couch, "or would you feel more comfortable at a table."

"This is fine," a little too comfy, Jewel thought, feeling a little uncomfortable as she sat down.

"What do you want to drink?"

"I'll just have a club soda, thank you."

"You don't drink?"

"Not really, except for champagne on holidays or special occasions."

"Maybe I should order champagne then, because I feel like this is a special occasion," Tyler said as he went to get Jewel's club soda.

"So, is this like your favorite hang out place?" Jewel asked.

"I like it here. They usually have live jazz music on Thursday nights. The atmosphere is mellow, and I can come relax, unwind and chill, so to answer your question, yes, I think this is my favorite hang out place. I hope you'll like it as well."

They sat quietly together, shoulders touching, while listening to the music and getting acquainted. Tyler put his arm around Jewel, or on back of the couch. Jewel wasn't sure which, but it was nice.

Jewel spent a lot of time in the next few weeks thinking about Tyler, whom she had begun to call Ty.

They talked every night on the phone and the weekends they went to the movies, dinner, for walks and talks. She felt more relaxed with Tyler than she ever had with any man she had been with in the past, even Brad. She use to think about Brad a lot, but now Brad was becoming a vague memory in her mind.

"So Jewel, tell me how such a beautiful woman, such as yourself, escape the attention of a steady male companion?

"Only if you'll tell me how come you have not been snatched away by some beautiful woman." Tyler laughed, but didn't answer.

"Oh, so there is someone."

Tyler looked into Jewel's eye and said, "not anymore," as he kissed her on the lips.

Jewel insides did flip-flops.

Jewel was afraid that a relationship so soon in her career would affect the effectiveness of her work, but it didn't. It actually did the opposite. Even the people she thought despised her notice her new disposition and were willing to work with her. She was no longer coming off as a small Atilla the Hun, as it was being said around the office.

"You and Tyler are moving faster than me and Edmunde. There seems to be something wrong with this picture," Ebba said to Jewel one day at lunch.

"I know and it's scary, but it's good at the same time, you know."

"I know."

"So how are you and Edmunde getting along?"

"I don't think it's going to work out between us."

"But you're still seeing him."

"Yeah, I think we want to make sure that it's not going to work, before we call it quits."

"Maybe it will."

"I don't think so."

"I feel bad, especially since you introduced me to Ty."

"Don't be silly," Ebba said, "at least something good came out of that night."

"Have you ever been to a poetry jam?" Tyler asked Jewel.

"No, I haven't. What's it about?"

"Just people reading poetry with music playing behind them. It's quite interesting and entertaining. Would you like to go to one?"

"I guess," Jewel said hesitating.

"It's not a trick. It is quite interesting."

"I'm sorry, I was just thinking."

"About what?"

"Nothing really," Jewel said, but she had been wondering for days what was bothering Tyler.

When she asked him what was bothering him, he said nothing, but she knew something was troubling him from the crease in his forehead and how he massaged his temple, when he thought she wasn't looking. She was beginning to read his body languages.

The poetry jam was held at the club where Jewel and Tyler went on their first date. They said something about open mic, but Jewel didn't know what that meant.

One after another, men and women got up and read or recite their own, or someone else's poetry, while the band played, mostly jazz, in the background. Some were good and some were bad, but some were really good.

The MC announced each poet.

Jewel heart pounded fast when she heard the MC said, "let's welcome our next poet to the mice. Let's give it up for Tyler Gustav."

Jewel looked at Tyler shocked and he acted like he knew nothing about it.

He got up to the mike and in a soft alluring husky voice said, "I'll like to read a poem I wrote, entitled, My Jewel."

Jewel felt her face go hot and hotter as Tyler began to descriptively share with everyone in the room his feelings for her.

The girls in front yelled, "I'll be your Jewel, Tyler."

He stopped momentarily smiled at them and searched the audience for her face. When he found it, he finished the poem while staring into her eyes, as she stared back.

He got a hearty applause from the audience, as Jewel got up and gave him a kiss, when he got back to his seat. He looked around and announced to everyone looking, "this is Jewel."

The girls sighed, "aaahhh," with disappointment, but they all clap as well.

Jewel couldn't remember a time when she felt this good.

Tyler took her to visit his parents in Brixton. She couldn't remember meeting nicer people than the Gustavs, except maybe the Jamisons. They welcome her in their home. They seemed genuinely interested in her, wanting to know all about her and her family.

Tyler had other brothers and sisters, but most of them were scattered about, but two of his sisters and a brother lived in Brixton with their spouses and children. They were at the dinner, to meet Jewel no doubt.

"You must bring her back on Sundays for dinner Tyler," Mrs. Gustav said.

"I will Mother," Tyler said.

"Sunday is a big dinner day for us," he said to Jewel.

"We have the same tradition in Tennessee," Jewel said.

Jewel and Tyler went over to his parents almost every Sunday afternoon for dinner, then they would take walks to the park half a mile away and played in the park like children and then sat and talk for hours.

"My job is almost finished here Jewel," Tyler said one afternoon, as they were sitting on the park bench throwing bread to ducks in the pond. Jewel was quiet.

"I think a month or two more."

Jewel heart sank, it couldn't be ending this soon, she prayed. It's just too soon, "so what does that mean exactly?" Jewel asked, trying to be cool about it.

Tyler got up and stretched and continued to make long throws in the pond.

"It means that I've finished the assignment that my job has sent me here to do, and I go back to the States, to my apartment and my life in Connecticut."

"I thought you had a life here," said Jewel.

Tyler stopped and sat back down and looked at Jewel, "I do, with you, but my job is back in the States. We knew this day would come, when we got involved."

"That's right, I wasn't suppose to hope for something more, besides that's where she is, isn't it?"

"Jewel I told you it was over between me and her."

"It was over while you were here. Are you telling me that you're not going to see her when you get back to the States?"

Tyler was suddenly sorry that he told Jewel about his old girlfriend back in Connecticut. It was over before he left. That was one of the reasons he took the assignment, to create some space between him and her. He did not want to talk about an old girlfriend. He wanted to talk to Jewel about the two of them and what his leaving London meant.

"I guess I'll see her around, but I don't want to talk about her. I want to talk about us. Where does this leave us?"

"I don't know, because my life is here."

"But I thought this job was only temporary. You're thinking of making London your home, when all of your family is in the States."

"Your family is in London, but that didn't stop you from making a life in the States, besides I have a strong feeling that in a year or two, I'm going to make junior partner."

"Wow, I didn't realize that. That's big. I certainly know what your career means to you. Do you believe in long distance relationships?"

"Do you? Is there any way you can continue to work for your company in London?"

"Jewel, I don't want to stay in London. I was born here, and all my life I wanted to go work in the States. When I got a scholarship to go to school in the States, I jumped on it and there was nothing anyone could do to talk me out of it. I love it there. It's my home now, and besides," Tyler pause not sure if it was the right time to tell Jewel what he was about to tell her.

"Besides what?"

"I have a daughter. Her name is Brianna."

"A daughter?" Jewel sat forward a little on the bench, so she could look Tyler in the eyes.

"I'm telling you this, because I want you to understand that it isn't because of another woman that I need to go back to the States, but it's because of my daughter."

"Her mother?"

"Her mother's name is Teri. She's okay, but we separated a year after Brianna was born. We wanted to do the marriage thing, but we were just two different people with nothing in common but the physical thing. We're still friends. We didn't want to put Brianna through any of our changes. She's five."

Tyler reached in his back pants pocket and pulled out his wallet. He opened it and showed Jewel a picture of Brianna.

"She's pretty."

"Yes, she is."

"Why didn't you tell me before?"

"Well at first, I didn't know how close we would get, before I had to leave and when we got closer than I thought we would, I didn't want to scare you off."

"Now what? What do you expect me to do? You have already started a life in Connecticut. I want to do the same here."

"I want you to come back to the States with me."

Jewel looked at Tyler puzzled wondering what exactly was he purposing. They were not sexually intimate. They had nothing binding between them, but Jewel knew she didn't need a sexual relationship with Tyler to know she loved him.

"I want you to marry me, Jewel."

The statement didn't take Jewel totally by surprise, but she was hoping he didn't put it out there.

"Tyler I'm not ready to be married to you, or anyone else right now. I understand that you have to go back to the States, but you have to understand my need to stay here."

"I understand. I know what your career means to you. I don't want to pressure you, or give you any ultimatums, but I'm not taking the proposal back. Why don't we just enjoy the rest of my time here together and you can think about it. I won't bring it back up, even if I have to leave here without hearing your answer. I know you feel for me the same as I do for you and we're going to have to find a way to make it work, or," Jewel looked at Tyler.

"Or what?"

"Or we are going to be two people on earth, unnecessarily walking around with broken hearts," Tyler said as he smile and put his arms around Jewel and drew her closer to him for an embrace and a long kiss.

Jewel deliberately blocked out the fact that Tyler may be leaving in a month or two, but she made sure she spent every spare moment she had with him.

Tyler came over regularly to her apartment and they spent hours on the couch talking and watching TV until one of them fell asleep in the others arms and eventually the other drift off as well. He would wake-up two, three and sometimes four in the morning and sometimes just stayed the rest of the night and got up early to go home to get ready for work.

The project Tyler was working on defaulted and he had to prolong his stay in London, until after the holidays.

On New Year's Eve, Jewel and Tyler showed their faces at each one of their office parties. After they made their rounds, they had reservations at a quiet restaurant with a live band playing soft music to bring in the New Year.

Tyler ordered a bottle of champagne.

"I remember you said that you only drink champagne on special occasions. Is this a special occasion?"

"This is a special occasion," Jewel answered.

"You look so lovely. I've never met anyone as beautiful as you."

"Tyler Gustav, you don't need to go there. I saw your daughter and her mother couldn't be a dog."

"Are you insinuating that I couldn't produce a beautiful child by myself?"

"I'm saying you couldn't produce any child by yourself." They both laughed.

"But seriously. You look like a Nubian Queen. Your skin is so smooth," he said touching her face, "and chocolately, I could eat you up." Jewel smiled embarrassingly. "Your hair is so blue black that I can see the blue radiating from it."

"It's the Indian in me, I guess."

"Really, I didn't know you have Indian ancestors. I guess that's where it comes from, but you didn't get that smile from the Indians. That's a true African smile, perfect and even white teeth. You make my heart leap when you smile, and your body."

Jewel suddenly felt her face on fire as well as the rest of her body.

"I'm not going to go there, Jewel, because as dark as you are, I can feel the heat radiating from your face."

Jewel was hot with embarrassment. No one had ever described her in such detail.

"But I will say this, your body, well let's just say that over the last several months, I can only say that if they were giving out awards for the most resolved in a difficult situation, I would win hands down, because it has been most difficult for me to watch you and want you and still respect your desire to remain a virgin until you're married."

Jewel smiled, "and I thank you for understanding. If I had an award, I would give it to you, but please don't think that it has been easy for me. I probably want to be with you that way, even more. When I first saw you, I thought, a male god, and I can't believe that I'm saying this," she said, as she let out a quiet little embarrassing laugh.

The waiter came up with the bottle of champagne. "Would you like me to pour the champagne now, sir?" Tyler looked at his watch. It was almost midnight.

"Yes, please." He said, staring into Jewel's eye.

The waiter filled the glasses and left the table.

Tyler reached over and took Jewel hands, "this is going to be a night that I'll never forget."

"Neither will I."

A big clock went dong and the band began to play, "Auld Lang Syne."

Tyler stood up and reached for Jewel. He took her in his arms kissed her and said, "Happy New Year."

"Happy New Year," Jewel replied.

Tyler reached for the champagne glasses and gave Jewel hers, and said, "To us."

"To us," Jewel repeated.

Tyler waited for her to start drinking and he followed, all the time he had his eyes glued on her. When she reached the bottom of her glass, a hard cold object slid into her mouth. She held her head down quickly, to make sure she didn't swallow whatever it was that was in the glass.

She spit the object back into the glass and stared at a huge sparkling diamond ring. She looked up at Tyler who was smiling from ear to ear. She suddenly became so nervous she thought she would drop the glass on the floor.

She sat down and held her head, as it began to spin. Tyler sat in the chair next to her and took the ring out of the glass and twirl it around in his hand for a few seconds, until he was sure Jewel had regained her composure.

Knowing Jewel had already practically said no, he proceeded to ask his question, without fear, "Jewel, I am asking you to marry me. I'm not asking you to leave with me in a couple of days, and maybe we will not be married for another year or two, and maybe in between that time, we are going to have to travel back and forth to see each other. I don't know. All I know now is that I want to marry you. I want you to be my wife. I can't imagine going back to the States without you, but I know I will have to, and I need to know that this will not be the end of us, but the beginning." Tyler waited.

"Are you finished with your speech?" Jewel said with tears in her eyes.

"I guess, but I'll talk all night if I think it will get you to say yes."

"You won't have to, yes."

"What did you say?" Although it was the answer Tyler was hoping for, he was not expecting it.

"I said, yes." Jewel place her hand on the side of Tyler's face. "I don't want this to be the end. I want this to be the beginning."

"Yahoo! She said yes," Tyler yelled out and everyone in the restaurant looked at them.

He placed the ring on Jewel's finger and pulled her up out of her seat and kissed her.

Then he turned to the people in the restaurant that were looking at them and said again, "she said yes. She will marry me."

Everyone started to clap. One man got up and proposed a toast. They were the last to leave the restaurant. They were still dancing as the band began to pack up.

A waiter came over and tap Tyler on the shoulder and said, "we're getting ready to close sir, and besides there is no more music."

"Oh yes there is," Tyler said, "You just can't hear it."

He was right. Tyler and Jewel stopped dancing to the band's music long before they stopped playing. They were dancing to the music that could only be heard in their hearts.

Chapter Twenty-Five
Lois

Lois made money hustling during the nights and she and Owen spent the days moving from crack house to crack house. Every now and then, they use some of the money to rent a room to take a shower, but that was not regularly. For the most part they stayed on the streets, to save their money for drugs.

"Where are you going?" Owen asked Lois.

"I'm going to rent a room for tonight. I need a shower and so do you."

"How much money do we have?"

"Not that much, but I need to take a shower," Lois said scratching herself trying to bring home her point.

"I think we need to spend our money sparingly."

"Sparingly," Lois said with a laugh, "maybe if you contributed we would have more money to spend. I haven't had a nice bath or shower in a week. I need one."

"Don't get smart with me. Who do you think got you back on the streets? If it wasn't for me you wouldn't be out there. Some pimp would have done you in by now," Owen said while preparing some crack in a pipe to smoke.

"Well, I'm not going to get any business smelling like this, and I need to buy some personal things."

"I guess you're right. Aint nobody wanna mess around with someone, who smells like fish," he said laughing at his comment while smoking on his pipe.

He past the pipe to Lois and she took a long draw, before Owen snatched it from her, "come on girl, don't be greedy."

Deb met Stephanie and Richard at the airport. They hugged and greeted each other before Stephanie began to cry again.

"I'm sorry, but have you heard anything from Lois yet?"

"No Steph I haven't"

"Come. I'll take you guys to your hotel, so you can take a shower and get rested up, and then you can come over to my apartment for dinner."

"That sounds good," said Richard.

The next day was a big day for Stephanie and Richard. They had petitioned the court for custody of Danijel. They met with the social worker and the lawyer early that morning.

"Mr. and Mrs. Johnson, it's good to meet you in person," Diane, Danijel's social worker, said as she greeted the Johnsons with a hearty handshake.

She looked at Deb and the lawyer and greeted them as well.

"Were you able to gather all the records that we're going to need today?" Diane asked Stephanie.

"I think so," Stephanie replied, "but I don't see how the courts can deny me custody of my own grandson."

"We need to be prepared for anything, Mrs. Johnson," Peggy Bekow, Danijel's guardian Ad-litem said. "The courts are only interested in doing what's best for the child, and Danijel don't know you. The only connection he has with you was telephone conversations."

Stephanie heart sank. How many summers past that she pleaded with Lois to bring Danijel for a visit, or let him come for the summer for a couple of weeks.

She was so protective of Danijel. Stephanie couldn't imagine how she could have just left him like this. To think of what state of mind her daughter was in to do such a thing was beyond Stephanie's imagination.

"I understand" Stephanie said weakly, realizing now that she should have listened to her heart and visited her daughter, but Lois always made an excuse as to why it wasn't a good time for her to come visit.

"Mrs. Hall I'm glad you could come as well," the lawyer said to Deb, "since you have already been before the court to petition for Danijel, maybe the courts will recognize the connection, and realize how much your family wants Danijel to be in their care. It can't hurt."

"I hope so," Deb said, "I just hope it turns out positive this time."

The judge turned Deb down because she was a single mother with three children, with little income.

"It has to Deb," Stephanie said. "We have placed our petition before God, and now it's in his hand."

"Yeah, we got everybody back at our church praying," Richard added.

"Everybody ready?" the lawyer asked looking at everyone. They all nodded yes, as she open the door to the court.

"What's your problem?" Owen said jerking Lois off the bed.

She was soaking wet from her shower, lying on the bed in a fetus position crying, with nothing on except the tower she had around her from her shower.

"I'm sick of you and this crying, you know. I don't need this!" Owen yelled at Lois as he shook her making her cry more.

"You stupid broad!" Owen said as he shoved Lois back on the bed, "you probably don't even know why you're crying. It's pathetic. Here," he said throwing a vial of crack on the bed for Lois, "this should help you get it together. You have to go to work soon. You can't stay here all night drowning in your sorrows," he said walking away.

"I've reviewed the documents before me and I've heard the petition of Danijel Edward's maternal grandparents, Mr. and Mrs. Richard Johnson." the judge pause as he looked down and flipped through some more paper, "It has been brought to this court's attention that the parent, Lois Johnson, who had sole custody of Danijel Edwards, have not come forward to claim the child, since the day the child was taken in custody by Family Social Services. It is also clear to this court, that the father cannot be located and notified of the child's situation," the judge flipped through some more paper, "I believe a sufficient time has gone by in which to locate the father and I can see that everyone involve has done their due diligence to do that." The Judge looked up, took off his reading glasses and addressed the Johnsons and the court.

"This court has found that given the circumstances, Mr. and Mrs. Johnson should be awarded custody of Danijel Edwards. The courts also recognize that the child will have to leave the state of New York to live with his grandparents, where they reside in Tennessee. While this is acceptable and within the laws, this does not mean that the Family Social Services are released of their duties to make sure the child, Danijel Edwards, adjusts to his new surroundings and that social services in…," the judge barely put back on his reading glasses, as he flipped through some pages, then looked up again, "…and the social services in Brickenbrat, Tennessee are aware of the child's case being moved to their venue and that regular follow-up on the child be done by them as well. Case close," the judge said, as he closed his file and looked up at the Johnsons again.

"I want to commend the Johnson's for stepping up to take custody of their grandchild. It is always with great pleasure, when this court can award custody of an abandoned child to relatives."

The word abandoned stuck in Stephanie's heart like an ice pick, but everyone started hugging each other and congratulating each other and her heart welled up with love. The thought of being able to take her grandchild home with her was overwhelming.

"Why don't we go pick up your grandson." Diane said.

"We can do that now?" Stephanie asked in surprise.

"We certainly can. You have custody. Unless you want him to stay with his foster parents, until you're ready to leave."

"Absolutely not," Richard said, "he has stayed with strangers long enough."

"Well, just keep in mind that you're going to be strangers to him as well."

"Not for long. Not for long," Stephanie said as Richard took her hand and squeezed it tightly.

"Hi Mrs. Johnson. I'm so glad you won custody of Danijel."

"Kelly. How are you? I'm surprise to see you here. How did you know about the trial?"

"I've been keeping in touch with the Agency. I've gone with Deb a couple of times to see Danijel, so they know me."

"I see," she said looking at Richard who looked a little puzzled, "I'm sorry excuse my manners. Richard this is Kelly. Cadera?"

"Caldera," Kelly corrected as she held out her hand to Richard, "glad to meet you Mr. Johnson."

"You're Lois' friend."

"Yes sir."

"Then how did you let this happen to our little girl?"

"I'm sorry, Mr. Johnson, but I…"

"Richard, we don't need to blame anyone. We just need to find her," Stephanie said coming to Kelly's defense.

She didn't feel it right to blame anyone, especially since they didn't know the circumstances that led Lois to do what she did.

"Have you heard from her?"

"I'm sorry, but I haven't."

"We should be going," Diane broke into the conversation.

"Thank you Kelly, for everything you've done for my daughter and for Danijel."

Kelly began to cry. It was the first time that anyone of Lois' family said anything nice to her, "I wish I could've done more."

"I know you do," Stephanie said as she hugged Kelly.

"Mrs. Johnson, do you think it might be possible for me to see Danijel, before you take him back home?" Kelly asked.

"I think we can arrange that. You can contact Deb. She will know where we are."

"Thank you," Kelly said, as Adrienne came beside her and placed her arm around her.

"Who were you calling?" Owen demanded.

"None of your business!" Lois said hanging up the phone. Owen took Lois by the hair pulling it until Lois was moaning in pain.

"When are you going to get it? You are my business and I need to know everything you do. Are you trying to two time me or something?"

"I was calling an old friend," Lois said between her teeth, gasping from the pain.

Owen let go of her hair and asked, "was she home?"

"No she wasn't," Lois said.

"Who is she?"

"Why? You don't know her."

"That's my point. I don't know anything about you. It would help if I did."

"Help what?" Lois asked.

The thought of letting Owen know anything about her life, especially about Danijel, made Lois shiver.

"Help to understand you better. Maybe if I knew you better," Owen said rubbing on Lois in places that made her jerked away in disgust.

"I don't think so."

"You think I'm any worst than the men you are with every night."

"I think you're worst, and you don't pay. It's not free." Owen burst out laughing as Lois walked away.

Lois had dialed Kelly's number. The phone rang several times, but no one picked up. She didn't know if she would've said anything, if Kelly had picked up. Did she want to know if Kelly knew anything about Danijel? Would Kelly tell her if she did know something, or would she condemn her for leaving?

Richard and Stephanie stayed at the hotel the rest of the week. Danijel stayed with Deb at night and they came over early in the morning to spend the day with him. They wanted him to feel comfortable with them, before they took him home.

The social worker thought it would be a good idea to do it this way, so he could associate them with Deb and Kelly, who Danijel already knew.

They hoped he could make the connection that Stephanie and Richard knew his mom, just like Deb and Kelly.

"How old are you Danijel? He put down his spoon and held up four little fingers, while his mouth was full of cereal.

"Do you know how many that is?" Stephanie asked.

"Four," Danijel said, "but I'll be five soon and then I can go to real school."

"You like school?"

"hmm hmm."

"Say yes, or no Danijel," Richard corrected.

"I know what to say, but I can't talk with my mouth full of food," Danijel corrected back.

"You sure can't," Richard said rubbing his head, "so I guess we need to wait until you've finished eating to talk." Danijel just looked up and nodded in a way that suggested they could do whatever they wanted.

"All done," he said finally and picked up a napkin to wipe his mouth. "Do you know my mommy?"

"Yes Danijel, remember we told you that I am Lois' mother, just like Lois is your mother, which makes me your grandmother."

"Is she at your house?"

"No she isn't. We're not sure where your mom is right now."

"Then how will she find me?"

"Your mother knows where we live Danijel and as soon as she can, she will come get you."

Danijel looked confused and tears began to well up in his big black eyes.

Richard took him and sat him on his lap and said, "Danijel I know this is all a little confusing for you, and I know that you don't know us yet, but we love you just like we love your mom and your mom would want you to come stay with us."

"I think you're going to really like it where we live, Danijel."

Danijel didn't say anything, as his little heart fluttered with fear of not knowing what was in store for him next.

"Did you take care of the room?" Stephanie asked Richard as she checked again for anything they may have left behind.

Deb got Karen to take them to the airport.

Richard jumped out of the car, "I'll go take care of the luggage. Y'all go ahead and say your goodbyes."

Richard took care of the tickets and met everyone in the waiting area.

"Flight 1452 to Atlanta is now seating all passengers with a handicap, or small children."

Stephanie got up, "That's us. Deb, I can't thank you enough for all you've done."

Danijel was holding on tightly to his stuff dog, looking through the windows at the planes while holding on to Stephanie's hand. When they got up to the counter, Richard only produced two tickets. Stephanie looked puzzled, so did the airline worker.

"Sir, are you not traveling with us today?"

Richard was looking at Stephanie, not the airline worker when he responded, "No maam I'm not. I have a daughter I need to find before I go back home."

"Richard?" Stephanie looked confused.

"Excuse us please," some people behind them said, wanting to board the plane.

Richard pulled Stephanie aside. "I have to do this. I can't go back home without looking for her, and I don't need you around to do that. I've been where Lois is, and I may know how to find her."

"But, but…," Stephanie said shaking her head.

"If I told you I was staying, you would want to stay, and one of us need to get Danijel home and settled and get back to the kids, before they take over the house."

Stephanie looked over at Deb and said, "Did you know?"

"Yes I told her, but I asked her not to tell you what I was planning."

"You're a good man, Richard Johnson," Stephanie said reaching over to kiss her husband.

"Hey Danijel," Richard kneeled down to talk to him, "you think you can get your grandmother home safely for me."

"Yes sir."

"That a boy," he said, "giving Danijel a big hug."

"You coming too?" Danijel asked.

"I'm not going with you guys today, but I'll be home real soon. Okay."

"Okay."

"Final boarding for flight 1452 to Atlanta," the announcement came.

"Well, that's you guys." Richard said, letting go of Stephanie hands as she and Danijel boarded the plane looking back at him and waving bye.

Richard stayed with Deb, because he didn't know how long his search was going to take. He knew he had to first get some information. He talked extensively with Kelly. He found out what he had already suspected, that Lois was heavily into drugs. He found out some other things about the Agency as well. Things he had already suspected. This is why he didn't want Stephanie to stay. He knew, if she found out what Lois had gotten herself into, it would break her heart. The less she knew now, the better. He just hoped he could find Lois before it was too late.

"What, what are you doing? Stop! Stop! Please stop!" Lois screamed as the man kept on hitting her with a whip chain.

"Scream in pain, you whore, Go 'head scream for help. No one is going to hear you."

The man kept on hitting Lois as she tried to reach the door.

"That's right, scream you demon, but tonight you will leave this tortured girl's body! I command you to come out of her, you foul lusting demon," the man said, while he kept on hitting Lois.

Everything was becoming blurred. Lois knew she was about to pass out and if she did, the man would surely kill her. Out of the corner of her eyes, Lois saw an object on the floor. She wasn't sure what it was, but she reached for it and threw it at the man. It hit the man right between his eyes, as he was regaining his balance, Lois pulled the whip out of his hand and began to hit the man with it.

She blindly saw the door from out of her blood-covered eyes, so she made a run for it.

As she was fingering with the locks on the door, the man got up and grabbed her from behind and said, "You can't run from me devil!"

Lois turned and kneed the man in the groin and as he wrenched in pain, Lois finally got the door open and ran for the nearest exit. She ran and ran, not knowing exactly where she was. She knew she needed to go to a hospital for help, but she couldn't run anymore, as she slipped and fell down on the concrete.

She woke up in the county hospital. Her head was still pounding, but she could see her surroundings.

"You awake?" A nurse asked her. Lois nodded her head.

"Who did this to you?"

"I don't know," Lois said.

The nurse acted like she didn't hear, "Boyfriend? A john? Pimp?"

Lois raised herself up a little on her elbow, "I said I don't know."

"Yeah right," the nurse said. "I'll get the police officers, so they can take your statement."

As soon as the nurse left the room, Lois began to look for her clothes. She found them underneath her bed, but they were stained with blood. Lois got up out of the bed and eluded nurses and doctors, as she searched rooms for something decent to put on. The emergency room was so busy, no one really noticed her. She found a blouse and some nurses pants in the nurse's station. She put them on and slowly walked out of the hospital, holding her side.

She went to the motel room that she and Owen had rented a couple of days ago. She didn't know where her keys were, so she had to knock on the door.

"Who is it?" Owen asked.

"It's me, Lois."

"Lois?" Owen asked opening the door. "Where have you been? I thought you met a rich john and skipped out on me," he said half laughing until he saw her, "hey what the heck happened to you?"

Lois didn't answer; she just pushed him aside and head for the bed, holding her side as she fell on the bed.

"I was at the hospital. They were going to get the cops, so I could make a report, so I left."

"You did the right thing. We don't need any cops sniffing around in our business."

"I need help Owen. I need something real bad."

"I got what you need babe," Owen went to the nightstand and pulled out a couple of vials. "I'll fix you up."

Owen mixed a couple of different drugs together and gave it to Lois to take.

"This will put you out of your pain."

Lois felt like she was asleep for days, or she died. She wasn't sure which. She had wild, delusional dreams; she dreamed about Danijel; she dreamed she died; she dreamed she got married to Peter and everyone was there, even Matt, but all the dreams ended the same; she ended up spinning and spinning and she couldn't stop, or she was falling, but never fell.

Lois was in and out for two days, when she came back, Owen insisted that she get back on the streets, because they only had a couple of dollars left.

After Kelly found out that Richard stayed behind to look for Lois, she began to call up old customers, trying to get someone to help him.

"I know someone who could help you Mr. Johnson."

Kelly said to Richard. She had talked to an old customer, who was a police captain. He agreed to let one of his men show Richard around, where the drug pushers and prostitute usually hang out.

"I could use all the help I can get."

"He's a police officer. You have a pen and paper? I'll give you his number and you can call him tomorrow. Tell him where you are and he'll come pick you up."

"Thanks Kelly," Richard said, as he hung up the phone.

"I think I might be getting somewhere," Richard said to Deb.

The police officer showed Richard around the next day.

"Actually your best bet is to come back at night, although I don't suggest doing it alone. We don't patrol these streets at night, unless we get a call. These streets belong to the drug dealers, pushers, the users and the prostitutes at night, and we only come on the scene when someone is killed."

"So you know this, but you do nothing about it." Richard said.

"Man it's too many of them and two few of us, and the people at the top have their own agenda, if it's not going to make headline news, it's not worth the man power."

"Some system."

"That's just the way it is."

"I'm not going out tonight, or maybe not even tomorrow, MAYBE NEVER!" Lois screamed at Owen.

Owen backed up, "okay, you don't have to go crazy on me or nothing like that. I understand you need some rest, sure just rest. I'll go see if I can't get us something to eat. I'll be back."

When Owen left Lois got up, "I won't be here when you get back," she said, as she began to gather up what little things she had, put it in a bag and left.

The next couple of days, Lois floated around from crack house to crack house, she had kept some money from Owen. She wanted it to be over. She wanted her life to be over. She tried everything, mixing everything.

"Hey you! You better not do that. That could be lethal, if used together," one of the drug addicts from the crack house said.

"I hope so," she said, "I hope so."

"Man that girl is suicidal."

"Who is she?"

"I don't know. She came in. She had money. I sell."

"I've seen her around here before with some guy name Owen."

"He a pimp?"

"Hers only. He's a two bit low life, who's known for latching on to some poor girl and sucking her dry."

"No one will suck me dry again," Lois mumbled to herself as she slowly drifted off.

"She said something?"

"Man, I don't know what that broad is mumbling, just leave her alone, the way she's mixing those drugs, she'll be gone by morning, then we can just put her body out in the back dumpster; just another soul out of their misery." The others agreed as they left Lois crawled up in a corner.

"Richard I don't think you should go out there this time of night by yourself. Let me see if I can find someone to go with you." Deb pleaded.

"I'm leaving now Deb. I can't wait until you find someone to go with me."

"Then, I'll get Mrs. Washington to watch the children and I'll go with you."

"Absolutely not. You are not going with me."

"What will I tell Stephanie when she calls? You know she calls every night the same time."

"Tell her I'm following up on a lead."

"Are you?"

"Am I what?"

"Following up on a lead."

"Yeah, I've been showing some pictures around during the day and there were two people that recognized her and said she sometimes comes around that way at night."

"What's in your bag?"

"This?" Richard held up the bag, "Or just some things I'm going to need."

As soon as Richard got down stairs, he pulled out some old clothes that he picked up out of the Salvation Army bin the day before. He layered on clothes, trying to look like a bum, so that he wouldn't look out of place and draw attention to himself.

After two weeks of looking, he felt like he had a really good lead. A girl said the last she heard, Lois had dumped her pimp and was alone. The girl also said that if she continued to be a loner, some of the pimps wouldn't like it and they may do her in.

Richard felt something in him telling him that Lois' time was running out. He had to find her soon, or he didn't think she would be found alive.

Richard looked in every crack house he remembered seeing during that day. He was on the streets for almost three hours. It was cold and approaching three in the morning. He wanted to give up and go back to the apartment, but something urged him on.

"That's her?" The pimp asked.

"Yeah that's her. They say she's Owen's girl."

The pimp looked at the drug dealer and said, "Owen doesn't have any girls on this side of town, besides I've seen this girl around here before. She works alone. I promise myself the next time I see her will be the last."

The pimp pulled out a stiletto knife clicked it open and looked around. Lois was out dead to the world.

"Maybe she's already dead," the dealer said.

"She's alive," the pimp said, noticing the slow, spasmodic movement of Lois' chest rising and falling.

"Hey man, don't do her in here. You'll have the cops all up in my business by morning. You know how hard it is to find a good place and establish new customers."

The pimp looked at the drug dealer and said, "then take her in the alley. I'll give you five minutes, then I'll come back in and do it right here," he said as he walked out back.

"God, show me. Please show me where to go God. I know she is here, but I'm so tired. I don't know where to look anymore."

Suddenly a gust of wind blew Richard's hat off his head and he stooped to pick it up, the wind blew it farther away, annoyed Richard picked up his pace to get the hat, before it went any further, but it kept blowing and blowing away and as Richard kept following it, the wind finally stopped and Richard stooped to pick up the hat and looked up into the pimp's steely eyes.

"What are you doing round here ole man?" The pimp asked, annoyed at Richard's intrusion.

"My hat," Richard said, as he place the hat on his head, "gots to have me hat, so cold, so cold."

Richard began to shiver more, as he noticed the pimp's hands behind his back, something was about to go down, but he didn't know what.

"You think they mind, if I come out of the cold maybe?" Richard said, barely able to see inside the dark crack house.

"I don't own this place, but you may be better off finding yourself a corner somewhere ole man."

"So cold though, so cold, I 'fraid my ole bones freeze by morning."

The pimp, annoyed, grabbed Richard with his one hand and shoved and kicked him in the crack house, "then get your butt in there, if you so cold," he said laughing.

Once Richard was in the crack house, he immediately saw a man trying to wake, or drag a woman from her resting place. He knew that on the streets, survival was minding your own business, but just the same he walked over to the woman's aide.

"Excuse me sir, but it doesn't seem like she wants to cooperate," Richard said tapping the man on the shoulder.

"What the…," the drug dealer said looking at Richard, "who ask you?"

"I just…," Richard said, as he looked at the girl and recognizing immediately that it was Lois,

"Lois?" he said.

"You know her?" The drug dealer asked. She was dirty and filthy and not the little girl that left their home eight years ago, but he recognize her red hair hanging out an old sweater cap.

"Yeah, she's my daughter," Richard said.

The drug dealer froze, then realizing what the pimp had said about coming back in to do her, he said hurriedly to Richard, "look man, if you and your daughter want to get out of here alive, you'd better get her and get out of here now, because there is a mean pimp out there who's waiting for me to drag her out there, so he can do her man."

Richard didn't ask any questions. He had already looked into the steely eyes of the pimp and wondered what he was holding in his hand hidden behind his back. With strength he didn't know he had, he grabbed Lois up into his arms. She was practically weightless.

"Where is the front entrance?" He asked the drug dealer.

"That way," he pointed, all the while looking for the pimp to come back in any minute.

"Hurry up man, get her out of here," he whispered heavily, his heart beating rapidly, wondering if the pimp would do him in instead.

Richard made it through the front entrance, but he knew the pimp would come looking for them, so he had to find a place to hide. Richard walked a couple of blocks, but he knew he wasn't going to get far carrying Lois, even though she was frail and light, her dead weight was more than he could carry far.

He saw a man and a woman going into the building across the street and ran over to them, before they entered the building.

"Sir, sir," Richard called out to the man.

"Look," the man said immediately pulling out a gun, "we don't want no trouble, but if you try something, I promise you I will shoot."

"I don't want any trouble either. I'm just trying to find a place for me and my daughter to hide for a few minutes. Could you please let us into your building?"

"Do we have stupid written over our face?"

"Please, sir, maam," Richard said, pleading to the woman as well. "Please, I mean you no harm. We just need a place for a few minutes that's all."

Richard heard hurried footsteps from behind and knew the pimp wasn't far behind.

"He's trying to kill my daughter maam," Richard said pleading to the woman only.

"Come on in, we'll call the cops for you. He won't bother you inside," the woman said.

"What do you think you're doing?" the man asked.

"You got the gun in your hand and he has his daughter in his, what can he do? All I know is that we all need to get inside now!"

"Okay, but if you try anything, I'll shoot the girl first," the man said.

"Thank you sir. Thank you maam," Richard said, as he followed the man and the woman inside the building. The door closed in the pimp's face.

"You can't hide in there all night ole man," the pimp said.

"I have a number. It's the number of a police officer, if you call him, he will come for us. Just tell him it's Mr. Johnson and he has found his daughter and needs a ride."

Richard put Lois down on the floor and reached in his pocket.

"Hold it!" said the man, "let me see your hands," Richard held up his hand.

"Where is the number?" The man asked, not trusting Richard to go into his pocket.

"In my wallet, in my back pocket."

The man put the gun to Richard's head and reached in Richard's back pocket and took out the wallet. He gave it to Richard. Richard took out the police officer's card and gave it to him.

"Is your daughter all right? Should we call an ambulance?" The woman asked.

"She's going to be alright," Richard said, "thanks for asking. You don't know how much I appreciate this. I think you may have saved our lives tonight."

The man took the woman's hand and they walked up the stairs, the woman looked back and asked, "Can I get you or your daughter something?"

"No thank you maam," Richard declined, sitting next to Lois exhausted, from running and carrying her, "you've done more than enough."

Two police cars pulled up with their lights flashing. The pimp who was standing outside the door, hoping for another tenant to come in and open the door, slowly began to walk away from the building, as if he was just passing by. He held his head down and out of the corner of his eye, he watched to see what the police officers were going to do.

The police officer that knew Richard got out of the car and shined his flashlight, while looking into the building.

The other kept his eyes on the pimp walking away, "just keep walking," the officer said, not wanting any trouble from the pimp.

When Richard saw the light, he jumped up and opened the door for the officers.

"So you found your daughter," the officer said shaking his head at Richard in approval.

"If more people cared like you, a lot more girls would be saved from these streets. Come on, just tell me where you want to go."

"Is she okay?" The other officer asked, "maybe you need to get her some medical attention."

"I think she'll get all the attention she'll need from now on."

He grabbed Lois' other hand and helped Richard put her into the squad car and drove them to the Bronx.

"Oh my God!" exclaimed Deb covering her mouth with her hands.

She had given Richard a key, but Stephanie kept her awake all night. She kept calling to find out, if Richard had returned. So when she heard the key turning in the door, she got up and waited for Richard to come in, all the while praying that he would have Lois with him.

The officer helped Richard bring Lois upstairs. "I hope everything works out for you and your daughter Mr. Johnson," said the officer.

"Thanks for all your help," Richard said to the officer.

"No problem, glad to help," said the officer before he left.

"Where did you find her?" Deb asked once the officer left and Richard and Lois were inside the apartment.

"I'll tell you in the morning. Right now I'm cold and exhausted. I just want to take a shower and get some sleep."

"You can put her in my room," Deb said, not wanting to wake her daughter

"No, just give us some blankets, sheets and a pillow and I'll lay her on the floor and I'll lay on the couch next to her until morning." Richard said.

Deb went to get some things to make up a bed for Lois and Richard.

"Steph wants you to call her as soon as you get in."

Richard looked up at the clock and said, "It's too late, if she doesn't call anymore tonight, I'll call her first thing in the morning."

"Is she all right?" Deb asked, noticing Lois' irregular breathing and her unresponsiveness.

"I think she is, but we'll have to wait until the morning to know for sure. If I can prevent doctors and cops from getting involved, I may be able to get her home sooner. The longer she stays here, the higher the risk of her getting away from us and going back to familiar places." Richard said, and Deb nodded in agreement.

The phone rang about an hour and half into Richard's sleep. He jumped up to get the phone, not wanting to wake anyone else, but he noticed lights were already on in Deb, the boy's room and the bathroom. Deb was in the bathroom taking a shower, while the boys were in their room getting dress.

"Hello,"... Richard said trying to wake up. "Stephanie?"..."I know. It was late, so I wanted to wait until the morning."..."Yes, I found her."

The phone went silent. "She's alive and she's going to be fine."... "I know. I know."..."No, you can't talk to her now."..."Go on to work and I'll call you later. Call my job and tell them I should be back by Monday morning."..."I know. They have been very understanding. I guess it's just God's favor."..."I love you too."..."Okay, I'll talk to you later."..."Yes, I'll call you at work. Bye now." Richard hung up the phone and Deb came out of the bathroom with a heavy thick terry blue bathrobe.

"That was Stephanie," Richard said.

"I'm going to get the kids off to school, then I'll take the rest of the day off to help you with whatever you need. You think you may leave today?" Deb asked.

"I'll have to see what kind of condition she's in when she wakes up. I don't know what she took last night, but she looks like she's going to be out for awhile."

Richard wasn't too worried. Ever since he was free from drugs, he has helped others who wanted to get free, so he had seen a lot worst than Lois. He wanted to get her home as soon as possible, before she started to experience withdrawals. She wouldn't be able to fly like that, without someone noticing she needed help.

Deb was back home early, but Richard had already made a round of phone calls.

"What's the plan?" Deb asked.

"I called the place where I've gotten a lot of addicts in to get clean. They can take Lois in as soon as she gets there. I'm hoping to take her straight there."

"You mean you won't take her home first."

"No. They don't recommend that. I told them the entire story and they suggest she get help before she return to a family environment, especially before she sees Danijel. Just one thing," Richard said.

"What's that?" Deb asked.

"She has to want the help. They don't take anyone that doesn't want help, and that may be a problem."

"What do you mean?"

"I don't know what state of mind Lois will be in when she wakes up. If she doesn't want the help, I'm not sure what else to do? If I take her home in this condition, things won't get better. She'll make our lives, especially her mother's, hell."

"What can you do?"

"I'm not going to assume anything now. We'll just have to wait until she wakes up. I'm going to take her to a hotel, until we leave. I don't want your kids to have to experience something ugly."

"Let's wait and see. It's only ten o'clock. The children get out of school at three o'clock, then they go to their after school programs. I don't have to pick them up until six, at the latest."

"That's good. That will give us some time. In the meantime, do you have anything she can put on?"

"Yes, although she looks like she's lost a lot of weight." Deb said looking at Lois' almost lifeless body wrapped up in a blanket on the floor. "I have some clothes that are too small for me. They should fit her."

"I'm going to give her a cold shower. I'll need your help for that, and then the other thing."

"What other thing?"

"The people at the center said I should get her something. I shouldn't bring her back home cold turkey."

"You mean give her drugs."

"It'll be better than have her go through withdrawals on the plane."

"I don't agree with that."

"I don't either, but they know what they're doing."

Lois started to turn and moan in her sleep, but she didn't wake. Deb was busy freshening up her apartment and preparing something for dinner, when Richard came in and said.

"I'm going to put her under the shower. I need your help."

Deb got some towels and some clothes ready. Richard brought Lois in the bathroom with her clothes on. He sat her down, so that she wouldn't fall down when the cold water hit her.

When she was settled in the shower, Richard looked at Deb and said, "If this doesn't work, we'll have to change her into dry clothes quickly and take her to an emergency room. I'm getting a little worried."

Richard turned the shower on first and then turned on the cold water. The cold water didn't move Lois. She sat stone face and motionless in the tub, as Richard held her up.

Richard looked at Deb, who was crying, and said, "there's no way anyone can sit under cold water like this and not show any response. I think we need to get her to a hospital."

Richard began to pull Lois up, "cut the water off?" He said to Deb.

Deb had her hand on the shower knob, as Lois began kicking, screaming, and flaying her arms at Richard.

"Help me! Help me!" She yelled in a screeching voice.

Deb tried to cut the water off, but Lois kicked her and a startled Deb, recoiled in the corner of the bathroom, with tears streaming down her face.

"I need you to help me hold her!" Richard yelled at Deb, but when he looked at Deb, he knew she wouldn't be able to do anything. Taking his eyes off Lois was a bad idea. With strength, Richard couldn't comprehend from such a frail body, Lois grabbed him around the neck and pulled him into the bathtub with her.

"I told you I'm not going back out there!" Lois screamed.

Her eyes were closed, but she wouldn't have recognized Richard, if they were open. Richard tried desperately to constrain her, but she was like a frightened, trapped animal.

"Lois," Richard began to call out her name, "Lois, you don't have to go back out there," he repeated several times, before it finally registered.

She finally opened her eyes and looked into Richard's eyes. Before Richard could figure out if it was recognition, or fear, he saw in her eyes, her eyes rolled upwards and she passed out.

Richard held on to her and yelled at Deb to cut the water off. Deb was finally able to regain her composure.

"Towels," Richard said, as he held an unconscious, but shivering Lois in his arms.

Richard managed to get her out of the tub.

"Can you gather up as many blankets, as you can? I'll need you to warm a couple at a time in the oven."

"I'll have to go next door and get some from Mrs. Washington. I don't have that many," Deb said as she hurried out the door.

She was glad to separate herself from the scene in the bathroom. When Deb came back, she began to warm the blankets in the oven and gave them to Richard two at a time. Richard used one to wrap Lois up in to get her body temperature back to normal, but he used one for himself as well.

Richard spent the rest of the afternoon holding Lois and wrapping her in warm blankets.

After a few hours, Lois opened her eyes. "Am I alive?" she asked.

"You're alive," Richard answered.

"Where's my mother?" She said in a shaky, weak and teary voice

"She's home," Richard said, as Deb came into the living room and sat on the couch next to Lois. Lois held down her head and placed her hand in her head and began to cry.

"I'm glad she didn't see me like this."

Deb put her hand around Lois.

"How did you find me?" She asked Deb.

"I didn't. Richard did." Lois looked at Richard confused.

"I'll tell you all about it later, but now I need to know some things?"

"Like what?" Lois asked.

"For one, do you want help? If so, would you be willing to go back home and get the help you need?"

Lois began to cry, as she began to shake her head and answered, "yes, I want help, but I don't know."

"Don't know what?" Richard asked. "You have to decide now. You can't afford to wait."

Lois stood up on shaky legs with the blanket still wrapped around her, "I can't just leave now?"

"Why not?" Deb asked.

"I have to find Danijel. I can't leave without him." Richard and Deb had forgotten that Lois didn't know where Danijel was.

"Lois sweetie, Danijel is with your mother back home," Deb said getting up to comfort Lois and sit her back down before she fell.

"Home? With my mother?"

"Yes Lois. I stayed behind to find you." Richard filled in, "Deb can fill you in on the rest, but I need to call the airlines and see if we can get on a flight out tonight."

Deb gave Lois as much information as she knew. Richard was able to get a flight for later that evening. She explained to Lois that she would have to go straight to the rehab center

"I want to see Danijel first."

"Danijel is doing fine and you don't need to see him in this condition. You could go into withdrawals at any time, and I think you wouldn't want him to see that."

Lois thought of another time, when she went into withdrawals, because she didn't have any money to buy drugs. Danijel was so petrified and stood crying, as he peed in his pants as he watched her.

"I guess you're right, but when will I be able to see him?"

"The rehab director will decide base on your progress."

"What about my mother?"

"I don't think she needs to see you like this Lois. That's why I'm trying to arrange for you to go straight there from the airport. Do you still want to go through with it?"

Lois began to cry again, "I can't go on like this anymore, I just can't."

Marty Sinkler, from the rehab center, met them at the airport.

"Hi, I'm Marty," she said, "you must be Lois. How was your flight?"

"It was okay," Lois said.

"How are you doing Richard?" she asked.

"I'm doing good, I think."

"Well, you look beat. I have a suggestion that will make it easy on both of you," Marty said.

"What's that?" Richard asked. She looked at Richard and said, "you take a cab home and I'll take Lois with me. There is no need for you to go to the Center, matter of fact, I think it best that you leave Lois in my care now," she went on before Richard could protest.

"I, I, was hoping to see her settled in," Richard said, "but if you think that's best, then okay, I guess…"

"I think it's best."

"Okay then," Richard said, as he went over to Lois to hug her for the first time since he had found her.

When he put his arms around Lois, she began to cry and said, "please daddy don't leave me. Don't let me go by myself."

Richard felt his knees buckled underneath him and his heart melted away. Lois had never referred to him as daddy before.

Marty assessed the situation and quickly tapped Richard on his shoulder, "Richard, this is the best thing. You've trusted many people in our care, now let us take care of your daughter."

Richard pulled away from Lois with tears in his eyes, as tears were streaming down Lois' face.

Marty took Lois' arm and said, "this way Lois. Do you have everything?"

Lois barely said, "yes," as Marty helped her into the back of the car, and she got into the front on the passenger side as the driver pulled off leaving Richard at the airport curb to get a cab.

Richard didn't tell Stephanie exactly when he was coming home and he told Deb to stall her until he got home.

He didn't want her to meet them at the airport. It was three o'clock Saturday morning, when Richard got home. Everyone was asleep and the house was quiet. He took off his clothes, got into his pajamas and slipped into bed next to Stephanie.

She sat up in the bed and asked, "Where is Lois?"

Then she got up and grabbed her robe. Richard reached over to stop her.

"Where did you put her?" She asked.

She was still deciding on where Lois would stay when she got home. She didn't want to put her in the rooms with the girls. She had planned to move Maggie out of her room and let her sleep with the other two girls until they came up with a better solution. She talked to Maggie about it and Maggie was willing to share a room with her other sisters, if that meant Lois was coming home to stay with them.

"She's not here Stephanie," Richard said.

"I don't understand. She didn't come back with you? But you said..."

"She came back with me, but she's at the McClellan's Rehab center. Marty met us at the airport."

"You didn't bring my baby home?" Stephanie asked in a wavering voice.

"I did bring her home Stephanie, but I brought her home to get help. This is the right thing to do. When she is well enough, you can go and visit her."

Stephanie sat back on the bed and cried into her hands.

Richard put his arms around her and said, "Baby, this is the right thing to do. She'll get the help she needs."

Although Stephanie knew Richard was right, it brought her little comfort.

Chapter Twenty-Six
Jewel

Jewel didn't know what to do with her extra time, after Tyler left to go back to the States. She felt like she was going around in circles trying to find something to occupy the times she would have spent with Tyler, so she did what she knew; she buried herself in her work, once again alienating herself from the people she worked with.

"Hey, don't snap at us, because Tyler left for the States and left you with only that big rock on your finger," Ebba said, after Jewel yelled at them to get her point across concerning a case they were discussing.

"I'm sorry," Jewel said really apologetic.

"You can snap at Eb, but don't snap at me. I didn't set you up with Mr. Right, who turned out to be Mr. Wrong," said Chad.

"Okay, I said I'm sorry, but he's not Mr. Wrong. He's in another country, not another Planet." Chad laughed.

"What's so funny?" Jewel asked, getting annoyed.

"That line should be, he's in another city, not another country." This time Ebba laughed.

"I'm glad you guys think that my lonely, broken heart is a matter for punch lines."

"We don't mean any harm Jewel, but if it was me, I would be in Connecticut with that man." Ebba said.

"I wouldn't have left without you," Chad said.

"He understood my need to pursue my career, as well as I understand why he had to leave."

"Can't you pursue a career in the States?" Ebba asked.

"Probably a more successful one at that," Chad added.

"I'm leaving," Jewel said, getting up and putting on her jacket, "I can find a lot of reason to be miserable without any help from you two."

"So shoot us for not letting you feel sorry for a situation that you could've prevented."

"Ahhhh!" Jewel screamed as she opened her phone bill. It was the first phone bill with a full month of calls to Tyler, her sister and her parents.

"This is definitely not going to work. If I talk to Tyler before they cut off my phone, we're going to have to make some new arrangements for phone calls. This one is not working for me."

Jewel sat down on her couch and started flicking through the television, "Ah shucks," she said, as she picked up the phone and dialed Tyler's number.

"Hi."... "I know, me too."... "I just got my phone bill. It's bad, really bad."... "I know. I should've waited for you to call."... "No, I don't need you to send me any money."... "No Tyler not even for a one way ticket to the States."... "I do have some vacation days coming up. I wanted to go visit my parents."... "Whose there with you?"... "Yeah, let me speak to her."

"Hi Brianna. My name is Jewel." ... "Yeah I'm a friend of your dad. You and your dad doing something special today?"... "That sounds like fun."

"Okay, it was nice talking to you."

"I can't wait to meet her," Jewel said when Tyler got back on the phone. "You thought that I wouldn't."... "I'm glad I called too."

Jewel and Tyler spoke for an hour, before Jewel looked at the time, "Tyler I'd better go, besides you have your daughter there. You don't want to waste your time with her by talking to me on the phone."... "Thank you."... "That's right. I forgot. Your day is just starting. She's there early."..."I see. Well, I'd better go just the same. It's that phone bill thing, remember."..."love you too." She hung up the phone and went to her bedroom to do some work, before she fell asleep.

Jewel buried herself in her work taking on extra assignments. She got home too late to call Tyler on weekdays, which Tyler was clearly not pleased with, so she began to only call on the weekends. On occasions, she was invited to dinner at the Jamisons and sometimes she had dinner with Tyler's parents.

She finally made up her mind to visit Tyler in Connecticut, who wished it was more than a visit.

"Do you still want me to visit?"… "I know what you would prefer, but I can only visit."… "I can come for the fourth."… "A week or two."… "I don't know; I want to visit my parents for a week at the end of the year, so let me think about it."

Jewel ended up taking two weeks. Bridgeport, Connecticut was beautiful in the summer. The weather was perfect. Tyler took her all over. She was a little skeptical about staying at his place, but he had more than enough room. He stayed in a two story condominium. You could see the view of the river from his guest bedroom, as well as his room, which Jewel painstakingly tried not to notice, but she couldn't help to notice how elegant his home was decorated.

"I'm embarrassed," she said to Tyler.

"Why?" he asked.

Compare to your condo, my apartment must look like a rat hole."

"Don't be ridiculous, but you could use some decorative skills."

"Tyler, my apartment isn't decorated. I just have some convenient furniture thrown around the room, not for beauty, but because they serve a purpose."

"Well don't worry about changing it now."

"Why?"

"I don't want you to have to think twice about leaving it."

Resting in his arms, on his swing on the back porch, overlooking the river, the thought of leaving Tyler, after her visit, was what she needed to be concerned about.

"I like it here Tyler."

"The condo, or Bridgeport?"

"Both.

"Don't like the condo too much. We won't be staying here once we're married."

"No?" Jewel asked, wondering what he meant by that.

"No. We're going to find us a home of our own. I moved into this condo after my daughter was born contemplating marrying Teri, but when that didn't work out, I decided to keep it, so that when Brie came to visit she would have some space."

"Aren't you going to hate giving it up?"

"Not at all, especially if it means starting a new life with you."

Jewel didn't say anything else; she hoped the smile on her face wasn't as wide as the smile in her heart.

Jewel and Brianna hit it off well. The three of them went to the park together and when Tyler had an emergency call to the office, Jewel agreed to keep Brianna, even after Tyler told her that he always had a back up plan for Brianna, when he was on call and she was with him.

Tyler left his car and took a taxicab just in case they wanted to go somewhere. They went to the store and bought food for dinner and Brianna was delighted that Jewel asked her to help prepare dinner, although she was kind of worried whether or not Jewel knew what she was doing.

Tyler complimented them on dinner, although both Jewel and Brianna apologized for how lousy everything tasted.

"It really isn't that bad," Tyler said.

"You think you still want to marry me?" Jewel asked when they were still alone.

"Even if you'd burnt down the house."

"That's not saying much, seeing that you want to move anyway," They shared a moment of laughter, as Tyler reached to embrace her.

"I can't believe two weeks is already over. Can't you call and ask for another week, or some more days or something," Tyler pleaded.

"I have to go Tyler."

"I'll take you to the airport."

"No way, just call me a cab and let's say our goodbyes here."

"It's never goodbye. It's just later," said Tyler hugging Jewel tightly, as he kissed her.

A month after Jewel returned home. She received a strange letter from a law firm in Hodgeport, Connecticut. She picked up the phone, and dial Tyler's number. "Hi Tyler."… "Yeah I miss you too."

Jewel wanted to cut through the small talk to get to the reason she called. "Tyler, did you give my resume to a law firm in," she looked at the address on the envelope again, "Hodgeport, Connecticut?"… "You gave my resume to a lot of firms!"… "How did you get my resume?"… "I think you'd better tell me."… "I don't want you to look for me a job."… "Yes, I'm mad."… "No, don't call me back later. Answer my question now."… "No, you should not have done this."… "No, I won't even consider it."

"Bye. Tyler."… "Bye, I don't want to make you late for work."

"What's the big deal Jewel?" Ebba asked.

"What's the big deal? I don't want Tyler looking for me a job. He doesn't know what I would look for, if I was looking."

"You're going to be looking one day, are you not?"

"That's not the point."

"It is the point, Jewel. What's it going to hurt to know what's out there now and who is interested?"

"I don't want to talk to you about it." Jewel had a thought. "Did you send Tyler my resume?"

"How would I get it? That's personnel stuff. I don't have access to that." Ebba lied, knowing she could get into some serious trouble, if Jewel was really mad about this and decided to report it to the administrative office.

She had told Beebe about Tyler's request and she and Beebe updated Jewel's resume and sent it to Tyler, who placed his final touch on it and sent it across the Internet requesting responses from only specific areas surrounding Bridgeport. He knew he was threading on thin ground and it may seemed like he was pushing Jewel, but he felt she needed a push. He didn't want to wait until her career was well established, before they get married.

A month later, Jewel received a phone call from someone from the law firm that wrote her the letter.

"Meet with you?"… "I'm sorry I don't even know you."… "That's public enough, but…" the man on the phone was making the meeting a real mystery. "If I decide to come, can I bring a friend?"

…"I'll be the African American." Jewel said, opting not to be mysterious. If he was going to discriminate, she wanted to know that now. The man did not acknowledge Jewel's description of herself, but was genuinely pleased that Jewel was beginning to sound interested in meeting with him.

"Who is this mystery man Jewel?" Ebba asked. "I don't know, but you owe me one, so just shut up and behave."

Ebba pouted and Jewel looked at her smilingly.

They were looking around the restaurant for a man sitting alone, but there were a few men sitting alone. A waiter walked up to them and asked, "are one of you Mrs. Stone?"

"Miss Stone," Jewel said, "and that would be me."

"I'm sorry. I didn't mean to offend you."

"You didn't," Jewel smiled.

"Follow me," the waiter said as he turned to walk to a table, where a well-dressed gentleman was seated.

"Mr. Madison," the waiter said, the gentleman looked up and immediately got up out of his chair to greet the two women, "this is Miss Stone and her guest."

"I'm glad to meet you Miss Stone. I'm Carl Madison."

"Nice to meet you Mr. Madison. I think," Jewel said, "this is my friend, Ebba Knight."

"Ms. Knight," Mr. Madison address Ebba, "ladies, please be seated." The waiter helped Jewel and Ebba to be seated.

"I'm sorry about all the mystery," Mr. Madison said, "but I was told that I would never get to meet you, if I told you who I was up front."

"I suspect that you are from the law firm that wrote me a month or two ago. Other than that, who are you?"

Mr. Madison pulled out a card and gave it to Jewel, the card read,

'Carl Madison, Attorney at Law." Jewel past the card to Ebba, who read it and returned it to Jewel.

Jewel was about to return it to Mr. Madison, but he said, "please keep it, just in case you want to use it later."

The lunch went better than Jewel thought it would. Mr. Madison didn't ask Jewel to come work for them. He told Jewel all about his firm. He told Jewel the reason he was in London was because his firm was thinking about starting a law firm in London and was looking for young and competent lawyers to work for them. He did mention he knew she had connections in Connecticut, but he would not talk of any position for her there, if she wasn't interested.

Jewel didn't feel pressured. She wondered if Tyler knew Mr. Madison wouldn't be trying to get her to leave London.

After the lunch, Mr. Madison told Jewel he would like to see her again before he left and he even asked Ebba to send him a copy of her resume, if she was interested as well.

Jewel did agree to meet with him again. This time it was dinner and he was definitely fascinated by Jewel, although he seemed a little too flirtatious.

Mr. Madison talked more about his firm in Connecticut this time than the one he wanted to start in London.

"Part of our training would be that you come to Connecticut for at least a six month period, before we let you out on your own here."

"Sounds like an interesting offer."

"I'm glad you're interested Jewel."

"I didn't say I was interested. I said it was an interesting offer, surely something to think about."

"I couldn't ask for more than that now, could I?"

"You could, but you're probably playing your cards the way you want."

"You are a smart woman, and beautiful to tops."

"Thank you."

Jewel and Mr. Madison said goodbye. He was leaving for Connecticut in two days, and wouldn't get to see Jewel again before he left. He told Jewel he might call, if she took too long to respond, but it would only be an attempt at one last try.

"Did you hear that Maddie Pinkerton just got offered junior partnership?" Casey, a tall blonde, who was an associate at the law firm whispered to Jewel and Ebba as they were having lunch in the law firm's cafeteria.

Jewel, Casey, Maddie and two other associates practically arrived at the law firm the same time.

"You have got to be joking," Jewel said surprised.

"He's a total idiot," Ebba added.

About that time Beebe came over and sat down next to them.

"What are you girls whispering about?" Beebe asked.

"Did you hear that Maddie Pinkerton was offered a junior partnership?"

"You girls know I can't talk about things like that. That's office gossip." Beebe said smiling hoping that the girls would pursue her for information, because then it would be more fun.

"Come on Beebes, you know the deal," Ebba, who was friendlier with Beebe pushed on.

"You girls don't play the old boys game. It could be because you're not men, or because you like having lunch with secretaries, or administrative staffs."

"What?" Jewel asked incredulously, thinking Beebes was teasing them.

"She's right, you know. That's what it's all about," Casey said.

"What do you know about it? You haven't been here that long," Jewel said to Casey.

"But it's true Jewel," Ebba agreed.

"But Lila is a junior partner and she is a woman," Jewel pointed out.

"But have you ever seen Lila have lunch with any of us, or you guys for that matter," Beebe said.

"That's ridiculous. She just works hard that's all," Jewel said.

"Yes harder than any man whoever made junior partner," Beebe said," and I should know. I've been here longer than any of you. In the States they call it male show 'nough a pig"

"That's male chauvinist pig," Jewel corrected.

"Same thing," Beebe said.

"I can't believe people play those games in real life," said Jewel, "those things only happen in the movies, or TV."

"And where do you think TV get it stories from?" Beebe asked. "This is it Jewel. Welcome to the real world."

"Beebes right," Ebba agreed.

"I know I am," said Beebes, as she turned to finish her lunch letting the other women know that the conversation was over.

The next couple of days, Jewel secretly reviewed some of Maddie's cases. He did some sloppy work. First year law students could have done better. Jewel began to observe the relationship of Maddie and Lila and some of the other junior partners, or even those whose goal was to make junior law partner. She worked harder than all of them, but Beebe was right. They did not associate with the same people that Jewel did.

"I guess I can reconsider my association," Jewel said to Beebe one afternoon after she had dinner with the Jamisons. She was helping Beebe do the dishes, while the guys were watching sports.

"Look at us Jewel," Beebe said.

"What?"

"Here we are, women, in the kitchen after dinner cleaning up, while my lazy behind son watch television with his dad. That's how it is in London, unless you are rich and wealthy and can buy your position." Beebe pointed out.

"But Lila," said Jewel.

"You can't compare Lila with the other women in the firm. She is practically a dike. She acts like them. She smokes like them and she probably drink and party harder than them."

"This is not encouraging," Jewel said sadly.

"I just don't want you to be naive about what is going on. Lila was with the firm ten years before she made junior partner. Maddie has been there how long? Some of the women associates have been there for twenty years and they still have not made junior partner. In about the next ten year, Lila may be offered a full partnership, but Maddie will probably get an offer in five or seven."

"Surely Reed pushes for equality."

"Reed Prescott might as well be a silent partner. She may have a voice one day. She's fair and not afraid to stand up to her brothers, but right now she is just too young and the louder she yells, the harder they try to ignore."

The next several weeks were an eye opening for Jewel as she began to see things the way they really were.

She decided to talk to Miles and Haddan Prescott.

"Miss Stone, come right in." Haddan Prescott said as Jewel knocked on his open door and asked if she could have a couple of minutes with him.

Haddan Prescott was middle aged and loved his cigar. He had a somewhat rugged good look, but nothing to write home about.

Miles, on the other hand in his early forties with already peppered hair, was always well-tailored, clean cut with a slight mustache and hazel brown eyes that always seemed to be smiling. He was eyed by every female associate in the office, but from what Jewel heard, he was happily married.

Good, Jewel thought, they were both in Haddan's office, so she didn't have to ask him to call Miles in.

"What's on your mind Jewel?" Miles asked sweetly.

"I just want to say upfront that I like working here. I like the people and you have been fair with me in given me good cases."

"We're so happy that you're happy here," Haddan said, smiling and looking at Miles.

"Thank you. I just wanted to understand something, if you don't mind."

"Go right ahead Jewel. We certainly don't want our associates confused about anything around here. Wouldn't be good for business,"

Haddan laughed, and she could see out of the corner of her eyes, that Miles also had a slight smile on his face.

She hoped they weren't taking her visit as something to add amusement to their boring day. It took all the courage she could muster up to come to their office. People said that Haddan was somewhat of a jerk, but Miles more than made up for Haddan by being understanding, sincere and genuine.

"I've done some reviewing around the office," Jewel said, hoping that didn't sound like snooping, "and I wondered, how is it that Maddie Pinkerton was offered a junior partnership over myself and Casey Lowry? Compared to the work Maddie has done, our work seems to exceed his in quality, as well as quantity."

"What kind of things did you reviewed Jewel?" Haddan asked.

His question sent cold shills down Jewel's spine, but Jewel had gotten this far, she was not about to back down. She pulled out some paper work that she had with her in a manila folder that compared her and Casey's work with Maddie's. Haddan looked over the paper then passed it on to Miles.

"Well Miss Stone. I can see where you would be concerned about being passed over, but let me assure you that we are well pleased with your work and we reviewed the same things you reviewed to make our decision," Miles said, as Haddan jumped in.

"You see Miss Stones as owners of the firm, we have to look at all scenarios and all aspect. We were replacing one of our top junior partners, who had received another lucrative offer with another firm. He did a lot of trial work for us, now whereas Ms. Lowry is beautiful to look on, she lacks the presence that it takes to dominate a court and win the attention of jurors," Haddan said, while Jewel was looking for discrimination in their every word.

"Jewel, what Haddan is trying to say is that we have accompanied the court room on at least one or more of each associates. We have not gotten around to viewing any of your trial cases first hand as of yet, and time was pending that we replace Mr. Moore, because he was working on cases with some of our biggest client. We have a system of getting around to each associate's trial cases," Miles said, laughing embarrassingly, "I must say that our system is rather elementary, but it works and it keeps everything fair. You see we do it alphabetically and the letter, 'S,' just hasn't come up yet on this round of associates. As Haddan has said, we have reviewed Miss Lowry cases and we find that she is going to be an excellent lawyer someday. We will work with her to help her build up her confidence in court, but we needed someone now, someone who already has that confidence. That could have very well been yourself but," he laughed embarrassingly again, putting down his head and covering his mouth with his index finger, "as I said, we just haven't gotten around to your letter yet, but we assure you that we are certain, by viewing the records on your trial cases that you will soon be a junior partner and for sure a full partner someday."

"Have that answered your question Miss Stone?" Haddan asked smugly.

"I think it did," Jewel said getting up to leave.

"I'm glad that we could oblige you with a satisfactory answer," Miles said, "like we said, it is certainly not good for our associates to be confused on matters in the firm. We are one big happy family and we want everyone to continue to be happy. Now if there is anything else that we can do for you, just let us know," he said as he place his hand on Jewel's upper back, politely walking her to the door, or showing her to the door, Jewel wasn't sure which.

"Satisfactory!" Ebba said, "I can't believe they fed you that bull!"

"Oh yes they did. They were careful not to make any discriminating statements, dominance in the court and alphabetical reviews, what a bunch of crock. You think they just made that up on the spot, or they plan that speech for any woman who comes in to challenge their decision?" Jewel asked Ebba.

"Probably made it up on the spot. I don't think there has ever been a woman who has challenged their decision. I can't believe they were even careful not to make discriminatory statements. They are so smugged. They probably think they could win over any woman who took them to court on the bases of gender discrimination."

"You think?" Jewel asked.

"You better believe I think," Ebba replied.

Jewel had a lot to think about over the next few weeks. One night when she was about to go over a briefing, she received a call from Carl Madison. This time he didn't do any formalities; he went right into his pitch.

"Miss Stone, we would really like to have you on board. We are in desperate need of some bright lawyers. I like you when I met you, and your resume and test scores say that you would be prime for this job."

He went on to share what his firm was offering, "Matter of fact, I think we're going to bring the next person on as a junior partner. It depends on the person of course. Someone like you would have no problem coming in as a senior associate, but like I said, we need to move along with our search, but I certainly don't want to pressure you to make a decision today. Let's say I give you until the end of next week to think about it, and you can call me. You still have my number don't you."

Jewel responded, yes.

They set up a time for Jewel to call him, "and like I said Miss Stone, if you decide against us, just don't call. It's as simple as that."

The next thing Jewel heard was the click of the phone, as Mr. Madison said goodbye.

Jewel had the remainder of the week and the following week to decide. She decided not to tell anyone, except Tessa.

Tessa would be the only one that would be objective, "Hi Tessa."... "How's it going?"... "Really?"... "That's really great, so how are you and what's his name."... "I thought you liked him."... "So it's Denny now."... "Okay, I don't know how you expect me to keep up with all of your boyfriends."... "Tyler is doing fine the last time we talked."... "Nothing much, I just got a really good job offer from that law firm in Hodgeport, Connecticut."... "Yeah, the one I told you about."... "I don't know. I have until end of next week to decide."... "Tyler doesn't think anything."... "I didn't tell him."... "Because you know he's not going to be objective."… "No, I didn't tell mom and dad either, like they could be objective. They would want me back in the States, no matter where."

Jewel and Tessa talked for a while. Tessa filled Jewel in on her life. "You did call Lois."… "What do you mean you tried?"… "Vaguely."… "She did."… "Well yeah, I guess I am surprise. Lois vowed never to go back home."… "Yeah, I guess. I certainly can understand being homesick, but it's nothing like family to cure that."… "Take it any way you want."… "No, I don't think I'll be going home for the holidays. I spent my two weeks with Tyler remember."… "Yeah, we both need to get off this phone. I'll let you know of my decision."… "Love you too, Sis."

Tessa was great to talk to. She never forced or even offered her opinion. She just listened.

"Where are you going?" Ebba asked Jewel as she walked into Jewel's cubicle. Jewel was putting on her jacket.

"To court."

"I didn't see your name on the schedule to be in court today."

"I'm not, but Maddie is, and I want to see the boy genius at work for myself."

"Good idea. Mind if I tag along?" Ebba asked.

"You don't have any work?"

Ebba cut her eyes at Jewel, who responded, "dumb question, you never have any work."

"I do," Ebba was about to protest, "sometimes."

They both laughed.

"Can you believe that?" Ebba asked, "Probably wouldn't, if I didn't see it for myself," Jewel responded.

They were referring to the mess Maddie made of his case. He was not prepared and the judge called a recess, until the next day and told him that he expected him to be ready.

"Maybe we should check out Casey just for argument sake." Ebba said.

"You think? She has a trial case on Monday."

"Let's," Ebba insisted.

"We'll tell her that we're there for support." Jewel suggested.

"That's a lie. We want to spy her out."

"Support, sounds better," Jewel said.

Casey welcomed their presence, "matter of fact, why don't you sit up here with me."

"I don't think we should do that?" Ebba said.

"Why not? It could be part of my strategy to let them think that we have an entourage of lawyers on the case. It couldn't hurt me."

"It's a good strategy. I like it. I have to remember that for future." Jewel said.

"What happens when we're asked what we were doing?" Ebba asked.

Both Jewel and Casey responded simultaneously, "support."

Jewel and Ebba never told Casey their real reason for wanting to be with her in court that day, but they learned a lot.

"Well they were right about one thing," Jewel said.

"What's that?" Ebba asked.

"Casey is certainly pretty to look at in court."

"But she's no dummy," Ebba said.

"That she isn't, and for them to say that she doesn't dominate the court is a bunch of crock. Her beauty alone is dominance."

"I agree."

"So, why did they feed me all that bull?"

"To keep you quiet."

"But there are other male associates better and smarter than Maddie."

"Then maybe we should do some more digging," suggested Ebba.

Jewel and Ebba found out that Maddie's family had ties with the Prescott and their goal was to prep Maddie to one day be a member of the parliament.

"That'll be the day." Ebba said.

"Too bad I won't be around to see him fall on his face." Jewel said.

"What do you mean?"

"I think I'm going to take that job offer in Hodgeport."

"Really!"

"Yes, Really."

"Tyler must be ecstatic."

"He will be when I tell him."

"He doesn't know yet? How did you keep it from him?"

"Easy, I just didn't tell him. I told you he wouldn't bring it up."

"So when did you call, Mr. whatever his name?"

"Actually, Mr. Madison called me about a week ago and made me a lucrative offer."

"Are you going to be training for the London firm, or are you going to stay in Hodgeport?"

"He didn't say much about London. I don't think it turned out the way he had hoped. He just said that they are short in their office in Hodgeport and was looking for some new and fresh lawyers for that office."

"Wow, I'm happy for you," Ebba said sadly.

"Don't sound too thrill. I might think that you're happy for me."

"I am. I'm just going to miss you around here. When are you giving your notice?"

"After I talk to Mr. Madison I'll know better."

"You're going to invite me to the wedding, right."

"Girl, you better start saving up your money, because you're going to be in the wedding and I'm not going to buy your dress." They both laugh.

It was a day early, but Jewel wanted to get it over with. She had talked to Tessa, who convinced her that waiting until the last day was nonsense. Obviously Mr. Madison already knew she was not anxious, or over zealous for the job, so she took her little sister's advice and called Mr. Madison, who was pleased to hear from her, and confirmed that she would get the senior associate position.

They agreed that Jewel would start a month from the following

Monday. A month seemed like a long time away. After she got off the phone and began to go over all the things she would have to do, she began to wonder if a month was long enough. Mr. Madison did offer her an extra week, if she needed it. She was already thinking she would.

"So what did they say?" Ebba asked Jewel about giving her resignation to the Prescotts.

"Not much. They didn't even seem surprise. Just your usually cordiality, like we're sorry to see you go. Wish you much success. You know, the usual, I guess."

"Yeah, what else could they say," Ebba added, "sorry to see you leave, but it worked out for both of us. We didn't want to have to fire you, because it would look bad on your record, but we don't want you tripping on us later about the partnership offer that you will never get."

Jewel debated over when would be a good time to tell Tyler. Should she just show up and surprise him. She wasn't planning on staying with him. She was going to find a place to stay before she got there. She hoped.

She told her parents, who were very happy that she was moving back to the States, but not so happy that it wasn't the state of Tennessee. Her mom was fishing to see if she was going to give away any hints, as to whether or not she was moving in with Tyler.

Not to Jewel's surprise a month came around very quickly. She didn't actually worked two full weeks at the firm. She hurriedly rapped up what she could and passed her other cases on to the other associates, and Maddie Pinkerton.

Her new job offered to pay all moving cost. She didn't have much furniture. The few little odds and ends that she did buy, she gave to Ebba and Chad. Chad was getting married soon. The rest she boxed up and mailed to her new job. She decided to surprise Tyler after all.

She made her rounds of goodbye making sure Tyler's parents understood that she wanted to surprise him. She gave the Jamisons, a nice oxford crystal vase, as a gift for their hospitality; she and Beebe had become good friends.

"You have everything?" Ebba asked Jewel as they were looking around the apartment for anything that she might have missed, "because if you leave something, it's history."

"I know," said Jewel looking around for the last time.

She looked in her purse. "I got my passport and my ticket, and I can't see anything that I'm missing. If I leave anything, I'll just convince myself that it wasn't that important."

"Well let's go then." Ebba announced. She was driving Jewel to the airport. "Is your apartment ready?"

"Yeah, believe it or not, they mailed me a key. Isn't the Internet great! The things you can do on it."

"I'll say. I can't believe you found a furnished apartment and everything on that thing. I just hope you like it."

"I should, besides, I'll probably be at Tyler's most of the time. We'll set our wedding date and then I'll be out of there before I'm in there."

"You should've called and tell him."

"It's going to be much better this way."

"I hope so."

Jewel's plane arrived on time. She wanted to get off the plane and call Tyler to pick her up, but she was too tired from the trip. She took a cab to the apartment building and prayed that it wasn't some torn down building in the ghetto.

She reached over and tapped the cab driver on the shoulder, "excuse me sir."

"Yes."

"Do you know the area where I'm going?"

"Yes. I know the area. You think I'm trying to stiff you maam."

Oh God, Jewel thought. The last thing I want to do is get this big Rastafarian man mad with me.

"No sir, I'm sorry. It's just that I'm new to the area myself and I was just wondering what it was like."

"It's a nice quiet neighborhood. I've driven there plenty of times, even to your building, nice apartment buildings."

"Thank you."

"First time in Connecticut?"

"No actually, my fiancé' lives here."

"Oh, you're getting married."

"I'm engage, yes."

"Congratulations."

"Thank you."

The driver didn't say much after that and Jewel wasn't about to push any further, after she wriggled her way out of what seemed like an insult to the man.

The building was nice. It had a security entrance and a security guard. Jewel was given all the codes that she needed to get in, and the security guard new her name. She was definitely impressed.

"I was told that we were going to have a new tenant. I'm Charlie, nice to meet you Miss Stone."

"Please, just call me Jewel. Thank you."

"Okay, Jewel. I'll help you upstairs with your luggage."

Once they were upstairs, Charlie asked if there was anything else he could do for her. Jewel was warmed by his welcome. She thanked and tipped him. She looked around the apartment and was well pleased with what she saw. The rent was a little steep, but she was offered a really big salary by Mr. Madison and would be more than able to swing it.

"I'm just not use to this jet lagged," Jewel said to herself before crashing on the bed and not waking up until early the next morning.

She was surprised she slept so soundly in a new place. She usually would be up all night her first night in a new place, but like her first day at the Jamisons after her flight to London, she just trust that everyone was above board, because nothing mattered at that point except getting some rest.

The next day was Saturday and Jewel got dressed hurriedly and called a cab. She just couldn't wait any longer. She had to see Tyler.

On the way to Tyler, Jewel played all kinds of scenarios over and over in her head. She found out that she lived about twenty minutes from Tyler, but right now it may as well been an hour. Of course Tyler would be glad to see her, but what if he was seeing someone else while she was in London, because he couldn't hold out any longer. Jewel began to tremble inside. She didn't know what she would do, if another woman was there with him.

"Miss, Miss," The cab driver called to Jewel snapping her out of her thoughts.

"This is the address you gave me." Jewel just sat in the cab wondering what she should do.

"I can wait for you, if you like." Jewel was suddenly relieved.

"Would you?"

"Yeah, I can for about fifteen minutes."

Jewel thought in her mind that would be enough time for Tyler to be shocked or surprise to see her. She would know right away. She paid the cab driver, and got out the cab. Then as a second thought, she gave the cab driver another tip for the fifteen minutes that he said he would wait.

Jewel went up to the door and stood looking at the door and looking back at the cab to make sure the driver was still waiting.

She noticed a black Saturn parked behind Tyler's silver Mercedes. Her inside felt like they would drop out. There was obviously someone there. She didn't know if she wanted to know who, maybe she should just go back to her apartment and call him from there and never know who was in the apartment with him, but then she would always wonder.

She looked back at the cab driver. He held up both his hands to gesture that she should do something, so she rang the bell.

She waited for about thirty seconds and then she heard a woman yelling, "Who is it?"

Jewel didn't say anything. She just stood there, wanting to run. She started backing up a little and then she heard the click of the door.

"Yes," the woman said, seemingly annoyed, "look, I don't mean to be rude, but if you're a Jehovah witness this isn't my house, but I'm sure the owner has no time this morning either."

Tears were about to well up in Jewel's eyes as she took another step back, then she heard Brianna screamed, "daddy! Daddy! it's Jewel," as she came running out of the house and wrapping her arms around

Jewel, as Jewel continued to stare at the woman at the door, who suddenly had a change of expression, but it was friendlier.

"You're Jewel? I should've recognized you from your photos."

"Yes," Jewel said in a shaky voice as she snooped down to hug Brianna, then she heard Tyler's voice.

"I said who is it Teri, you deaf or something?"

"Or something," Teri said.

Tyler came to the door and for a moment couldn't believe his eyes. He ran outside and picked Jewel up and began to kiss her.

He finally put her down, took a look at her and said, "If this is a dream, please God don't let me wake up just yet."

"This isn't a dream Tyler," Jewel said.

Tyler picked Jewel up again, and Jewel wave at the taxi driver and mouthed, "thank you."

The taxi driver smiled and drove off.

Chapter Twenty-Seven
Lois

A month after Lois went into rehab she was allowed visitors. She didn't want to see Danijel while she was in rehab, but she felt that it was time to see her mother. Lois was unsure about the visit. Richard was coming with her. For some reason, she found solace in knowing that. She had found an ally in Richard, someone who truly knew what she was going through.

Lois walked into the waiting area hesitantly.

She looked around and thought they had not arrived yet, or maybe they weren't coming at all, but as she was about to do an about turn, she heard, "Lois, baby," and she looked to see her mother hurriedly walking up to her.

She grabbed Lois and hugged her tightly. Lois didn't reciprocate the hug. She was still feeling unworthy of anyone's love and understanding, especially her mother.

Stephanie and Lois' first visit did not go as Stephanie hoped, but she was not put off by Lois' lack of response, or reserve. She kept coming back again and again. She brought messages from Lois' brothers and sisters and reported on how Danijel was adjusting to life with them.

"Have you told them about me?" Lois asked.

"I told them you are not well and as soon as you get better, you'll be coming home. They're all excited about that."

"Are they Mother?"

"Of course, why wouldn't they be? You're their big sister and they look up to you."

"Will they continue to look up to me when they know the truth?"

"We can't change the past sweetheart, but we can help you get through this, and you will. Marty said your progress is really good."

"Physically I'll get through this, but mentally, I'll always be haunted by the things I did."

"Lois, God will forgive you, if you ask him, but you will also have to forgive yourself."

Lois stared at her mother as if seeing her for the first time.

"You don't understand Mother. I've done unspeakable things. Things you don't talk about at your church meetings. Things you can't even bring yourself to ask people to pray for," Lois said as she began to cry uncontrollable. Stephanie took her in her arms and began to rock her back and forth.

"Lois, Jesus knows it all. Nothing is unspeakable to him. You can tell him anything and he will understand. You just have to open up and let him into your heart."

Those words stuck with Lois for weeks after her mother's visit.

She called Richard at work one day and asked him to come to visit her without Stephanie.

"I can't say that I'm not a little surprise that you call," Richard said.

"I didn't mean to sound mysterious. I just wanted to talk to someone who, who…"

"Who knows what you're going through?"

"Yes, but now I'm not sure. I know you were on drugs, but you didn't do half the things that I did."

"Lois, I did worst things. I stole food out of my children's mouth. I hurt your mother. I even tried to sell my daughter's body for drugs."

Lois began to cry as Richard held her in his arms.

"But now you've forgotten it all, and you believe God has forgiven you?"

"I don't know that I will ever totally forget the things I've done, but I know God has forgotten and forgiven me. I have a peace within my soul about my past, and I've forgiven myself."

"I forgive you too. I do, and I'm not just saying that because it's one of my steps, but I really do. I didn't know what it was like to be out of control, to not care about anyone or anything except the next high. I forgive you."

Tears welled up in Richard's eyes, as he held his head down. It seemed like he waited forever to hear Lois say those words. He was even resolved to the fact that he might never hear them. Richard kept his head down and it was Lois who took him in her arms and held him.

"I want to know forgiveness like you know it Richard."

Richard looked up and said, "You can." He took Lois' hand and said, "You can have it now. All you have to do is open up and let Jesus in your heart."

Lois knew the procedure; she had faked it before, like so many of the youth did, only to laugh about it afterwards, but this time was different. She really wanted that peace Richard had. She knew she wouldn't be able to live without it.

"I want to," Lois said.

Lois closed her eyes and bowed her head feeling not even worthy to look up, while Richard led her through the sinner's prayer.

When Lois opened her eyes, nothing had changed on the outside, but she knew a lot had changed inside of her. She just couldn't explain it yet.

"I'll like to tell mom," she said to Richard.

"Well you better hurry up, because I know this is one secret I can't keep." He kissed Lois on the cheek and said, "welcome to the family of God."

"I have good news for you Lois," Marty said.

Lois was called to her office for a special meeting. She was a little nervous. In the past, her special meeting with Marty was to tell her she was not pleased with her progress and was concern about letting her go home, even though Lois was free to go when she wanted to.

"I think you're ready to take on the world," Marty was saying, and Lois couldn't believe what she was hearing.

"What do you think?" she asked Lois.

"I don't know. If you think."

"I think so Lois, but it's what you think that matters."

Lois got up and looked out the window. She longed to hold her son in her arms again and tell him how much she loved him.

"Are you thinking about Danijel and how he's going to react to you?" Marty asked.

"Yes."

Marty got up and went over to the window and put her arms around Lois.

"I wish I could tell you that he's going to be so glad to see you, but you can't tell with children. He may be ecstatic, or he may resent you for abandoning him and leaving him for strangers to take him. Whatever he feels, you're going to have to find out about it soon, so you can begin to work with him to build that trust again."

Lois looked at Marty with tears in her eyes, "I have so many relationships to mend."

"Well you can't do them in here, besides I need the space."

"So you're kicking me out," Lois said wiping her eyes with the back of her hands.

"The truth is I get a little shaky every time one of you leaves here. It's easy to be drug free in a controlled environment. The test comes, when you're face with the real pressures of life, and every body has to take that test. As much as I hate to see them go, I don't want to ever see them back in here, unless it's to visit or help out. Unfortunately, everyone has not made it out there, but I got a good feeling about you Lois. You have good family support, which is so important. I think you're going to do okay."

Richard came to pick Lois up. Stephanie stayed home to prepare a big dinner and a little celebration. She was busy putting up balloons and the girls were busy putting icing on the cake.

"Danijel, guess what?"

"It's my birthday!" he screamed jumping around the room. The other children laughed at him. He was such a delight.

"No, Danijel that was last month," Stephanie said grabbing him as he ran around her.

She sat him down in her lap.

"I sit next to you. I'm a big boy. Big boys don't sit on lap."

Stephanie let him sat next to her, as she eyed Tony, now 12, who was probably responsible for Danijel's vie for independence. He folded his arms, crossed his legs and looked up at Stephanie. He was so serious. It was hard for Stephanie to keep a straight face.

"Danijel, your mommy is coming home."

Danijel didn't say a word. He uncrossed his arms and his legs and a sad look came over his face.

"You're my mommy now. I don't want to leave you."

"I'm your grandmother Danijel. I've explained this to you before. I'm your mommy's mom, and you were staying with us until she get better, remember."

"You're my mommy! You're my mommy!" Danijel yelled as he ran out of the room.

Stephanie placed her hand on her head. She wasn't expecting this behavior from him.

She prayed this didn't set Lois back, but how do you explain these things to a five year old."

"I'll get him Mom," said Maggie, who practically made herself totally responsible for taking care of Danijel, when her parents were not around.

Maggie was a beautiful and responsible seventeen year-old. She was not the whiny little sister that got on everyone's nerves when she was younger.

"I'll help her," said nineteen year-old CJ, who was in his first year of college.

Stephanie looked at him and said, "thank you," then she said to him and RJ, "thank you both for coming tonight."

CJ practically stayed there when school was out, but most of the time, he stayed at the dorm at the state college he attended about two hours away.

RJ, twenty-one, went to a technical school, learned computers and landed a good job with a large company, as their computer technician.

He had his own apartment and was planning on going back for his bachelor degree, at the expense of his job.

Dwan was a wild fifteen year-old that Stephanie prayed would end soon.

Baby Teona, who was ten and ready to fight anyone who still called her Baby.

Everyone was waiting in the living room for Richard's signal. He was going to accidentally blow the horn, so they could know he was there.

"Wow, this is a big house," Lois said.

"That's right," Richard acknowledged, "you've never seen our new home."

As he parked, he pretended like he was looking for something and accidentally hit the horn.

"You ready?" he asked Lois. "I'm as ready as I'm going to be."

As they entered the room, Richard had to flick the light, Lois was a little relieve when she thought no one was home, but a little disappointed as well, but then everyone jumped out from behind couches and doors and her mother came in with a lighted cake and they all yell, "Welcome home Lois!"

They all ran up to her hugging her and telling her they were glad she was better and that she was home.

Maggie broke down and cried, "I miss you so much."

Lois was not prepared for this, as tears began to stream down her face. RJ grabbed a napkin as he pulled Maggie away.

"Okay Maggie, give the rest of us a chance to tell her how much we've missed her, and then rag her out for not coming home sooner."

"I can't believe how much you guys have grown. You don't even look the same," said Lois.

"That's a good thing, seeing that RJ was a snotty nose brat," CJ said, who got hit in his head by RJ for the comment, "besides it has been what, nine, ten years, but whose counting," he said as he hugged Lois.

Lois was looking around the room. She didn't see Danijel.

"You looking for something, or someone?" Richard asked, as he sort of looked crossed eyed towards the door.

Danijel was peeping from behind the door. Lois took a deep breath and walked towards the door. He saw her walking towards him, but she didn't let on that she had seen him.

When she got up on him, she said, "Hi Dandan."

Danijel felt cornered, as he managed to run around Lois screaming, "you're not my mommy, you're not, and I'm not going anywhere with you! Go away! Just go away!"

He ran to Maggie and wrapped himself around her waist. Stephanie was about to intervene, but Richard grabbed her by the shoulder.

Lois took another deep breath, trying not to cry. Marty warned her concerning Danijel's first reaction to her return, but she was still not prepared for it.

"I'm not taking you anywhere you don't want to go Danijel. I," she wanted to say that she promised, but how many times had she said that to him and broke the promise. She stepped a little closer to him and watch him hugged Maggie a little tighter.

"Danijel, I'm sorry I left you. I'm going to make it up to you if it's the last thing I do, but you can't wish me away baby. I am your mother and I love you so much, and I'm here to stay and take care of you, like I use to do, before I got sick."

Danijel loosened his grip on Maggie, but he kept holding on.

"When you're ready we'll talk, but only when you're ready, okay."

"I'm starving," Richard said, "Is dinner ready?"

"Yes it is," Stephanie said, as she led them into the dining room.

"I can't wait to eat your cooking again Mom."

"Then let's not wait another minute," RJ said, as he hugged Lois around the neck and escorted her in the dining room.

Maggie picked Danijel up and carried him into the dining room and sat him down in a chair next to her, which was not close to Lois.

"Boy you're getting heavy."

"He certainly has gotten bigger," Lois said, "gotta be from eating mom's cooking."

"You know that," CJ said, as he began to dish out food, as Stephanie took a spoon and knock him on his hand "what?"

"We haven't prayed, and we have a lot to be thankful for tonight," Stephanie said, as she reached for Lois' hand on one side of her and Richard's hand on the other.

As all the children began to join hands around the table, Richard went into a heartwarming prayer of thanksgiving for all of their children being presence at the table with them once again, including their first and only grandson, Danijel.

Danijel kept his eyes fastened on Lois, who tried to meet his gaze as much as possible, while talking and listening to the others. When their eyes locked, she knew they were making a connection. She was grateful for that. She knew in her heart that he would come around soon. He had too.

"Should we ask her if she wants to go with us, or you think that would be pushing it?" Stephanie asked Richard as she was preparing for church.

"I think we should wait and see what she wants to do. You may be surprise. I'll see you downstairs."

Richard picked up his jacket and walked down stairs for his second cup of coffee, as he usually do while waiting for Stephanie to get ready for church on Sundays.

Breakfast on Sunday changed, as the children got older. Except for Danijel, everyone pretty much prepared breakfast for themselves.

"Good morning." Lois said to a surprised, but delighted Richard as he observed that she was already dressed.

"Good morning to you. I'm surprise to see you up so early."

"I thought that I would get a ride with you guys to church this morning, if that's okay."

"That's fine. We have enough room in the van."

"I like your new Van."

"Yeah, it was Stephanie's mother day present. We needed one. You want something for breakfast?"

"I'm just having toast and coffee. How about you? Would you like me to make you something?" Lois asked.

"I'll take some of that coffee, if you don't mind."

"Not at all," Lois said as she reached for another cup, "this isn't the Sunday mornings I remember."

"I know. As children begin to leave the nest, routines change. It's more stress free for your mother, with everyone responsible for getting themselves ready and making their own breakfast."

"I can imagine. You let Danijel make his own breakfast as well?" Lois said observing the mess on the kitchen counter top and remembering when he had to do it himself many mornings.

"No, not at all. He gets up with your mother and I."

"He can you know."

"Oh, we know that. Put on his own clothes too, as he so adamantly likes to point out."

"I guess that's my doing, because of me he had to fend for himself many times."

"Lois you can't dwell on the past. You have to focus on the future."

Stephanie came down at that time, "look whose up and ready to go with us to church this morning sweetheart," Richard said to Stephanie, as he went to the stairs and yelled down for the rest of the children to come down.

That was the first of many Sundays that Lois attended church services with her family. Richard and Stephanie told her that she could stay with them as long as she needed. They wanted her to wait on looking for a job and insisted she spend more time with Danijel, but since he was going to school for part of the day, Lois decided to look for a job in the mornings.

She was there when he came home from school, so he wouldn't have to go to daycare in the afternoon. She was slowly building back a strong relationship with him.

"I have to go back to New York," Lois announced one afternoon after the other children had left the dinner table.

Stephanie looked panic stricken, as Richard remained calm. Richard and Lois were developing a strong bond between them. They stayed up late at nights for long heart to heart talks. There were a lot of issues the two of them had to resolve, and as a result they grew closer.

Richard became more supportive and easy to talk to, as oppose to Stephanie's over protectiveness and questionings.

"Mamma, please don't look as if I said I'm not save anymore or something. I need to go back to New York, not to stay, but to finish something I promised to someone."

"You don't owe anyone anything Lois. You must think about you and Danijel now." Stephanie said.

"I know Mom, and I am thinking about him."

"You don't need to be in that environment anymore, or around your old friends."

"Mom, believe me when I say, it wasn't my friends that influence me to start doing drugs. It was because I couldn't face reality, but I don't want to get into all that right now. I love you and appreciate all you've done and are doing for me and Danijel, but I need to do this and I'm taking him back with me."

"Now that's ridiculous!" Stephanie said as she got up to start clearing off the table. Lois got up with her and began to help.

"Mom, it's not ridiculous. I want him to be with me. I'm not going to do anything that will jeopardize what has taken me weeks to rebuild, and I know he still doesn't trust me. That's why I can't leave him."

"He'll understand."

"He's five Mom. He won't understand. You know that."

"So what'll you do, and where will you stay?"

"I'm hoping Aunt Deb would let me come back." Actually Lois knew she would, because she had already discussed it with her.

"Well considering…," Stephanie began.

"Considering all that I've put her through it's a wonder that she would," Lois finished her mother's thought. "She might."

"What do you think Richard?" Stephanie asked, looking for Richard to be on her side.

"It's Lois' decision dear. I'll leave you two to finish talking about it." He said as he got up and left the table.

Lois shared with Stephanie her reason for wanting to go back. Stephanie was still a little concern, but she knew Lois may have changed in some ways, but she was still her strong willed daughter and once her mind was made up about something; it wouldn't be changed easily, if at all.

The Sunday before Lois left for New York, at the pastor's invitation, Lois got up and publicly gave her life to the Lord. She asked the pastor if she could say something and he gave her the microphone.

"I know you all want to go home, and I'm surprise Pastor Fischer gave me the mic, but since I have it I just want to thank you all for your prayers. I know you all were praying for me while I was in New York trying to destroy my life, but like they say, I got away. I already confessed Jesus as my savior, but I want everyone to know that your prayers for me were not in vain, and all I'll say to you young people is, listen. They do know what they're talking about. I knew very little when I was your age, but I thought I knew it all, and I learned the hard way that I didn't. Thank you for letting me take up some of your time," Lois said giving Pastor Fischer back the mic.

"Lois I pray that one day you will talk to our young people and tell them exactly what it is that they don't know about."

He hugged Lois and asked the congregation to get up and embrace her as well; many did. It was a heart-wrenching day for Lois, as even some of her old youth group members, now adults, came up as well.

Chapter Twenty-Eight
Jewel

It wasn't long after starting her new job that Jewel was in court. She was becoming known for being a hardball. She would rather fight it out in court, than make a deal. She was just what the firm wanted. She made it her business not to associate with the secretaries and any of the associates. If they weren't own their way up, Jewel didn't know their names.

She was hanging out more with her lawyer friends than with Tyler, who was becoming increasingly unsatisfied with the way she was changing.

One night she called Tyler to pick her up, because she had too much to drink.

"I only had two drinks baby," she said.

"Maybe, but two is too much for you. You know that," Tyler replied.

The truth was she had more than two.

"Why do you have to hang out with those guys anyway?" Tyler asked, after she was in the car.

"Come on Tyler, I'm just trying to fit in and make new friends. I enjoy talking to them, especially when we talk law."

"Even if you're so drunk that you don't know what the heck you're talking about." Tyler said annoyingly.

"Especially then, because we're too drunk to know that we don't know what we're talking about," Jewel said as she laughed hysterically.

Tyler took her home and spent the night at her apartment on the couch, so he could take her to pick up her car the next morning.

"Ooooooww!" Jewel yelled as she saw a form on her couch the next morning.

Tyler jumped up half asleep yelling, "what? What?"

"Tyler!" Jewel yelled, "You scare me. What are you doing here?"

"I brought you home last night and decided to stay." Tyler said as he got up off the couch.

"I called you?"

"Yes you did."

"Oh," Jewel said embarrassingly, "thank you for coming to get me."

"You know I would come get you no matter where you were. I just wish you were staying with me, and then I wouldn't have to spend the night on your uncomfortable chair."

"It's not a bed. It's for style, and I don't want to get into this with you right now. My head is about to disengage from my neck, and my eyes are about to pop out of my head, so I don't feel like arguing with you about setting a wedding date now. When we set our date, I want to be focus. There's going to be a lot of things to do, like planning the wedding, a honeymoon, and buying a house. I just don't have the time to do those things right now. I haven't gotten settled on my job yet. Give me some time, please."

"In other words, you want enough time to make it to the top first."

"I'm not going there with you this morning Tyler. You act like you don't know what motivates me."

"I know alright, that's why I want to marry you now, while I think it's still attractive."

"Maybe you don't know me as well as you think. It may be in your best interest to wait, if that's your attitude."

Tyler came over and hugged Jewel.

"Oh come on Jewel. I don't think there's anything that you could do that would make me not want to marry you. I just have to accept the things that I don't like. I'm sure there are things about me that you don't like."

Jewel tried to think in her pounding head, what could be some of those things, but she couldn't think of anything. He was almost too perfect, maybe too perfect for her.

"I just hope that one of those things that I don't like about you don't become a habit," Tyler finished saying.

"Like what?" Jewel asked, and Tyler screamed at the top of his lungs into her ear.

"Drinking!"

Jewel jerked out of his arm, "not funny," she said holding her head.

"I thought it was." Tyler said as he headed for the bathroom to wash his face.

Jewel's pursuit for success and power became intense. She always pushed for the quick trial in her cases, whenever possible, which meant she had to put in a lot of time researching and preparing briefs after hours. Tyler began to see little of her, even on weekends. She didn't allow time for leisure.

She was called in for a meeting with Carl Madison one day after she was on the job for about six month. She only saw him once a week at the staff briefings. It was said he never met with anyone, one on one. Whatever he had to say was said at the briefings.

Dale Bertrie, administrator and partner, met with the associates once a week, so Jewel was a little nervous about this meeting.

"Come in Jewel," Carl said to her as she became a little more nervous at seeing all the partners in the room, "I've asked the other partners to be here for this as well."

Jewel nodded to everyone in the room, as Carl pulled out a chair for Jewel. They were all seated around the smaller conference table in Carl's office, where he met with the partners once a week.

"Well there's no need to hold up this meeting any longer," Carl began, "Jewel you've been here for what now? five, six months?"

"Six months, sir."

"I must have made you nervous Jewel. I'm sorry. There's no need to be nervous."

"Excuse me sir."

"Sir. You're addressing me as sir, and I've never recall you doing that before. Carl will be just fine."

"Yes sir, I mean Carl," the other partners laughed and Jewel used the distraction to adjust herself in her seat, making herself a little more comfortable as she took a deep breath and calmed down, something she learned from her sessions with her psychiatrist.

"I, we," Carl said indicating all the partners, "just want to tell you what a great job you're doing here. We're pleased with your work, and I think all of us, except maybe Florence have seen you in action in court. You have a killer instinct. Some people just have that charisma and some have to learn it. I don't know which category you're in, but you have it, and it's just what we want on our team. We've also heard compliments from our peers concerning your work. You're the kind of lawyer they want in their firm, which brings us to why we've called you in here today. We want to offer you a new position. It's actually a created position, created especially for you. As you know, Dale here is our administrator, and he keeps things running around here. Well, he has his hands full, now that we're growing. We have what?" he looked at Dale for an answer before he even asked the question.

"We have three junior partners and four associates and we're looking for at least one or more associates." Dale answered.

"So you see, we are expanding. We would like to offer you the position of head junior partner. You'll be given your own office space with a window, no more cubicle, and you'll be sharing Sue, Dale's and Florence's secretary, with them getting first bid on her of course. If we need to hire another secretary or something we'll do so, but for now, we'll see how this works out. You will also be given a corporate account for you and your staff expenses. Your staff will consist of all the associates. You will coordinate their assignments, with the other junior partners and they will report directly to you, and you will continue to report to Dale. Dale will still do the recruiting for all new associates, but you will have an opportunity to interview and help make the final decisions as to who is hired or let go, but we've never hired anyone that we've had to let go, because as you know, we try to hire the best the first time. If it was possible, we would offer you a full partnership today, but we can't because of our company's policy. We don't consider any junior partner for senior partner until at least a year after they made junior partner, but we wanted you to know that we appreciate your work and are pleased to have you on our team. Now that I've done all the talking, do you have any questions?"

"I, I don't know what to say," Jewel was totally at lost for words.

"Well from what we've seen of you in court, that must be a first," Gregory Amerson, VP, said, as everyone in the room laughed.

"I just wasn't expecting anything like this," Jewel said.

"Well Jewel, everyone in this room have left good firms, because they did not recognize our talents and abilities as more than just good lawyers," Florence said, "and one of our goals are to reward our good lawyers to encourage them to do better, not to leave us."

"Well if no one else has anything to say, this meeting is adjourned," Carl said as he got up out of his chair.

Everyone followed suit and so did Jewel. As they made their exit, they each shook her hand and congratulated her.

As Jewel was about to walk out the door, Dale called to her, "Oh, Jewel, one more thing. I will meet with you in a couple of days to discuss your raise and your office move, until then you can celebrate with your fiancé, but let's keep this under wraps until we've shared the details with the entire staff at the next office briefing."

Jewel shook her head in agreement and heard someone say, "she's still at lost for words," as she walked out of the office, she felt like she was walking on air.

She decided not to celebrate until all the details were worked out and the staff was told. After her meeting with Dale, she still couldn't believe it. She was given a big increase in salary, making her the highest paid junior partner and was told by Dale to save some of it, because partners have to make a monetary investment in the company.

The news caught all the junior partners off guard, because they all were there before Jewel. The partners made it seemed like it was something promised to Jewel upon hire, but Jewel couldn't recall. She was sure nothing of the sort was in her hire contract, but maybe Carl did say something during the interview. She knew he did mention the possibility of becoming partner, but nothing about a promotion in six month. The associates were not happy with the announcement, although no one said anything at the meeting. Everyone congratulated Jewel on her promotion when the meeting was over, but there was talk in and out of the office concerning which one of the partners she had to sleep with to get the position.

The junior partners asked Jewel to join them at the bar and grille after work, and she did, thinking they wanted to take her out for a congratulatory drink. She also saw it as an opportunity to size up the competition.

"So Jewel, which one of the partners you slept with to get that cushiony position?" Stanley O'Brien, the junior partner who was there the longest posed the question.

"Excuse me?"

"I think you heard the question counselor," said O'Brien.

Jewel looked at them around the table and realized they were all waiting on an answer. She immediately assessed the situation. They didn't ask her out for a drink, because they wanted to congratulate her; they obviously had alternative motives.

"Is this an inquisition? And what happens if I confess to sleeping with one of the partners? Will that make you all feel better, or sleep better, and what if I don't confess. Are you going to beat it out of me? Well, I'll tell you," Jewel said, as she got up and picked up her briefcase, "I have to disappoint your lust for blood. If you have a problem concerning my promotion, you should take it up with the partners, or Dale. I don't think that I need to stand here and listen to your accusations and I don't need to defend myself, because the evidence stares you right in the face. You come here everyday, and you laugh and drink and go back to work and goof off the rest of the afternoon. I know, because I sat right over there most of the time listening to you, while I work on a brief and prepare for my court cases that were scheduled for the afternoon. So, while you went back to the office to watch the clock, until it was time to go home, so you could be right back here to drink some more, I was working. And I can almost bet my position, that none of you have anything in your briefcase to work on later, while I, on the other hand have two cases that I plan to review before I call it a night, and that ladies and gentlemen will be the reason that I will make full partner before all of you. Now if you will excuse me, I got work to do."

"Why that little witch," Stanley said, as they watched Jewel leave.

"Did she just talk down to us?" Cynthia asked.

"I think she did." Chin answered.

"I'm not going to let their jealousy and lack of ambition stop me from enjoying my promotion, if I have to toast myself, I will." Jewel said to Tyler, who took her out to dinner to celebrate.

"I don't think that's necessary baby," Tyler said, as he picked up his glass and said, "here's to my baby."

Jewel held up her glass and said, "To me."

"Is there any way you can work it out with those guys? I mean, can you afford to have all of your peers as enemies?"

"All they want to do is work just enough to justify having a good time at the end of the day. I want more and I'm going to get more. If they want more, then they can stop bellyaching and work for it."

"What about the associates?" Tyler asked.

"What about them?"

"How are you going to win them over?"

"I don't have to win them over Tyler, I'm there boss. If they like me, fine. If they don't, well there is nothing I can do about that, now is there?"

"Maybe you can."

"Like what?"

"Like being a little easier to get along with."

"Tyler, please don't start with your criticism. Let me enjoy my promotion. Is this one of those things that you don't like about me or something?"

"Or something," Tyler said, "but you're right, I apologize. This is a night for celebrating. You deserve to be happy with your promotion. You worked hard to get it."

"Thank you," Jewel said holding up her glass to Tyler.

The evening ended in Jewel having too much to drink and Tyler having to practically carry her to her apartment.

Jewel did not take Tyler's advice and the associates resented having her as their boss, but she was smart and they respected that.

"If she was as nice, as she was smart," said Clayton Brown, one of the associates, as they sat around one day waiting for Jewel to come to their weekly meeting, "I would have no complaints about her at all."

Patrick Conry looked at his watch and said, "she's late again as usual, but she'll come in as usual and start the meeting, without any apologies, as if her time is more valuable than ours."

"Unfortunately guys, it is from what I understand." Clayton said.

"What is it that you understand Clayton," Jewel came in putting her brief case down and hanging up her jacket.

"We were just talking about the case that you're working on, and I was just saying that from what I understand one of us maybe working on it with you." Clayton said trying to bale out, as the others put their heads down smiling.

Jewel knew the game and she knew that was probably not what they were talking about. She was sure the topic was about her.

"Well you're absolutely right, Clayton, but it won't be you," Jewel said.

She had not made up her mind yet on who would work with her, but had just decided it wouldn't be Clayton.

"Patrick and Craig will work with me on this case. It's going to take a lot of running around and research. Clayton you will be working with Chin on a case he just got this morning. I know you all are already working with others on other cases. If you have too much on your plate, let me know now. Dale is currently looking for two new associates, but until then we have to work with what we have. I don't have anything else on my agenda, unless there is something one of you would like to discuss?" She asked looking around at them.

They all sort of held their heads down, except Clayton, as they nodded negatively.

"Then this meeting is adjourned. Thank you for your time."

"You're not welcome," Clayton said, once outside the door.

"Lighten up Clayton," Craig said.

"You don't see the injustice in all this?"

"What injustice Clayton?" Patrick asked.

"Our boss, a black female, giving orders to four white males and assigning one of us to work with a chinch."

"Like Craig said Clayton, lighten up. This is a changing world and she's a good lawyer. I'm just not going to look at the negative, but maybe if I can learn from her, I can get where she is as fast as she got there," Patrick said.

"Believe that if you want to. All this is about is a thing call affirmative action and glass ceilings, placing a black woman in an executive position to make the company look good with the liberals."

"Clayton, believe what you want," Craig said as he walked away not giving ear to Clayton prejudices.

Without another word Patrick walked away as well, not wanting to give Clayton any more fuel.

"What are we celebrating tonight?" Tyler asked Jewel as he met her at the restaurant.

"I won the case!" Jewel nearly screamed in a low voice.

"Wow babe. That is reason to celebrate. You really thought you would lose this case."

"I know, but the prosecutors practically gave me the case, when they put their girl on the stand. I didn't think they were that stupid."

Tyler had known about this case. It was all Jewel talked about for the past several week. It was involving a young girl who was badly beaten and presumably rape by some boys from a high school football team. Jewel was the lawyer for one of the boys, whose father was a prominent citizen in the community and an important client of Jewel's law firm. Tyler knew Jewel was hoping that the prosecuting attorney would put the girl on the stand. She was sure that her cross-examination of the girl would make her testimony seem not credible.

"She became totally confused, and practically admitted to knowing what she was getting into."

"You badgered that little girl on the stand?" Tyler asked unbelieving.

"I wouldn't call it badgering; I just asked her some tough questions."

"She could have been Brianna."

"But she wasn't." Jewel said coldly.

Tyler looked at her sadly and got up from the table.

"Where are you going?" Jewel asked. "This is one celebration I can't join in with you? Do you need a ride home?"

"No. I don't," said Jewel annoyed, "I think I'll stay and have dinner and have a couple of drinks to celebrate."

"Then have the waiter call you a cab," Tyler said, as he threw his napkin on the table.

"Oh, you need not worry Tyler, I won't call you. Matter of fact, maybe it would be better if you didn't call me either."

Tyler heart sank. The last thing he intended was to break up with her. He just couldn't celebrate this with her and he knew if she could do something like this, there would be many more celebrations he wouldn't have with her.

"Maybe I shouldn't," Tyler said as he walked out of the restaurant.

Chapter Twenty-Nine
Lois

Lois had a promise to keep, so she and Danijel went back to New York. She and Deb made arrangements to attend a business school during the day. They had to attend five days a week from nine in the morning, until three in the evening, but they arranged it with the school to take classes through lunch, so they could get out earlier.

Deb changed her shift at the factory from day to night and Lois stayed with the children. The twins, now fifteen, and Bridgett, 13, were a big help with Danijel, so Lois had the easiest night job.

Lois got a cleaning job with an agency for Saturdays and did errands for elderly people on Sunday afternoons to earn some money to help with her and Danijel's expense.

On Sundays Lois and Danijel walked to a nearby church, while Deb and her children went to their church.

One Sunday Lois decided it was time for Danijel to meet his other grandmother.

"We're going to church with you guys today," she said to a surprise Deb.

Deb knew Lois was still heart broken over the way things ended with her and Matt and even more hurt at the way Matt's mother treated her, but Lois wanted to make an attempt for Danijel to meet his father. She knew it was going to hurt her more than it would Danijel, if Matt still rejected him, but she wanted to give it one last try.

She could feel the eyes staring at her as they came in to find a seat. Danijel stayed with her, until they dismissed the children to children's church.

Lois knew Deb had asked the members of her church to pray for her, but how much they knew or thought they knew, she didn't know. She never discussed it with Deb. Every time she found herself looking in the direction of Patricia Edwards, Matt's mother, she felt like her eyes were boring through her. She made a mental note to avoid looking her way.

The sermon was good and after the service, the minister called her out, "Lois, we're certainly glad to see you back in our midst."

The church clapped and Lois felt liked she turned three shades redder.

When they were outside, Deb asked, "Are you going to talk to her?"

Lois knew she meant Mrs. Edwards.

"Not today. Maybe another time," but before Lois finished her statement, she heard her name being called.

"It looks like it's going to be today," Deb said as she smiled and walked away.

"Don't leave," Lois tried to plead with Deb, but she just smiled and kept on walking.

Patricia Edwards walked up to Lois and as if it was a second thought, put her arms around Lois and gave her a hug.

"Lois, it's so good to see you baby."

Patricia Edwards had a tired expression on her face, which made her look older than she probably was, thought Lois.

Before Lois could speak, Danijel came racing up to her showing her something they made in children's church.

"Look mommy, I made an angel just for you. Here, keep him close to you always and he will protect you and you will never be sick again." Lois reached for the angel and bend over to hug Danijel, as she looked at the angel.

"I'm going to place him right in my bible, where he will always be safe."

"But he's suppose to keep you safe."

"That's why I have to protect him from getting torn or misplaced, and what better place than the bible, where God will watch over his angels with his words, so that the angel will always be able to protect me."

"Okay, let me have your bible."

Lois gave Danijel the bible and he gently placed the cut out angel into the bible.

"Danijel, I want you to meet someone."

Danijel looked up and covered his eyes from the glare of the sun.

"Why she crying mommy?"

Lois looked up to see tears in Patricia's eyes, as she wiped them away.

"I'm not crying sad tears Danijel. I'm crying happy tears. Do you know about happy tears?"

"Yeah, my mommy cried them a lot when she came home, after she got better."

"Well, I'm crying them because the good Lord is allowing an old fool like me to correct a wrong."

"What's a fool?" Danijel asked, with his hands still over his eyes every time he looked up at Mrs. Edwards.

"Well you never mind about that now sweetie."

"What's your name?" Danijel asked.

"You can call me grandma."

"I have a grandma," said Danijel.

"Oh, but God is so good that he gives everyone two sets of grandparents," said Mrs. Edwards, as Danijel continued to stare up at her, trying to block out the glare of the sun.

"I'll explain it later Dandan," Lois said.

Danijel seemed to be satisfied with that answer and got tired of staring up at Mrs. Edwards

"Can I go with Kevy and Micky?"

"Yes, but don't pester them. If they're with their friends and don't want to be bothered, come back okay."

"Okay," but Danijel knew there was no way Kevy and Micky would think he was bothering them, so off he ran.

They treated Danijel like he was a big boy and he liked that.

"Where are you staying?" Mrs. Edwards asked Lois, as she watched Danijel run off.

"We're staying with my aunt for now, but it's only temporary. We're going back to Tennessee in about five months from now."

"Do you think it would be possible for him to come spend some weekends with me?"

Lois was taken back by the request. She didn't want Danijel to meet Matt for the first time without her, and she didn't want to ask Mrs. Edwards anything about Matt.

"I'll have to think about it," Lois responded uneasily.

"That's good enough. At least you didn't say no." Mrs. Edwards was grateful.

"I should go, because I have to go to work."

"It was so nice to see you Lois, and you look so well. I just want you to know that I'm sorry. I hope that you can forgive me for the way I acted when…"

"I forgive you Mrs. Edwards," Lois said.

"When I saw Danijel come into the church with you today, it was like a flashback of when Matt was his age. He looks just like my Matt."

Lois didn't want to hear this. It made her heart hurt even more, to think that Matt did not want to even see his son; the son who was the very image of him.

"I'd better go," Lois said.

"Yeah, go ahead, but you think about it now. I sure would like to have him come spend some time with me."

On the train, Lois tried to get some information from Deb.

"Mrs. Edwards seemed different, more, more, I don't know, sadder or something."

"I know. A lot has happened to her. You know her son, Craig, was killed and now Carla, her daughter, has a little girl. She's now living on her own. Carla tries to stay away from her mother as much as possible. They don't get along that well. She brings the baby to church some times, and Matt, I honestly don't know. I heard he doesn't keep in contact anymore. He did what she wanted him to do concerning you, but he's not been back home since. No one knows how he's doing."

"Wow, I didn't know."

"Were you hoping to see Matt while you were here?"

461

"I kinda hope, but I guess that won't happen."

"Anything's possible to them that believe." Deb said. Lois had a lot to think about the rest of the trip.

One Sunday afternoon, when Lois didn't have to work, she told Deb she was going to take Danijel to the city to see his godmother.

"You think that's a good idea?" Deb asked.

"In spite of everything, Kelly was there for me. If it wasn't for her, who knows where I would be and Danijel may still be in foster care somewhere," Lois looked off, "I don't want to even think about the what ifs, but Kelly got in touch with you and because of that, my son got out of the system and my father came looking for me and may have just saved my life that night. I owe a lot of that to Kelly, regardless of how you feel about her."

After she was on the train, Lois wondered should she have called first. Kelly worked unusually hours and may not even be home.

"Maybe we'll have dinner together, go see a movie and try again later," she said to Danijel, as if he could read her thoughts.

He looked up at her and said, "but I thought we going to see auntie Kelly"

"Yeah, but if Auntie Kelly isn't home, maybe we'll do something else until she comes home, okay."

"Okay," Danijel agreed.

Lois was a little nervous ringing the doorbell. She suddenly felt like this was not the thing to do. She looked around her. The building and the surroundings were bringing back unpleasant memory.

She took Danijel's hand and said, "I don't think she's home Danijel let's go."

She began to walk fast towards the elevator, almost pulling Danijel. She placed her hand on her head as she felt a prickling of a headache.

Danijel kept looking back and calling, "mommy, mommy," and then Lois heard footstep racing behind them.

She almost ran, but then the voice caught up with her, "Lois? Danijel? Oh, my God!"

Lois stopped, looked back and let go of Danijel's hand as he ran back to greet Kelly. Kelly picked him up and swung him around, as he began to giggle loving the excitement. Kelly walked up slowly to Lois and they hugged each other in a long embrace.

"We'd better get back into my apartment. You know how nosey these people are around here."

Lois felt a spirit of calmness come over her and she was grateful for it.

"We'd better," she replied as they headed back to Kelly's apartment.

"Wasn't it nice to see Auntie Kelly, Fran and Adrienne, Dandan?"

Danijel just shook his head, as he was absorbed in the game Kelly gave him. She had bought it for his birthday and was meaning to get the address from Deb to mail it to him.

Lois looked down at him playing with his toy, as she rubbed his head and sat back on the train to relax for their long ride home, as pleasant thoughts of her visit played in her mind.

Kelly couldn't wait to get back into the apartment to call Adrienne and Francesca, who raced over shortly after. They laughed and talked about some of the good times they had together. No one wanted to talk about the bad, but Lois needed to thank them for all they did for her and Danijel.

Lois told them how Richard had found her at her lowest and about the close relationship she was forming with him. She told them she was saved and that it was the best thing to happen to her. She felt like she should've said more, but she wasn't sure. She told them she had found a better way and even though it didn't pay as much, "you can't buy the peace that I'm experiencing."

They all seemed a little uncomfortable about her talking about being save and peace, so she didn't want to sound preachy, so she moved on to a lighter subject, like school and her future plans. They all agreed to get together again before Lois leave New York and Lois hoped they would. She really wanted to say more to them about the Lord.

Lois began to go to church with Deb every Sunday. Mrs. Edwards picked Danijel up almost every other Friday afternoon and kept him until church on Sunday. One Sunday Carla came to church with her and brought the baby. She was a beautiful little girl, nicknamed Peaches.

Carla came over to speak to Lois after the service, "Hi Lois. It's good to see you again."

"I'm glad to see you too," Lois said.

After all, she didn't hold any animosity against Carla. Carla pretty much stayed out of her brother's relationships.

"I, aaamm, I mean," Carla was trying to get something out, but was finding it awkward to do.

Lois misread it and said, "Carla you don't owe me any apologies."

"I know. I mean, what I'm trying to say, I guess, is that I hear from Matt a lot."

Lois looked surprised.

"You've probably heard that we don't hear from him, but it's really not the truth. He doesn't call mama, because she always want to be up in his business, but he calls me to see how she's doing."

Lois still looked at Carla surprisingly. Not knowing why she was sharing this information with her.

"Well, I guess, I'm glad that someone hears from him and that he's alright."

Lois wasn't sure whether she cared to know if he was all right, or not.

"Mom has always been overprotective of me and Matt, ever since Craig got arrested not wanting us to get in any trouble, but to make something of our lives and then when Craig was killed; she went from over protective to possessive. It was just too much to live with her." Carla tried to explain.

"You don't owe me any explanation Carla, really."

"I guess I just need to come out and say what I want to say."

Lois looked at her even more puzzled, she seemed to be missing what Carla was trying to say.

Lois laughed at Carla and said, "Maybe the direct approach would be the best approach Carla."

Carla felt a little at ease and laughed, "I know Matt hates himself for not ever seeing his son. He talks to me about it all the time. He hates himself for the way he treated you. He really never meant to hurt you. He was just caught up in trying to please mama that things just got so mixed up. What I was wondering is, well, do you think it would be all right if I told Matt that I've seen you and Danijel. If I do, he might want to call you or something, I don't know. I don't like getting involved with Matt's business, but I think he would want to know that you're back in New York."

Lois didn't know what to say. Was this one of those times, when God test you to see if you've really changed?

Something inside of her wanted to scream, tell Matt he'll never see Danijel, but she heard herself saying, "I don't have a problem with Matt knowing that we're in New York, I guess if he wants to call me, that's up to him, but I don't think it's a good idea to meet his son over the phone."

"I'll tell him then," Carla said, "well I'd better go and get Peaches out of the nursery."

The conversation with Carla kept Lois occupied all the way home on the train, as she played it over and over in her mind.

As they were walking home from the train station and the children were walking ahead of them, Deb commented, "I saw you talking to Carla after service. You seemed pretty occupied after that. Everything all right."

"I guess. She wanted to know if it would be all right to tell Matt that Danijel and I were back in New York. I didn't know he knew we were gone."

"Well I sort of told some of the people in our prayer group that you were back home with your parents and doing well."

"Mrs. Edwards in your prayer group?"

"Yes, but I didn't think she talked to Matt."

"She doesn't, but she talks to Carla and Carla talks to Matt. Apparently more than Mrs. Edwards knows."

"I see. So how do you feel about that?"

"Don't know."

"What will you do if he wants to see Danijel?"

"I don't know. I thought I wanted them to meet, but now, I just don't know. Carla made it sound like he resented not ever seeing his son, but

I wasn't stopping him from seeing Danijel, you know," Lois looked at Deb for understanding.

"I know."

"Are you ready to quit your factory job, Aunt Deb? Are you ready to be bless?"

Lois was saying to Deb one Sunday afternoon after hearing a powerful message on, 'God's gonna bless your socks off. Deb laughed at Lois. She was jumping up and down more excited than Deb had ever seen her.

"What has gotten into you?" Deb asked laughingly as the children joined in imitating the Pastors message.

Danijel started jumping up and down as well, even though he wasn't in the service for the message. Deb just laughed at their silly acts.

"We have two more months Aunt Deb, and they are already starting to look for jobs for us, well you anyway. I'm not staying here. I'm going back home, but can you stand to leave that factory?"

"Oh, I can stand it. Let me tell you, I can stand it," said Deb.

"Then get up and shout your socks off!" Lois said pulling Deb out of the chair and holding her hands while they went around in circles, saying, "the blessings of the Lord is going to knock my socks off."

"I can't believe you'll are acting like that," Micky said in a disgusted tone.

Deb grabbed his hands and all the children joined in to form a circle and sang. The phone rang and everyone fell down on a chair, or the floor and just began to laugh.

"Y'all be quiet," Deb was motioning from the phone, "I can't hear," she said sticking one finger in her ear, as she knew the noise wasn't going to quiet down any time soon, but it did when Deb yelled, "Matt?" and looked at Lois, who suddenly went quiet, as the nerves in her stomach recoiled.

"What's the matter Mommy?" Danijel asked.

"Nothing sweetie, Auntie Deb is on the phone."

Deb said, "hold on," and stuck the phone out to Lois. Lois got up and hesitantly took the phone and twirled it around before putting it to her ears.

"You're where?"... "In New York?" Lois turned from the piercing eyes that were on her and face the wall. "I don't know."... "I understand that."... "No. I don't owe you anything," Lois was getting annoyed. "Call me when you get to Carla's."... "I didn't say I would. I just said to call me. It'll give me time to think about it, bye," Lois said as she hung up the phone.

"Come on mommy, let's do the circle again, come on!"

Kevy and Micky sense something was up and Micky took Danijel's hand and said, "come on Danijel let's go to our room and play on the Nintendo."

Danijel liked that better, so off he went with the boys.

"Can I play too?" Bridgett asked.

"Come On, but you'd better not whine, or out you go," Kevy said.

"Decisions, decisions," Deb said.

Lois just looked at her not wanting to talk about it just yet, but Deb intended to have her say.

"I know how you feel girl. Can you imagine how I felt when the boy's father came back into their lives when they're almost grown wanting to be their father. I almost laughed in his face, but it really wasn't my decision to make. I had to give him a chance. If he screwed it up, it wouldn't be me pushing him out of their lives, the kids would do that for me, but I have to say, he did changed, a wife, a son, and a daughter later. I wanted to hate him for that too. I mean, why couldn't he have changed earlier and marry me, so that we could be a family. I ask God these questions over and over, but I get no answers, and I may never get an answer, but I'm all right with that. I've come to terms with it. Do you still love him?"

"Wow, where did that come from?" Lois got up and went into her defense mode.

"Are you? There's nothing wrong with you, if you do. It's just one of those things. We can't turn off our emotions as easily and quickly, as they can. All they need is another..., well you know. They think they've found love, but all they've found is someone to satisfy their lust, because we've wised up and decided not to play that game anymore. You know."

"I've never heard you talk like this, Aunt Deb."

"Sometime the truth will set a soul free. Even my soul," she laughed as she went into the kitchen to do the dishes leaving Lois to make her decision.

Lois did. She agreed to let Matt meet Danijel at Carla's apartment. When Carla opened the door, Danijel headed straight for the room where Peaches slept.

"Danijel stop!" Lois yelled. "Just where do you think you're going?"

"To see Peachy," he said looking at her as if she didn't know his routine, when coming to Carla's, but Lois didn't see Matt and she didn't want Danijel running into him alone.

"It's okay. She's awake with them big eyes looking up at me, when I want her to go to sleep," Carla said.

"I know how that is," Lois laughed.

"Come on in, Matt went by mama's."

"Are they talking?" Lois asked.

"Matt wants to do the right thing, you know," Carla replied.

Lois thought, a lot of doing the right thing going around.

"He should be back any minute now."

Lois hoped he would never show, then she would be justified when she never give him another chance.

"I forgot how cold this place gets." Matt came in shaking himself and taking off his coat, when he looked up Lois was standing up.

She didn't want to feel any disadvantages.

He stopped and looked behind him, as a little girl came running up behind him, "daddy, you left me!"

Matt looked at his daughter and said, "I thought you were right behind me."

Lois didn't know what to expect, as her heart sank. There were so many emotions trying to take over her all at once. The sight of Matt brought back the strong feelings she once had for him, but seeing this little girl calling him daddy, and knowing that she had to have a mother not far behind made her heart ache, yet she was going to be tough, so she held her head up.

Matt reached down to help the little girl take off her coat.

"Is Peaches awake yet?" the little girl asked Carla.

"Yes, she's in her room, why don't we go check on her and bring back some one who's here to meet your daddy." Carla said.

"Hold still for a minute Tiffany. I want you to meet someone." Matt said, still trying to take the antsy little girl coat off.

"Tiffany this is Miss," Matt looked up at Lois and asked, "Is it still Miss?"

"Yes it is," Lois said with a stiff upper lip.

"Tiffany, this is Miss Lois. She's an old friend of mines."

"Hi Miss Lois," Tiffany said, "Now can I go see Peaches."

"Hi Tiffany," Lois managed to get in before Tiffany tore out of Matt's hand and headed to Peaches bedroom.

"How old is she?" Lois asked.

"She's almost three." Matt said, "Please sit back down."

Lois looked at the chair wondering how she was going to get out of there with Danijel, before this became any worst than it already was. Matt sat next to her and took her hand and Lois withdrew them, as if a bolt of electricity had just gone through her, because that's what it felt like. Could he hurt me anymore? Lois thought.

"Lois, I can't imagine what you might be thinking about me right now. It's probably not good, but I want to apologize for not being there for you, for leaving you to be alone and raising our son alone."

Lois wanted to scream at him that Danijel wasn't his son and she came here to tell him that, but how could she lie. It would be so cruel to do that, but didn't he deserve her cruelty. He didn't deserve her sitting there, while he made empty apologies.

"I'm glad you agreed to meet with me and bring him here, so we can finally meet."

"His name is Danijel. I thought you knew that?"

God help me to act in a Christ-like manner. How did I put myself in this position? What was I thinking? The thoughts just kept going through Lois' mind.

"I'm sorry, Danijel. Yes I do know his name."

Matt stopped, trying to think of what else to say. He knew Lois was responding out of hurt. When he first saw her, he thought he saw a welcome in her eyes and a smile on her lips, but when Tiffany ran in, it all seemed to go. Matt was thinking that his fiancé was right. He shouldn't have brought Tiffany with him, but he wanted his children to know each other.

"Lois I'm sorry. I wasn't thinking of you when I brought Tiffany here."

"That wouldn't be the first time you didn't think of me Matt."

Matt held his head down. This was definitely not going the way he hoped.

"I think I should go," Lois said as she got up.

"Lois, please give me a chance. I know I'm the reason things didn't work out between us, and I can't do anything about that now. I just want to be straight up with you now. I'm in love with someone else. We're going to be married. It's Tiffany's mother, but I really want to know my son. That's why I asked for this meeting. Hate me. Yell at me. Tell me what you really think of me, but please don't keep me from being a father to our son. Maybe if my father was around, I would've known how to stand up to my mother back then," Matt paused, "no, no, I'm not making excuses, Lois. I refuse to make excuses for the way I treated you. You did not deserve that. You didn't. All I can offer you now is an apology. Please forgive me."

Oh God no, Lois thought. He was asking her to forgive her. Why God? She didn't want to forgive him. She wanted to hate him, to hit him, to hurt him. To do anything, except forgive him, but she knew she had to do it. That no matter what he'd done. God required her to forgive. Her drug rehab steps required her to forgive. It was the only hope of a future for her. Isn't this really why she came back to New York, with the hopes of seeing Matt and forgiving him, even if he didn't ask it.

"I forgive you Matt," Lois said with tears welling up in her eyes.

She took the back of her hand and wiped her tears as she looked away. There was nothing else for them to say. It didn't matter now why he did it. It was done and over with and it was time to move on. Lois knew this feeling she was having now all to well. It was a feeling of insurmountable peace.

"Let me introduce you to your son. Danijel!," she yelled his name, as she heard his feet running to her

"Are we leaving now? I'm not ready yet. I want to stay and play with Peachy and Tiff."

Lois looked at him and stooped to his level to fix his shirt in his pants, "One day you will learn that it's not polite to shorten people's name. Her name is Tiffany, isn't it?"

"Yeah, but Auntie Carla calls her Tiff."

"I see. Well I want you to meet someone," Lois stood up and looked at Matt while holding Danijel's hand.

"Danijel this is your father."

She looked down at his son, who was speechless and said, "Matt this is Danijel, your son." She looked back at Matt. "I'm going to leave you to explain to him why you're just meeting him for the first time."

She stooped back down to Danijel and said, "I'm going to do some errands, then I'll be back to pick you up."

"No!" Danijel finally spoke up. "I don't want to stay with him. He's not my father! You're lying!"

"Danijel, I wouldn't lie to you. Didn't I tell you that one day you would get to meet your father? Well, this is that day, but if you don't want to stay, then I won't make you sweetie."

"Promise."

"Of course, I promise," Lois said crossing her heart.

"Danijel, I know you don't know me and that's my fault, but I want to get to know you. Your mommy won't be long, but if you want her to stay, she could."

"I want her to stay." He said.

"Why don't I go say hello to Peaches. I'll be right back," Lois said.

"Don't mommy!"

"I'm just going right here sweetie. No where else."

Danijel wasn't sure of what was going on and he was not happy to be left with this man, but he thought if his mother was only going in the next room, it should be okay.

Lois gave them about thirty minutes. Carla had put Tiffany to sleep by reading her a book, and she gave Peaches a bottle and she finally went off to sleep.

Carla and Lois talked for a little and Lois decided that it was long enough. When she came out of the room, Danijel and Matt were on the couch and Matt was telling him about his job and where he lived. Danijel was asking lots of questions.

"You ready?"

Danijel looked at Matt. He wasn't about to let Lois leave him, but he was now curious about this man who said he was his father. Matt was sensitive to what was going on. He knew he hadn't won Danijel over yet, but he felt that he had scored some points.

"Why don't you go with your mommy now, and maybe tomorrow after church, you could come home with Carla and we could all go out somewhere."

"My mommy too?" Danijel asked.

"If your mommy wants to," Matt answered.

"Mommy will you want to?"

"I don't know sweetie. We'll talk about it later. I have to work tomorrow, because I didn't get to do it today. Now why don't you say goodbye to Auntie Carla, and be careful not to wake the girls and then we'll be on our way."

"Everybody sleeping?" Matt asked.

"Everybody except Carla. You have an impressionable little girl."

"You've done a great job with him."

"Thanks. I had a lot of help and I know you know that I had it rough for awhile, but I'm okay now, and we're going to be fine."

Matt didn't give any indication of knowing anything, although his mother tried to fill him in on what she thought she knew when he went to see her earlier. She was actually telling Matt not to hurt Lois anymore. Matt thought how ironic, since he would've never hurt her in the first place, if she had stayed out of his life.

"I'm glad everything is working out for you Lois. You deserve the best."

"Thank you," Lois said. "Matter of fact things are working out for us, and you're right, I do deserve the best."

Danijel came back, said his goodbyes to Matt and they left, with Lois still feeling an overwhelming sense of peace. It was over. That part of her life was now behind her, now she was ready to move on. She wanted to shout and leap. She was expecting good things for her and Danijel.

Chapter Thirty
Jewel

It had been months since Jewel last seen Tyler. The last time they talked, Tyler suggested they have a cooling off period, especially since Jewel kept refusing to see him.

Jewel lay in her bed for the first time in months with nothing to do, no briefs to go over, no research to do. She was thriving in her new position and the partners couldn't be happier with her. She had to constantly knock head with Clayton, but she refused to let his prejudice stand in her way. She assigned him to menial task with the intention of changing that, when he acknowledge her authority.

Jewel picked up the phone to call Tessa, but she got her answering machine, "Yes Tessa, this is your big sister. You should consider calling some time. Talk to you soon."

She got up, raided the refrigerator and surfed the TV. She looked in the paper for any good movies playing. She couldn't remember the last time she went to a movie, but she also didn't want to go by herself. She couldn't think of one person she could call to go with her. The thought of not having one good friend scare her.

All of her life, she was surrounded by people. There was always someone around, a girlfriend, or even a boyfriend, but now there was no one. She thought of calling Tyler, but decided against it. She picked up the phone and dialed her parent's number.

"Hi Mom."... "No, everything is alright."... "I do call."... "I admit it has been awhile, but I'm busy. My job is very demanding." She got up off of her couch and began to pace around the room. She almost resented calling her mother. She always gave her the third degree. "No maam. I haven't found a church to go to yet, but I'm looking." She knew that was a lie, but it was better than having her mother faint over what she really thought about going to church. "Tyler is fine," she said, "I guess," she said softly and quietly. "I said, I guess he's fine. I haven't talk to Tyler in awhile."… 'We're going through a cooling off period."… "Mom I really don't want to get into that with you. What's going on in Brickenbrat.?" … "Lois?"… "Really. Do you know her number?"… "Her mother?"… "Do you think she's still living there?"… "New York?"… "I'll call."… "Wait let me get a pen and paper to take down the number."… "Matter of fact, I think I'll call after I hang up from you."… "Love you too."

The phone kept ringing and ringing. Maybe no one was home, Jewel thought, as she was about to hang up, someone picked up.
"Hello?"… "Is Lois there?"… "May I speak to her?"
Jewel waited for Lois to get to the phone. A strange feeling came over her, a feeling of nervous anticipation.
"Lois?"… "Is it really you girl?"… "This is Jewel."… "Jewel Stone."… "Yessss!"… "I've been trying to get in touch with you for the longest. What's going on with you?"
Jewel spent almost two hour on the phone with Lois. They had so much to catch up on. Jewel told Lois about college, law school, her new job and her prospect of getting married. Lois told Jewel about New York and Danijel. She wasn't ready to share anything else. She told Jewel she was saved.
"Honestly Lois, I probably can count the times I've went to church since High School."… "I don't know. I guess I've changed."… "I still can't shake the way I was raised and believe it or not, I'm still a virgin, but I'm not ruling out church, or something. I need to know what religion is best for me."… "Yeah, yeah, I know, me, the good little Sunday school girl."… "Well I was always someone good little something. It's just time for me to be myself, and find out what works for me. I've even gone to a shrink."… "It really helped me. Maybe you should try it sometime. I know you had a lot of issues with your stepfather."…

"Really. I'm glad to hear that. Your mother must be happy."... "I'd better let you go Lois."... "He is?"... "Well we can't let this be our only call."... "Call me sometime."... "Here take my number."... "If you can't afford to call, just write. It would be great to hear from you."... "You take care as well. Bye."

Jewel sat on her couch, as she reflected on her conversation with Lois. She hoped she didn't insult her, by insinuating that she couldn't afford to call. She couldn't believe Lois was saved. She never thought Lois would ever make that commitment. Jewel looked at the time and decided it was too late to go out, so she took a hot bubble bath and went to bed. She decided she would get up early the next morning and find a church to go to.

When she got up the next morning, she was too tired because she stayed up too late watching old movies on TV, so she just stayed in bed for most of the day.

Lois called Jewel the following week. Jewel was glad to hear from her, but uncomfortable when she talked about being saved. It bothered her more than when her brother, or mother tried to get her to find a church; finding a church was a little impersonal than what Lois was talking about. Lois was sensitive to know she was making Jewel uneasy and didn't want to push her beliefs off on Jewel, so she made sure she didn't talk about it too much. She didn't want to scare Jewel off, but she didn't want to miss the opportunity to witness to Jewel either.

Jewel tried to call Lois before she called her, because she knew Lois was looking for a job and probably couldn't afford the long distance bill. It was no big deal to her; she was doing well financially and was glad to have her old friend back in her life, even if they were miles apart.

Lois lightened up on preaching to Jewel. She too was glad to have Jewel back in her life. When they talked, it was as if the world stood still and they were right back in Brickenbrat together, giggling like silly little Sunday school girls again.

Lois told Jewel one night, as they were sharing boyfriend stories that she needed a head examination, if she let someone like Tyler get away.

It was a season of reunions for Jewel. One evening as she sat in a restaurant having a drink, with a client to go over his file for an upcoming case she was working on, she ran into someone from her past.

She was in the middle of a conversation with her client, when she heard a very familiar voice calling her name. She looked up and staring down at her was Brad. She had to shake herself, as she stared into his blue eyes. It reminded her of the first day of law school, when they first met.

"Brad? Oh my God, what are you doing here?" She said instinctively getting up to greet him.

"I was about to get some dinner," he said coming around to her side of the table, where they join in an embrace.

"No, I mean here, in Connecticut."

"I'm here on business, but I didn't imagine running into you here. What are you doing here?"

"I live here."

Jewel client cleared his throat.

"Oh I'm sorry," Jewel apologized to her client. "Brad I'm here with a client. Are you meeting someone?"

"No, I'm just having dinner alone."

"Well, when I'm finished here would it be okay, if I came over for a drink or something? I would hate it, if I didn't get an opportunity to talk with you, and catch up on old times," Jewel smiled, knowing some of those old times were better left in the past.

"I don't plan on leaving this restaurant, or letting you leave until we've catch up," Brad said.

"Good, then I'll see you in a little bit."

"Sounds great," Brad said as he left to go to his table, where the waiter who was seating him was standing patiently.

Jewel was totally distracted.

"I've never seen you so distracted Miss Stone," Jewel's client acknowledged.

"I'm sorry. It's just that we go back a long way and I'm taking back a bit at seeing him tonight."

"Then why don't we wrap it up for now and reschedule this. We still have time, don't we?"

"Yes we do, but are you sure? It's your time that I'm concerned with Mr. Benito."

"I'm perfectly fine with meeting another time. Just call my secretary and set up something," he said as he was getting up.

"Thank you Mr. Benito and I want to assure you that I'm on top of your case. This is just a routine court hearing. Everything is going to go smoothly."

"I have confidence in you and your firm, Miss Stone. Have a good night with your old acquaintance."

"Thank you again, and you have a good evening as well."

Jewel took a deep breath, as she began to put her file back in her brief case. She motioned for the waiter.

"Could you please bring me the check?" Jewel had her things together, when the waiter return with the check.

Jewel took a quick look at herself, in her purse mirror and got up and smooth out her very chic two-piece skirt suit that fitted her tightly and smugly. It was one of her best suit and she was suddenly glad she wore it. It was her dress to impress suit. The one she wore when meeting a new client.

She asked the waiter who sat Brad, to show her to his table.

"Yes maam. I believe he's waiting on you," the waiter said.

Jewel wondered what that meant. It was at least fifteen minutes since he had come in, was he waiting on her to have dinner. Jewel smiled. It would be a Brad thing to do, to presume she would have dinner with him.

"Hi Brad," Jewel said in a voice she barely recognized. It sounded deep and sensual.

Brad got up while the waiter seated her.

"I'm glad your meeting didn't take long. I didn't see any plates on the table, so I decided to wait to order hoping you would have dinner with me."

Jewel smiled, "Observant as usual. No, I haven't had dinner and yes, I would love to have dinner with you."

Jewel's heart was pounding so loud, she could barely hear the background music.

"You look good Jewel."

"Thank you, so do you."

"I didn't know you were back in the States, and how did you ended up in Connecticut of all places?"

"I think we'd better order, or we could be here all night," Jewel recommended.

"I'm already wishing we could," Brad said as his blue eyes caught Jewel's.

Jewel opened her menu trying to avoid his deep blues, but he kept his eyes on her as if in disbelief. The waiter came over and they ordered. Jewel ordered a club soda, knowing that she already had a glass of wine with her client on an empty stomach and Brad had never seen her drink before, except champagne at holidays.

"This is certainly a nice coincident," Jewel said.

"This could never be a coincident Jewel. Of all places and of all the restaurants we could've gone to, here we are. I honestly don't think this is a coincident at all."

"What is it then," Jewel asked eyeing Brad, "fate?"

"Destiny."

Jewel held her head back and laughed a dainty laugh, "destiny? Now there's a term I don't think I've heard since…, since…, I guess since my mother's pastor preached it the year I graduated from high school." Jewel held her head down with a puzzled look, "which is even more strange that I would remember that sermon now, of all times."

"Then I know its destiny."

"Let's just get caught up and get through dinner."

Dinner was over and they continued to talk about what had transpired in their lives, since they last saw each other. Brad had accepted a job with the District Attorney's office. They were prosecuting someone who did crimes in Connecticut, New York, New Jersey, Maryland and Atlanta. Brad was in Connecticut tracking the criminal's crimes to report back to his superiors any thing they could find to tie the man to the crimes in Atlanta.

"Sounds like an interesting case," Jewel said.

"I don't know if it's interesting, more grisly than anything. Our suspect has committed some gruesome murders and I don't want to talk about that tonight," Brad said taking a deep breath, "I'm still trying to make the connection."

"What connection?" Jewel asked.

"How did you end up in Connecticut, Hodgeport, of all places? What's your strategy for becoming a big time lawyer in Hodgeport? I thought if any place, you would have ended up in LA, Chicago, New York, or even Atlanta, but a quiet little town like Hodgeport, Connecticut. You might as well be back in Brickenbrat."

"Strange isn't it? I don't know. No connection. I sent my resume out over the internet and this guy from Connecticut was in London and interviewed me. I wanted to come back to the States and get my feet wet, before I jumped in to play with the big boys."

Jewel mentally decided not to tell Brad about Tyler and she wasn't sure why. Did she believe what Brad said about destiny? She wasn't sure, but she didn't see any point in getting into all that now.

Brad looked at his watch, "Oh man, it's getting late."

Jewel looked down at hers, "Is that the right time?"

"I think it is. I know you have to get up for work tomorrow and I got to meet with some guys in Bridgeport tomorrow. I hate to leave. Can we get together tomorrow?"

"How long are you going to be in town?"

"I don't know, probably less than a week, but I'm sure going to stretch it out as much as possible."

"Then I gather you're not going to trial anytime soon on this one."

"No. We need time to make our case stick."

"Well, if I can help you with your research, let me know, in the meantime, between work, maybe I can show you around town, that is, if you don't already have a tour guide."

"If I did, they would be fired as of right now." Brad took care of the bill and they both got up and head for the door.

Brad took his phone out and began to call for a cab, but Jewel offered to take him anywhere he wanted to go.

"This your car?" Brad asked as they approached a red BMW.

"Yes it is," Jewel said.

"Exactly what I would imagine you to be driving."

"I missed my red mustang."

"I'm sure you do. I hope your driving is a little tamer."

"Get in and I'll take you for a spin. You be the judge."

Jewel was on a whirlwind with Brad and she didn't take time to analyze just what it was she was feeling seeing him again, but she liked it.

Brad managed to extend his time in Connecticut. He requested some vacation time that he had due and they granted it. While Brad was working they spent every afternoon going to dinner and just driving around and seeing the sights.

When Brad requested days off, Jewel took a couple of days off as well, and they toured as much of Connecticut as possible. It felt good being with Brad and they knew the day would come when Brad had to leave, but neither one of them wanted to talk about their expectations beyond that point.

Brad and Jewel spent an afternoon on the Pier downtown from where Jewel worked, watching the sun go down. Brad stood behind her with his arms around her waist and Jewel wished the evening would never end.

"I don't know about you," Brad said, "but I think I'm starving and the smell of fishes has given me a taste for fish."

"Only you would smell fish and want to eat it, but you're saved. I know of a great seafood restaurant around here."

"Then what are we waiting on?" Brad said, as they left the Pier hand in hand and walked to the restaurant, which was right around the corner.

It never occurred to Jewel that she was doing with Brad the very thing she and Tyler use to do. She and Tyler would sit for hours on the

Pier on Saturday afternoons waiting for the sun to set and then they would walk around the corner to the restaurant, which was Tyler's favorite seafood restaurant. She wanted to show Brad a good time, but she didn't know much about Connecticut herself, except the places where Tyler had taken her.

They sat in the restaurant under low light at a table for two. They were leaning over the table laughing up close, at the stories they shared with a glass of wine in one hand and hands slightly touching across the table, as someone interrupted.

"Hi," the man said as both Jewel and Brad looked up.

Tyler was standing over them and Jewel's heart felt like it escaped her chest.

She almost dropped her wine glass, as Brad caught it, and asked, "You okay?"

Jewel shook her head trying to regain her posture, "yes, I'm fine. I'm sorry. I didn't waste any on you did I?" She asked Brad.

"No," Brad said helping her to wipe up the spilled wine, as Tyler stood waiting to be acknowledged.

Jewel was hoping he would go away, but he didn't, so she looked back up at him and said, "Hi Tyler. What are you doing here?"

Tyler was more hurt than annoyed, as he answered, "I always eat here. The question is what are you doing here?"

Jewel suddenly wondered the same thing. How could she have forgotten this was Tyler's favorite place to eat, or did she sub-conscientiously come there, because it was?

"I…, we were in the neighborhood and got hungry and I remembered this restaurant around the corner."

Unbelievable, Tyler thought, she remembered. How could she forget as often as he brought her here?

"I'm Brad Connors," Brad said standing up to shake Tyler's hand since it seemed that Jewel was taking her time at introducing them.

"Oh, I'm sorry. Brad this is Tyler."

"Tyler Gustav," Tyler finished the introduction of his entire name wondering if it would ring a bell with Brad, the way Brad's name did with him.

Jewel had told him all about her relationship with Brad, but unawares to Tyler, she hadn't told Brad anything about him. He was going to say he had heard all about him, but since Brad didn't say it first, he didn't.

"Have y'all had dinner yet?" Tyler asked, "because I just walked in and I don't have a table yet. Do you mind if I joined you?"

Jewel looked at Tyler with her eyes quenched. She couldn't believe he was asking to sit at a table for two, especially when he knew who Brad was.

"This table is sort of small," Brad laughed uneasily, looking for Jewel to object, but she was somewhat in a daze.

"That's not a problem," Tyler said, as he turned looking for a waiter, "can you find us another table? We would like to sit together," then he turned back to Jewel and Brad remembering that they did not agreed to anything yet, "I'm sorry, how presumptuous of me, I mean of course, if that's alright with the two of you," he said looking at both Brad and Jewel.

Jewel came out of her daze and was steaming under her breath and at a lost for what to do or say. She should've just said no, but she didn't.

"I guess it's okay with me, if it's okay with you Brad?" Jewel asked, hoping Brad would say no.

"Well I guess I've had you to myself long enough. It'll be nice to have dinner with someone you, work with?" Brad said, as he looked at Jewel for an explanation.

"I don't work with Jewel," Tyler corrected.

"I see," but he didn't.

He couldn't understand why Tyler was insisting on having dinner with them, when he obviously knew he had walked up on them having an intimate moment and preparing for an intimate dinner.

The waiter came back and said, "I have found you a table, right this way please."

Jewel took another deep breath. She was so irritated with Tyler that she was near tears. What did he think he was doing and why was he doing it, to embarrass her? This just seemed so out of character for Tyler.

They were seated at a round table with Jewel in the middle. Tyler asked Brad what was he doing in Connecticut. How long he was staying and Brad obliged him with answers. Tyler really didn't want to play like he didn't know anything about Brad, so he only asked questions he knew he didn't have the answers to, but he still didn't let on that he knew about Brad. Brad obliged Tyler with much more than answers to his questions. He told Tyler how he came to run into Jewel in Connecticut and the great time they were having together.

Brad sense there was much more between Tyler and Jewel than either one was going to tell him. He wondered if Tyler thought he was stupid or something. No one interrupts an intimate meal between two people without having an ultimate motive, so Brad decided to call them both on it.

"Tyler I have to tell you. I know Jewel don't believe in destiny and all that, but I know it's nothing short of God's will that we've met like this again. You know, I almost asked Jewel to marry me once." Brad cupped Jewel's chin in his hand and raised Jewel's face to look at him, "I don't think I've ever stop loving this woman and I'm hoping this isn't two old friends just running into each other and catching up, because it's much more for me, much more," he said, staring into Jewel's eye.

"So, is it Jewel? Is it much more for you as well?" Tyler asked Jewel, who, in spite the fact that she thought her heart had escaped her chest earlier, heard it beating even louder now.

"I think Brad deserves to know, don't you?"

"Well actually, I have a couple more days. I guess I can wait and let her think it over."

"How noble of you, but you see Brad," Tyler said, placing his hand on Jewel's shoulder and turning her to face him, "I've waited long enough for an answer, and I'd rather hear her answer now."

Tyler didn't realize he was squeezing Jewel's shoulder.

"Tyler," Jewel said, trying to move Tyler's hand from her shoulder, "you're hurting me."

"That was never my intention Jewel," he said staring in her eye.

"I'm not sure how long you two want to continue to play this game, but I would think that one of you would have the decency to let me in on what's going on here." Brad said, having about enough of Tyler's questions and Jewel's solitude.

"You're right Brad. The game is over, and I think I'd better go."

Tyler got up and took some money out of his wallet and threw it on the table.

"I apologize for intruding on your intimate reunion. It was rude of me to do so. Dinner on me," he paused, almost turning to leave and then he turned to Jewel and said, "Goodbye," and it was so final Jewel didn't dare look up, because her eyes were filled with tears.

As Tyler walked away, Jewel finally got up and called, "Tyler!" but he was gone.

She stood staring at the door, until Brad pulled her back down to her chair.

"Why didn't you tell me about Tyler? I got the feeling he knows about me." Brad said hoping Jewel would come clean.

"He does," Jewel felt the need for a confession.

"You love him?"

"Yes," Jewel said, covering her eyes with her hand as they became teary, "but it's over between us. It's been over for a long time now."

"Is it Jewel? Is it over?" Brad asked placing his hands on the top of Jewel's trying to comfort her.

Brad made reservations to leave the next day and stopped by to see Jewel before he left. "It's been really nice being with you," He said to her.

"I had a great time too."

"But I showed up too late, didn't I?"

"If it wasn't for Tyler, Brad, you could have showed up in Connecticut at anytime and not find me. I moved to Connecticut because he was here."

"I see, so what now?"

"I don't know."

"You think there's any chance for the two of you?"

"I don't know," Jewel said honestly, "I didn't set out to hurt him, but I did. I just don't know what to think anymore. I mean, I thought it was over between us, then he showed up."

"Yeah Jewel, he showed up at a restaurant that he always goes to eat. Was the sunset yours too?"

Jewel held her head down. "The sunset the other night was ours Brad, but I guess I do have some unfinished business with Tyler."

"Let me know how it works out, but don't invite me to the wedding," Brad said as he leaned over to kiss Jewel on her forehead.

"Daddy it's the doorbell?" Brianna said, as she sat on the couch watching television. Tyler came out of the kitchen, wiping his hand in the kitchen towel and went over to the TV to turn it down.

"You can't open the door. Is something wrong with your hearing as well?" Brianna just rolled her eyes at her dad.

It was a silly question and she wasn't going to answer it. Tyler walked over to her and messed in her hair, as the doorbell rang again.

"Dad, just get the door okay."

"Okay," he said, opening the door without asking who it was.

Jewel stood at the door with two-dozen bouquets of white roses. Tyler stood staring at her.

"May I come in?" She asked.

Tyler stepped aside and Jewel walked in. Brianna didn't want to open the door, but she was kneeled on the couch watching.

"Hi Brianna," Jewel said.

"Hi," she said and turned and continued to watch TV, "I hope you haven't come here to hurt my daddy again?"

Jewel didn't know what to say. She didn't know how much Tyler shared with her. She felt awkward standing there, not sure if to ask to sit, or just stand.

"Here, these are for you," she said giving Tyler the flowers.

"Brianna, find a vase for these please and go watch TV in your room," Tyler said.

"Oh man, the TV in my room is too small," she complained.

"The TV in your room is not too small. Please do this for me without giving me any flack. This won't take long."

Jewel heart sank when Tyler said it wouldn't take long. Was he just going to tell her it was over and ask her to leave? Jewel began to feel like this was a really bad idea. She should've called like Tessa said to do, but instead she listened to Lois and decided to do the 'take him by surprise' thing, like Lois knew anything about men.

"All right, but you'll owe me," Brianna said, taking the flowers and going to her room.

Tyler caught her as she was passing and hit her on her backside with the towel.

"Oouch!" she yelled, "that hurts."

"I intended it to hurt, and it'll hurt even more, if you continue talking to me that way young lady."

"Sorry," she said with a frown on her face.

"You want to sit?" Tyler asked Jewel.

"Yes, thank you." Jewel looked around, "Brianna is growing."

"I guess she is. You haven't seen her in awhile."

"Is she mad with me?" Jewel asked.

"I'm not sure."

"What did you tell her?"

"That we weren't going to get marry," Tyler got annoyed at Jewel's questions and came right out and ask, "why are you here Jewel? Are you apologizing for taking your old boyfriend to our favorite restaurant, or maybe you're apologizing for taking him to our favorite spot on the Pier, or did you come to apologize for wanting to go back to Atlanta with him?"

"I'm apologizing Tyler. I didn't do anything intentionally to hurt you, but I'm definitely guilty of being insensitive, but so were you. I mean, inviting yourself to have dinner with us. Don't you think that was sort of cruel?"

"You came all this way to tell me I was cruel for what I did."

Tyler got up picked up the phone and listened for the dial tone and extended the phone, so that Jewel could hear it too.

"The phone works, or did you lose the number. Well whatever it is. Thank you for letting me know how cruel I was. I appreciate that. You never can get enough criticism you know," he said walking to the door and opening the door, "I guess I'll see you around, when I show up in your life and do something else cruel. If I were you, I wouldn't invite me to your wedding. I just might show up and do something cruel, now if you're finished," he said bowing with his hand curved to the door showing Jewel the way out.

Jewel was becoming increasingly upset with Tyler's attitude. She got up and walked to the door. If he wanted it this way then fine, just let it be over with, but when she got to the door, Tyler had straightened up and was looking at her and before she knew it, she was pouring her heart out.

"I came to tell you I love you Tyler, and I don't want it to be over. I wanted to know if there was some way we could work things out," she was talking loudly as tears ran down her face.

"I know I'm not the easiest person to get along with, and I know you don't like some of my courtroom tactics. I don't know how much I can change, but I want to do whatever it takes for us to be together. I'm sorry about Brad. I don't know what happened. I felt so alone without you. I don't have any friends here. Brad showed up when I really needed a friend, and I guess I just confused that with old feelings. I don't know what else to say, except I'm sorry," she finished with a deep breath.

"So why didn't you say that when you first came in," Tyler said, taking her in his arms and kissing her.

"May I come back out now?" Brianna asked after watching the entire door scene.

"No you may not," Tyler said, "and if I thought you were at that door listening to our conversation, you're going to be in big trouble missy."

"It wasn't my fault. I heard yelling and came to see if everything was alright."

"No one was yelling," Tyler said, smiling at Jewel and talking to Brianna with his back to her.

"But I thought," Brianna continued.

"Brianna," Tyler said in an "I'm warning you" tone.

"Okay, Okay." Brianna said, as she closed the door and went back into her room.

Tyler wiped Jewel's face with his shirt.

"I'm sorry too. I acted like a jerk. I don't want you to change for me." Tyler said as he wrapped his arm around Jewel again, "Are you hungry?" He asked.

"Yes, I am." She said sniffing up her runny nose, while taking the tip of her finger to wipe the tear from her eye.

"Great. I was just cooking. You can come help, or just watch, or just talk so I can know that you're really here."

"Brianna! Brianna! Or now she doesn't hear. That child of mind," Tyler said.

"Yes daddy dear," she finally came out of the room.

"The TV and the living room are all yours. Jewel is staying for dinner, so we're going into the kitchen to finish cooking."

"Are you two going to get marry or not?" Brianna asked.

"Are we?" Tyler asked Jewel.

"Yes we are," Jewel responded loud enough so that Brianna could hear.

"Yes!" they heard Brianna said as they walked into the kitchen smiling at each other.

Jewel took her ring out of her purse and placed it back on her finger, "you think we can set a date for this wedding tonight?" she asked Tyler.

"Oh, I think that can be arranged," he responded pulling Jewel tightly to him and embraced her as he kissed her again.

Chapter Thirty-One
Lois

Even though Lois was please with the decision she made to go back to New York, so that she and Deb could go to that business school, she was glad to be back home.

They finished top of their class and the school offered her a job right away. The office administrator for the school fell on some ice and sprained her ankle. The school's Dean asked her to fill in while she was out. She didn't take the job, but Deb did and it wasn't long after, they found Deb a job working in the Mayor's office. Deb was excited. They were paying her three times more than she was currently making at the factory and because it was a city job, it had excellent benefit.

She found a job as an administrative assistance to one of the CEO of a big corporation. They were looking for someone with good typing skill. She had no office experience, but the fact that she could type sixty-five words per minute was very impressive and just being fresh out of school didn't hurt either. It wasn't paying as much as Deb's job, but then Brickenbrat wasn't New York.

For the short time that Matt stayed in New York, he created a bond with Danijel and when he left, he promised to call Danijel at least once a week and he kept his promise. He also kept the promise he made with Lois concerning child support. Lois was grateful for the help.

She didn't get to see all the girls from the agency before she left, but she did get to see Kelly again. Kelly came to visit them one weekend, while visiting her family in the Bronx. Lois tried to convince her to get out of the agency and do something on her own.

Kelly had given up on her dreams. She seemed sad and wanted the peace that Lois had found, but was sure she never would. She said the agency wasn't talking about sending her to California, as much anymore. She didn't think the plan to expand was going to happen, but she didn't think she could run an agency that was really built on a lie. They really never intended to help any of the girls pursue a modeling career. It was all just a lie. She also found out how much kickback the agency was getting for the sexual favors the girls perform with their client, even though they adamantly claimed a strict policy against it.

Kelly also found out that the girls they boasted became models through the agency were also a lie. They simply got smart, quit the agency and pursued their own modeling careers.

In a couple of month, Jewel would be coming home to have her wedding. Lois was excited to be reunited with Jewel, even if it was only over the phone. Lois was going to be Jewel's maid of honor. Lois was pleasantly surprise when she asked, especially since they hadn't kept in touch for all those years, but once they started talking again, it seemed like they picked up where they left off.

Jewel was going all out for her wedding. Lois had to fight resentment, at times, when she thought of Jewel's success. It seemed that all of Jewels dreams had come true. She had become a successful lawyer and was marrying a wonderful man, who loved and adored her and she managed to keep herself a virgin for her wedding night.

Lois thought of the times they shared concerning their dreams. She felt her only success was Danijel and being born-again. Her life couldn't compare to Jewel's materially, but spiritually, she felt she had more. She hoped the material would come one day, if not for her, then for her son.

"I don't know why you and Dandan couldn't continue to stay with us?" Stephanie asked Lois, as she helped her move into her new home. "Our home is big enough," she said brushing away dust from a windowsill.

"Mom, I have a good job now. I thank you and Richard for all that you've done for us, but this is what I want. I don't want to be dependent on you and Richard forever."

"It won't be forever, just until you save up enough money to buy your own home."

"That will happen one day Mother, but for now this will do."

"Is this neighborhood safe?" Stephanie asked wiping the windows with a cloth to see out of it better.

"This neighborhood isn't any worst than the one we grew up in," Lois pointed out.

"Why do you think we worked so hard to get out of it?"

"We're going to be fine Mom." The phone rang and Danijel came running to answer it.

Lois and Stephanie watched him. He talked for a few minutes, then he said goodbye and hung up.

"Daddy said hi," he said and off he went back into his room.

Lois went back to cleaning as her mother looked on, "I hope to get to meet his father someday." Lois made no comment, "How did he get your new number, so quickly?"

Lois stopped cleaning and looked at her mother, with one hand on her hip, "What exactly do you want to know mother?"

"I was just asking how he got your new number so soon. I didn't realize you were talking that frequently with him, that's all."

"I don't talk to him at all mother, unless it has something to do with Danijel. He calls Danijel almost weekly and Danijel gave him our new number, so he would know where to reach him."

"I'm glad he wants to be a part of Danijel's life. That's good for him."

"Good for who? Danijel or Matt?"

"Well Dandan of course, since I don't know Matt. It's hard for me to say what would be good for him." Stephanie commented trying to match her daughter's sarcasm.

They both smile at each other. Lois looked at her mother. It was good to be able to talk to her mother about this. They were becoming friends and Lois liked it.

"Mom, I'm sure one day you will get to meet Matt, but if you're fishing around to see what the story is with me and Matt. Here it is. Matt wants to be a part of Danijel's life. We've agreed on an amount for child support that he'll be sending for Danijel. He's doing really great and he wants to send Danijel to a private school. Danijel will spend part of the summer with him, and every other holiday, if I can stand to let him go. As for me and Matt there is nothing, matter of fact, he's getting married soon to his daughter's mother and I wish them all the best."

"I see," Stephanie said, "are you sorry it didn't work out for the two of you?"

"I thought Matt was the love of my life, so I would be lying if I said I wasn't. I don't know why things work out the way they did, but I have to move on. All that matters to me now is Danijel, and I'm glad Matt got it together to be a part of his life. I'm not going to be stuck in the past."

"Well there are certainly enough single men at the church. I'm sure…"

"I'm sure that when the time is right God will put someone in my life, until then Mother, I'm not going to let it be my number one goal."

"I was just saying."

"I know, and I want you to understand where I'm coming from on this."

Stephanie threw her hands up, "okay, you've made your point and you're right. God will place someone in your life, when you're ready."

"Did Mrs. Stone call you?" Stephanie asked.

"She's always calling," Lois said laughing, "I hope she's calling Jewel as much as she's calling me. I think she's losing it."

"It's not everyday that one of your daughters get marry."

"I guess, but she calls all the time. She calls me when she can't reach Jewel, which is most of the time. Jewel always seems to be working, she says."

"She's a busy lawyer, so I heard."

"Yes she is, and from what I understand a good one. Do you wish that my life had turned out like Jewels,' mom?"

Stephanie walked over to her daughter and placed her hand on her shoulder, "sweetheart, no mother wants her daughter to go through what you went through. I'm just grateful that all of that is in the past now. I am blessed to have you as my daughter. You're smart, beautiful and a good mother. I couldn't be more proud of you and pastor Fischer is so pleased with the work that you're doing with the young people at the church."

"I don't do much." Lois said modestly.

"The time you take with them is worth a whole lot. You share your story with them. They can relate to you. Pastor Fischer is thinking about making you one of our youth pastors."

"Pastor! Are you kidding me Mom? I hope you are. I don't want to be no one's pastor. I just want to share with them what I went through and hope it will spare, if just one of them, from going the wrong way and making wrong choices."

"I wasn't supposed to say anything. Pastor Fischer said it would take time, and only when you believe it's what God is calling you to do, and he won't approach you about it until then."

Lois took the back of her hand and wiped her forehead, as she pretended she was pouring sweat, "thank God for the wisdom of the pastor, because I'm definitely not ready for anything like that."

They went back to cleaning.

"I can't wait to see Jewel though. I don't know. It's weird, but I've really missed her."

"She was always a good friend to you. She never criticized, or stuck her nose up at you. I've always liked Jewel."

"Yeah, she was good like that, even now, after she's made it big and has heard what I've been through, she still wants me to be her maid of honor."

"You talked to her about what you went through?"

"Yeah, I did. I wasn't sure for a while if I wanted to, or not, but I knew when she came home, people were bound to talk to her about me, especially our old friends from the church, so I wanted her to hear it from me. When I started to share it with her, it was as comfortable talking to her, as it was when we were in high school."

"I'm glad you have someone like that to talk to. It's important you know, to have good friends."

"Yeah, me too," Lois said, then added, "but I'm more glad that I have you to talk to."

They smiled a warm smile at each other, as they went in separate rooms to do some more cleaning. Neither one thought they would ever see the day that they would be able to communicate openly with each other.

Well, almost openly Lois thought, after all, she's still my mother.

Chapter Thirty-Two
The Heavenlies

As the scene on earth unfolded and came to a conclusion before the loving eyes of the Father and the Son, Lucifer feared he would not have a case after all his blundering attempts. He hoped the Almighty would not be able to see through his ultimate goal.

The Almighty thunderous voice sent shock waves through the heavenlies as he spoke, "and why O' Lucifer, do you stand before me today? It seemed that you have had your chances and have been defeated. What is your cause?"

The Son stood up making Lucifer trembled as he spoke, he bowed before the Almighty and said, "well Almighty, this church has set forth an all out attack against my kingdom, and I should only have the right to defend myself."

"Rights!" The son interjected furiously, at the audacity of Lucifer to think he had any rights in the presence of The Almighty, "I think you have mistaken your position O' Lucifer, for you have no rights. The only rights you have are what my Father gives you, and you have proven a very weak case before us this day."

The Son looked towards the Father and said, "I adjure you Father to kick this fallen angel out of your domain once and for all."

The Father eyed the Son with respect and pride knowing all to well that it was the Son's job to intercede earnestly for the souls that he gave his life for.

"What is your ultimate goal here Lucifer, and don't bother to stand before me and utter your lies, because I can see right through your wicked black heart."

Lucifer began to fear that he would soon be kicked out of the Kingdom, so he decided his only choice was the truth.

"This church," he pointed his wicked finger toward earth, as the scene before them had been suspended for their viewing only, "this church has declared war on my kingdom, and it is only because they have not had to endure any pain or lost. I want one last chance to discredit this church. I don't think their hearts are pure towards you. It is all a pretense to be noted in the community."

The Son stooped to Lucifer's level and eyed him, "Do not speak of man's heart, because you do not know the hearts of men. Only the Father has such power, and to whom he gives it and you he has given no such power!"

Lucifer dared not think of what he wanted to do with the Son at that moment, knowing that all his attempts of destroying and discrediting the Son had failed. If he gave in to his thoughts of evil towards the Son, The Almighty would dismiss him without another word; he knew he had to stay focus on why he was there.

"Forgive me Almighty, but your Son is correct. You have not given me such power, but you usually allow me the privilege to come up against whoever comes up against me."

"And how does these two," The Father turned to the suspended scene on earth as he looked at Jewel and Lois, "fit into your plan. You have failed in your past attempts, why should I give you another chance."

"Oh great One," Lucifer pleaded, "because you are a fair God. You have pre ordained all things to be. I have fairly won authority over the earth realm and it is my right, at your prerogative, to defend my domain."

The Father stood up and motioned to the Son to stand by his side. It was clear that he had made a decision.

"I will allow you to defend your territory."

"Almighty, please I ask one last thing." Lucifer said.

"And what is it?" The Father thundered, tiring of Lucifer's whimpering and pleading.

"That I be allowed to loose the death angels."

All heaven stood still, as The Son moved once again to intercede.

"He has proven no cause for such an action upon this body of believers and I plead with you Father not to suffer this to be so."

The Father eyed the Son lovingly, but He knew He had to allow Lucifer this last attempt. He was expecting Lucifer to ask it. It was the only thing he hadn't been allowed to do yet, and he knew he wouldn't be successful in any more attempts, without the death angels. It would be futile to try anything else.

"You may release the death angels." The Father said at the Son's dismay.

"Then we should be allowed to release the warring angels. This church has proven that they deserve this defense," The Son pleaded.

"Then let it be so," The Almighty uttered.

At the sound of the warring angels preparing for battle, Lucifer almost wanted to rescind his request, but he was stupid enough to try once again to defeat God's warring angels. He quickly made his exit through the clouds of smoke gathering in the throne room.

Lucifer:

Lucifer felt a false sense of victory, as he usually does. He was at the meeting place standing proudly, with death angels standing post around him.

As the other demons arrived, they knew things had stepped up a notch. The atmosphere was solemn and stanch of the smell of sulfur, mildew and the smell of a swampy pond.

Lucifer stood grinning from ear to ear, "It is time to move in for the kill," he said with a robustious laugh. "We have been given the opportunity to bring this church down to our level! Tonight we come up with a strategy!"

He turned to the death angels and said, "Death. Soon this church will feel your sting!"

As he said it, one of the death angel came forward blowing fire from his nostrils.

"Are we going to burn them Satan?" One of the demons dared to ask.

Another demon jumped forward excitedly, "what do we do? What do we do?"

"Shut up!" Lucifer yelled, "you have all failed in your sorry attempts to discredit and destroy this church, now we call on the experts. They will know what to do and they will instruct each one of you, as to your role."

"But what about them?" one little imp came close and whispered, pointing outside to giant figures standing around the building of the church basement, where they were holding their meeting.

"What about them?" Lucifer snarled, as the little imp coward away.

"Well, your great Lucifer, they have doubled in number," another demon pointed out.

"And so have we!" Lucifer shouted, "We will not be defeated by them! Their power is only as strong as the prayers of the Christians!"

"So how do we get them to stop praying?" Another demon asked.

"We don't get them to stop. We let them continue to pray, but we make their prayers ineffective?" One of the death angels answered.

"How do we do that?" The little imp asked.

"We use what we got," Lucifer smiled, "Strife! Bitterness! Jealousy! Hatred! Contention! Disunity! Come forward!" Lucifer called out to his spirits, "you will go forward and whisper and whisper AND YELL IT, IF YOU HAVE TO! But I want you to make sure that you make your presence known in the ears of those so called prayer warriors."

"How?" Bitterness asked.

"Bring things back to their memory. Flood their memories with past hurt, past failure, manipulate friends, lovers, mothers, brothers, sisters, cousins; I don't care who, just use them as needed!" Lucifer instructed, "but you'd better remember that if you don't do your jobs, you may be the one that ends up in the hands of these guys!" Lucifer said with clenched teeth, looking towards the death angels. "Now fall in line for your assignments! The death angels have been busy surveying the congregation and they will be giving each one of you a Christian from the church. If you fail in your assignment, you want have to worry about those guys out there," he looked up at the window where a Warring angel was looking in, then turned back to his followers and yelled, "BECAUSE I WILL DESTROY YOU MYSELF!" He said blowing out fire from his nostrils, scorching one helpless little imp scurrying to get out of the way.

Some of the other demons ran over to help put him out. He got up burned to a crisp, but limply walked away holding his scorched off hand in the other.

"Let's go!" Yelled the death angels as the demons received their assignment and dissipated away.

Chapter Thirty-Three
Jewel and Lois

"Mother I just got here. Please let me get some rest. I promise, one hour and I'll be at your command" Jewel pleaded.

Ever since Stephanie picked her up from the airport, she had non-stop questions. The wedding was two weeks away and her mother acted like it was tomorrow. She was there in plenty enough time to take care of last minute details. All she wanted now was a little rest. She had been buried at work with cases, right up to an hour before her flight. Tyler would arrive the early part of the following week with Brianna.

She took four weeks off from her job. They had no problem with her taking some time off to get married. She had certainly deserved the time. She hadn't taken any real time off since she started working there, except for a couple of days here and there.

She and Tyler were headed straight to Hawaii for a week the day after the wedding and then she would have a week to get settled into their new home.

"Mother you know this is why Tyler and I hired a wedding planner, so you wouldn't have to be so stressed out."

"A wedding planner. If it wasn't for me...," Theresa began, but Jewel cut her off.

"If it wasn't for you, I wouldn't have to be called every other day," Jewel said smilingly, as she kissed her mother lovingly on her cheek, "but I love you anyway."

"Wasn't it you that said I shouldn't stress out over planning your brother and Saida's wedding, because that was Saida's mother job, and that I should wait until you and Tessa got married? Well, you're getting married and I was not going to be left out of the planning because you hired a wedding planner."

"Okay Mom, you have certainly made that clear, but still, can I just get a little rest," Jewel said holding up her thumb and index finger to show the sign of a pinch.

"I'm sorry dear, you must be tired. Why don't you go ahead and do that. I have to call Tessa anyway."

"When is she getting here anyway?" Jewel asked.

"She said Friday, but you know your sister. Let's hope she made plans to get here at least by the rehearsal."

"So Jewel is getting married." Jarod stated.

"Yes, she is." Lois replied.

"So, who's left? Jarod asked.

"Actually, just you and me, if you count Ashley out, since she's currently divorced again."

"Well she had her chances."

"Jarod!" Lois pretended to be shock, "that's not a nice thing to say."

"Maybe not, but it's the truth and you know it."

Lois laughed. Ever since she ran into Jarod at the movie theatre one weekend, he had been calling her. She finally decided to go out with him.

Jarod was chief operations officer of the company he worked for.

"I make sure everything runs smoothly, so that the profits keeps coming in," he said to Lois, explaining his job duty.

He was also their "go to" computer guy. He was very computer literate. He often talked about starting his own computer business one day. He just wasn't sure which approach he wanted to take with it.

Lois welcomed his friendship and he got along well with Danijel. He even took Danijel out a few times to the movie, the park, or McDonalds to give her some time to herself. Matt wasn't pleased with hearing Danijel talk about all the things he did with Jarod, but he was glad there was a man in his life. He sometimes talked to Lois, after talking to Danijel to see where the relationship was heading. He told her he didn't think she should introduce Danijel to guys she was not serious about, because when they left, it meant they left Danijel as well.

Lois was annoyed at his suggestions and said she was not going to stop her life, because he didn't think she should date anyone except potential husbands.

"Do you want to go come over on Thursday? Lois asked, Jewel is coming by."

"I don't think so. You ladies probably have a lot to catch up on."

"Actually we've done all of our catching up over the phone."

"Then you'll talk about the wedding."

"Probably, but there's not a lot more to talk about."

"I still think you girls need some time alone. You haven't seen each other since right after graduation."

"I guess you're right."

"You know what I was thinking?" Jarod said in a seductive tone.

"What?" Lois asked, looking at Jarod sideways with her slanted eyes.

"Since we're the only two in the group that hasn't gotten married yet, maybe we should just marry each other."

"Don't Jarod. I've had some really hurtful experiences with men, and I'm just not looking to get into a serious relationship right now. I just want to raise my son and be a good mother."

Lois and Jarod had this conversation before and Lois knew that before she and Jarod moved forward in their relationship, she would have to tell him everything that happen to her in New York and she was not ready to do that, nor did she thought he could handle it.

"I can wait. Maybe nothing will ever happen between us, but I have to know that, maybe this is our destiny. Maybe everything you've gone through has brought you back to Brickenbrat to pick up where we left off, maybe it's supposed to be me and you forever."

"Destiny. The last I heard that was…," Lois pause to remember where she heard that phrase. She laughed, "actually the last time I can remember anyone talking about our destiny was Pastor Fischer the Sunday before I left for New York. Wow, how ironic is that?"

"Nothing's ironic about destiny Lois. It just is."

"I guess, if you believe that. I don't know that I do. I'll have to do a bible study on that one day."

"Well you do that. In the meantime, I'll wait on you," Jarod said looking at his watch and getting up.

"You leaving?" Lois asked disappointedly.

Yeah, I got to research some things on the Internet for an early meeting in the morning. Tell Dandan I'm sorry I missed him, but I'll catch him this weekend."

"Okay." Lois said getting up to walk Jarod to the door. "Thanks again."

"Hey maybe we all can get together on Friday or Saturday afternoon. If Jewel is not too busy with her wedding things," Jarod suggested.

"That sounds like a good idea. I'll ask her."

"And I'll get in contact with Ashley and Brian."

"Great'"

"Let's talk again, say Wednesday to see if anyone wants to. We'll meet at the Mall."

"Don't you think we're too old to hang out at the mall?" Lois asked.

"Speak for yourself. We'll meet at Fridays restaurant in the mall."

"Sounds good."

"Hi!" Jewel screamed as she came running up the steps of Lois' house.

"Hi!" Lois said in return, as she ran up to Jewel and gave her a hug, as they jumped up and down holding each other like they were eighteen again.

Lois was patiently looking out of the window for her to arrive. She gave Jewel good directions, but she wanted to make sure she didn't pass her house, while looking for the numbers on the houses.

"Come on in," Lois said welcoming Jewel into her home. "It's not much, but it's my abode."

"Oh, don't be silly, Lois. It's quite quaint."

"Small and old is the word you're looking for," Lois smiled, "but it'll do for now. We're content here."

Jewel looked around, "where is he. I can't wait to meet Dandan," She said, using his pet name.

"Danijel!" Lois yelled, "We have company. Come out and meet her."

Danijel came running out of his room and stopped in front of Lois and Jewel and began to stare up and down at Jewel."

"Dandan, this is a very good friend of mine. Her name is Jewel."

"Hi Dandan," Jewel said holding out her hand to shake Danijel's hand not sure what to do when introduced to a six year old.

Danijel took her hand and said, "nice to meet you Miss Julie."

"Jewel sweet heart," Lois tried to correct Danijel's pronunciation of Jewel's name. "He never seemed to get people's name correct the first time."

"Jewel." Danijel said.

"That's it," Lois said pleasingly as she looked to Jewel, "believe me that's a first."

Jewel had a nice visit with Lois and Danijel. Danijel had become quite a talker and Jewel loved hearing his animated voice, but his long thick eyelashes couldn't keep his big round eyes open much longer, as he yawned his way through a story about something that happened at his school.

"I think that's it for you," Lois said getting up and taking him by the arm.

"Can't I stay up and visit with Jewel some more Mommy?" he asked between yawns.

"Not tonight sweetie, maybe another time. She'll be here for a while. We'll see if we can't get her to come back for another visit before she leaves."

"Can you, please." Danijel pleaded.

"I think I'll have time to do that," Jewel said, pulling Danijel back to her for a big bedtime hug. He complied and off he went to bed.

"That's my son," Lois said, after she came back from tucking Danijel into bed, "can I get you another soda."

"Oh no, thank you. I'm good. I try not to drink too much of this stuff."

"I know. I only buy it to have something to offer people to drink, when they come over and Maggie drinks much too much of it."

"Danijel is such a sweetheart Lois. You are doing a great job with him."

"God I hope so. How about you and Brianna?"

"Brianna can be an angel, but she has a quick tongue. I think she gets it from her mother, but other than that we get along very well. She may stay with us after we're married."

"Oh, why is that?"

"I'm not sure why. I think it's because Tyler is getting married and she isn't, or it's because she wants to focus more on school. She's going back to medical school."

"How do you feel about that?"

"I don't have a problem with it. I just hope everyone understands that I'm not going to take the place of Brianna's mother. When I'm ready to be a mother, I'll have a baby. I still have a lot I want to accomplish as far as my career is concern."

"You've already made partner in your firm."

"Junior partner, but enough about me. What's going on with you and Jarod?" Jewel asked.

"We're just friend, and speaking of which, he suggested that we all get together on Friday."

"Who's we?"

"You, me, him, Ashley and Brian."

"Will Brian's wife let him out of her sight?"

"She may."

"It sounds like a great idea. I'm in, if I can get away from my mother."

"I feel for you."

"You don't know the half," Jewel looked hopelessly at Lois.

Jewel and Lois talked until midnight, "I'd better get out of here. You have to work tomorrow." Jewel acknowledged.

"I wish I could take some time off from work and visit with you some more," Lois said.

"Why don't you?"

"I've already requested a day off in preparation for the shower. I'd better not push it. I don't have as much clout on my job as you do on yours."

"Okay, but let me know about Friday. I'm definitely interested in getting together with those guys and Friday is a good day. I don't think I'll be able to do it next week."

Everyone was seated after standing to greet Jewel and Lois. They talked and laughed about Ashley's two-failed marriages and Brian's possessive and jealous wife. They all had drinks, except Lois and Jarod.

"I can't believe you two," Ashley said, "are you two the goody two shoes or what?"

"Oh what," Lois said. Lois made it her business not to socialize with Ashley since she came back. They saw each other at church, but Ashley was just a church attendee. She asked Lois out several times, but Lois' constant refusal discouraged her from asking again.

Lois was getting worried that Jewel was on her second drink. She wasn't aware that Jewel drank. She rode to the restaurant with Jewel, but she felt comfortable that if Jewel drank too much, she would let her drive them home. Jarod would either take Ashley and Brian home or call a cab for them. Once she assessed the situation, she was comfortable to sit back and enjoy the rest of the evening.

"So is the next wedding going to be Jarod and Lois?" Lois blushed at Brian's bluntness

"Oh come on Lois. There is no need to try to act like you two don't see each other." Ashley said.

"What about you?" Jewel asked Ashley, coming to Lois' rescue.

She knew Ashley and Lois never got along, now she knew why. Ashley was too pretentious. Lois only put up with Ashley because of Jewel, but Lois seemed to be keeping her composure better than she use to.

"I'm done with marriage." Ashley said.

"Oh come on. You're too young for that. I don't believe that for one moment." Jewel said.

"Believe what you want." Ashley said matter of fact. "So what's your fiancé like? Lois makes him out to be some prince in shining armor."

"That's because he is." Jewel said with her head tilted up, proud to say so.

"Only good little Jewel would live the fairy tale." Brian said sarcastically.

"It's not a fairy tale Brian if you work hard for it. I've been through some relationships that wasn't made in heaven." Jewel defended herself.

"And tonight it doesn't matter, because we're here tonight to toast and celebrate the bride to be." Jarod said cutting in.

Jarod was sitting quietly back listening to the conversation. He was only introduced to the group, because he went to school with Jewel, who wanted him to meet Lois. He wasn't sure what kind of relationship the four of them had. All he knew was that they went to the same church and went on youth trips together, but tonight he was sensing hostility from Ashley and Brian towards Jewel and Lois. He almost regretted his suggestion for them to get together, but every now and then the conversation would lighten up and they would talk about the things they did when they were younger.

Jarod poured every one some champagne, even a little for him and Lois for the toast to Jewel.

"To Jewel, I wish you all the happiness, if anyone deserves it, you do." Lois said with all sincerity.

"To Jewel, everyone's little princess, who will soon be someone's queen," Brian said.

"The best to you," Ashley said.

"To you Jewel. May God bless your marriage and everything the two of you put your hands to do," Jarod toast.

"Thank you all," Jewel said with tears in her eyes.

"I'll drive you home and maybe Tessa or your dad could drive me home." Lois said.

"Why?" Jewel asked looking puzzled.

"Because you've had too much to drink," Lois stated what she thought was the obvious.

"Don't be silly, besides my dad would have a fit, if I let anyone drove his new Mercedes. He didn't even want me to drive it around."

"I think he would understand" Jarod said as concerned about Jewel's drinking as Lois was.

He had already put Ashley in a cab and Brian called his wife to pick him up. Brian stood waiting for his wife to pick him up at the far end of the mall. He knew she would probably go off on him and he wanted to avoid having his friends hear it.

"I didn't have as much to drink as Brian and Ashley you guys. I'm okay, really. I know my limit, and believe me I didn't reach it." Jewel said.

A sudden down pour of rain began to fall, "Oh darn it!" exclaimed Jewel, "Now my hair will get wet, another thing to worry about. You want to run for it?" She asked Lois.

"I could drive Lois home," Jarod offered, seeing the concern still in Lois' eyes, "and save you the trip Jewel."

"No way am I going to let you take my friend. You get to see her all the time, besides we have to talk some more about that little fiasco in the restaurant," Jewel said, "what was that all about?"

"I don't know. They're your friends, remember." Lois said.

"Oh, they're my friends now, see how you are," they both laughed.

Lois turned to Jarod and said, "It's okay. We'll get home safe. I'll just loose our angels to watch over us."

"Okay, you want me to go get your car, so your hair won't get wet?" Jarod asked Jewel

"Would you? That would be great," she gave Jarod her keys.

When Jarod made a dash for the car Jewel looked at Lois, "how can you not be interested in him? He's your knight in shining armor."

"I know," Lois said, "but I just have to make sure my mind is clear of all the mess. I don't want to hurt him and I sure don't want to get hurt."

A bolt of lightning lit up the skies as the thunder rolled and Jewel jumped behind Lois for shelter, "you still afraid of the lightning girl."

Jewel laughed and came from behind Lois, "Not really just a quick reaction, I guess."

"Liar," Lois said, "are you sure you don't want me to drive?"

"I'm not afraid of the lightning anymore," Jewel tried to sound convincing, "promise," she said smilingly.

Jarod drove the car up to the sidewalk of the restaurant. He had drove by his car and retrieve an umbrella. He got out the car and walked Jewel to the car, then came back for Lois.

"You didn't have to do that," she said, as he stood there soaked.

She leaned over and kissed him on the lips.

Jarod was surprised, "if I knew that was what it would take, I would have gotten soaked in the rain for you sooner."

Lois smiled at him and got into the car, "call me later," she mouthed softly to him, as they left him standing in the rain with his umbrella and a big grin on his face.

"Don't say anything," Lois said to Jewel, seeing her staring at her out of the corner of her eyes.

"I'm not saying a word, but I think you've just given Jarod some hope."

"I hope so," Lois said, not even sure why she was having a change of heart all of the sudden, maybe it was Jewel. Hearing her talk about her wedding, Tyler, and the life they were planning together, made her desire the same thing, and there was nothing wrong with wanting that with Jarod. He was caring and good looking. He had a good job and wanted a home, a family, and his own business and one day he would have all those things. Lois wondered why couldn't he have those things with her and he was saved, that was the biggest plus, maybe it was time to give him a chance. She would tell him how she felt tonight. She could hardly wait to get home. She even felt a little guilty for wishing Jewel had agreed to let him take her home.

"So what was that all about?" Jewel asked Lois, who was off in another place and time.

"What? Jarod. I don't know yet."

"Well I do, but I wasn't talking about Jarod. I meant Ashley and Brian."

"Oh that. You mean years of jealousies finally venting."

"You serious?"

"Of course. You couldn't or didn't want to see it, but they were always jealous of you. I guess that's why Ashley and I never hit it off. I talk to her sometimes now, but she's got a lot of issues, you know?"

"Like what?"

"What do you mean like what, two divorce, no career, to name a few? We just have to keep her in our prayers."

"I don't know if I can pray for someone who has so much hostility towards me."

"You can, if you love them."

"You are really into this church thing aren't you?"

"It's not a church thing Jewel. It's a heart thing. It's what I believe to be the truth."

"Okay, but don't try to sell me on it tonight. I can hardly see through this rain, let alone concentrate on what you're trying to preach to me."

The rain was coming down in a torrential down pour.

"You smell something?" Lois asked Jewel as she began to look down and around her sniffing in the car.

"Yeah, I do, but it can't be coming from my dad's new car."

"Are you suggesting that it's me?" Lois laughed as she held up her arms and began to sniff her underarm and her clothing.

"I don't know what it is," Jewel said as she began to sniff as well.

Jewel suddenly made a turn off the main road.

"Where are you going?"

"I know a short cut."

"But this road is so dark. Maybe you should just pull over for awhile until the rain let up a little."

"I hate doing that, because you know it's probably not raining as hard a mile, or so down the road."

"What's that?" Lois asked putting her face up against the window shield wiping the fog from off her side of the glass, with her hand.

"What did you see?" Jewel asked as she began to finger with the defogger knobs in the car.

"Turn on your defogger. I don't know how you can see anything out of your window. It looks like something might be in the road up ahead."

"I don't see anything and I don't know why this defogger doesn't work. I have it on. Dad's got to take this car back to the dealer and have it look at. Wait. I think I see what you're talking about."

"Slow up Jewel, until we know what it is. Jewel!" L o i s yelled as they approached the object in the road.

"Oh my God!" Jewel screamed as she turned the car quickly to miss what looked like a person lying in the road.

She lost control of the car and both girls began to scream, as the car crashed into a big tree along side the road.

"Oh my God," Lois said looking down at herself. She was not scratched or bruised. She looked at her arms and hands and felt her face. Everything seemed to be in tack, but she seemed to be frozen in her spot. She was not able to move her legs. She looked down at her legs and felt them. They felt fine, but she still couldn't move them and she needed to move them. She needed to get to the car to help Jewel out of the car.

There were others there also, a police car and another car. The police officer and the man were trying to pry the car door open.

"Jewel!" Lois yelled.

They were trying to help Jewel and she wanted to go help them, but she couldn't move. She just couldn't move. It was so frustrating that she couldn't help her friend. It looked like the car was on fire. She heard sirens and she looked around to see a fire truck and an emergency vehicle approaching.

The lights shone towards the car and as Lois looked again, she saw Jewel standing on the opposite side of the road, looking at the car as well. She was screaming, but Lois couldn't hear her. She put up her hands to wave at Jewel wondering, who the rescuers were trying so frantically and desperately to rescue; somehow she had to let them know that there was no one else in the car, before the car caught on fire and someone got hurt. The car was already smoking. It surely would burst into flames any minute.

Suddenly Lois stood even more frozen as the rescue workers pulled someone out of the car. She turned her head to try to see who it was, suddenly there were two men on both sides of her. They were tall men in all white.

Each one took one of her arms and said, "It's time to go Lois."

There voices were like nothing Lois had ever heard. They sounded like they were singing a hymn. It was almost melodic. Lois was suddenly aware that she was not afraid of them, matter of fact, she felt a peace like she had never experienced before and for some strange reason, she wanted to go with them, but she had to try to help Jewel before she go.

"I need to help my friend," she said to both men.

"There's nothing you can do for her now Lois," they both said the same thing and as Lois looked across the road again at Jewel, she saw there were men with Jewel, as well, but Jewel was fighting them.

"No! Let me go!" Jewel screamed at the two men standing in all dark clothing.

Their faces were all but covered with the dark hood they were wearing and when they placed their hands on Jewel their touch felt like fire. They grabbed Jewel by the hand and Jewel began to kick and scream for Lois to help her.

"Help me Lois! Don't let them take me! Please Lois! Don't let them! I'm so afraid! Help me!"

She screamed over and over and she couldn't understand why Lois wouldn't help her, or why the rescuer workers were so busy messing with the car, while she and Lois were being abducted against their will, only Lois wasn't screaming like she was. She just stood there as if everything was all right. Jewel never felt so confused in her life.

The hooded men in black pointed towards the car and said, "look."

Jewel looked towards the car and she recognized herself being pulled out of the car by the rescue workers.

"Oh my God!" she began to scream. "What is happening? Am I dead?"

Both men looked at her and revealed their hideous face to Jewel, "In that life, you are," they snickered, "and God isn't the one you should be calling on now."

They picked Jewel up and turned her around and began to walk away, with Jewel kicking and screaming and calling out for Lois to help her.

As Lois saw the men taking her body out of the car, she realized what was happening. She looked at the two men, who nodded in agreement to Lois. They began to turn Lois around.

"You do not have to concern yourself with that." They said.

"I want to help my friend," Lois said, as she saw the two men roughly handling Jewel, who was obviously screaming and kicking, even though Lois couldn't hear her screams, "Can't you guys help her?" she asked.

The two men looked at Lois and said, "there's nothing to be done now," and they slowly walked away with Lois, who once turned around from the scene, had no desire to look back. She wasn't even sure why she wasn't sad for Jewel, but all she knew was the peace and calmness she was experiencing, as she willingly walked away with the two men.

The Accident Scene

The Rescuers:

"They're both gone," said the rescue worker as they place white sheets over both girls bodies and place them on stretchers.

"Get their ID's we'll have to notify the families to identify the bodies."

The Death angels:

The demonic world was rejoicing at their victory. There assignment was to only take out one of the girls, but something got screwed up and they began to congratulate themselves at their double victory.

The angelic Warriors:

"What got screwed up!" One of the Warriors asked the commander in charge.

"We got word at the last minute to let it be so, the other girl suffered too much injury from the impact of the crash. We could have survived her, but she would've been in a vegetable like state for years, so at the last minute we got word to let her come in. It was an executive decision."

Interlude

"And war broke out in heaven. Michael and his angels fought with the dragon; and the dragon and his angels fought, but they did not prevail, or was a place found for them in heaven any longer, so the great dragon was cast out, that serpent of old, called the devil and Satan, who deceives the world. He was cast to the Earth, and his angels were cast out with him.

Then I heard a loud voice saying in heaven, now salvation, and strength, and the Kingdom of our God, and the power of his Christ has come. For the Accuser of our brethren, who accuse them before God day and night, has been cast down. And they overcame him by the blood of the Lamb and by the word of their testimony, and they did not love their lives to the death. Therefore rejoice, O heavens, and you will dwell in them! Woe to the inhabitants of the earth and the sea! For the devil has come down to you, having great wrath, because he knows that he has a short time."

(Rev. 12:7-12)

9 781608 365241